CW00970666

The Impulse
of the Moment

by

Jann Rowland

One Good Sonnet Publishing
Publishers of Fine Romance
and Fantasy Fiction

By Jann Rowland
Published by One Good Sonnet Publishing:

PRIDE AND PREJUDICE VARIATIONS

Acting on Faith
A Life from the Ashes (**Sequel to** *Acting on Faith*)
Open Your Eyes
Implacable Resentment
An Unlikely Friendship
Bound by Love
Cassandra
Obsession
Shadows Over Longbourn
The Mistress of Longbourn
My Brother's Keeper
Coincidence
The Angel of Longbourn
Chaos Comes to Kent
In the Wilds of Derbyshire
The Companion
Out of Obscurity
What Comes Between Cousins
A Tale of Two Courtships
Murder at Netherfield
Whispers of the Heart
A Gift for Elizabeth
Mr. Bennet Takes Charge

COURAGE ALWAYS RISES: THE BENNET SAGA

The Heir's Disgrace

Co-Authored with Lelia Eye

WAITING FOR AN ECHO

Waiting for an Echo Volume One: Words in the Darkness
Waiting for an Echo Volume Two: Echoes at Dawn

A Summer in Brighton
A Bevy of Suitors
Love and Laughter: A Pride and Prejudice Short Stories Anthology

This is a work of fiction based on the works of Jane Austen. All the characters and events portrayed in this novel are products of Jane Austen's original novel or the authors' imaginations.

THE IMPULSE OF THE MOMENT

Copyright © 2019 Jann Rowland

Cover Design by Jann Rowland

Published by One Good Sonnet Publishing

All rights reserved.

ISBN: 1989212034
ISBN-13: 9781989212035

No part of this book may be reproduced or transmitted in any form or by any means, electronic, digital, or mechanical, including photocopying, recording, or by any information storage and retrieval system, without permission in writing from the publisher.

To my family who have, as always, shown
their unconditional love and encouragement.

PROLOGUE

July 1807

While it is often understood that a single man of good fortune must be in want of a wife, it is also understood that if that man is merely an heir to an estate, such concerns cannot be pressing. While a man in possession of his own fortune must be a specimen of much interest to young ladies of a similar station, the heir may escape much of that attention, though he is not truly free of it.

In the neighborhood surrounding the small town of Meryton in Hertfordshire, there were enough smaller estates that the aforementioned truth could not be relied upon. For young ladies of little dowry and few other benefits in life must take what they can get, not always what they wish. The society near that town boasted two families of moderate wealth among all the smaller estates. These estates, Longbourn and Netherfield, were about equal in consequence, producing something in excess of five thousand a year. Each estate also boasted a young heir of a little more than twenty summers, who were, thus, of interest to the ladies of the neighborhood.

It was unfortunate for those young ladies and their mothers that neither heir was yet considered a strong possibility for marriage. The elder, Mr. Thomas Bennet, was two and twenty summers and had only graduated from Oxford that spring. The younger, Mr. Charles Bingley, was still attending university at the age of twenty, with two more years before he too would graduate. Furthermore, though any developments were still some years away, it was also evident to the locals that each preferred the sister of the other. Mr. Bingley was often to be found with Longbourn's eldest daughter, Jane Bennet, while Mr. Bennet usually preferred the company of Miss Caroline Bingley, Mr. Bingley's younger sister. Both ladies were eighteen, possessed substantial dowries, and were content with the attentions of their beaux, with little interest in other gentlemen.

It was so unfair! Or at least that was what the other eligible ladies and heirs of the area could often be heard to lament. Longbourn and Netherfield were more than double the size of any other estate in the neighborhood—it was the height of selfishness for those two families to keep to themselves, rather than spreading their connections and wealth to other families of their acquaintance. Of course, in these lamentations, the locals did not consider the fact that had the two couples not been inclined to each other, it was equally likely they would have made marriages among wider society, as they were the only two families who boasted any kind of presence in London.

As the matches were not to come to fruition until some years in the future, the neighborhood consoled themselves with the knowledge there was still time to effect a change in their fates. In 1807 a new gentleman came to stay for some days at Netherfield, giving the ladies, at least, a new target for their matrimonial intrigues. Mr. Bennet was, at this time, away on the continent, engaged in that rite of passage, the grand tour, but Mr. Bingley was visiting his parents for the summer. It was his friend, a Mr. Darcy from Derbyshire, who was his guest. And it was to Mr. Darcy the interest of the young ladies was turned. Unfortunately, the young ladies and their mother could not have fixed on a subject more likely to bring them vexation, for Mr. Darcy was not of mind to pay *any* young woman any attention if he could possibly avoid it.

There were many points in Mr. Fitzwilliam Darcy's favor. Though he was a son and heir, the same as the aforementioned gentlemen, his father's estate was easily the size of Netherfield and Longbourn combined, and the family possessed other estates and interests, making their wealth and position in society one to envy. Furthermore, Mr. Darcy was tall, handsome, possessed of a noble bearing and connections to the nobility through his mother, the daughter of an earl.

What was not in his favor was his less than inviting demeanor and his manners which, though simple reticence and discomfort, gave the impression of haughty indifference or superiority. On the occasions when Darcy was in company with his friend, Bingley, he was a little more open, but with whose he did not know, he was akin to a closed book. The rumors of his family's wealth and position in society did not help either, nor did the ladies' obviously flirtatious attempts to garner his notice. His disinterested demeanor, rather than giving him concern about causing offense, was his shield against unwanted attention. He could not repine that which brought him a modicum of peace.

"I am happy you agreed to visit," said an exuberant Bingley one morning while they were riding the estate. "I know society here is not what you are accustomed to, and I appreciate your willingness to overlook the more rustic manners on display here."

"It is not all that dissimilar from my home," said Darcy. While he was not at all comfortable in society, he knew enough of it to know that truth. Truly great estates were not plentiful, and while the neighborhood about Meryton hosted more than the usual number of smaller estates, it was not so different from Derbyshire.

"I appreciate your attendance, regardless. I know your father does not exactly approve of your friendship with me."

It was the truth, and Darcy made no attempt to deny it. While the Bingley family was landed and had been so for longer than Bingley had been alive, his grandfather had been a tradesman, albeit one whose accumulation of wealth had been sufficient for his son to purchase their present property. Bingley still possessed some relations who were engaged in trade, rendering them much too near to the detested profession for some, including Darcy's more traditional father. The Bingley family would, unfortunately, bear the stench of trade for at least several more generations.

Not that the Bingleys appeared disturbed by that truth. The family were respected members of the second circles, and in some respects that was a point in their favor. Darcy was not enamored of high society, for their morals were lacking, avarice was their calling card, and they had a tendency to look down on those who were less in society's consequence. Even the Darcy family, possessing connections to the nobility, did not always escape the haughty eye of the highest members of society, even though the Darcy heritage was rich, ancient, and lengthier than that most nobles could boast.

"My father does not look down on you," said Darcy, feeling some urge to defend his absent sire, though Bingley's words were essentially the truth. "He has told me he considers you to be a good sort of man."

"But he is traditional and concerned with appearances," replied Bingley with a shrug. "I am not offended, you know. Many men of his station are the same. The few times I have met him, he has been unfailingly polite, which is more than I receive from some."

"That he is," replied Darcy. "Before you think I have deceived him as to my whereabouts, you should know he is well acquainted with my current activities. He may wish for me to associate with those of our circle, but he would never attempt to deny me the right to choose my friends."

"Never would I have thought it of him," replied Bingley. He paused and then laughed. "Then again, if he could see the attention you have received in the neighborhood since you came, he may have judged differently."

"It is nothing different from what he received as a young man himself."

"I am certain it is not. The fact that Caroline is enamored with Thomas Bennet must make you breathe easier, my friend. If she was not, Caroline is of such a determined disposition that had she focused on you, I doubt you would have a moment's rest."

"Your sister is all that is amiable and lovely, Bingley," replied Darcy. "Never has she given me the indication that she would act with anything less than propriety."

"As I said," replied Bingley, "she has been smitten with Bennet since she was twelve years of age. Even if you had wished to initiate a closer connection with her, you never stood a chance."

Darcy grunted and did not reply. There was nothing to say—Miss Bingley was a lovely woman, poised and elegant, and not lacking in accomplishments. Darcy was well able to acknowledge her assets and not have any further interest.

"Perhaps you should be grateful that I am not fascinated with Miss Jane Bennet," said Darcy in a teasing tone. "If I had, I might have tried my hand at turning her attention away from you."

A laugh was Bingley's response, as Darcy had intended. "Miss Bennet is a wonderful young woman, indeed! Never have I met such beauty, poise, kindness, and manners in one angelic package."

"Exactly," replied Darcy. "She would be the perfect future mistress of Pemberley with all these advantages."

Again Bingley chuckled. "If she takes your fancy, you are more than welcome to make the attempt, my friend. I should warn you, however, that she has been infatuated with *me* nearly as long as my sister has been with her brother. She will be perfectly polite, but I doubt you will find her easy to move."

"And your feelings?" asked Darcy with some interest. His friend was usually an open book, but in this instance, while he could easily discern Bingley's enjoyment of Miss Bennet's company, he was not certain that extended past his friend's easy manners with everyone.

"I enjoy Miss Bennet's company very much," replied Bingley. "But she is yet eighteen, and I am not yet one and twenty. After I complete university and finish my grand tour, my father will wish to ensure I am properly trained to take over Netherfield. When I return to the neighborhood, we shall see."

"It does not concern you that she may find another man in the interim?"

"There are hardly many men in the neighborhood who would meet her desires in a husband."

"Oh?" asked Darcy. "You know this of her? This account makes her sound mercenary."

"Miss Bennet is as far from mercenary as a lady can be," replied Bingley. "I simply mean that there is no one who would suit her temperament. The masters of lesser estates and their sons tend to be a rougher lot."

"And London? I assume she is not unknown there."

"No, she is not." Bingley shrugged his shoulders and took his hat from his head, wiping his brow and then replacing it on its perch. "If she should happen to find a man she wishes to marry, then I will content myself with wishing her every happiness. But if she is still unmarried when I am in a position to take a wife, she will be at the top of the list, I assure you."

Darcy nodded and allowed the subject to drop. Many a time Bingley had been called impulsive—it was good he was approaching this subject with the seriousness it deserved.

"Perhaps her younger sister would be good for you."

Bingley's voice intruded on Darcy's thoughts, and he looked askance at his friend. With a shrug, Bingley said: "Miss Elizabeth is still full young, of course, being naught but sixteen. But she is pretty and smart and possesses a rapier wit, the likes of which I suspect you might find irresistible."

"I am not looking for a wife, Bingley."

"Nor did I say you were," agreed his friend in his usually easy manner. "As I said, she is not ready to marry anyway and will not be for some years yet. I neither pressure you to consider her nor suggest you should pay court to her. In her, however, I believe I see a girl who would suit your interests. Furthermore, in a few years, I suspect she will blossom into a true beauty, akin to her elder sister."

Guiding his horse in close to Darcy's, Bingley nudged him with his elbow, waggling his eyebrows suggestively. "A young woman truly ought to be a beauty, if she can at all help it. Is it not so?"

The two men laughed together. "I suppose she ought, though she has no true control over the matter."

"Which is what makes a young woman of such attributes precious, especially if she is also possessed of a noble and interesting character.

"Well, you shall be able to judge for yourself," added Bingley. "I understand from Miss Bennet that her sister is to attend her first assembly tomorrow."

Darcy grimaced at the mention of that detested activity, which prompted his friend to laughter yet again. "Do not look at me that way, Darcy. It will be the perfect send off. Call it a last bit of society in thanks before you depart on Friday."

"Then I shall attempt to see it as such, though you know I am not at all fond of assemblies."

"I know you are not, Darcy. And it is greatly appreciated that you will agree to attend, in spite of your disinclination. Let us return to Netherfield, for I believe I have had enough riding today."

As Bingley heeled his horse back toward Netherfield, Darcy followed his lead. Bingley was nothing if not predictable, and Darcy supposed he could withstand one night with the man's neighbors, even if he would not enjoy it. It was all part of being a gentleman, his father would say. Robert Darcy, who was much like his son, did not enjoy assemblies either.

The first glimpse Darcy had of the temptress was within minutes of entering the assembly rooms of Meryton. It was impossible to avoid noticing her, so brightly did she glow in her simple but elegant muslin dress the color of sunshine. It was immediately evident she was the younger sister of whom Bingley had spoken the previous day as her looks were similar to that of her elder sister.

But while the similarities were easily seen, the differences between the two women were equally striking. Miss Bennet was calm and quiet, akin to a softly bubbling brook, flowing with nary a ripple to the sea. Miss Elizabeth was anything but calm and quiet. Oh, she was not improper by any means. But she was lively and happy, flitting from one person to the next, with a smile and a jest on the tip of her tongue and a joyous smile bestowed upon all.

Even using the term temptress was pushing reality, Darcy was forced to concede to himself as he watched her. The term implied a woman using her wiles to draw men into her sphere, especially if she meant nothing more than flirtation. Miss Elizabeth did none of these things—it seemed to Darcy that playful manners were simply part of her character. Many men might have found her manners anything but fashionable, he supposed. But having endured simpering ladies who agreed with his every word in order to ingratiate themselves to him, Darcy found her openness refreshing.

It was doubly amazing, considering this was her first taste of society, according to his friend. He walked along the length of the dance floor, watching as Miss Elizabeth's graceful form spun along with the other dancers, marveling at the mastery she already displayed of the steps. Georgiana, Darcy's younger sister, was still but twelve years old, but given her shy nature, Darcy suspected she would not fare so well in her first assembly. Miss Elizabeth seemed as if she was a veteran of ten seasons.

"Well, Darcy? What do you think now?"

Darcy turned, noting his friend's eyes on him twinkling in amusement. When Darcy did not immediately reply, Bingley's smile grew larger, and he nodded in Miss Elizabeth's direction.

"Did I not tell you that she is a delightful girl?"

"She is tolerable, for a girl just out of the schoolroom," replied Darcy. For some reason he could not quite understand, he had no desire to concede the truth of Bingley's words. "Given her age, I suspect it might be better if she spent at least another year preparing herself for society."

"If this were London, I might agree with you," replied Bingley. "But if there is any girl who is ready to be in a society such as this, I declare that girl to be Miss Elizabeth.

"Look at her!" exclaimed Bingley. "Does she not bewitch them all with her ways? I cannot imagine any man can resist her."

"She *is* lively," acknowledged Darcy.

"Then shall I introduce you?"

The reticent in Darcy did not wish to be introduced at all, especially when he was certain the young woman would likely say ten words for every one of his. The man whose interest was piqued by a sparkling young woman, however, did wish to know her. She was too young, being only sixteen years of age. But that did not prevent a man his age from being known to her. In the end, knowing it would be churlish to refuse, Darcy accepted. Bingley did not seem to understand Darcy's internal debate; he did nothing more than grin and lead Darcy toward where the girl had been left with her elder sister by the side of the floor at the conclusion of the dance.

"Miss Bennet, Miss Elizabeth," said Bingley with a grin, the return of which spoke to his familiarity and comfort with these ladies, "my friend has indicated a desire to be introduced to Miss Elizabeth."

While Miss Bennet, true to character nodded in her calm fashion, it seemed to Darcy that Miss Elizabeth found his application irresistibly hilarious, for her grin was as bright as the sun. The ladies acquiesced and Bingley performed the office.

"I am happy to make your acquaintance, sir," said Miss Elizabeth, wasting no time in raising her voice to teasing. "You have a firm friend in Mr. Bingley. He can rarely speak a full sentence without injecting your name into the conversation."

Bingley, predictably, laughed at her sally. "I do not speak of my friend *that* much, Miss Elizabeth."

"Perhaps not. But sometimes it seems you do."

"I understand this is your first taste of society, Miss Elizabeth," said Darcy, more due to the lack of anything intelligent to say.

"My first taste of dancing, yes," replied she. "But I have often attended parties and dinners. Do you enjoy society, Mr. Darcy?"

"With the right inducement," Darcy found himself saying.

Bingley laughed, but Miss Elizabeth tilted her head to the side, as if trying to puzzle him out. "And what would that be?"

"Perhaps *you* should attempt to determine the right inducement, Miss Elizabeth," said Bingley. "I am sure Darcy himself knows nothing of it."

"Is that so, Mr. Darcy?" asked Miss Elizabeth, arching a brow at him.

"I find myself uncomfortable in the company of those with whom I am not acquainted," replied Darcy, feeling more than a little foolish. "But I am by no means as bad as Bingley would tell you."

The snort with which Bingley made his feelings known spoke to his opinion of the matter, and Darcy found himself becoming more than a little annoyed with his friend. It was akin to what he often felt when his cousin Fitzwilliam turned his teasing on Darcy. Darcy never knew if he would have acted as he did if he remained unprovoked, but in a large part to prove his friend wrong, he addressed Miss Elizabeth.

"I am pleased to stand up with you if you are willing. Might I have the next dance?"

"Our father stipulated that she is only to dance with a few close friends," said Miss Bennet, seeming a little embarrassed. "It was the compromise on which our mother and father agreed to allow Lizzy to attend."

"But surely if I vouch for Darcy's character, it would be acceptable," protested Bingley. "After all, I am on the list of approved partners for Miss Elizabeth, and I am well acquainted with my friend."

Though Miss Bennet appeared dubious, Miss Elizabeth beamed at Bingley and was quick to say: "Then it is settled. I would be happy to accept your hand for a dance, Mr. Darcy!"

While Miss Bennet's misgivings were readily apparent, she did not attempt to dissuade her sister. For a moment, Darcy wondered if it was wise to partner her—would a vengeful father, intent upon protecting his children suddenly appear to rebuke him for daring to stand up with his beloved daughter? It seemed Bingley had seen Darcy's indecision, for he leaned close.

"Mr. Bennet is usually to be found in the card room, and Mrs. Bennet will not protest."

The time for considering the matter was at an end as the strains of the next dance floated over the assembled. Having no other choice, Darcy extended his hand, grasping Miss Bennet's, and leading her to the floor, Bingley and Miss Bennet close by.

In later years—or even the very next day, as it was—Darcy would be unable to remember of what they spoke, the particulars of the dance, or even what he felt during his time with Miss Elizabeth Bennet. It seemed likely, given the volubility of the young woman's never-ending stream of words, that Darcy said little. A short time in her company suggested that nervousness prompted her constant stream of commentary, but it was equally possible that she was simply this talkative at all times. Either way, Darcy found himself utterly charmed by her manner, for she was lively and intelligent, and at sundry times in their dance, her observations of her friends, Bingley, and even herself, were rather droll.

At the end of the dance, Darcy delivered her to the side of the floor where her sister joined her, thanked her for the dance and walked away. He felt, rather than saw, her eyes upon him as he did so and wondered if she had been affected as much as he had himself.

And so, the evening continued. Darcy noted that Miss Elizabeth danced a few more times, though seemingly not so many as she might have liked. For his own part, Darcy decided he had done enough to acquit himself that evening, having danced with the Bennet sister, and was content to watch the rest of the evening. If his eyes strayed more to the young woman's person than any other part of the room, Darcy decided it was best not to examine his behavior too closely.

That, of course, turned out to be his undoing. For Miss Elizabeth, seeing him standing by the side of the floor, seemed to take it into her head that he should stand up again with other ladies of the company.

"This is an assembly, Mr. Darcy," said she on more than one occasion. "As a man, it is your duty to ask a woman to dance, for she may not do so without an invitation from a gentleman."

"I have no further interest in dancing, Miss Elizabeth," said Darcy. "I am quite content where I am."

"But it is silly for you to stand about in this manner!" cried she. "You had much better dance."

"Am I mistaken," said Darcy, turning an exasperated look on her, "or have you not danced your fill tonight?"

"That is hardly the point, Mr. Darcy," said she, disapproval evident in her tone.

"That is exactly the point," countered Darcy. "I am not inclined to dance at the best of times. I have done my duty by you and your sister and am content to watch the rest of the evening."

"But, Mr. Darcy—"

"That is enough, Miss Elizabeth. I have no more intention to dance this evening."

A huff escaped the young woman's lips. "I have no notion of why you are so unsociable. It is gentlemanly to ask young ladies to dance, is it not?"

"Leave me be!"

Miss Elizabeth shrugged and turned to stalk away. Soon, she was in the company of the young lady she had attempted to induce Darcy to dance with, and by the way they were giggling and looking at him, Darcy surmised that he himself was the subject of their conversation. Darcy continued to watch her, but while she had spoken to him with ease earlier in the evening, now her manner was distant, and she avoided him. And while Darcy was annoyed with her at first, thinking she had been the one to importune him, he soon realized that he had been short with her. It was, indeed, ungentlemanly conduct.

The evening was nearing a close when Darcy saw his chance to speak with her again. He had been watching her stand beside the dance floor for some moments, and suddenly she was not there any longer. Surmising that she had stepped out onto a balcony, Darcy made his way to the location he had last seen her and stepped out through a small exit into the darkness beyond.

The light was dim as there was only a sliver of a moon that night. Beyond the hall, the balcony looked out over a waving field of grain on the edge of the town. Darcy waited for a few moments while his eyes adjusted, noting the slender figure of Miss Elizabeth stood by the balustrade, looking out onto the gloomy night. When he thought he could walk without running into her, Darcy stepped forward, calling her name softly.

At the first sound of his voice, she let out a little cry and spun about, her hand rising to cover her breast. When she saw it was he, she directed a heated glare at him and drew herself up to her full diminutive height.

"Have you never been taught that it is dangerous to be alone with a young woman?
If we are discovered, it could be the ruin of my reputation."

"No one saw me leave the room, Miss Elizabeth," said Darcy.

"You do not know that, sir!" exclaimed she. "I must insist you return to the assembly room."

"First, I wish to apologize."

"I care nothing for your apologies!" exclaimed she. "There is a real possibility of compromise."

"Will you not simply be silent for a moment, so I can say my piece and return?" demanded Darcy, becoming cross with her once again.

"It is not necessary," said Miss Elizabeth. "Leave at once!"

"Are you always this infuriating? Can you not be silent for even a moment?"

The two combatants stood stock still and glared at each other for one long moment. Then the fateful words spilled out of Miss Elizabeth's mouth.

"Perhaps I might, but it is better than being silent at all times, is it not? Or perhaps you prefer to stalk stupidly about the dance hall all evening, looking down on all and sundry like the Prince Regent himself. Or it may simply be—"

Whatever she was about to say would forever remain unsaid. Darcy, desperate to silence her, acted on impulse and without thought. He leaned forward and kissed her full on the lips.

Miss Elizabeth's eyes widened, and she looked up at him in shock. For perhaps the first time that evening, she said nothing, though her mouth worked with the words which were begging to be released. But they were not.

Then, just when Darcy thought to speak to explain himself, or maybe just to apologize, Miss Elizabeth darted around him, fleeing through the doors at his back. And Darcy was left by himself, wondering what had just happened.

CHAPTER I

July 1811

A splash of color flashed through the foliage. Elizabeth stopped, standing stock still, senses alert for any further indication her solitude was to be interrupted.

The trill of a bird called loudly overhead, and while Elizabeth might normally have looked toward it, marveling in the joyous release of happiness, the needs of the moment took precedence. Her aunt and uncle were somewhere on the other side of the line of trees and shrubbery where Elizabeth now walked, but the color she had seen did not seem to be the color of her uncle's coat.

Carefully, unwilling to be seen, Elizabeth edged her way forward, eyes alert for any sign of what she had seen, ears open to any sounds to disturb the air. A breath of wind fluttered against her cheek, blowing a few loose hairs back to tickle her ear. Impatiently, Elizabeth pushed them away, careful to make the movement slow and unobtrusive.

There! The sound of voices caught her attention, drawing her forward, still careful to keep the hedges between her and the source of the sound. Through a hole in the greenery, the image of a couple, her aunt and uncle, came into sight. They were speaking with a man, tall and forbidding. The man turned slightly, his profile visible to Elizabeth's gaze.

He had come. The heir of Pemberley had returned to his home.

Elizabeth had known all along that it was foolhardy to visit Pemberley. The name, long known to her, brought in its wake memories she wished to forget. Memories she could not banish.

The years since *his* coming to Hertfordshire had been hard in some respects. While Elizabeth had found her courage in those years to face society with her head held high, the sibilant whispering in her ear spoke to her own humiliation and ruin. What else could it be? Though she had not known it as a happy and carefree girl of sixteen, she now well knew that a woman was subject to the whims of men. Even all the care in the world — which she had certainly never exercised when she had yet been innocent — might not be enough to protect her from the depredations of rakes of the world. In all, Elizabeth was still a happy woman, and she did not think to excess of what had happened. But in the night, in dreams, she relived it time and again, and the memory never truly left her.

The loss of her mother to a sudden illness had provided a new crisis on which to focus, a family of six reduced to five in the blink of an eye. Mrs. Bennet had been a flighty woman, one not born to her married status of a gentlewoman. Though she had embarrassed them all on occasion, they had all loved her and mourned her loss. With two other sisters and a brother to commiserate, Elizabeth had endured the loss of a mother, emerging from the trial sadder, but with a more hopeful demeanor.

The Bennet family had not long emerged from their mourning when the journey to the north had been proposed, and while all had been invited, only Elizabeth had ultimately agreed to go. For others, there were valid reasons to remain in Hertfordshire. For Elizabeth, there was every reason to be gone for a time.

"We had thought to go next year," said Aunt Gardiner when the amusement had been proposed during Elizabeth's visit in the spring. "But your uncle's business has been very prosperous this past year, and I have determined he requires a holiday away from the concerns of business."

"It is good that uncle has a wife such as you," replied Elizabeth, "who knows when to insist he take a break."

The two ladies laughed together. "It is, indeed!"

"Where do you think your travels will take you?"

"The lakes are our ultimate destination. But in our journeys, I hope we shall take in the Peaks and have a little time to spend in Derbyshire."

The sound of *that man's* home county cast a shadow over Elizabeth's soul, but she did not allow anything to show in her countenance. "Is there anywhere in particular you wish to visit in Derbyshire?"

"You well know I spent many years in the town of Lambton in my youth," said Mrs. Gardiner. "My father was the rector there, and I remember it with great fondness. But you have heard me speak of it enough times that I should think you weary of it by now!"

Elizabeth laughed, and the subject turned to the delights in which her aunt expected to partake. For Elizabeth's part, she chided herself, thinking there was little reason to fear entering *his* county. The fates could not be so unkind as to impose upon her the coincidence of meeting a man she never wished to see again, could they?

It seemed they could. For when they arrived at Lambton on their way north, it had not been fifteen minutes later that Elizabeth heard the name. Pemberley. The great estate of the Darcy family was situated fewer than five miles from the borders of Lambton, and while the estates of the neighborhood contributed to that town's livelihood, Pemberley was spoken of with all the mystique of a mythical fairy kingdom.

"Are the family at home for the summer?" Elizabeth had asked a maid, feigning a sort of disinterested ennui, though inside she was all aflutter for the answer.

"No, Mum," was the blissful reply. "They were at home earlier in the year but have since departed for the residence of the Earl of Matlock. Lady Anne Darcy is sister to the earl."

"And is the earl's estate far distant?"

"Perhaps some thirty miles," was the reply. "Snowlock is on the southern border of Derbyshire."

Entirely too near, Elizabeth thought to herself. She comforted herself with the thought that they were not to stay in Lambton long — no more than three or four days, according to her aunt. There were several ladies who lived in the area with whom her aunt had lost contact, and much of the business of the visit was to re-establish those ties, as much as it was to explore a small market town.

Then disaster struck.

"You wish to see Pemberley?" asked Elizabeth, unable to fathom how the fates had suddenly turned against her.

"I do," replied Mrs. Gardiner. From the lack of response to Elizabeth's query, she thought she had hidden her discomposure admirably. "I did see it once when I was a girl, and I should like to see it again as an adult."

"Must we?" asked Elizabeth, again affecting boredom. "Were the wonders of Blenheim not sufficient to quench your thirst for large and imposing manors?"

"Pemberley must rival even those venerable estates," replied Mrs. Gardiner. "Even famed Chatsworth, which we shall see anon, is no finer than Pemberley. And the grounds are as lovely as any I have ever seen." Mrs. Gardiner grinned at Elizabeth and nudged her with an elbow. "I am well acquainted with your ways, Lizzy. The grounds of Pemberley must be an irresistible lure for one of your love of nature. The park is ten miles around, from what I understand!"

"And do you propose to see it all?"

Her uncle and aunt laughed. "I have not your ability, my dear. But perhaps I can content myself with the gardens while you take a longer circuit, though I am afraid we cannot allow the full ten miles."

"Is it wise to visit the place without an invitation?" asked Elizabeth.

"Was the lack of an invitation a problem when we visited those other estates?" asked her uncle.

"We were not known to the families that live there."

"Ah, yes," replied Aunt Gardiner, "your brief acquaintance with Mr. Darcy the younger. It *was* brief, was it not? And the acquaintance has not been maintained?"

"I have not seen Mr. Darcy since his visit," replied Elizabeth, striving to maintain her composure.

"Then I see no problem with it."

When Elizabeth hesitated, it seemed her relations finally grew concerned. "Do you dislike the scheme, Lizzy? Having heard of the place, I might have thought you would be interested to see it."

"Mr. Darcy spoke little of Pemberley," replied Elizabeth, feeling defensive.

"That is not a reason to avoid it," said her uncle.

"I have no true dislike for the proposal," said Elizabeth. "If you both wish it, we may go to Pemberley. I am sure, given your account, that I shall be delighted by the grounds and will find some way to lose myself within them."

Though her relations directed a long look at her, in the end it seemed they decided her recalcitrance was not something to cause alarm. Thus, to Pemberley they were to go.

The incident with *him* was a closely guarded secret. Not only was it shameful to Elizabeth in particular, but she was well aware of how a reputation might be ruined with nothing more than a word. Elizabeth might have preferred to keep it strictly to herself. But one of the disadvantages of having a close sister with whom she shared everything was a distinct difficulty in keeping secrets. Wonderful Jane, who was all that was lovely and good, eager to see the good in others, was nevertheless observant and intelligent and had immediately seen that something was wrong with Elizabeth. Thus, only a few days after the event, Elizabeth had told her, but not without insisting upon the strictest of confidence.

"Perhaps there has been some misunderstanding," Jane had said, wringing her hands in distress.

Dearest Jane! Had Elizabeth sought to predict her sister's reaction to her tale, she could have done it with a high degree of accuracy!

"I know not how you can see anything of misunderstanding in what I have told you," was Elizabeth's reply. If she was a little short, Elizabeth thought she had more than enough provocation.

"But Mr. Darcy seems to be everything that is good! How could he behave in such an ungentlemanly manner?"

"I know not," replied Elizabeth. "Nor do I care. He did — that is the salient point."

"How can Mr. Bingley be so imposed upon?"

"Do not blame Mr. Bingley," said Elizabeth, patting her sister's hands to comfort her. "Though I cannot say for certain, I do not think Mr. Darcy is the rake this action paints him as being."

"Did you fear for your safety?" asked Jane. She leaned in and put an arm around Elizabeth's shoulders to provide the comfort of an elder sibling.

"I do not know. The only thought I had was to preserve my reputation, for I doubt he could have been worked on to remedy it should his actions become known. It was nothing more than impulse, I think. But I did not wish to test the theory."

"Lizzy," said Jane, her manner as earnest as Elizabeth had ever seen, "you must tell Papa."

"No!" was Elizabeth's emphatic reply.

"Papa is responsible for our safety. He cannot remain ignorant of this."

"What good would it do to inform him?" Elizabeth crossed her arms, the stubbornness for which she was renowned coming to the forefront and settling in her breast. "No one knows what happened and my reputation is intact. Mr. Darcy has already departed from Netherfield, and if we are very lucky, he will not return."

"He is Mr. Bingley's close friend," argued Jane. "He may very well visit frequently."

"That is a possibility," replied Elizabeth. "But I shall not be taken unaware again. I have learned my lesson."

"Lizzy—"

"No, Jane. You promised to keep my confidence. I wish to forget this incident and act as if it never happened."

But to forget proved impossible. Jane had not liked Elizabeth's strictures, but she had, in the end, kept her word, allowing the matter to rest. It was fortunate, Elizabeth decided, that Jane had not seen fit to raise the subject again, and as Elizabeth had acted as if she was not affected, Jane had seemed content to watch and wait. Mr. Darcy had not returned, not the next year or the one after, and after a time, Elizabeth suspected her sister, while she did not forget, considered the matter closed.

The matter was not closed, however, at least in the confines of Elizabeth's heart. In time, the memory grew distorted, as all memories must with the passage of time, and she found less evidence to suggest that Mr. Darcy was impulsive and more fear to justify his being a rake. As the months passed, Elizabeth grew more fearful that he would return to finish what he started, to compromise her irrevocably. To ruin her in society.

But then, as she left the awkward teenage years and became a young woman, endured the loss of her mother and attained the age of twenty, that fear gradually lessened and ceased altogether. If Mr. Darcy meant her any harm, surely, he would not wait years before taking action. That did not mean Elizabeth lost her sense of caution—far from it. She took great care in her dealings with men in general, endeavoring to avoid being alone with any of them. But the fear, which had lodged itself in her breast at the age of sixteen, had dissipated by the time she reached twenty.

Which brought her to the present. While Elizabeth had not anticipated the visit to Pemberley, she found the estate to be everything her aunt had said, and more. The small prominence from which she first caught sight of the manor in the distance was breathtaking, and the house and gardens were enough to inspire awe.

The Gardiner party applied to the housekeeper to see inside, to which the woman agreed with cheerful alacrity. Mrs. Reynolds was clearly a retainer of longstanding, for she possessed intimate knowledge of the estate, guiding them from room to room, sharing anecdotes and bits of family history. With interest, they toured the principle rooms, noted the room where Mrs. Darcy wrote her letters, the pianoforte where the young Miss Darcy practiced all day long, the long gallery filled with centuries of family history. And her words of the family themselves were even more interesting to Elizabeth, for it painted at least one of them in stark contrast to her long-held opinion.

"They are a wonderful family," said Mrs. Reynolds, eager to share what she knew of them. "Lady Anne is, as you must know, the daughter and sister of an earl. And while the Darcy family has no title, theirs is arguably the more illustrious of the two, for it extends back centuries to the time of William the Conqueror."

"You have been with them long, I take it?" said Mr. Gardiner. Elizabeth could detect no amusement in his manner. Mr. Bennet, Elizabeth knew, would have taken the housekeeper's assertions for conceit.

"I was a junior maid in this house," replied the housekeeper with more than a hint of pride. "It is the current Mrs. Darcy who raised me to my present position more than ten years ago."

"I have long heard nothing but good of the family," said Aunt Gardiner. Her own connection to the area had been made known to the housekeeper within minutes of their arrival. "Whenever they came to Lambton, Mr. and Mrs. Darcy were always kind and considerate. But I have less news of the younger generation."

"They are just like their parents," said Mrs. Reynolds. "Miss Darcy is a little shy, but she is generous and affable to those who know her. And as for the young master, he is as good a man as was ever seen and shall be an excellent master of the estate when his time comes."

"That must be a relief," replied Mr. Gardiner. "So many young men these days care only for their own pleasure and nothing for that which gives them their benefits in life."

A shadow crossed the housekeeper's face. "I cannot say you are mistaken, Mr. Gardiner. There is a young man who has been attached to this household for most of his life who is of that ilk. But young Mr. Darcy is nothing of the sort. No one among the tenants or servants will give him a bad name. He is one of the best young men I have ever met."

This account of Mr. Darcy stayed with Elizabeth throughout the rest of the tour. When they were consigned to the care of the gardener and left to view the gardens, Elizabeth continued to think on the matter to the exclusion of all else. When Mrs. Reynolds had made her claim, Elizabeth had been curious, then understanding. He would not wish for his actions to be made public, after all, especially since his father did not sound like the kind of man to tolerate such failings in the son.

Do his virtues include stealing from young maidens that which they can most ill afford to give? thought she in the confines of her own mind.

And then Mr. Darcy himself arrived. Situated as she was, away from the main path and behind some foliage, Elizabeth determined at once that she would not call attention to herself. Why would she once again put herself into the position of vulnerability to the man's schemes? Elizabeth was, however, close enough that she could hear the conversation. Curious as to what she would hear, she edged closer.

"I am just returned myself," Mr. Darcy was saying to her aunt and uncle. "My family is staying at my uncle's house in the south, but a problem arose, and my father dispatched me to meet with our steward."

"Then we apologize for trespassing, sir," replied Mr. Gardiner. "We were assured the family is not in residence."

"It is no trouble, sir. We were to remain absent all summer, and only the matter of which I spoke drew me back. Mrs. Reynolds knows when the house might be shown — she would have turned you away, had the timing been poor."

"We are happy to hear it, sir," said Mrs. Gardiner. "It has been many years since I toured Pemberley. It would have been sad had we been unable to visit."

"You have seen Pemberley before?" asked Mr. Darcy, the interest evident in his tone.

"Lambton was my home for many years. My father was the rector there."

"Then you must be the daughter of Mr. Plumber," said Mr. Darcy.

"Indeed, I am, sir."

"Then I welcome you back, Mrs. Gardiner," said Mr. Darcy with a bow. "His sudden passing was a tragedy. He has been missed very much."

They continued speaking in this vein for some moments, the conversation largely carried by Mr. Darcy and Mrs. Gardiner, centering about some common acquaintances or their shared understanding of the town. As he spoke with them, Elizabeth noted he seemed more animated than she remembered seeing him during their short acquaintance in Hertfordshire. Did he realize they were of the trade class? Elizabeth could not be certain, but she suspected not—Mr. and Mrs. Gardiner were quite fashionable and easily able to pass themselves off as gentlefolk when they wished. In truth, Elizabeth was forced to conclude it might not make a difference even if Mr. Darcy knew. Mr. Bingley was his friend, and his father had been a tradesman before he purchased Netherfield, after all.

"But we are keeping you from your tasks," said Mrs. Gardiner after they had been speaking for some minutes.

"It is no trouble. I believe the situation will be resolved without difficulty."

"I am happy to hear it, sir. For the present, however, I believe it would be best if we found our niece and departed."

"You are traveling with another?" asked Mr. Darcy, looking about with some interest.

For a moment, Elizabeth thought he must see her, even though she thought she was well concealed. But his eyes passed her location without any hint of recognition, and she breathed a sigh of relief.

"Shall I have the gardeners look for her? The grounds are quite extensive. I would not wish for her to become lost."

A laugh was Mrs. Gardiner's response. "Our Lizzy is well able to retain her bearings, regardless of where she walks. She is quite renowned for being a great walker of the paths near her father's home. I dare say she could find her way back to Lambton in the darkest night, should the situation demand it."

A flash of recognition passed Mr. Darcy's countenance, and for a moment Elizabeth entertained the wild thought that he knew it was she. But then reason reasserted itself—he could not know the connection, and Elizabeth was a common enough name that it could not point to her. With a short pause and a long look, he bowed to her relations.

"Should you have any difficulty in locating her, please to not hesitate to ask Mr. Stevenson for assistance. He knows these paths like the back of his hand."

The Gardiners assented, and with a few last words, the man departed, allowing her uncle and aunt to continue walking along the avenue. Elizabeth stayed in her place of concealment, watching as his long strides took him away toward the house. Then, taking thought to her situation and unwilling to allow her aunt and uncle to know she had been watching the exchange, Elizabeth set off away from the house, taking a long way around the strand of trees, and then found her way to the path. In a few minutes, she had come upon her aunt and uncle.

"Ah, Lizzy," said Mr. Gardiner. "You will never guess whom we met!"

"Given your tone of voice and the suggestion in your words, I might suppose it was Mr. Darcy or Lady Anne herself."

It seemed Elizabeth was successful in her obfuscation, for her relations laughed at her sally. "You are far too quick, Lizzy," said Mrs. Gardiner. "Indeed, you are correct in general, though not in particular. We met the younger Mr. Darcy, who had just returned from his uncle's estate."

"Did you?" asked Elizabeth. "And what did you think of him?"

"Very civil," said Mr. Gardiner. "He asked after us and spoke to your aunt of Lambton for some minutes."

"In looks, he is much like his father," added Mrs. Gardiner. "Though in temperament, I would suggest he is friendlier, more like his mother. Mr. Darcy the elder is a good man, but his countenance is more severe, his manners, more reticent."

"Had you been with him, he might have recognized you," said Mr. Gardiner.

"Perhaps," replied Elizabeth. "But it has been four years. I was much different as a girl of sixteen."

"Change is a part of life." Mr. Gardiner paused, looking at Elizabeth closely. "If your acquaintance had been a more substantial one, I might have mentioned it to him. As it was, it would have sounded like an impertinence, and very likely it would have been."

"I agree," said Elizabeth.

"Well, Lizzy," said her uncle, "what do you think of the place?"

The warmth in Elizabeth's breast was all for the estate and had nothing to do with her feelings for the heir. "It is very beautiful, indeed. I thank you for insisting we come, for to leave the area without viewing it would have been a tragedy."

"I am glad you think so," said Mrs. Gardiner. "For my part, however, I believe I should like to find our carriage and return to Lambton, for all this walking has tired me."

"Then that is what we shall do," replied Elizabeth, thankful she had not been forced to insist on their departure.

"I might have thought you would protest," teased Uncle Gardiner.

"No, sir," replied Elizabeth with a grin. "The woods are beautiful, and I am glad to have seen them. But there are so many beautiful places we have seen that I am sure there are more delights just around the corner."

"That is the spirit, Lizzy!" exclaimed Aunt Gardiner. "Soon we shall see Dovedale and visit Chatsworth. While I will still assert they are no better than Pemberley, they are very fine themselves. And then we will go on to the lakes, which I am certain you will find no less than charming."

"That much is assured. I anticipate them keenly."

And with much laughter, the trio departed to seek their coach. But in Elizabeth's heart, she could not help but be relieved she had managed to encroach on the man's very doorstep, and even into the halls of his hallowed home, and escape unscathed.

CHAPTER II

$\mathcal{L}$ulled as he was by the staccato rapping of the horse's hooves against the hard gravel road, Darcy allowed himself to drift back into the thoughts which had plagued him since the previous day. There was something familiar about the couple he had met—or at least about the man. The woman, Mrs. Gardiner, was familiar, indeed, and Darcy was certain he had seen her in Lambton at times when he had been a child. No, it was the man that particularly confounded Darcy at present.

Unsure what it was, Darcy considered the matter. It might have been nothing more than fancy, but he thought he recognized a hint of something about the man's jaw and nose which jarred his memory. Something in his eyes spoke to good humor and intelligence. And then there was the mention of their niece. Lizzy.

The mention of that name jarred other memories loose though they had never truly left him in the years since he had last seen her. Was Mr. Gardiner related to Miss Elizabeth Bennet? He had never heard tell of any relations, but that did not mean anything either. He was not on so intimate a footing with the family that he would know the state of their connections in any great detail. It seemed unlikely—Lizzy was not an uncommon nickname. The connection to Lambton was another point in opposition to the possibility. While the couple had seemed fashionable, that she was the daughter of a parson suggested that they were not, in fact, of the gentry themselves. Would the Bennets' relations not inhabit the same level of society they themselves claimed? No, the coincidence seemed too fantastical. Darcy put it from his mind.

What was not so easily banished, however, was the remembrances of "Lizzy" that the events of the previous day had prompted. Indeed, though it had been nearly four years since his visit to Bingley's home, it seemed a rare day when memories of the young woman did not intrude upon his senses. She had been a diminutive sprite of a girl, beautiful dark eyes, slightly plump cheeks, still carrying a hint of the child she had been. Miss Elizabeth had been sixteen at the time — Darcy could not help but wonder if the promising prettiness she had displayed as a young girl had blossomed into true beauty now that she was a woman. Given her sister, Darcy suspected it likely that he would be rendered stunned should he see her now.

A gust of wind nearly knocked Darcy's hat from his head, and he reached up to fix it in place. His steed, a trusted animal Darcy had ridden for the past five years, nickered and lashed his tail to and fro. Darcy patted the beast, earning another whinny in response, and he settled once again into the rhythm of man and beast, the swift canter eating the miles which remained between himself and his uncle's home.

The problem was, Darcy thought to himself, the incident which had occurred between them the last time he had laid eyes on Miss Elizabeth Bennet. Charmed by her manners and exasperated by her continual teasing, Darcy had allowed his baser nature sway, stealing a kiss in a most ungentlemanly manner. His father would not be pleased should he learn of his son's behavior, and rightly so. He had been taught better.

It was for that reason Darcy had not visited Bingley again. Bingley's invitations had been plentiful, but Darcy had found a reason to refuse every time. In the interim, Bingley had even visited Pemberley, not that Darcy's father had appreciated the visit. Oh, he had been civil and respectful. But Mr. Robert Darcy had definite ideas about the proper acquaintances for himself and his family, and he was not at all a friend of his son's association with the likes of Charles Bingley. That he recognized that Darcy, as a man in his own right, possessed the ability, intelligence, and will to choose his own friends was the only reason why Darcy's friendship with Bingley had not become a source of strife between them. But his father did not approve, and Darcy was certain he never would.

An invitation had arrived again—it was among Darcy's correspondence which had been held for him at Pemberley. As he always did, Darcy had immediately begun to search for ways to avoid attending Bingley in Hertfordshire. He would have to face *her* if he allowed himself to be lured there, and while a part of him would like nothing more than to see her again, the scene of his shame was one to be avoided.

At least Darcy thought this way until memories of the conversation with the Gardiners had surfaced, with mentions of Lizzy. Again and again he reminded himself that there was nothing attaching her to them. The Lizzy they had mentioned was almost certainly a different person entirely.

But in Darcy's breast had been awakened a desire to see her again, to judge for himself if what he suspected of her beauty was correct. And perhaps even more importantly, he wished for the opportunity to gage whether he might make an apology to her for his actions. Even if she was not injured by them, his honor demanded he offer it, regardless. The notion to go and see her was nigh overpowering.

By the time he could see Snowlock rising through the trees, its façade open and welcoming, Darcy had convinced himself to go, alternately talking himself out of it, more than a dozen times, it seemed. Eager to put such thoughts behind him, Darcy consigned his steed to the care of a groom and climbed the stairs two at a time, eager to be with his family again. Surely, they would provide a respite and a distraction from his thoughts.

"Fitzwilliam," intoned his father as he entered the sitting-room upon making himself presentable. "Sit with me and tell me of matters at Pemberley."

Knowing his father would demand an accounting of him, Darcy sat close to his father and informed him of his actions. The problem had not been a difficult one—a particular pair of tenants had a history of disputes between them, such that Darcy was certain their current strife was more a matter of habit than true disagreement. Darcy had soothed ruffled feathers and restored peace between them—amity was too much to ask for.

When the explanation was complete, Robert Darcy grunted. "It is well that Stearns and Cooper will be turning their farms over to their sons before too many years have passed. Their constant petty rivalry is grating on the nerves."

"Given what you have said of them," said Darcy's uncle in a jovial tone, "I do not doubt their sons will carry on the tradition."

Darcy's uncle was a large contrast to his father, though the two men had been close friends from the days they had been at Eton together. If the elder Darcy was akin to a closed book, the earl was one which lay open. Robert Darcy was calm and rational, reticent and quiet, and while the earl was also a rational man, he was garrulous and happy, quick with a joke and kind to all. Mr. Darcy was not unkind, but he was more apt to remain silent. Silence was a term with which Jacob Fitzwilliam, Earl of Matlock, shared little acquaintance. These traits were shared to a lesser extent with his sister, Lady Anne Darcy, though Lady Anne was more likely to smile and speak with affection than laugh. With their other siblings, Darcy was not as well acquainted. The earl had one elder sister, Lady Catherine, who Darcy had never cared for, due to her autocratic manners, and two younger brothers, one a bishop, and the other, a gentleman who had inherited an estate in Wiltshire from an elderly relation.

"Actually, Uncle," said Darcy, "the sons are known to me. Though their fathers prefer to butt heads like the sheep on our estate, the sons are known to be friendly with each other."

"Then perhaps you should encourage their fathers into retirement. There are few things more frustrating than tenants who continually quarrel with each other."

Privately Darcy agreed with his uncle. His father, however, seemed ready to allow the subject to drop, and Darcy did so. They sat in general conversation for some time, the sounds of his sister playing the pianoforte providing the background for their conversation. His mother sat with Lady Susan, speaking of inconsequential subjects, while the men discussed their estates and the expectations for this year's yields. The earl's three eldest children were all gone from the estate, his son James on his wedding tour with his new bride, while his son, Anthony, had been called away to business with his regiment. Of the two daughters, Rachel was at another house party with her husband, while Charity was somewhere on the estate or with Georgiana in the music room. There was some talk that his cousin's regiment would soon be called up to duty on the peninsula, and while Darcy knew his aunt would fret, he also knew Fitzwilliam would not consider shirking his duty.

"Was there anything else that requires our attention?" asked Darcy's father, turning back to him some time later. "No correspondence which must be handled?"

"Nothing that I could see," said Darcy. "There was, however, an invitation for me to join Bingley at his father's estate in Hertfordshire."

"Bingley," said his father, his voice flat. "Is he still importuning you?"

"He is my friend, Father," said Darcy, his tone a little more pointed than he had intended.

Mr. Darcy grunted. "Perhaps he is, at that. As you have not seen him for some time, I had hoped you intended to allow distance between you."

"It is not to be supposed since I have not seen Bingley lately that I do not still consider him a friend." Darcy met his father's eyes evenly, not in challenge, but with a look which was meant to convey his firmness on the subject. "I enjoyed my stay the last time I was in Hertfordshire and mean to accept the invitation this time."

Although his father's lips tightened in displeasure, Darcy was more focused on surprise that he had come to a decision in such a manner. He was now committed, he realized, though he had not been decided at all when he walked through the door. But it felt right, he decided; it had been four years since he had gone, four years of thinking, of remembering, of longing. Yes, longing. It was time to return, to see what time had wrought. Time to consider new possibilities.

"You know I have no issue with the man himself," said his father, drawing Darcy's attention again. "Mr. Bingley seemed like a gentlemanly man. But I am not convinced it would be best to encourage such a close association. The Bingleys are not of our sphere."

"I thought him a perfectly lovely man," said Lady Anne.

Husband and wife shared a look, one which Darcy had seen many times between them. Theirs was not a relationship in which Mr. Darcy, as the master and husband, dominated his wife. Lady Anne had her own opinions and was not shy about sharing them, and her husband, to his credit, was a man who listened to his wife and esteemed her as an equal. That she was more open to those of Bingley's ilk was interesting, for the Fitzwilliams were the titled family, after all. Mr. Darcy had never attempted to impose his will on his wife, not that she would have been cowed anyway.

"As I said, I know nothing ill of the young man. But the fact that he is not of our level of society is incontrovertible. The Bingley family is new money. Their standing in society is of the second circle at best, and that only because of the wealth they brought with them when they purchased their estate. It will be generations before they are fully accepted. The consequence of the Darcy family can only be lessened in comparison when we associate with people of their station."

"Times are changing, Darcy," said the earl. "While the gentry fight tooth and nail to maintain their rank in society, tradesmen amass prodigious fortunes and buy their way into the upper echelons. I know you do not like it, but I find that the contents of a man's character are far more important to his worth in society than the matter of his birth. Take Baron Godwin, for example—though his family is lower on the societal scale than many, I would not associate with him were he the Prince Regent himself, so low are his morals."

Mr. Darcy grunted his agreement. He turned back to Darcy, his gaze piercing. "Will they attempt to push one of their daughters on you? I understand there are two."

"One is already married," replied Darcy, "and the other is now engaged."

"To some local landowner, I will wager. Will she be content, or will she turn to the greater prize when you are before her?"

"Since the marriage is to take place before I am to arrive, I highly doubt it."

The dryness of his reply set the earl to laughter, and even his mother and aunt smiled fondly at him. It appeared his father was no happier with his son's intentions, but at least he appeared resigned.

"You will do what you wish, I suppose. You always do. Is it too much to hope that you remember your place and avoid entanglements with young ladies of the neighborhood? I know too much of such local societies to think that every woman of marriageable age will not immediately set her cap at you."

"I shall be circumspect, as always, Father."

"Very well," replied Mr. Darcy, and the subject was dropped for other matters.

It was later that evening, when the company was together after dinner, that Darcy had an opportunity to speak with his sister. Georgiana was a lovely girl with honey blonde hair—lighter highlights due to the summer sun—a tall and womanly form, and an affectionate heart. In the past several months, seeing the woman she was growing into had aroused a protective instinct in Darcy. Soon they would be forced to allow her to spread her wings, to move in society, and soon after, she would undoubtedly catch the attention of some young man, marry, and make her own way in the world. Darcy did not know who was good enough for his beloved sister, but he knew he would be required to let her live her own life, not that he would ever dream of stepping in her way.

When informed of her brother's intention to visit Mr. Bingley later that summer, she appeared interested, though knowing her father's opinion of that family, she refrained from displaying her delight. "I know how you enjoy Mr. Bingley's company, Brother. When do you leave?"

"Not until the beginning of August," replied Darcy. "Bingley's elder sister is about to be married, and I would not dream of intruding on them while they are in a frenzy of preparations."

"I wish I could meet Mr. Bingley's family," said Georgiana. "He was very kind when he visited. Are his family much the same?"

While Darcy informed her of what he remembered of Bingley's immediate family, the unspoken matter between them was that their father would be unlikely to allow it. In the future, when Georgiana was grown and possessed more autonomy from their parents, it might be possible. But until she came out, Darcy judged it unlikely that she would be allowed to be in the Bingleys' company, and Darcy knew that she was well aware of this fact.

As they spoke, Darcy could not help but notice his mother's eyes upon them. The look she was giving them suggested she was aware of the content of their discussion. While Darcy did not think she precisely disapproved, he knew she would follow her husband's lead concerning Georgiana ever meeting Mr. Bingley. Thus, Darcy was not surprised when Lady Anne made her way across the room.

"Georgiana, Fitzwilliam," said she when she joined them, sitting next to her daughter. "May I ask to be included in your conversation?"

"Of course, Mother," replied Georgiana, apparently unaware of her mother's level look. "William was just telling me of Mr. Bingley's family."

Lady Anne smiled at her daughter. "I did enjoy Mr. Bingley's company when he visited us, Georgiana, and believe he is a very good sort of man. But I hope you do not esteem him more than you ought."

There was an inherent question in his mother's voice, though it was clearly a statement. But it was the subject which caught Darcy by surprise. Georgiana was no less shocked, for she blurted:

"Do you think I admire Mr. Bingley?"

"This interest in him is suggestive, my dear," said their mother. "He *is* an amiable man, well-favored, and just at the right age to attract the interest of a young girl of your age."

"I am not infatuated with Mr. Bingley," said Georgiana, her cheeks burning in embarrassment.

"And Bingley has long been enamored with the daughter of his closest neighbor," added Darcy. "Even if Georgiana should have some youthful infatuation for Bingley—"

"Which I do not!" protested his sister.

Darcy grinned at her. "Even if you did, it would come to nothing."

"That is well, then." Lady Anne fixed them with a pointed look and said: "Your father would never stand for it."

"I am still but sixteen," said Georgiana, her grumpy tone prompting a smile from her mother. "There is no thought in my mind for any young man when I am not even out."

"Good. Let us keep it this way." Lady Anne smiled at her daughter and caressed her cheek with a light touch. "I find I am not ready to lose you, Georgiana. I would appreciate your company for some years yet."

"There is no reason to rush," agreed Georgiana.

Lady Anne took this admission as the end of the subject, and they moved to other topics, Darcy listening to the conversation, though participating little. After a time, he began to pay less attention to his family, his thoughts of his now confirmed engagement filling him. The thought, however fleeting, of how Miss Elizabeth would be received by his family flitted across his mind. His mother and sister, he thought, would love her, though his father would decry her as unsuitable. But he had spent only a few moments in her company and knew little of her—he could not be serious in his interest. Thus, he forced the matter from his mind.

"Fitzwilliam," said his mother, drawing his attention back to her. "There is something of which you should know."

When Darcy directed a questioning look at her, Lady Anne responded: "Your father received another letter from Wickham this morning."

Annoyed by the mention of the libertine, Darcy felt his good humor fleeing. "What does he want this time? I suppose his request was for money?"

"Your father said nothing of that," replied Lady Anne. "But he has asked for a visit to Pemberley. Furthermore, the letter was directed to your father's attention at Snowlock."

Darcy felt his scowled deepen, but that was nothing new when it came to the mention of Wickham. "I suspect he has some contact at Pemberley who is willing to feed him information concerning our movements. Or at the very least, our location when we are not home."

The look Lady Anne bestowed upon him was considering. "You know I am taking your account of Wickham on faith, Fitzwilliam. The sort of vices of which you have informed me have never been betrayed in my presence, nor that of your father."

"That is because Wickham takes great care to hide it from you," was Darcy's short reply. "Wickham knows my father's character and understands that if he should betray his true nature, his association with the family would end. As I am near to him in age and have had the opportunity to see him in unguarded moments—and was in his company for several years at university—he is less capable of hiding his character from me."

Georgiana gasped. She had fond memories of Wickham, Darcy knew, and while he did not wish to destroy her innocence, perhaps it was best that she now understand exactly what kind of man he was. For her part, Lady Anne simply watched Darcy, saying nothing. Darcy took it as an invitation to expound upon the matter.

"I ask you to trust me in this matter, Mother. Wickham is not a good man. Shall I show you the receipts I have of his debts I paid before I departed from Cambridge? He is too clever to allow his accounts to be in arrears in Lambton where Father would soon become aware of them, but I have little doubt he has incurred them in other places where he is not as well known. And consider his request to leave his livelihood after only a few months out of our company. Does his position at the solicitors mean so little to him?"

"I do not question you, Fitzwilliam," said his mother with a sigh. "But your father will hear nothing against him and will not speak on the subject."

"Father's blindness with respect to Wickham is obvious," replied Darcy shortly. Georgiana once again looked at him with shock, but Darcy smiled at him and addressed his mother: "I have no notion of ever convincing Father, and thus I give it little thought. For myself, I will no longer associate with him.

"As for his position in London, I know very well he only studied the law when Father made it clear that it was the law or the church. Even then, his studying was rudimentary, and his position at the solicitors was bought by Father's connections, and not any virtue of Wickham's.

"Furthermore, I am well aware of Wickham's expectations in life."

Darcy paused, bitterness welling up within him. The matter of George Wickham was the one subject on which father and son could not agree. Darcy was confident in his father's love for him, and all of Wickham's taunts, his claims of being the elder Darcy's favorite, were nothing more than wishful thinking on Wickham's part. But the fact that his father would hear nothing against Wickham dismayed and angered Darcy, especially when his father put great weight in his opinion otherwise. Even with Fitzwilliam's support, Darcy had never been able to make his father see the truth of his favorite.

"Do you know he disdained the offer of the Kympton living?" said Darcy at length, his words even, regardless of his desire to give in to his anger.

"The manner in which he refused it made it evident," replied Lady Anne.

"It is one of the few times I have ever seen Father treat the blackguard firmly." Lady Anne's countenance darkened, but Darcy was adamant. "You know it is true, Mother."

"It is. But I would appreciate it if you would modify your tone."

Darcy bowed his head, but he kept his countenance even. "Wickham expected more than the Kympton living, a valuable living that one such as he would not normally be in a position to expect. For a man of his background, an income in excess of three or four hundred pounds a year is equivalent to a king's ransom."

Darcy grimaced as he remembered the leach's reaction to Mr. Darcy's suggestion. "He was even less pleased with the offer to study the law. But he knew my father would soon learn of his proclivities should he accept Kympton, and therefore settled on, in his eyes, the lesser of the two evils. I do not know the content of his thoughts, for he would never confide in me, but I suspect he thought Father would bestow upon him a gentleman's income. Perhaps Rosedale or Pine Bluff."

"Does he think he is a second son?" demanded Lady Anne. It was apparent she was growing offended. Perhaps Darcy should have shared these thoughts with her previously. Though he had no notion Wickham would attempt anything with Lady Anne—though Darcy thought there were few other women in the kingdom who were safe from him—knowing his nature was a protection against his depredations.

"He has been treated as one all his life," said Darcy.

Though it was apparent his mother did not appreciate his words, Darcy knew there was little disputing them. "Your father means to refuse him."

"Good," replied Darcy. "Hopefully he will continue to do so." Darcy turned to Georgiana, who was watching them with the wide eyes of one whose previously held opinions were being stripped away. "If Father should give in to the libertine's pleas, I would particularly suggest Georgiana take care in his presence."

"Surely you do not expect her to be his target," protested his mother.

"For her fortune of thirty thousand pounds, Wickham might risk it," replied Darcy. "She would be his means of obtaining a life of ease, and that might be enough of an inducement."

Lady Anne's eyes searched Darcy's for a few moments before she grimaced and looked to her daughter. For her part, Georgiana looked back, more than a little fearful. Darcy watched it all with satisfaction of knowing his warning had been soberly received. While he did not wish his sister to be forever walking the path of life afraid for what lay beyond the next hill, her wariness of Wickham could only be beneficial.

"You may be assured that I will be chary of Mr. Wickham," said Georgiana.

"And I shall keep her safe," said Lady Anne. "In the meantime, I will advise your father that Wickham should remain in London. He is not that long in his position that he can leave at will for weeks at a time. Your father understands this."

Darcy responded with a curt nod. "If something happens, let me know. Or Anthony can intervene if he is nearby.

The subject was then dropped. Though Darcy had no notion that Wickham considered Georgiana a target, he also knew the man was an opportunist. Should he ever entertain the notion of attempting to woo Georgiana for his own gain, he would find his wheel well and truly spiked.

Chapter III

*L*ongbourn Estate, near Meryton in Hertfordshire, was a respectable estate, and one of the two largest in the neighborhood. It had not always been so, having been much smaller only two generations earlier. But an unexpected and sizeable inheritance had allowed the master at the time to make extensive purchases of land, including one small estate in full, whose master decided to move his family to the Americas in search of a better life.

As a result, the manor house was an odd mixture of older sections intermingled with a newer, more modern wing, which boasted a ballroom for entertaining. It was not so imposing as the house at Netherfield Park, that building having been constructed as one single entity, standing tall and handsome amid groves of trees. Longbourn was a more rambling house, seeming smaller and humbler on first glance, when in fact it was the larger of the two.

The current master of Longbourn, Mr. Henry Bennet, was a retiring man past his fiftieth year and had been master of the estate since not long after his son was born. Having been born a younger son, Henry had been destined for academic circles, having eschewed the traditional professions most younger sons pursued. When his elder brother had perished in a riding accident, he had returned to the estate and taken up the reins of management. But whereas his brother was perfectly suited to be an estate's master in temperament and talents, Henry was much more at ease with others of his collegial interests. In short, his interest was more in books and learning, than estate accounts, tenant concerns, and the intricacies of crop rotations.

While Mr. Bennet had managed the estate successfully in the years he had been its master, his penchant for the written word had drawn him to his bookroom more often, meaning his management was often indifferent. A good steward had made this lack less severe than it might have been. Lately, his only son, Thomas, had largely taken over the reins of the estate, allowing Mr. Bennet to settle further into his retirement. This seemed to suit both gentlemen, for Thomas was much more interested in the workings of their holdings, yet his father was available should he require assistance.

Of Mr. Bennet's status as a widower there was not much to say. An oddly matched couple from the start, it had been assumed by many that Mr. Bennet had not possessed much affection for his late wife. This assumption was incorrect, however—for all that Mrs. Bennet had been a flighty woman of indifferent intelligence, she had kept his home for more than twenty years, provided him companionship, and borne his children. Whatever she lacked in cleverness, she had more than made up for in her ability to manage a house and entertain guests, though Mr. Bennet was not at all one who enjoyed a great deal of society. He missed her a great deal, but his philosophy, that change was inevitable, and all were destined to meet their maker someday, allowed him to endure his loss and take comfort in his children and his books.

As has been previously noted, the Bennet family of Longbourn had long been close with the Bingleys of Netherfield. Their sons and daughters were of similar ages, often in company with one another, and the parents enjoyed cordial relations. In the case of Mrs. Bingley and Mrs. Bennet, they had been excellent friends until the untimely loss of the latter. The existence of the assumed matches between said sons and daughters was not in any way an impediment to their shared felicity. Indeed, it was widely thought in the neighborhood that Miss Caroline Bingley would likely already be married to Mr. Thomas Bennet, had Mrs. Bennet not suddenly passed the previous year.

The couple was now engaged, however, with the date of their wedding rapidly approaching, while the younger couple of Mr. Charles Bingley and Miss Jane Bennet appeared well on their way to joining the aforementioned in their state of engaged bliss. While the Bennet sisters' mother was no longer present to put her stamp on the coming wedding celebration—and it was well understood in the neighborhood she would have stood for nothing less than a fête the likes of which the town had never seen—her daughters stepped into the void, planning their brother's wedding alongside Mrs. Bingley with a will. The exception being, of course, Elizabeth, who was currently away touring the lakes with her relations.

On a particular day in July of 1811, the younger Bennets arrived at Netherfield for a visit for the purpose of furthering the plans for the coming celebration. In actuality, Jane Bennet knew that most of the arrangements had already been made and there was little left to be done. The visit was more an excuse to gather together as their families were wont to do, and her brother's presence—who, like his father, had little tolerance for talk of wedding preparations—suggested the more informal nature of the visit.

As they entered the sitting-room at Netherfield, Jane watched her brother as he approached his affianced, noting the eagerness and quick step with which he left his sisters' sides. Thomas was a kind and attentive man, but he was not given over much to frivolities. His marriage to Miss Bingley was what was important, not the flowers, foods at the wedding breakfast, or any other secondary concerns.

"Miss Bennet, Miss Mary," said Mr. Bingley, welcoming them as they entered the room. "How do you do today?"

Jane felt a fluttering in her heart as she did every occasion she was in Mr. Bingley's company. The sensation had started about the time she was fifteen years of age and had not ceased since. Though she well understood the reasons why Mr. Bingley had not yet made his addresses to her, Jane could not help but be impatient for them.

"We are very well, Mr. Bingley," said Mary, speaking when Jane did not immediately respond. "I see I will need to find something with which to occupy myself today. My brother's attention shall not be pried from your sister, and I have no doubt you and *my* sister shall soon be lost in each other's eyes."

Feeling the heat rising in her cheeks, Jane shot a censorious glance at Mary. For her part, Mary did nothing more than grin and step away to find herself a seat on a nearby sofa. Of the three sisters, Mary and Elizabeth were much more alike than Jane was to either. Mary was a little quieter than Elizabeth, more interested in spiritual matters and her devotion to her pianoforte. But they both possessed a teasing manner, one which manifested itself the most in their dealings with their family, Jane in particular.

"Now, now, Mary dear," said Mrs. Bingley, shooting a sly glance at the pair still standing by the door. "You shall sit with me. I would not wish you to feel left out in such a company as this."

"Had I any notion I was being excluded of a purpose, I might feel snubbed," replied Mary. "As it is, I have seen their looks too many times to misunderstand them."

"That is a fact," said Mrs. Bingley while smiling at her progeny. "If only your dear mother were here to witness this realization of all her hopes. I dare say she would have been so pleased and proud of you all!"

As Mr. Bingley drew Jane to a nearby seat, she reflected on the truth of Mrs. Bingley's words. Mrs. Bennet would indeed have been pleased as punch at the upcoming nuptials of her eldest and been eager to see Jane disposed of in marriage too. The pang of her missing mother was one with which Jane was familiar by now, but it had eased to a dull ache of longing.

Mary, it seemed, was pleased with Mrs. Bingley's attention, for she sat with the matron willingly, and soon they were engaged in lively conversation, which, from Jane's perspective, seemed to consist mostly of Mrs. Bingley's inquiries as to any beaux in Mary's life. Jane smiled fondly at her sister—Mary had always been the awkward child, and many had been the comments of her plainness compared to her sisters' beauty. But in the last year or so, Mary had matured, blossomed into a young lady who possessed her fair share of beauty. At this time in her life, at the tender age of only eighteen, Jane knew that Mary had little desire to be courted. In the future, she would make some fortunate man an excellent wife. But there was no rush.

"Is your father out on the estate today?" asked Jane of Mr. Bingley.

"I believe Father is in his study," said Mr. Bingley. He grinned and added: "Though my father is more open in company than Mr. Bennet, it seems his tolerance for wedding talk prompts him to mirror your father in avoiding it."

"I believe my husband has spent too much time in the company of your father," said Mrs. Bingley. "Wedding talk, indeed! The arrangements have been largely complete for at least two weeks!"

"And yet Papa avoids our sitting-room when our dear friends come," said Caroline. "Perhaps he fears an outbreak of such talk whenever we are together."

They all laughed at Caroline's observation. "It may be best if you encourage him to visit Longbourn when we are here," said Jane. "Then they may commiserate without enduring the danger of being infected by such subjects."

"But what of the times when the Bingleys visit us?" asked Thomas. "You know Father does not like to trade the comforts of Longbourn's library for Netherfield's."

"Not to mention the fact that ours is not suitably enough stocked for Mr. Bennet's taste," added Mr. Bingley. "None of us Bingleys are great readers."

"I enjoy a book when I can get it," said Thomas. "But there is always so much to be done on the estate. And I can never hope to hold a candle to Lizzy or Mary when it comes to the written word. I am as educated as the next man, but sometimes hearing them speak with Father, I might think the book they are discussing is in Greek!"

"At times it is," was Mary's prim reply, prompting laughter among the company. "I dare say, you all would benefit from a little literature at times."

"Perhaps we would, Mary, dearest," said Thomas.

"Personally," said Mr. Bingley, "I take issue with your claim of possessing an education. I cannot imagine that so-called university you attended can claim anything so lofty as to be able to impart an education."

"How dare you debase Oxford's good name!" exclaimed Thomas in mock affront. "I will inform you that Oxford is the older, more venerable institution."

"Cambridge's charter was granted in 1231," noted Mr. Bingley. "Oxford was not granted until 1258."

"Ah, but Oxford was instructing as early as the late eleventh century, my dear Mr. Bingley. Cambridge did not begin offering their pitiful attempts at higher learning until the early thirteenth."

"Boys!" scolded Mrs. Bingley. "I shall not have you debate the relative merits of your respective universities in my sitting-room!"

The two men only grinned, however, ignoring Mrs. Bingley and continuing to throw facts back and forth. Mrs. Bingley, accustomed as she was to their friendly debate, shook her head and turned back to Mary. Jane watched her brother and her beau with some interest. She had never felt the desire to become more educated than she was at present though she knew Lizzy would have jumped at the chance to attend either of the universities. Jane was by no means uneducated — she had learned alongside all her sisters at the instruction of their governess and had spent some time at school in Caroline's company. But she had never craved knowledge for its own sake, which she knew Lizzy, and to a lesser extent Mary, always had.

"Well, I shall soon have another to back me up regarding the relative merits of our educations," said Mr. Bingley, drawing Jane's attention back to the conversation. "And I know *he*, at least, has the right opinion of the matter."

"One of your university friends, no doubt," said Thomas, shaking his head in apparent disdain. "Given your own lack of education, I can only assume he will share the same, and he will be just as ignorant of it as you."

Thomas paused and looked critically at Mr. Bingley, apparently deep in thought. For his part, Mr. Bingley waited for him to speak. Jane knew he enjoyed their verbal sparring matches with Thomas as much as Thomas did himself. The men were firm friends; neither would take offense at the teasing of the other.

"In fact, I am afraid I have proof that your education is lacking, my friend," said Thomas at last.

A laugh was Mr. Bingley's response. "Please, share this insight with me. In what way has my education been lacking?"

"Why, in the fact that you cannot even write a coherent sentence!" said Thomas, his manner suggesting triumph. Mr. Bingley laughed and shook his head. "I have had occasion to read your letters, my friend."

"Oh, Charles is most careless when he writes!" exclaimed Caroline, looking at her brother with unmistakable fondness. "It seems he leaves out every third word, and as the rest are blotted, it is impossible to decipher their meaning."

"It is a fault I will own without disguise," said Mr. Bingley, ruefully shaking his head. "Whenever I write, I do so with the firm intention of making it legible. But my thoughts flow so quickly, my pen cannot keep up."

"There," said Thomas, leaning back, his countenance alive with satisfaction. "It has been proven. You have no choice but to retire the field in defeat, my friend."

"Or perhaps it is simply my own personal failing. Not *all* men educated at Cambridge are the same. My friend, Mr. Darcy, for example, writes letters that are nothing like mine. They are clear, concise, and filled with words, the meaning of which I am only dimly aware!"

Jane felt her heart lurch within her chest at the mention of that particular gentleman's name, though she did not allow it to show on her countenance. It seemed she had been successful as none of the rest of the party noticed. In particular, Thomas regarded Mr. Bingley with apparent interest.

"Is Mr. Darcy the friend of whom you spoke only minutes ago?"

"He is," replied Mr. Bingley. "I received a letter from him just yesterday, accepting my invitation for him to visit us this summer. With your wedding approaching, I did not feel it was right to invite him before, but he shall join us soon after."

"Mr. Darcy is such a gentlemanly man," said Mrs. Bingley. "I would be happy to have him attend my daughter's wedding, but I can understand why he might be made uncomfortable. Though he is Charles's friend, he is not well known to the rest of the family, after all."

"He *did* stay with us," replied Caroline. "If you write him again, Charles, inform him we would be happy if he would attend, if he wishes."

"Given your brother's skill with a pen," said Thomas *sotto voce*, "I doubt he could decipher it in time to make the journey."

"I *do* possess the ability to write legibly, when I choose," said Mr. Bingley, leaning back in his chair and fixing Thomas with a grin.

"And yet, you informed us that ability deserts you when you attempt to utilize it!"

Again, they all laughed. For her part, Jane's was forced, for the matter of Mr. Darcy's upcoming visit was foremost in her mind. Jane still, after four years, did not know what to make of the matter. That he had imposed upon her dearest sister most improperly was beyond dispute—Elizabeth would never speak a falsehood about such a thing. But what manner of man was he? Jane still wished to believe there had been some extenuating circumstance. But Lizzy's peace of mind was the most important consideration. Could Lizzy be easy with that man in the neighborhood?

"I doubt he would accept an earlier invitation, regardless," said Mr. Bingley. "It is my understanding his family is visiting their uncle's estate at present. I shall be content with his arrival in August, for it has been some months since I have been in his company."

"It seems to me you are engaged in some great conspiracy, Bingley," said Thomas.

"How so, my friend? And what could this intrigue hope to accomplish?"

"Why, to prevent me from meeting this Mr. Darcy of whom you speak," replied Thomas. "Your words of him have been frequent and your attachment firm, and yet I have not made this gentleman's acquaintance. It always seems that I am in town when he is not or vice versa, or that I arrive at the club only moments after he has left. Even when he visited, I was on the continent and did not return until after he had departed. And now, you propose to invite this gentleman to visit when I am honeymooning, and I shall miss him yet again!"

"I have never thought of it that way before," replied Mr. Bingley with a chuckle. "It does seem you have just missed him several times in the past.

"Thus, my reference to a conspiracy. It almost seems to me you have imagined this gentleman in his entirety."

"Well, this time you shall make his acquaintance," averred Mr. Bingley. "Darcy shall stay some weeks with us, and as he will not arrive until a week or more after your nuptials, I think it likely he will still be here when you return."

Jane could not help but shake her head in dismay. Mr. Darcy would be here, and Thomas would not even be present to protect Lizzy!

Unfortunately, her action was witnessed by Mr. Bingley, for he turned a questioning gaze on her. "Did you not find Mr. Darcy all that was gentlemanly and amiable, Miss Bennet?"

"Yes, he was gentlemanly, indeed," replied Jane. In the confines of her mind, she added: *To me. Lizzy did not find him nearly so gentlemanly.*

"Mr. Darcy is a good man, indeed," said Caroline. "I am anticipating making his acquaintance again."

"I am not surprised you would," said Mary with a sly look at her future sister. "For it seemed to me that you spoke of Mr. Darcy so much when he visited that I might almost have thought you held a tendre for him!"

The sparkle in Mary's eye reminded Jane greatly of Lizzy. It was a tease Lizzy might have made had she been present. And had she not been importuned as she was at the hand of the man of whom they spoke. Caroline was prepossessed enough to shrug off Mary's words, though her gaze in response suggested future vengeance.

"It seems to me all young ladies share an interest in a man new to their acquaintance," said Thomas, grasping Caroline's hand and squeezing it. "Had I any doubts of your future sister's affection, Mary, I might be jealous. As it is, I have no doubt, it shall not bother me a jot."

"Of course, you should not, dearest Brother," said Mary, fixing him with an affectionate smile. "I think half the neighborhood was in love with Mr. Darcy, as he *is* remarkably well favored. If Caroline was affected by him, I should not blame her at all!"

"Just you wait until I am mistress of Longbourn, Mary Bennet," said Caroline with a sniff. "I shall ensure you live in the coop with the chickens, and that you subsist on nothing more than dry bread and water."

"I am anticipating your move to Longbourn too, dear Caroline," replied Mary.

While the friendly banter continued all around her, Jane found herself too immersed in her own thoughts to participate. This news of Mr. Darcy coming again to Netherfield was worrisome. It may be that Jane's hope of exculpating circumstances would prove true, but she knew that Lizzy's peace of mind would be affected with Mr. Darcy's coming.

Had Jane not promised to keep her sister's confidence, she would have informed her brother of the matter. Jane thought Thomas *should* be informed, for it was his—and their father's—duty to protect them. But Jane could not bear to think of breaking Elizabeth's trust, especially when she was so uncertain of the worthlessness of the young man's character.

But one thing was certain—Lizzy was due to return to Longbourn within the next few days with their aunt and uncle, and Jane did not relish the prospect of informing her younger sister of the gentleman's imminent arrival. There was little doubt that Elizabeth would protest that she was well and Mr. Darcy's presence did not affect her. But she would almost certainly be affected by him, enough that she would avoid him and endeavor to protect herself by always being in company with others. For one as free and spirited as Lizzy Bennet, such restrictions would be difficult to endure.

There was not a hint of doubt in Jane's mind that Elizabeth would continue to be the strong, determined individual that she had always been. But Jane, who knew Elizabeth as well as any other person in the world, had been with her sister these past four years. She knew that Elizabeth did not always possess the strength she projected. Many times, Jane had witnessed her wariness when in the company of gentlemen, and while such care was prudent, there was something more to it than simple caution. Elizabeth had been changed irrevocably by the experience. And now the gentleman was to come again.

Jane did not know what to do.

CHAPTER IV

The sights had been seen, the delights savored, and now it was time to return to the south. Of the places they had visited, Elizabeth knew she would always hold fond memories, though she might never visit them again. Elizabeth had even learned to look back on Pemberley, which had seen the coming of a man she wished to avoid, with a certain fondness. It *was* a beautiful estate, after all, one of which anyone would have the right to be proud.

The distances were long, and the time to travel back to Longbourn and then London was not insignificant. As a result, the travelers amused themselves as best they could. While Elizabeth was often to be found gazing out the window at the passing scenery, there was much conversation to be had. For their experiences were still fresh in their minds, and their observations concerning what they had seen readily given. In all, it was pleasant to journey in such a manner with such company.

The discussion of their experiences, Elizabeth found she could well tolerate, for her aunt and uncle were intelligent and observant, and their conversation always interesting. When the talk turned to the situation to which they would return, Elizabeth found herself growing a little less comfortable, though she was unable to determine exactly why.

"Well, Lizzy," said her uncle as he noted the carriage crossing into Bedfordshire, "we shall be home before long. Though we have enjoyed our tour, I assume you must be eager to return to Longbourn."

"I am, I will own," replied Elizabeth. "The charming vistas you have shown me will always remain fond memories, and I thank you for inviting me. But the return to one's own home must be savored, I think."

"A good home it is," said her aunt. "Are you as eager to see your family as you are the paths you often walk?"

"Indeed, I am. And I am gaining another sister within the month. It is a reason to celebrate."

"That is a subject of which I have meant to ask you," said her uncle. Elizabeth noted his interested look, wondering what it might portend. "With your brother's marriage, his wife will assume the management of the house, considering your mother's passing. That will be a significant change for you and Jane, will it not?"

"More for Jane than me. Jane was the one who took up the role of mistress when my mother passed."

"But it will also be a change for you, Lizzy," asserted Mrs. Gardiner. "Jane is your sister by birth, one trained by your mother to one day manage a house. Miss Bingley is, though she has been known to your family for many years, a newcomer to the estate, and her ideas of what should be done might not mirror your own."

"I hardly think that would be a cause for strife," said Elizabeth with a shaken head. The conversation was confusing, for she could not determine what her relations meant by speaking in such a manner. "Caroline is a sensible woman, and if she serves dinner at a different hour or instructs the maids to their duties in a way I might not, what is it to me?"

"Nothing, I presume," replied her aunt. "And yet, there is always the possibility for misunderstanding, and if it is not corrected, discord."

"And if I recall," added her uncle, "you have not always been friendly with Miss Bingley. Is that not correct?"

"That was a long time in the past," replied Elizabeth. "I will own that Caroline and I have not always seen eye to eye, but it has not led us to overt conflict. I am quite friendly with her now."

"We are happy to hear it, Elizabeth," said Aunt Gardiner. "Hopefully the transition will proceed in a manner which is easy for you all."

"Excuse me," said Elizabeth, eying her relations with open curiosity, "but I wonder to what these questions portend. Surely you do not suggest we shall be overset with dissention by the introduction of my brother's wife to our home."

"No," replied Mrs. Gardiner. She turned a fond look on her husband before once again addressing Elizabeth. "It is only that I have experienced such in the past and wished to ensure you are prepared for it. When my mother passed away, I was only a girl, though old enough to remember my mother very well. When my father remarried, it was different—an adjustment for us all."

"That is different from my brother marrying and bringing his bride home to our house."

"Yes, it is. But it is also similar in many ways. There are always little things which can disrupt a house, particularly as you do not truly know someone until you have lived with them and endured their quirks of character. I do not say that you will rue Miss Bingley's entrance into your home. But there will almost certainly be times when you disagree or when hard feelings may arise."

"If you should require distance," added Mr. Gardiner, "you are always welcome to stay with us in London. For that matter, should Jane or Mary require a respite, they are welcome to come too."

Elizabeth shook her head and directed a wry smile at her relations. "What you say has merit, I will confess. For myself, I thank you for the invitation. As Caroline and I are both of a stubborn bent, I suspect there will be times when we do not agree, and Mary may agree with me. As for Jane—can you imagine her ever being at odds with *anyone*, enough to wish to flee to the safety of your home?"

They all laughed at Elizabeth's observation, which was no less than the truth. Jane was the soul of contentment, one who could never imagine being anything other than amiable with everyone she met, particularly one she had considered a friend for many years.

"Perhaps you are correct with respect to Jane," replied Uncle Gardiner.

"As for my brother," said Elizabeth, "I am quite happy for him, regardless of the changes it will bring to my home. Though I have, in the past, butted heads with Caroline, I consider her to be good for my brother. He has admired her for many years. If it should become necessary, I will consider your invitation and will be happy to impose upon your hospitality." Elizabeth grinned and arched an eyebrow at her relations. "In fact, I suspect I shall impose upon it in any case, as I have many times."

"And we shall be happy to have you, Lizzy," said Aunt Gardiner, patting her hand with affection. "Only send us a note, and we will receive you at any time."

"What of your elder sister?" asked Mr. Gardiner. "It seems to me Thomas has not been the only one admiring another. Do you expect Mr. Bingley will ever come to the point with Jane?"

"I suspect he has wished to for some time," replied Elizabeth. "He is yet a young man — not even five and twenty. After university and his grand tour, I believe he thought it essential to learn all he could of the management of Netherfield before he could offer for Jane. Once the harvest is in and he is able to focus more of his attention on her, I suspect they will come to an understanding quite quickly."

"Your happiness for your sister is evident, Lizzy," said Mrs. Gardiner.

"Who could not be happy for Jane? Yes, I am very happy for her, for she is most deserving of it. And she has admired Mr. Bingley for a very long time. Consequently, I suspect she will not be required to endure Caroline's management of Longbourn house for long, for she will undoubtedly be engaged before the end of the year."

"Then what will your future be?"

Her uncle's question took Elizabeth by surprise, and she faltered for a moment in confusion. "I do not know," replied Elizabeth when she had gathered her wits. "There is no one in Meryton or its environs I could see myself marrying."

"Not even your father's cousin?"

Elizabeth shook her head in amusement. "Not even him. While the estates in the neighborhood are much smaller than Longbourn or Netherfield, you know I would be happy if I truly esteemed the man I was marrying. But there is no one there in whom I have the slightest interest. Even Samuel Lucas, who is a cut above the rest of the gentlemen in the neighborhood, would not suit me, nor I him, though I know his mother would eagerly accept me as a daughter."

"Then perhaps it is to London you should look to find a husband," said Aunt Gardiner. "Your family is well known in the circles you keep."

"Perhaps," said Elizabeth, careful to remain noncommittal. "But I am not yet one and twenty, and I have no desire to search for a husband at present. For now, there is Thomas's wedding to consider, and then Jane's will follow not long after. Once my elder siblings are safely married, I might consider my future."

"I hope you successfully find a husband, Lizzy," said Mrs. Gardiner with affection. "It is correct that you still have plenty of time. But you have so much love to give—it would be a shame if you remained unmarried."

"I shall attempt to avoid disappointing you," replied Elizabeth with a grin. "The notion of marriage is not onerous, I assure you. I simply do not believe I must be in a rush to find someone at present. But while I am not impatient to look for a husband, if a suitable man comes along, I shall not spurn him."

The Gardiners seemed to accept Elizabeth's assurances, and for a time, they were silent. For Elizabeth's part, she felt all the lie of her own words in the deep recesses of her heart. It was true that she did not feel any need to rush into marriage at the present time. But when she thought of marriage and considered the possibility of it, especially when compared to the easy manner in which her elder siblings had found their life partners, she wondered if it would be as simple for her to do likewise.

If Elizabeth decided not to marry, she knew she could live comfortably and not regret that which did not come to pass. Her brother would forever welcome her at Longbourn, she knew, and she could always live with Jane. Furthermore, her dowry was such that if she was required to do so, she could live in comfort should she choose it.

In the back of her mind, in a dark recess of which she did not like to think, nor would she confess to anyone—even dearest Jane—the thought of marriage would bring the image of Mr. Darcy to mind. Given the actions of that gentleman and the secret she had hidden the past four years, Elizabeth wondered if marriage was even a possibility.

Elizabeth's homecoming was all she could ever wish. Welcomed by family she had long missed, she and the Gardiners were accepted into the bosom of the family with the true pleasure of those sundered, while the children, who had been at Longbourn during their tour, were clearly happy to see their parents.

As they settled in after their long journey, the Gardiners were given a room to stay and rest themselves for the final leg of their journey back to London. Elizabeth was eager to return to her own room with its familiar comfort to rest for the remainder of the afternoon. They made a boisterous company that evening, with even her father joining them, informing Elizabeth how happy he was for her return. As Elizabeth had always been his intellectual companion in a way that even Thomas had not, she accepted his welcome, informing him that she was glad to be returned to her home.

The only blight on the evening was the behavior of her dearest sister, Jane. While all three Bennet daughters had always been close, Jane and Elizabeth had shared a relationship which was profound. Mary, who might have felt excluded by their close friendship, had always looked on their relationship with fondness but no envy. In every way that counted, they were the closest of sisters, and both Jane and Elizabeth made every attempt to include their youngest in everything.

As such, Jane's behavior that evening was concerning to Elizabeth, for she knew not how to interpret it. Anyone watching from the outside would have seen nothing amiss — Jane was eager to greet her sister and welcome her home, eager to be in her company as ever. But to one who formed half of the pair, Elizabeth could see little signs that her sister's behavior was not quite what she might have expected. She was hesitant, careful in Elizabeth's company, as if she had some great weight settled on her shoulders. Elizabeth looked at her sister askance more than once, but Jane affected contentment, pretending not to see Elizabeth's curiosity.

The next morning the party broke their fasts together after which the Gardiners departed for their home. Returned, as they were, to their usual family party, Elizabeth lost no time in confronting her sister. As typical for Jane when they were alone, she sighed and confessed something was bothering her. Elizabeth could not imagine what it was until her sister confided in her.

"It is only that I have received some troubling news which I know will be of distress to you."

"Then you had best share it!" exclaimed Elizabeth. "While I know of nothing which would cause my beloved sister such pause, I know it must be serious, for I have rarely seen you in such a state."

"When we visited Netherfield the other day," said Jane, "I learned that they will receive a visitor after the wedding. A visitor whom I know you will wish to avoid."

For a moment Elizabeth was at a loss to understand Jane's meaning. Then the memory of seeing Mr. Darcy once again after four years, coupled with the memory of that night on the balcony of the assembly halls, flooded into her mind. Elizabeth felt her color rise, and she looked away, contemplating the utter irony that she would escape meeting him at his estate, only to have his company thrust upon her mere weeks later.

"Are you well, Lizzy?"

Jane's panicked voice reached Elizabeth's ears, and she pushed her confusion away. "I am quite well, Jane," said Elizabeth, catching her sister's hands up in hers and resting them between Jane and herself on the mattress on which they sat. "Why should you think I care one way or another whom the Bingleys invite to stay with them?"

"Oh, Lizzy!" said Jane, shaking her head. "Your reaction to this news betrays you, Sister dearest."

"I *was* confused for a moment," confessed Elizabeth. "But truly, I do not know why I should concern myself over Mr. Darcy's coming. The more I think of *that* matter, the more I believe there is nothing about which to worry myself. If Mr. Darcy had truly meant any harm to me, he could have returned at any time to do as he wished. That it has been four years with no sign of him suggests I am nothing to him but a diversion."

"Lizzy," said Jane, her tone slightly censorious, "I think I know you well enough to recognize your obfuscation quite well."

"I am in earnest, Jane!"

"Yes, I dare say you are," replied her sister. "As it is a subject we canvassed often after the event, you are aware that I do not think you to be in any danger from Mr. Darcy." Elizabeth nodded. "While I know you think me simple for attributing it to misunderstanding, I cannot but think there may be something more to Mr. Darcy's action than you are suggesting. He never appeared the rake when he was here."

"Not where anyone but me could witness it," muttered Elizabeth.

"Be that as it may," continued Jane, as if Elizabeth had not spoken, "I am still wary of the man and would not have my sister hurt by him."

"Thank you, Jane," said Elizabeth. "I do not intend to put myself in the position of being hurt by Mr. Darcy. Whatever he may do, I care not, for I mean to avoid him. The less consequence and notice I give him, the better I will feel."

"And your scruples do you credit. But, Lizzy, I wish you to consider something you may not have." Elizabeth's nod was sufficient for Jane to continue. "With Mr. Darcy's return to the neighborhood, I am concerned for your wellbeing. I know you preferred not to speak to my father of this matter, but I would ask you to reconsider. If Mr. Darcy *is* a threat, should Papa not be informed so he can better protect you?"

"My reasons for keeping this from Papa are still valid, Jane."

"You cannot think to take this all on your own shoulders." It was not often that Jane became frustrated, but her tone indicated it, nonetheless. "And surely you do not think Papa would force you to marry him."

"Nor did I think he would after the event," replied Elizabeth.

"He would never do that," agreed Jane. "Unless, of course, there was some consequence to your reputation which, of course, there is not. Now that Mama is no longer with us, the threat of her saying something imprudent has been removed. Do you not think it is time to inform Papa and allow him and our brother to perform their duty by protecting you?"

It was a powerful argument, and for a moment Elizabeth felt herself wavering. But there were other matters to consider. Elizabeth thought her state of mind or wellbeing would remain uncompromised by Mr. Darcy's coming and the thought of what would ensue—particularly by her brother, who would be quite upset—stayed her hand. There was no reason to suppose Mr. Darcy meant her harm and every reason to believe he would pay her no mind whatsoever. As such, Elizabeth could not bear the thought of the tumult which must result from such a confession.

"I understand your reasons for wishing to tell Papa, Jane. But I am convinced it is not necessary. There is little to be gained from such an action. What would Papa do? Demand Mr. Bingley put Mr. Darcy from his home and never allow him entrance again?"

"Of course not, Lizzy. But he could ensure your protection."

"If there was some danger, I might agree. But I am convinced there is not. Four years absence between visits supports my theory. No, Jane, I have no desire to provoke such a scene when I am convinced it is unnecessary."

Jane appeared hesitant as if she were considering arguing the matter further. So Elizabeth played her trump card.

"Please, Jane—you promised to keep my confidence. I simply wish to forget about it. There is nothing to fear from Mr. Darcy's coming."

A long look was Jane's response, after which she grimaced and nodded. "Very well. But heed me well, Lizzy—if I think there is some danger which you will not acknowledge, I shall not hesitate to act in your defense."

Feeling a little choked up by her sister's support, Elizabeth threw herself into Jane's arms, accepting the caress of Jane's hand on her back, the love of an elder sister. She had been so blessed—Elizabeth did not know what she would have done without Jane's support.

As might have been expected, later the day after Elizabeth's return saw a pair of visitors descend upon Longbourn. While it might be reasonable to suppose they came to see *her*, given her recent return, it was also evident that at least one of the ladies came to see someone else in particular. Thomas certainly did not seem to mind the presence of his fiancée in the slightest though much of her attention was on Elizabeth. The other visitor was Charlotte Lucas.

It was an interesting dichotomy among the four ladies, thought Elizabeth as she greeted her friends with unfeigned enthusiasm. Jane and Caroline, being of age, had always been the particular friend of the other, perhaps because it had long been assumed that each would marry the other's brother. Charlotte had always been Elizabeth's friend first and foremost, though each of the sisters was quite friendly with the other's friend, and Charlotte and Caroline had always been pleasant to each other. Elizabeth and Charlotte were younger and older than the other two ladies respectively, Elizabeth still being twenty, while Charlotte was four and twenty. With Mary, Thomas, and Mr. Bingley in attendance that morning, the ladies renewed their friendship.

"I see you have been returned to us in good order," said Caroline as they sat down to visit. "No beaux have snapped you up while you were visiting the north?"

"Unfortunately not, Caroline," replied Elizabeth with a laugh. "It seems you must endure my presence in your new home, at least for a little while."

"It is of no matter," said Caroline with an airy wave. "The responsibility to see you safely married must now rest with me. I believe myself quite equal to the task."

"Elizabeth does not need a reincarnation of our mother," said Mary with a roll of her eyes once the laughter had ceased. It was an ongoing joke with Caroline that once she became the mistress of the estate that she would take on their departed mother's role of matchmaker and see them married.

"No, I dare say she does not," said Charlotte. "I am quite confident in her ability to attract a man without any interference at all."

"This presupposes I actually wish to attract a man," said Elizabeth. On one hand she was amused. On the other, the joke was old and had become tiresome.

"Very well," replied Caroline, holding her hands up. "It seems you are not to be teased. The subject shall be raised at some time or another, so I shall let it rest at present. Let me just say that I am glad of your return, Elizabeth. It would not have been the same had you not come back in time."

"There was never any question of it," replied Elizabeth with genuine warmth. "Missing my brother's wedding was not to be considered."

"As I informed you, Caroline," said Thomas in a manner which suggested his affection for the woman.

For some time, the company devolved into smaller conversations among themselves, Caroline with Jane as was to be expected, while Charlotte sat close to Elizabeth, with Mary in attendance. They were much more similar in temperament than the others, though Elizabeth was forced to acknowledge that regardless of Jane and Caroline's dissimilarity, their friendship was just as close.

"Can you tell me of the places you saw, Lizzy?" asked Charlotte.

And so they spoke of Elizabeth's tour. But Elizabeth avoided the mention of Pemberley, the same as she had the previous evening. While the man himself might be coming to interrupt her serenity and invade her peace of mind, Elizabeth did not wish to give anyone any hint of the discomposure she had experienced while visiting the place.

"You are very fortunate," said Charlotte after they had spoken for some minutes. "I should like to tour those places you have seen. But my father has not the means for such frivolities and is content with Meryton and his occasional excursions to St. James's Court."

Elizabeth shared a wry smile with Charlotte—her father's knighthood and admittance to that exalted company was one of his favorite topics. The man was too busy being civil to all to contemplate anything beyond his immediate purview. Elizabeth suspected Charlotte was completely correct—there would be little chance of her ever seeing such sights.

"Perhaps not," replied Elizabeth, feeling the need to reassure her friend. "But I suspect one way or another, you will be allowed to become acquainted with such sights, even if it is only a passing acquaintance. If nothing else, perhaps you and I may tour them sometime by ourselves."

"That would be lovely, Lizzy," replied Charlotte. "But I shall not hope, lest I be disappointed should it not come to fruition."

At that point, Caroline commandeered their attention again, and the conversation turned to general topics. After some little time, Caroline brought it around to that which she had originally meant to take it, in Elizabeth's opinion. Unfortunately, it was not one she would find palatable.

"As you know, we shall be gone for some weeks after we are married. I shall count on hearing from you, Jane, of certain events which shall take place while we are absent."

"Perhaps Elizabeth can be counted on as well," said Thomas with a grin for his sister. "My father, unfortunately, is not a great letter writer. He avoids it at the best of times."

"I should think it unlikely there will be much to discuss," said Charlotte. "Meryton is not exactly an area of great excitement, after all. My father *has* informed us that a company of militia are to quarter here for the winter, but I do not believe they are to arrive until after you return."

"That is because you are not aware of the impending addition to our party here." Caroline paused for dramatic effect, and Elizabeth knew at once what she would say, the sly glance at Elizabeth telling her all she needed to know about the woman's reasons for speaking in such a way. "My brother, you see, has asked Mr. Darcy to visit, and the gentleman has accepted. He will arrive after we leave and will likely stay until after we have returned."

"If you ask me," said Mary *sotto voce*, "it is fortunate that Caroline will already be married to my brother before the gentleman comes, given her behavior the last time he was here."

Elizabeth snickered while Charlotte and Thomas laughed outright. Pleased that her sister had diverted Caroline's tease so effortlessly, she reached out and squeezed Mary's hand in thanks.

"You were not at the assembly — the first your sister ever attended, I might add." Caroline smirked at Mary and then winked at Elizabeth. "I rather thought the gentleman was quite interested in your sister, for he danced with her, you know."

"I seem to recall that he stood up with you, too," replied Charlotte.

"He had a duty to his host's daughter," insisted Caroline. "To me, he was all politeness. In his eyes when he looked at your sister, I am certain I saw the true light of admiration."

"For a girl of sixteen?" demanded Elizabeth, feeling a little uncomfortable at her future sister's continued teasing. "Of course, any man of his age would feel nothing but infatuation for a young, awkward girl, just out in society."

"You have never been merely an awkward girl," said Caroline. Everything in her tone suggested she was entirely sincere in her praise. "Even as a young girl, you sparkled, Lizzy. If you decided to turn your attention on him, I have no doubt you would charm him utterly."

"Thank you, Caroline," said Elizabeth, feeling equal parts vexed and pleased. "But you forget I may not be amenable to it."

"That is why it is my role to act in your interest." Caroline's grin told Elizabeth she was at least partially jesting. "If you will be so unnatural as to refuse."

"I must inform you, my dear future sister," said Elizabeth, "that you are in very great danger of being as disagreeable to me as when you called me an 'insufferable bluestocking in the making' when I was ten! Cease this talk, I beg of you!"

Caroline's laughter was echoed by their companions, and with evident affection, she reached out and clasped Elizabeth's hand, squeezing it tightly. "Then I shall be silent, though I am surprised you remembered that. I had quite forgotten it myself!"

"We Bennets do not forget such slights," was Elizabeth's arch reply. "You should remember that, if you wish to join this family."

"Then I will take care to remember."

At that moment Jane, who had seemed somewhat uncomfortable with the direction of the conversation, changed the subject, asking Caroline some question of the arrangements for the upcoming wedding. Thus diverted, Caroline allowed herself to speak on that subject at great length. Elizabeth nodded at her sister in thanks. Jane truly was the best of sisters.

CHAPTER V

"*I*t is good you have returned, Elizabeth. The wedding would not have been the same if you had remained absent."

Elizabeth smiled warmly at the Bingley matron. "It was never my intention to stay away when my brother married your daughter, Mrs. Bingley. My tour of the north with my relations was planned specifically to ensure we were able to return in plenty of time."

"Excellent, my dear! I hope you have come today prepared to assist, for there is still much to be done for the upcoming wedding breakfast."

As it happened, that was precisely the reason why Elizabeth, along with her sisters, had presented themselves at Netherfield that day, and with a nod of her head, she set to it with a will. Most of the details, those concerning lace and flowers, decorations and other such fripperies Mrs. Bingley thought necessary, might have escaped Elizabeth's notice, had the planning been her responsibility. With her singular interests, Elizabeth had always known she was unlike most other young ladies of her age. But her education common to most young ladies essential to their future had not been neglected, and in such cases as these she was willing to learn, viewing this as an education she may someday be able to put to good use. The thought she would likely never marry whispered in the back of Elizabeth's mind, but she put it aside in favor of her present activities.

Mrs. Bingley was, in essentials, quite similar to Elizabeth's late mother. The two ladies had always been close, two peas in a pod, as it were, and while Mrs. Bennet had tended toward silliness and gossip, Mrs. Bingley was her pair in every way, though perhaps not so pronounced. When the Bennet matron had passed, Mrs. Bingley, while not donning mourning attire, had still given her late friend every honor in her power to give, not hosting dinners or other events for the time the Bennet sisters had been in mourning, often speaking her feelings of how much she had missed her friend.

As a result, she had taken on the Bennet sisters as her own daughters, providing for them a sort of surrogacy for the mother they had lost. All three girls loved her, for she was a good woman, if a little trying at times. She quite looked on the wedding of her daughter to Longbourn's heir as a feather in her cap, the second feather being, of course, the future expected marriage between Longbourn's eldest daughter and her own son. But the younger girls were not forgotten.

It could be expected that the necessities of accomplishing their work would lead to idle chatter among ladies of their station. This was precisely what happened that day—and many days after—at Netherfield. The demands of working with one's hands left the mind to other tasks, and as such, the ladies rarely stayed silent for even a few moments. For the most part, their conversation was desultory in nature, but on occasion something of more substance was said.

"Do you expect your other daughter to return home in time for the wedding?" asked Elizabeth of Mrs. Bingley when they had been working for some time.

"We do," replied Mrs. Bingley. "Louisa and Humphrey should arrive a week before." Mrs. Bingley paused. "While I do not see Louisa as much as I would like, at least they are to attend us for her sister's wedding."

While Elizabeth understood a mother missing her daughter, few others would repine her absence should she not come. If Elizabeth's relationship with Caroline when younger had been, at times, a little strained, there was little of a relationship to be had between Elizabeth and Caroline's elder sister. Elizabeth found Louisa Hurst to be more than a little vain, somewhat vapid, and possessing a mean streak which had passed the rest of the family by completely. For many years, she had set her cap at Thomas, resenting Caroline for the attention she gained from the gentleman so effortlessly.

While the matter had never been discussed openly, Elizabeth was aware that her brother had taken Louisa aside some years back and informed her he would not propose to her, advising her to cease her objectionable behavior toward her sister. Louisa had, at first, been inclined to discount his words, until he had publicly snubbed her at several events of local society and one infamous evening in town. Humiliated, Louisa had ceased to importune him, and for some time after had treated her sister with cold civility. Had she possessed any affection at all for Thomas, the matter might have been one to provoke pity for her lost hopes. But she had quite clearly only wished to be wed to the wealthiest man in the neighborhood and, as a result, had not garnered much sympathy.

This character flaw had been more than amply proven when she had promptly during the next season attached herself to the wealthiest man who would have her. Humphrey Hurst was a portly, balding man some fifteen years her senior. He was of suspect hygiene, little intelligence, and the most banal of interests. His principle virtues were a fondness of the finer things in life, including his new father-in-law's table, dishes rich and exotic in nature, and an ability to imbibe enough spirits to knock a bear into a month-long hibernation. It was not uncommon for the man to lie down on a sofa and snore the evening away, no matter who comprised the company.

After some months of marriage, Louisa had seemed to realize the flaw in her vengeance, for she had mellowed the few times Elizabeth had seen her since. While Mr. Hurst was fond of society—and more precisely fond of anyone who would feed his prodigious appetite—much of their time was spent at his estate in Norfolk. It was the simple and unfortunate fact that while Louisa had thought him to be wealthy enough to provide her a triumph over the man who spurned her, Mr. Hurst was a man of more fashion than fortune, his estate generating only a little more than half of Longbourn's annual income. A tendency to exceed his income due to his appetites and an unfortunate interest in the racetracks meant they could not afford to be in London, unless they were staying with family.

"I understand from my daughter there might be reason to expect an addition to the family in the near future."

"Is that so?" asked Elizabeth. "I will be sure to give my congratulations to the expectant mother when she comes."

Elizabeth's sisters echoed her words to varying degrees, from Jane's softly spoken but fervent congratulations, to Mary's more cynical well-wishes to her hostess's eldest daughter. Caroline, for her part, said nothing, the news already clearly known to her. It seemed she still had not forgotten nor completely forgiven her sister for her previous behavior. If there was any character flaw to attribute to Caroline Bingley, it was a tendency to remember slights and slurs, as well as an unwillingness to allow them to rest.

Of course, given Caroline's behavior when calling at Longbourn after Elizabeth's return, it was inconceivable that she should be spared similar jests, especially now her mother was in attendance. Though Caroline was never overt, the sly manner in which she spoke of Mr. Darcy, then encouraged her mother to continue speculating as to the gentleman's level of interest, was blatant enough to raise Elizabeth's hackles.

"He *did* dance with you, of all the ladies of Hertfordshire," said Mrs. Bingley to her daughter's provocation, her tone introspective. "Of course, he did favor Louisa and Caroline, but we knew he had no intentions in that direction, though Louisa did hope she might engage him."

"Louisa was deluding herself," was Caroline's blunt assessment.

"Yes, perhaps she was." Mrs. Bingley turned a speculative eye on Elizabeth. "What did you think of the gentleman, Elizabeth?"

"No more than we all did," interjected Jane. "He danced with me as well, if you recall."

"He did. But I am certain he understood my Charles's interest in you, my dear, even four years ago."

Jane blushed in response to this observation and could not say anything more. Elizabeth glanced at her sister, reassuring her that she was well able to speak for herself. It was her impression that Jane was grateful for the reprieve.

"As Jane has said," inserted Elizabeth into the silence, "I thought of Mr. Darcy no more than anyone else. While he did ask me to dance, it was nothing more than a dance. I could detect no peculiar interest in me, I assure you."

"But he is undeniably a handsome man," said Caroline.

"Oh, aye," replied Elizabeth. "I dare say there is no deficiency in his ability to attract the attention of those of the fairer sex." *Only in his ability to act in a gentlemanly manner to young and impressionable girls.* "But there is much more to attraction to a man than simply his countenance or his stature. It would be vanity to consider such things above all else."

"You are correct, I am sure," said Mrs. Bingley.

"So perhaps you would prefer a plainer man?" asked Caroline with an arch look. "Perhaps Mr. Collins is much more to your taste."

"There is nothing the matter with Mr. Collins," interjected Mary primly into the discussion. "But I do not think our Lizzy is considering *him* either."

"Nor would I have expected she would," said Mrs. Bingley. She turned a fond smile on Elizabeth. "I have nothing against the gentleman. But I am sure you could do much better for a husband than him."

"Such as Mr. Darcy."

Elizabeth directed a withering glare at Caroline for her continued attempts to tease. Though completely unaffected by Elizabeth's displeasure, Caroline shook her head, shot a grin at Elizabeth, and let the matter drop.

"Well," said Mrs. Bingley, "I shall not press you, Elizabeth. You still have all the time in the world to be married—if you find you are not inclined to it yet, then there is no need to rush.

"As for Mr. Darcy, I found him to be a gentlemanly man, one who would make any young woman a fine husband. Furthermore, according to Charles, he is an excellent catch—one of the most sought-after young men in the country. It would be a stupendous match if you were able to induce him to propose. But know that I shall not push you in his way, nor interfere in any way. Your mother, God bless her sainted soul, wished for the best for you girls, and I will do my part to guide you in her absence."

The arrival of the elder Mr. Bingley put an end to such discussion. Elizabeth found she could cheerfully forgo it though she smiled at Mrs. Bingley with pleasure and affection. Mrs. Bennet had been more of a matchmaker, and she had not been choosy about toward whom she had directed her daughters, though she had not been insistent on their accepting her chosen suitors. By contrast, Mrs. Bingley, though also eager to see her dear friend's daughters married, was in no way a matchmaker. She was much more content to illuminate her thoughts of who would make a good match and allow the girls to make their own choices. In the end, it was all done out of love for them, a fact which Elizabeth appreciated. Her interference could have been far worse.

In this manner, the final days before the wedding passed. For Mrs. Bingley, the delight of having her second daughter disposed of in marriage was tempered by the loss of said daughter to another man's house. This, in turn, was made easier by the fact that she would live only three miles away, allowing frequent opportunities to be in

Caroline's company.

Of further interest and satisfaction to Elizabeth was the behavior of Mr. Bingley with her sister Jane. The long-held expectation that he admired her was playing out before their very eyes—Elizabeth expected her sister to be engaged by the end of the year. In this expectation, she found that her sister had acknowledged the increased fervor of his attentions and had responded by increasing her hopes accordingly.

"I have always found him to be the most amiable man of my acquaintance, as you know, Lizzy," confided Jane the day before the wedding.

"Only a simpleton would be unaware of your feelings, Jane," replied Elizabeth. "And Mr. Bingley is no simpleton."

"But he has been more overt in his admiration of late." Jane's eyes lost their focus and a dreamy expression rendered her countenance hopeful and all the more beautiful because of it. "He has given me no indication by word, however, that he intends to propose."

"But in deeds, he has given his assurances amply," said Elizabeth. "I am happy for you, Jane. I suspect you will be a very happy woman, indeed."

A warm glow suffused Jane's cheeks, and she nodded to acknowledge Elizabeth's point. Though sorely tempted to tease her sister further, Elizabeth did not have the heart, so obvious was Jane's pleasure in Mr. Bingley's increased attentions. Soon, she would leave for her own home with a good man for a husband. But Elizabeth knew she had nothing to fear, for like Caroline, she would only be three miles from her ancestral home.

The next morning dawned bright and warm, a truly propitious day for a wedding. The Bennet family prepared for the day with laughter and not a little remembrance for the one member who had not lived to see it, the one who would have taken the most pleasure in it of them all—perhaps even greater than that of the groom!

"Mama would have been in a frenzy of preparations, would she not?" said Mary, the light of happy remembrance bright in her countenance. "We would have been up before dawn, chivvied from our beds to ensure we were ready in time, looking our best."

"She might have thought it likely that we would all catch our own beaux at the wedding," added Elizabeth. "For if Thomas would only invite his friends from town, surely we would all be thrown in the path of eligible gentlemen!"

"I cannot say you are incorrect, Lizzy," said Mr. Bennet as they all laughed. "This would have been your mother's crowning triumph, and as such, I think we should all dedicate it to her memory." Mr. Bennet paused and looked at Jane, winking and saying: "Then again, she would likely already anticipate Jane's marriage, which would undoubtedly supplant today's festivities as her *new* crowning achievement!"

Once again, the Bennet family laughed. Elizabeth found herself fighting back tears, for though it was cathartic to think of her mother in such terms and gratifying that the crippling sorrow her loss had caused was absent, still she missed her mother and wished she could be here for this day.

"I, for one," said Thomas, "will gladly cede the title to my sister. I am simply happy to be marrying a woman I esteem."

"And we are all equally happy, Thomas," said Mr. Bennet. "But while your mother is not here to chide us for the potential of arriving late, I have no doubt your new mother-in-law will take up the office should we tarry. Shall we?"

The Bennet family agreed, and they soon departed, making their way down the drive toward the church which lay nearby. An open carriage was pulled up before the door of the church to convey the happy couple to Netherfield for the wedding breakfast once the service was complete and from thence to Ramsgate where a house had been let for their honeymoon. Outside the church, the principle families of the neighborhood had gathered to see the union which had been expected for so long. Elizabeth was greeted cordially by those she had known all her life, and if there were those among the company who were disgruntled that they had been spurned by Longbourn's heir, they were thankfully few and possessed the good sense to keep their disappointment to themselves.

As she was making her way toward the gathered crowd to the church, Elizabeth caught sight of the parson and moved to greet him. He was a tall man, slightly heavyset, with neatly combed dark hair, which, unfortunately, was thinning at the back. He was dressed in the traditional cleric's garb, black upon black, which gave him a certain distinction. He was a young man, only five and twenty, and while he was not handsome, his features could be called pleasantly plain. Elizabeth also knew from experience that he was not a particularly intelligent man though not deficient either.

"Miss Elizabeth," said he with a bow. "How do you do on such a fine occasion?"

"I am very well, Mr. Collins," said Elizabeth with a fond smile. "I am very happy for my brother, for he is gaining an excellent wife."

"That he is," replied Mr. Collins. "I suspect Jane will also be following him to the altar before long?"

"Perhaps," was all Elizabeth would say in response.

"I hope she does," replied Mr. Collins. "She is deserving of every happiness in life, as is all your family.

"Might I escort you to the family pew?"

"Thank you, Mr. Collins. That would be lovely."

As she took his offered arm and accompanied him toward the front benches where the Bennets usually sat, Elizabeth considered the young man by her side. Mr. William Collins was her father's distant cousin, though Elizabeth did not quite remember the exact extent of her father's connection with the gentleman. Mr. Collins's father and Elizabeth's father had fallen out over a disagreement of some sort—Mr. Bennet had never been explicit as to the details—leading to a long estrangement between them.

When Mr. Collins had been fifteen years of age, his father had suffered a fatal accident, leaving the young master quite alone in the world. Upon hearing of it, Mr. Bennet, putting his grudge against the young man's father aside, had sent for him, installing the young man in his home, treating him as the family he was. William Collins had resided in their orbit ever since, as much a part of the family as any of the Bennet children.

Furthermore, Mr. Bennet had undertaken to educate the young man, who had come to them quite downtrodden. The elder Collins had been, from what Elizabeth understood, a miserly and abusive man with a revulsion for the gentry and a sense of dissatisfaction for his lot in life. Under Mr. Bennet's painstaking tutelage, Mr. Collins had grown to become more than what he had been when he arrived, receiving not only an education, but lessons in how to be a man of good character. He still, at times, possessed a certain servile streak about him, and he gravitated to others, craving their guidance, but he had been educated in a prominent seminary at Mr. Bennet's expense, and been installed as the rector of Longbourn when the incumbent passed away about a year before.

"Here you are, Miss Elizabeth," said Mr. Collins, taking up her hand and bowing over it. "I hope I shall see you after at the wedding breakfast? I have been reading in the gospel of Luke of late, and I was hoping to obtain your insight. And Mary's, of course."

"Then I would be happy to speak with you," said Elizabeth. "Until then, sir."

Once again, Mr. Collins bowed and took his leave to take his place at the front of the church, his welcoming smile bestowed upon all the congregation. Of his request, Elizabeth could not help but smile, though she was well aware that Mary's name had been thrown in by Mr. Collins as an afterthought. Though Mary was the Bennet sister with the most interest and knowledge of Holy Scripture, it was to Elizabeth that Mr. Collins turned.

The reason, of course, was that Mr. Collins admired Elizabeth and had for quite some time. While Elizabeth had noticed some inclination on his part before he even left for the seminary, it had become increasingly evident when he had returned, taken up the curacy, and subsequently become master of the parsonage.

It might have become difficult for Elizabeth to be the recipient of his admiration, for she possessed no similar inclination toward the gentleman. While she knew him to be a good sort of man and his situation was eligible, Elizabeth thought she required something more in a husband, something more challenging than William Collins could provide. Mr. Collins seemed to understand and accept her feelings, though they had never spoken of it, content to watch and esteem her from afar. Or at least it seemed that way. It was entirely possible that he was simply biding his time until he thought she would be receptive to his overtures. But Elizabeth thought it unlikely. The man was quite incapable of misdirection or guile.

Soon Elizabeth's family joined her, Mr. Bennet sitting beside her, while her sisters sat on her other side. The way Mr. Bennet regarded her, it was clear he had seen Mr. Collins's actions. Showing a protective side that he did not often display, he addressed the matter:

"Are you well, Lizzy? I hope your conversation with my cousin was agreeable."

"Quite agreeable," replied Elizabeth, well aware as to her father's thoughts. "Mr. Collins has always been perfectly amiable in my presence. I believe he wishes to discuss scripture with me when we go to Netherfield."

Bemused, her father looked up at the parson, and they both caught a glimpse of his eyes darting away. Elizabeth allowed herself a slight smile and a nod which proved, by his replying smile, that he remained aware of her presence.

"It is not, perhaps a commonly discussed subject at a wedding breakfast, though at the wedding itself it is, of course, expected. I suppose he would not ask it of Mary."

"Mary's name was mentioned," said Elizabeth. "But only once he had solicited my own participation."

Mr. Bennet grunted, and Elizabeth felt obliged to say: "He has never been insistent, Papa. I am quite able to speak with him with tolerable ease. If he wishes for something more between us, he has never attempted to impose upon me."

The searching look Mr. Bennet gave Elizabeth warmed her. "Very well. He is a good man, Mr. Collins, though not without limitations. If you truly wished for his addresses, you know I would not stand in your way."

"I know, Papa. I do not wish for them, and I think Mr. Collins knows that."

"Then there is nothing more to say. Should he become more insistent, please speak to me. Between us, I am certain we may handle his disappointment in a manner which is least damaging to his confidence. I would not have it destroyed after all the trouble and effort that went into its creation."

"Nor would I," replied Elizabeth.

The bride and groom soon entered the chapel, and the service began. Of the service, there is not much to say, other than that it proceeded in a manner much like many others had, from time immemorial. The significance to the Bennet and Bingley families was greater, of course, but of much more importance to both parties than the joining of their two families in tighter bonds, was that the two principals were so perfectly suited and deeply in love.

At the wedding breakfast, Elizabeth allowed Mr. Collins his time with her, to his very great delight, and consigned him to her sister's insights when she felt she had given him enough of it. The breakfast was a stupendous success for Mrs. Bingley, a fact which Elizabeth did not stint to ensure her hostess was aware.

When the time came to farewell the happy couple, they gathered on the drive and watched them depart, tears of happiness mingled with shouts of congratulations. The first hurdle had been surpassed. Now Elizabeth only had Mr. Darcy's coming over which to concern herself.

CHAPTER VI

Nestled among the hills of Hertfordshire, Netherfield Park rose in the distance. Still unsure as he was of the wisdom of coming here at all, Darcy gazed at it, taking in the sight with jaundiced eyes which were made all the more uncompromising due to his mood.

It was a handsome scene, he supposed, though the building itself was not especially pleasing to the eye. The manor house was squat and severe, its rectangular shape unremarkable, the reddish brick of its construction leaving much to be desired. No, it was not the house which drew his eye, but the place in which it was situated, which consisted of waving fields filled with the life which provided its prosperity, strands of alder and ash, and the glory of the sun set in a blue sky as if to welcome him. It was not Pemberley—nothing could be equal to Pemberley in Darcy's eyes—but the gently undulating terrain of Hertfordshire was appealing for different reasons, ones which Darcy could appreciate.

The crunch of the gravel beneath the wheels of the carriage brought figures to the door of the manor house, and Darcy saw his friend, accompanied by his parents, emerge to greet him. Bingley, true to form, was almost bouncing on his heels in his anticipation, prompting an amused shake of Darcy's head. His parents, though their countenances were beaming, were much more sedate.

"Darcy!" exclaimed Bingley as he descended from the carriage. "How excellent it is to see you again, man! Welcome to Netherfield!"

"Thank you, my friend," said Darcy, extending his hand, which Bingley grasped and pumped with much enthusiasm. He turned and greeted Bingley's parents, accepting their welcome and renewing his brief acquaintance. Then he was shown to his room in deference to his need to refresh himself before returning to the sitting-room to wait upon his hosts.

Upon joining them, Darcy found annoyance welling up within him, for it is perhaps a perversity that when one particularly wishes to speak of a certain subject, to hear certain information, nothing of that sort is brought up in conversation. When he descended the stairs, Darcy was not even aware himself of what he wished to speak. But the longer the conversation continued, the more his mood worsened, though he thought his efforts at hiding his pique were creditable.

First, Mrs. Bingley seemed to feel the need to wax long in her raptures concerning her younger daughter's recent wedding. It was not unusual for a mother to be proud of such an event, but it was not something Darcy could find especially interesting.

"It was such a beautiful ceremony," said Mrs. Bingley with a sigh after she had spoken on the subject for some minutes. "A mother is, of course, more than a little biased in such matters. But I confess, I care not if others think me entirely conceited when I consider how beautiful a bride my Caroline was."

"I am certain anyone who witnessed it could think no such thing," said the elder Mr. Bingley. "And Thomas Bennet suits her so well in every respect."

His interest suddenly pricked by the mention of the name Bennet, Darcy finally replied, saying: "Might I assume they have departed for their wedding tour?"

That proved to be a mistake. "Oh, yes!" exclaimed Mr. Bingley. "Mr. Bennet has let a house in Ramsgate for their honeymoon. Anything which can be done for my Caroline's comfort and enjoyment must be done in an instant! He is a good man, and I am particularly glad that he—and his family—are now our family."

This statement led to another lengthy discourse of Mrs. Bingley's expectations of her daughter's future felicity, the virtues of the Bennet family, and her speculations concerning how her daughter would enjoy her time in Ramsgate. She even hinted, in a manner which might have been gauche if she were only a little more explicit, how she anticipated the arrival of grandchildren before long. In short, she spoke of many things, but of the one subject of which Darcy wished to hear, she remained silent.

"I have not yet made Mr. Bennet's acquaintance," said Darcy during a lull in Mrs. Bingley's discourse.

"Oh, yes," said Bingley, grinning at Darcy. "Bennet mentioned something of that himself. If you can be convinced to stay long enough, you shall make his acquaintance." Bingley paused and fixed Darcy with a curious look. "You do mean to stay some weeks, do you not?"

"My plans are not yet fixed," said Darcy. "But there is nothing limiting my time here at the moment."

"That is wonderful news!" said Mrs. Bingley. "With Caroline now married and Louisa gone these past three years, now Charles is my only child at home." Mrs. Bingley turned a fond gaze on her only son. "At least he shall not leave me. And I have the hope that he too will soon bring home a bride."

Bingley appeared a little embarrassed at his mother's statement, but she did not notice. Instead, she launched into a long commentary on the charms of one Jane Bennet, the girl she thought she would soon obtain for a daughter. Again, Darcy listened with as much polite patience as he could muster. The simple fact of the matter was that had Mrs. Bingley spoken of *another* Bennet sister, she would have found Darcy much more interested. Though he had known the woman was a little flighty, Darcy could not remember her being *this* voluble. It must be the excitement of having a daughter married which had brought this change over her.

As he was close to despair of hearing what he wished, a strange change came over Mrs. Bingley. For while she was speaking, she suddenly paused, and her eyes found Darcy. Then, after a few moments, she began to speak yet again. This time, however, the subject was a little more palatable to Darcy.

"Of course, you have heard me speak of the Bennets and my pleasure at gaining them for a family. Why, the girls are so close to my Caroline, with her marriage to Thomas, I quite consider them all my daughters, especially with the passing of their dear mother."

"I was not aware of their loss," said Darcy, his thoughts returning to Mrs. Bennet. While he had not known the woman to any great extent, what he did remember suggested she had been similar to Mrs. Bingley. "When I meet the Bennets, I shall be certain to offer my condolences."

"It *is* a sad story, indeed," replied Mrs. Bingley. "It was sudden, you understand, which must have made it doubly hard for them. The girls, in particular, miss their mother keenly, and I long for my dear friend. Mrs. Bennet had been my friend since Mr. Bingley and I moved to the neighborhood, you understand, which was not long after she married Mr. Bennet. As our children are of age with each other, we have been close for a very long time."

"Yes, I understand." Darcy paused, thinking to prolong the discussion of the Bennets. "There are three girls, as I understand?"

"There are. Jane is the eldest, now two and twenty years of age." Mrs. Bingley turned a smile on her son, to which Bingley responded with a slightly silly grin of his own. "Had it not been for Mrs. Bennet's untimely passing, I am sure my Caroline would have been married to Longbourn's heir last year already, and Charles might have secured the hand of Miss Bennet by now."

It took all of Darcy's willpower not to gnash his teeth in frustration. The woman seemed determined to avoid speaking of the one of whom Darcy most wished to hear! Then she returned her attention to him, and the conversation took a turn for the better, in Darcy's opinion.

"After Jane, Elizabeth is the next eldest, and Mary, the youngest. They are both good girls though Mary is only now out in society."

"Miss Elizabeth had only just come out when I visited last," observed Darcy.

"She was! In fact, I seem to remember something of you dancing with her at the assembly before you left us."

Mention of the assembly brought to mind the *other* event which had happened there, and Darcy felt suddenly confused. The situation with Miss Elizabeth and his concern with how she might have got on after his departure was the reason why he had taken so long to accept Bingley's invitation. It was the reason he had refused at least two others. Why was he so eager to hear of her now?

"They are good girls," continued Mrs. Bingley, unaware of his thoughts. "Though my friend always lauded the beauty of her eldest daughter, I never saw it that way."

"Surely you must confess that Miss Bennet is the most beautiful lady in the neighborhood!" protested Bingley.

"Yes, your opinion on the matter is quite well known," interjected his father with a laugh.

"I do not dispute she is a very handsome lady," said Mrs. Bingley, patting her son's hand with an absence of mind. "But in my eyes, Elizabeth is her equal, though her beauty is of a different kind, to be sure. And Mary will make some fortunate young man an excellent wife and is not devoid of her own share of appeal."

Darcy felt Bingley's eyes darting to him. But he only nodded at his mother and said: "There is no disagreement to be had. All the Bennet sisters are quite handsome in their respective ways, though I will own a preference for Miss Bennet's gentle manners and calm demeanor."

"I know you do, Charles, and you could not choose any better." Mrs. Bingley smiled at him and turned back to Darcy. "But I am convinced there are others who will prefer Elizabeth's liveliness and darker features. The two eldest are truly akin to the sun and the moon, and while Mary is a mixture of them, she is no less handsome because of it."

"It seems to me," said Mr. Bingley with amusement, "that you praise the Bennet sisters to the heavens, but your words concerning your own daughters have been more concerning your happiness for their situations."

"Well, Caroline at least." Mrs. Bingley's lip curled with disdain. "I do not think much of Hurst."

"We have also produced handsome daughters," said Mr. Bingley.

"Of course!" exclaimed Mrs. Bingley. "But as I do not have to concern myself for their futures and the Bennet sisters do not have a mother to look after their interests, I am determined to be of whatever assistance I might."

"And an excellent advocate they shall have in you, my dear," said Mr. Bingley.

"The Hursts left after the wedding?" asked Darcy from politeness rather than any interest.

"They traveled to London after the wedding," replied Bingley. "But we expect them back soon, perhaps within the week."

Though from what Darcy had heard, he thought he would be quite happy to refrain from making Hurst's acquaintance, he accepted Bingley's information, saying he hoped they would enjoy the return of their family. His words were accepted, Darcy thought, with grace, but little enthusiasm, at least for the return of the husband.

"Regardless," said Mrs. Bingley, turning the conversation back to where Darcy wished it to go, "Miss Elizabeth is a handsome young woman, one who would grace the hand of any man who might offer for her. She is also known to be quite intelligent, so much so that many of the men of the area are almost intimidated by her ability to speak circles around them. If any man chooses to espouse an interest in her, he had best be aware of this, for she is not one to stay silent."

Bingley appeared uncomfortable throughout his mother's speech, but at the end he laughed and said: "That is the truth! Sometimes when I am speaking with her, I cannot make any sense of what she says."

"It is incumbent upon us all to ensure those to whom we speak understand what we are saying," commented Darcy.

"Oh, Charles!" said Mrs. Bingley. The matron glanced at Darcy and then back at her son, her tone seeming to suggest she was vexed with him for meddling in her matchmaking. "Lizzy is not unkind. She knows exactly what she wishes to say, and she is not shy about saying it, but I have never known her to speak in a fashion deliberately designed to be difficult to understand."

"I never said she did," replied Bingley, apparently unmoved by his mother's reproof.

"Be that as it may," interjected Mr. Bingley with a pointed look at both, "I believe we are beginning to bore Mr. Darcy with our constant comments concerning our friends."

"Not at all," replied Darcy.

"Let me say, Mr. Darcy," continued Mr. Bingley, "that I highly appreciate your friendship with my son. I am well aware that he makes friends easily," Mr. Bingley paused and smiled at Bingley, who reddened a little, "but it is also equally evident that not all friendships are equal. I understand you have kept him from trouble at times when you were both at school."

"My friendship with Bingley has been much to my benefit as well," replied Darcy. "Not that he did not need assistance with some of the scrapes he got into at university."

The family laughed as Bingley's face began to resemble a ripe tomato. He sputtered and protested his innocence, but his father only patted him on the back and returned his attention to Darcy.

"I am grateful for it, regardless. Please know that you are welcome here any time. We are happy to have your acquaintance."

Darcy was aware that Mr. Bingley's profession of appreciation might be taken with another meaning, should a man be the suspicious sort. Darcy's father, in particular, might have thought their pleasure was derived solely from the Darcy family's prominence in society. But Darcy knew better. Bingley was among the least pretentious people to whom he had ever been introduced, and he was certain the remainder of the family was the same. Thus, he accepted their thanks and professed his own pleasure at the acquaintance.

In truth, he was far from displeased with the conversation as a whole. While he had not considered it consciously, he was relieved to know that his impulsive action had not appeared to damage Miss

Elizabeth in any way. It seemed evident she had put whatever she had felt behind her, if she was easy enough in company as his friends had said. Darcy was gladdened, though he was forced to wonder if she had thought about him these past years, and if she had, what, exactly, was her opinion. Those thoughts stayed with him the entire afternoon and even after they had been called to dinner.

Darcy found that he enjoyed his time with the Bingley family. They were a happy, friendly lot, not given to airs or any other such nonsense. Considering the world Darcy inhabited, Darcy appreciated their lack of pretension, for higher society was full of it. Why, Darcy had often met daughters of mere tradesmen who thought the possession of a handsome dowry allowed them to look down on others as if they were descended from the king himself!

Being well aware of their history, Darcy knew that they were new money, and in many circles in London—especially the circles in which he moved—they would be considered usurpers. Many would think them less than worthy to be termed gentle folk, regardless of their possession of an estate. There were also many in the Bingleys' position who would affect even more haughtiness to compensate for the perceived lack of respect they received.

In some ways, Darcy enjoyed their company better than that of his own family. His father, for example, was not a man to look down on others for their position in society. But he was well aware of the Darcys' history and was accordingly proud of it. Even his uncle and aunt, who were about as unpretentious as any of their own position, were still cognizant of their position and prone to arrogance at times. It was, Darcy supposed, part of being noble.

That evening, after the elder Bingleys had decided to retire, his friend invited Darcy to his father's study for a nightcap. Darcy went willingly, his head still full of the thoughts which had been occupying him all day. Bingley seemed to be insensible of Darcy's introspection, for he spoke enough for both of them, and then others, besides. After some time of this, Darcy's interest was pricked by a comment made by his friend.

"With all this talk of Miss Bennet, I might have thought you would already be engaged to the girl."

Bingley blushed, looking a little silly. "I might have. But there was the whole business with her mother, you understand."

"I did not say married, Bingley," replied Darcy. "It is clearly improper to court a woman when she is in mourning. But she has been out of mourning for some time, has she not?"

"Yes," replied Bingley. "But there was always something holding me back." Bingley shrugged. "First it was my desire to learn more of the estate, then it seemed to me like she was still not ready for my addresses. In the end, I care not. We shall come to an agreement at some point in time — the timing truly does not matter."

"Are you certain of your affection for her?"

Bingley frowned. "You are disposed to think it best I not pay my addresses to her?"

"I am disposed to no such thing, Bingley," said Darcy. "The only person who can determine if Miss Bennet will suit you is you, yourself. I cannot attempt to direct you.

"The only caution I give you is that you have long thought yourself enamored of her, and it may have led you to neglect to consider any other options. Your slowness to move on your interest in her may suggest you are not as interested as you thought."

"Then you may rest easy, my friend," said Bingley with a wide grin. "In fact, when I was in London last season, I paid some attention to certain other ladies I met there, but none of them could measure up to Miss Bennet. I have, perhaps, not rushed to secure her, but that is because I am sensitive to her feelings. It is entirely possible that I will propose to her before you leave the neighborhood."

"In that case, you have my congratulations, my friend," said Darcy, raising his glass in salute. "There are few men who can claim to have found their partner in life with so little difficulty."

Bingley's grin grew wider, and they both drained their drinks. When he lowered his glass, Bingley's countenance was overset by a truly silly expression, one which prompted Darcy to laugh. His friend leaned forward with the decanter and filled their glasses once again. Accepting a little more of the amber liquid, Darcy sat back in his chair considering. In the spur of the moment, he decided he wished for a little more information about the girl who had dominated his thoughts since he had arrived. As such, he turned the conversation in that direction.

"Might I assume your intended bride's family are all in favor of the match?" Darcy paused and added: "Though I suppose they could hardly be opposed, considering the marriage of her brother with your sister."

"Exactly," replied Bingley, smugness overflowing in his tone. "While I shall be required to approach Mr. Bennet for his blessing and will no doubt be subject to his teasing manner, his consent is assured."

"Excellent, my friend," replied Darcy with a laugh.

Then Darcy paused and considered the matter for a moment, not certain how to raise the subject. As he was uncertain, he decided it would be best to speak openly.

"And what of the younger Bennet daughters? Are there any suitors for their hands at present?" Darcy laughed. "Or is your mother still searching on their accounts?"

Bingley reddened, and he stammered: "You have my apologies, Darcy. Usually my mother is not so overt. But I am afraid Caroline suggested you may be partial to Miss Elizabeth. She has latched onto the notion and seems to think you would make her an excellent husband."

"It is no trouble, Bingley," replied Darcy.

When he considered the matter, he supposed it was quite obvious that Mrs. Bingley had been attempting to recommend her late friend's daughters, and while Darcy still found himself more than a little uncomfortable, considering what had passed between himself and the lady, Mrs. Bingley's behavior was no worse than other matchmaking mama's.

In the deep recesses of his mind, the thought of paying court to Miss Elizabeth Bennet sprang to life. It was unthinkable. There were many demands on him, one of which was the need to make a good match, to choose a woman who would not only bring great fortune to the Darcy coffers but also great connections. Miss Bennet's dowry was respectable—or at least Darcy suspected it was. But she had no connections greater than a middle tier gentleman who was the first of his line to be a landowner. It could not be contemplated.

"I shall speak with my mother," said Bingley, drawing Darcy from his thoughts. "She is zealous in her desire to see the Miss Bennets married and settled, but she will not do anything but speak of it. It would be better if she did not speak of it at all."

"Indeed, I am not bothered," said Darcy hurriedly. "It is actually refreshing to meet a woman so concerned with another woman's daughters."

Bingley laughed. "Well, she *has* succeeded in seeing her own daughters settled. It is only natural she would then turn her attention on our nearest neighbors."

"From that perspective, you must be correct."

Draining his glass, Darcy refused Bingley's offer to pour again, instead rising and favoring his friend with a smile. "I thank you for this invitation, Bingley. In the coming weeks, I would be happy to renew my acquaintance with *all* of your friends."

It seemed Bingley understood his meaning. "Excellent. Then I shall be happy to reintroduce you. I am pleased you have come."

That evening, Darcy went to bed feeling strangely unburdened, such as he had not felt since before he last visited. With nothing more expected of him than a pleasant visit, Darcy thought he could meet with the people of the area and enjoy himself. And if a certain lively, dark-haired temptress featured in his dreams, Darcy felt he had little cause to repine. In fact, he had every reason to appreciate her appearance, despite how she teased and tormented him.

CHAPTER VII

The sensation of once again being in the same neighborhood as Mr. Darcy, of once again being within his reach, was a curious one. While Elizabeth chided herself multiple times, she could not help but look over her shoulder on occasion to wonder if the man were nearby, waiting for her vigilance to fail. He would hardly be lying in wait, ready to kidnap her and spirit her away from all she had ever known and loved. The sensation of watchfulness could not be dispelled, however, no matter how hard she tried.

Word that the man had arrived at Netherfield spread throughout the community as a grass fire driven before the wind, carried on the wings of gossip. Had her mother still been alive, Elizabeth knew she would have been among the first to learn of it. As she was no longer with them, it fell to their aunt, Mrs. Phillips, to inform them of the gossip—or at least she felt it was her responsibility. By the time Mrs. Phillips came bustling down the drive, all self-important excitement for her news, the Bennet sisters had already had the gossip from Lady Lucas.

"Yes, we have heard of it." Jane took it upon herself to make the reply for the Bennet sisters when their aunt had shared her news. "Mr. Bingley informed us of the time of Mr. Darcy's arrival when he visited on Tuesday."

"Oh, you already know, do you?" asked their aunt, seemingly disappointed at not being the first to inform them. "That is well then." She turned to Elizabeth and eyed her closely. "I seem to recall reports of you, in particular, being favored by Mr. Darcy's attentions, Lizzy. It would behoove you to make the best of the situation."

Elizabeth was amused by her aunt's baldly stated words. Mrs. Bennet truly had been like two peas in a pod with her sister Phillips. When she replied, therefore, Elizabeth's words betrayed her amusement, though it was unlikely Aunt Phillips would understand the joke.

"Very well, Aunt. When he calls, I shall sequester myself in a room alone with him long enough for us to be compromised."

Elizabeth's thoughts concerning her aunt's lack of understanding were proven correct when Mrs. Phillips scowled at her. "This is no time for your impertinence, Lizzy! From what I hear, Mr. Darcy inhabits a sphere high above that which your father can boast. It would raise your consequence to be courted by such a man, and as your mother is sadly departed, I must attempt to do my best by you."

How Aunt Phillips thought she could manage to do so was beyond Elizabeth's ability to understand, since she, as the country solicitor's wife, did not move in the same circles to a large extent, even in a country society such as Meryton. It was fortunate, therefore, that Mrs. Phillips was easily diverted. Nothing could do so like another piece of gossip, which Mary provided, though with a roll of her eyes at Elizabeth. Soon, Mrs. Phillips was happily speaking of a scandal involving the butcher's daughter and a young man of one of the tenant farms of the area, and Mr. Darcy was quite forgotten. Mrs. Phillips did not leave without a few more choice words to Elizabeth concerning Mr. Darcy, however, but at least she was spared the worst of her excesses by Mary's quick actions.

"I hope you are grateful for my forbearance," said Mary when their aunt left. "Gossip should not be endured nor encouraged, and yet I have done both this day."

"It is for a good cause," said Jane, smiling at her youngest sister. "Aunt Phillips might have gone on the entire afternoon had we allowed her to."

"That is why I spoke," said Mary, albeit a little primly. "Perhaps I shall suggest to Mr. Collins that he speak on the subject of gossip. I might, if I had any thought our aunt would heed him."

With those words and a smile, Mary rose and left the room, leaving her sisters grinning behind her. Mary had possessed a moralizing streak at the age of sixteen, but with the efforts of her father, brother, and Elizabeth herself, she had managed to relax her judgmental attitude. Now she employed it as more of a jest, a poke at her own previous tendencies.

But while Mary and her father remained oblivious to Elizabeth's discomposure, Jane, ever aware of Elizabeth's mood, did not. Though Jane did not speak of the matter aloud, Elizabeth caught her sister's eyes upbraiding her several times and knew well what they were telling her. But Elizabeth was determined to act as if Mr. Darcy had not come, as if nothing had ever happened between them. The man could hardly ride up to Longbourn, abduct her and carry her off to perform whatever nefarious harm her mind could conjure. There was no need to be concerned.

Thursday was the day Mr. Bingley had informed them that Mr. Darcy was to arrive. As there were no society activities, they were not to see Mr. Darcy until Sunday at church, unless the gentlemen took it upon themselves to visit Longbourn. Elizabeth was glad they did not, for she had no notion of what she might say to Mr. Darcy if he suddenly appeared in Longbourn's sitting-room.

It was with a sort of fatalistic acceptance that Elizabeth dressed that Sunday morning for church. Jane's query concerning her wellbeing was quickly responded to in the affirmative, and Elizabeth thought she must have been convincing, for Jane appeared to take her answer at face value. Soon after breakfast, the Bennet family gathered together in the entrance to make their way to Longbourn church.

The building was already filling by the time the Bennet family arrived. It was not a large church, but the stained glass in the windows and the fineness of the appointments, from the altar to the pews, crafted of solid English oak and polished to a gleam, spoke to the prosperity of the parish. The living had long been in the Bennet family's gift to give, and the lands of the glebe were nearby, a short walk should an industrious cleric wish to inspect the lands which supported him.

Mr. Collins was, as usual, standing by the doors, greeting the parishioners as they entered, his countenance beaming from the greetings of those entering. Then he saw the Bennet party, and his countenance fairly glowed at the sight of them. Elizabeth, who knew his pleasure was largely for her in particular, stepped forward, leading her family to the door to greet him.

"Hello, Cousin Elizabeth," said Mr. Collins with a low bow. "How happy I am to see you — all of you, of course."

"William," said Mr. Bennet. The Bennet patriarch directed a pleased smile at his protégé. "Are you prepared to instruct us all this morning?"

"I am, Mr. Bennet," replied Mr. Collins with a short bow, though not nearly so deep as the one he had offered to Elizabeth. "It is my duty to do so, and one which I accept eagerly."

"Excellent, sir!" said Mr. Bennet, clapping him on the back. "Then we shall seek our seats in preparation for your wise and holy words."

The beaming smile Mr. Collins directed at Mr. Bennet as he walked away with his family, except for Elizabeth, who lingered behind, showed his veneration for the elder man. Mr. Collins was a little too simple to understand the thrust of Mr. Bennet's understated jests, which was likely just as well. Elizabeth was well aware that her father truly liked Mr. Collins, for his humor tended to be much more biting with those for whom he did not care. In fact, Mr. Bennet considered Mr. Collins to be one of his greatest successes, and Elizabeth could not deny the claim, considering the state of the young man when he had arrived at Longbourn as a boy of only fifteen.

"Are we to dine at Longbourn tonight?" asked Mr. Collins, his attention once again on Elizabeth — if, indeed, it had ever been anywhere else.

"As we do every Sunday, Mr. Collins," said Elizabeth, completing the ritual which had happened almost every Sunday since Mr. Collins had taken the living. "We shall expect you at five."

"I shall be punctual, as always," said Mr. Collins. "Your brother is to return soon with his bride — is that not so?"

"In about two weeks," replied Elizabeth. "We have not heard much from him since he went away."

"That is hardly a surprise," said Mr. Collins with a grin. "I know of no man who would wish to take his attention away from his wife long enough to engage in excessive letter writing."

"No, I suppose not," said Elizabeth. "Be that as it may, unless some information comes to contradict their plans, we do expect him to return with his new wife."

"Another member of your family — particularly one so well known to her as the new Mrs. Bennet — must be welcome, indeed."

"Jane must think so," replied Elizabeth with a laugh. "I think we all anticipate their arrival, Mr. Collins."

"Myself no less than any other," replied he.

"I had better find my family," said Elizabeth.

Mr. Collins agreed, bowed over her hand, and turned to greet several newcomers. Charlotte, who had entered while he was talking with Elizabeth, shot her an amused smile, which Elizabeth returned with a hint of self-consciousness. It was well known that Mr. Collins had a particular regard for Elizabeth, meaning she was often the recipient of such looks. Elizabeth knew he would never press a suit unless she gave him some encouragement, which she would never do. They had settled into this comfortable relationship where he admired from afar, not expecting anything more, while Elizabeth was kind to him and occasionally embarrassed when her neighbors read more into the situation than existed.

The Bennets were seated in their usual pew at the front of the church, having long occupied that bench, their favored position as much a function of their position as the masters of the living as their status as one of the wealthiest families in the district. When she sat down with them, Elizabeth noted the bemused smile she was given by her father and the commiseration from her sisters. It was only then that Elizabeth looked about the church, seeing the faces of those she had known her entire life. And that was when she caught sight of him.

He was here.

Entering the church, Darcy found his eyes searching the confines of the edifice for the woman who had haunted his thoughts for the past four years. The parson, he noted, was a tall, young man, dark hair tending toward a little thinning at the back. He had been talking with a young woman whose back was to Darcy as they entered the church. But he had no attention to spare for the parson or the young woman to whom he spoke. His eyes were already searching for *her*.

It was not until some moments later, after he had sat down, that Darcy realized his error. Disappointment welled up within him as he looked about, noting the presence of Miss Jane Bennet, whom he remembered from his last visit. Of her younger sister there was no sign, leading to an unfathomable feeling of loss.

"What is it, Darcy?" asked Bingley, seeming to see that something had perturbed him.

Darcy was not willing to allow his friend to understand his innermost thoughts, but he turned to Bingley and gestured to the Bennets. "Your new brother is not present, of course, but I understood there were three Bennet sisters?"

"There are," replied Bingley with a grin. "We passed one of them on the way in, speaking with the parson."

Surprised, Darcy looked back toward the door, and the sight of a young woman entering, her mind seemingly focused on something else, caught his attention. It was Miss Elizabeth Bennet. She was here.

Eagerly, Darcy drank in the sight of the young woman. It had been four years and much had changed in that time—much for the better. A pastel green-hued muslin dress provided her attire that day, accentuating a light and pleasing figure, one which was now that of a woman, unlike the ungainly and slight figure she had sported as a girl of sixteen. While Miss Elizabeth had been pretty as a young girl, her beauty had matured, her face suffused with a healthy glow, hair dark mahogany, glowing in the light streaming in through the windows. She was exquisite. Darcy felt his heart beginning to pound within his chest.

"She is lovely, is she not?"

Startled, Darcy turned to look at his friend, seeing Bingley gazing at the Bennet pew with all the longing of a devoted suitor.

"Miss Bennet," clarified Bingley. "She is everything for which a man could ever wish: poised, beautiful, kind, engaging. She will be my wife one day, Darcy—I cannot wait."

It took Darcy a moment to realize that Bingley was speaking of *Miss Bennet* rather than Miss *Elizabeth* Bennet. For a moment he felt himself on the verge of a murderous scowl until his slow thoughts caught up and prevented it.

Silly was what it was, Darcy decided. Miss Elizabeth Bennet was not *his*. Nor would she ever be. As engaging, lovely, and desirable as she was, Darcy was well aware she was not what he required in a wife. He had best remember it.

Then Miss Elizabeth turned. Her eyes fixed on him, and all thought fled from Darcy's mind in favor of the intense pleasure of having her attention on him. Darcy nodded in her direction, witnessing the sudden bloom of her cheeks as her head whipped back toward the front of the room. And Darcy smiled to himself. She was not unmoved by his presence.

Elizabeth was a pious woman. While she could not claim to know the Bible so well as Mr. Collins or her sister Mary, she tried to be a good Christian, one who attempted to live by the principles the parson taught in church each Sunday. At the very least, she attempted to pay attention.

That day, however, she found it impossible. For *he* was there. When he had entered, she did not know, but he was there just the same. And the memories welled up within her, consuming her mind for the rest of the service.

It was generally acknowledged that Miss Elizabeth was a witty, independent sort of young woman. It had often been said that her courage rose with every attempt to intimidate her. Rarely had she found herself at a loss for what to do, how to think, how to act. And yet, the mere sight of this man, the man who had kissed her unbidden and unwelcome, set her mind racing. How she could withstand his visit she did not know.

At length, Mr. Collins's voice fell silent, and the organist took her position to play the hymn to close the service. Elizabeth sang along with the rest of the congregation, its words a soothing balm to her troubled mind. Then the congregation stood, and all too soon Elizabeth was confronted by Mr. Darcy's nearness.

It was Mr. Bingley's fault. With Jane so close at hand, the poor man, so besotted with her, could hardly be expected to refrain from approaching her at the earliest opportunity. He did so, of course, pulling his newly arrived friend along with him, bowing to them and greeting them with his usual enthusiasm and friendliness. And after a few words to Jane, which Elizabeth could not hear due to the overwhelming proximity of Mr. Darcy, he turned to introduce him again.

"I do not know if you recall my friend, so please allow me to introduce him again. Darcy, this is Mr. Bennet and his three daughters: Miss Bennet, Miss Elizabeth, and Miss Mary. Mr. Bennet, my good friend, Fitzwilliam Darcy."

"Ah, yes," said Mr. Bennet, his eyes shining with interest. "I *do* recall something of your visit, sir, though I do not believe I made your acquaintance at that time. It has been some years between your visits."

"It has," said Mr. Darcy, though Elizabeth noted his eyes flitted back to her as if drawn against his will. "But I was happy to accept Bingley's invitation this time, being quite at my leisure to do so."

"I *had* attempted to induce Darcy to visit several times since then," said Mr. Bingley. "After several rejections, I had begun to think Darcy disapproved of my neighbors."

"That is not the case, I assure you," said Mr. Darcy, seeming a little uncomfortable.

"Of course not, sir," said Mr. Bennet, his amusement quite evident. "Though it would be understandable if you were. According to Bingley here, your family is quite prominent and quite possibly owns half of Derbyshire."

Mr. Darcy shot a look at Mr. Bingley, who shook his head. "I am sure Mr. Bennet is exaggerating. You must accustom yourself to his jesting manner."

"Aye, that is the truth," said Mary. "Father is never happy unless he is able to uncover some folly which he can use for his amusement."

"You make me sound quite the misanthrope, Mary," chided Mr. Bennet, though with no real censure.

"I speak as I find, Papa," replied Mary.

Mr. Bennet laughed and leaned over to kiss his youngest daughter's forehead. "That you do, my dear. That you do. And it seems you know me very well.

"But in this case," continued Mr. Bennet, turning back to Mr. Darcy, "I speak nothing less than the truth. Those who are accustomed to the best society has to offer might find our little community less than satisfactory."

"That presupposes the one in question finds anything laudatory in 'the best' of society," rejoined Mr. Darcy. "I find them to be rather tiresome, to be honest, when I do not find their excesses distasteful."

Once again, Mr. Bennet was amused by the response. "It is interesting to hear you say that, sir. As my daughters will attest, I find myself in quite the same situation as you are, at least with respect to society in London."

"But that may be said for *any* society, Papa," said Mary.

Mr. Bennet grinned at his daughter and waggled his eyebrows. "It appears you have caught me out, Mary. Indeed, I am quite happy with my books. In general, I find them less foolish, less judgmental, and entirely better company."

The friendly banter continued for some moments, and slowly the party began to make their way toward the exit. Elizabeth found herself surprised at Mr. Darcy's behavior, akin to her feelings at Pemberley. The last time the gentleman had visited Meryton, he had seemed to Elizabeth to be above his company, as evidenced by his reticence in the assembly rooms and the scarcity of his dances. But this Mr. Darcy was seemingly at ease speaking with Mr. Bennet, and even had a few comments for Mary, who was the only one of the sisters who opened her mouth.

As for Jane, Elizabeth soon noticed that Jane was staying close by her side, her mere presence supportive. Elizabeth was grateful while at the same time annoyed with herself for her lack of fortitude. Why should she feel this way when in the presence of this gentleman? Where had her courage gone?

They had gained the outside of the chapel when Mr. Darcy turned his attention to Elizabeth, the suddenness of it rendering her speechless. "Am I to understand that you are also a great reader, Miss Elizabeth?"

For the briefest of moments, Elizabeth looked on the gentleman, dumbfounded by his sudden attention. The way her father was looking at her, mirth evident in his eyes, suggested he had made some comment to Mr. Darcy, which had prompted the gentleman to turn to her.

"Lizzy is a great reader," said Jane, as Elizabeth was drawing herself together to respond. "She and Mary sometimes have conversations with Papa that I cannot quite understand."

"You are well capable of understanding them, Jane," said Mr. Bennet with an affectionate glance at his eldest daughter. "But you lack interest, which is a necessary component for true understanding."

"It depends on the subject," replied Jane in her calm manner. "Though I enjoy poetry, Shakespeare, and other subjects well enough, Milton makes my eyes cross."

The company laughed at Jane's jest, prompting Mr. Darcy to say: "Then I understand that Miss Elizabeth enjoys Milton?"

"Indeed, she does," replied Jane, once again speaking before Elizabeth could. "She even attempted to explain it to me once, though I did not prove to be an apt pupil."

Mr. Darcy looked at Jane askance, seeming to be wondering at Jane's constant interference. For her part, Elizabeth was becoming a little annoyed with her sister. Did she not have the courage to deal with this man herself? Was she required to hide behind her sister's skirts?

"Perhaps we should discuss *Paradise Lost* sometime, Miss Elizabeth," said Mr. Darcy, again attempting to elicit a response from her. "I should like to compare opinions with a sagacious lady such as yourself."

"Are you certain it is quite safe?" said Elizabeth in a teasing tone, pre-empting Jane's words. "After all, a learned man such as yourself might be shocked into insensibility when confronted with a mere woman."

Mr. Bennet chuckled and shook his head while Mary grinned at Elizabeth. For their parts, it seemed Mr. Bingley was as amused as her relations, while Jane simply looked at Elizabeth, unease roiling under her calm demeanor. As for Mr. Darcy, it seemed to Elizabeth she had charmed him, which, while it was not precisely what she had intended, was good enough to push her unsettled thoughts to the side.

"On the contrary, Miss Elizabeth," said Mr. Darcy, "I thoroughly enjoy such discussions, regardless of whence they originate. I would be happy to speak with you on this, or any other subject, at any time."

"Careful, Lizzy," said Mr. Bennet, nudging her with his elbow, "I suspect this one is intelligent enough to understand, should you choose to make sport with him."

"I am quite at your disposal," said Elizabeth, though inside she wondered what she was doing.

"Excellent," said Mr. Darcy. "Until next time, then. I am certain Bingley will wish to visit your sister. I shall join him."

A few more words were exchanged, and then Mr. Darcy bowed and departed in the company of the Bingleys. Elizabeth watched him go, wondering what had just happened. Mr. Bennet and Mary began walking back toward the house, Jane and Elizabeth trailing behind.

"Are you well, Lizzy?" asked Jane.

"Perfectly so," replied Elizabeth.

She did not notice it, but Jane glanced at her with what would have been evident concern had she had any capacity to think of such matters. Instead, her thoughts were focused on Mr. Darcy. And for the first time, Elizabeth felt a warmth for the young man—or perhaps a thawing of her previously held opinions of him. So much still lay between them, but his behavior had been so far from what she had expected that day, she wondered if she even knew what to expect.

CHAPTER VIII

"Wickham!"

The sound of a harsh voice, coupled with its nearness, jerked Wickham from his contemplations. Wildly looking about the room, his eyes fell on Patterson, the man who had been set over the clerks, and he hastily suppressed a scowl.

"You are not paid to sit at this table engaged in pleasant reverie. There is work to be done, man!"

"I offer my unreserved apologies," replied Wickham smoothly, slipping into the persona he had built for himself as effortlessly as a man donned a nightshirt at the end of a long day. "It seems my thoughts got the better of me. I shall complete my tasks directly."

"See that you do."

Patterson glared at him, showing his utter contempt. The feeling was mutual.

"I should warn you, Wickham," said Patterson, stepping close and speaking softly. "You are not on firm ground. Wealthy patron's godson or not, the partners of this establishment will not continue to pay the wages of a man who considers himself too good to do the work of the office. If you do not complete your duties, you will be dismissed."

"Indeed," replied Wickham. "I shall take your . . . advice into consideration."

While Patterson's scowl deepened, he refrained from saying anything. Instead, he returned to his desk at the end of the room and sat, though Wickham was not misled for an instant by the man's seeming concentration on whatever document he held in his hand. No, Patterson was watching him, as he always was. And knowing he had little choice at present, Wickham turned his attention to his own work space. The other clerks — of which there were four — he ignored as not worth his time. Wickham was not well liked, and it bothered him not a jot. Let these small-minded men disdain him in their pettiness. Wickham knew he had always been meant for greater things.

In a fit of anger, Wickham thrust his pen into the inkpot, though he flicked the excess ink away carefully, knowing Patterson was watching him closely. The greater things for which he was destined seemed quite distant at present and growing ever more distant, the longer he was stuck in this wretched hole.

"I *am* meant for better things," muttered Wickham to himself.

A snort to his right told Wickham he had not been as quiet as he had intended. Wickham knew his fellow clerks would know of his words before the day was out, but their opinion did not concern him. Not for the first time, Wickham wished he could simply plant a facer on Patterson and depart this place forever. But Wickham's situation was not favorable at present. Thus, he was forced to bide his time.

As he worked — simply copying certain documents, which required little attention — he considered the events which had led him to this place. While many men would envy him in his position, Wickham was there only reluctantly. The firm of Mortimer and Sons was one of the most prestigious law firms in London. The solicitor and his progeny — of which there were four — were known to pay well and treat their employees like family. But Wickham had never thought he might actually be required to work for his bread.

"The stupid old sod," muttered Wickham, this time taking care to ensure he was not heard.

The author of his current distress was none other than his wealthy patron, Mr. Robert Darcy. Raised on Pemberley estate, Wickham had often been in the company of his patron's son, Fitzwilliam, and over the years, he had become closer to the man rather than to the son. Fitzwilliam Darcy, sanctimonious prig that he was, disapproved of Wickham's activities, taking no interest in the finer things in life, and while Wickham was forced to subsist on a mere pittance, Darcy was afforded as much capital as he could spend. Not that he ever used it, of course — Darcy was frugal and careful, though why he would be so was beyond Wickham's understanding.

It was fortunate, indeed, that Wickham had always possessed the ability to flatter the elder Darcy, for he was aware that the younger man had attempted to turn his father against him from an early age. The first few times Mr. Darcy had called Wickham into his study, his words had been spoken quite firmly. But Wickham's ability to curry favor with the man had stood him in good stead, to the point where Wickham knew he was a subject of contention between the two men.

But it was still not enough. If it had been enough, Wickham would not be stuck in this dingy office, slaving away, copying documents by the light of the sun filtering in through the small windows and a smelly taper. Treated as a second son all his life, Wickham had expected that treatment would continue once he became an adult. But it was not to be.

The memory of that fateful day caused Wickham to grasp his quill so hard, it was a wonder it did not snap under the strain. Wickham relaxed his grip and dipped it into the ink again before putting it to the paper. His mind, however, was quite distant from the task before him.

It had been a brilliant day, one which could only portend a good omen. Or so he had thought at the time. Freshly graduated from Cambridge, Wickham had returned to Pemberley and his future, eager to receive his just desserts. For a time, Wickham had lounged around the beautiful manor house, spoken with Mr. Darcy, flattered Mrs. Darcy and the girl, and ignored his erstwhile friend. But even as he had waited for Mr. Darcy to come to the point, Wickham had known his whole life lay before him. The income of a gentleman was there for the taking, whether it was a gift of money, or even one of the smaller estates which comprised the Darcys' holdings.

"Ah, Wickham," Mr. Darcy had said when he entered the study that morning. "Come in, come in, my boy!"

"You sent for me, Mr. Darcy?" Wickham had asked. His appearance had been calculated to show no foreknowledge of the subject his patron wished to discuss, though Wickham had no doubt of the matter.

"I did," replied Mr. Darcy. He directed Wickham to the pair of chairs which sat before the fireplace, though Wickham was disappointed the gentleman had not offered him a glass of the fine brandy he kept at hand. "Now that you have graduated from university, some thought must be taken for your future.

"As you know, I promised your dearly departed father that I would provide for you, which I have attempted to do to the best of my abilities." Mr. Darcy paused, a wistful look coming over his face. The two men had been close, more like friends and partners than master and servant.

"Yes, Mr. Darcy?" asked Wickham, interrupting his reverie. In truth he was impatient, having convinced himself that Mr. Darcy was about to offer him ownership of one of the satellite estates. Perhaps even Blackfish Bay, which was, to Wickham's thinking, the most prosperous of them all! Mr. Darcy's subsequent words, however, dashed such hopes.

"I have been thinking of the best way to accomplish this," said Mr. Darcy. "After much considering, I have determined to offer you the living at Kympton."

"Kympton!" exclaimed Wickham. In his shock, he was certain his mask had slipped. Fortunately, Mr. Darcy seemed to take no notice.

"The living at Kympton is a good one, George, one which a man in your situation could not hope to obtain until you were at least thirty years of age. The parsonage is large and is in good order, and the duties of the parish, while demanding, are not onerous. As we do not have any near relations for whom to provide, I think it an excellent opportunity for you."

Mr. Darcy's last remark stung, for it reminded Wickham that he was not truly a member of the family. Had they any near relations who required a living, it seemed *they* would have received preference rather than Wickham himself. But that thought was brushed aside—that Mr. Darcy would insult him with the offer of a parson's pittance was highly insulting.

"You wish me to become a priest," said Wickham, unable to keep the incredulous note from his voice.

"It is a highly respected profession, George," said Mr. Darcy, a note of censure in his voice. He had, apparently, recognized Wickham's tone.

Mr. Darcy continued to speak of the living, including his reasons why Wickham should feel privileged to have been offered it, but Wickham was no longer listening.

I care not if it is a respected profession! It is not what I am entitled to as a favored son. I was meant for more than to be a simple parson, droning on about the Bible and enduring the whining of the masses!

Though Wickham knew he could not say what was in his heart, he thought there was some way to bring Mr. Darcy around to the proper way of thinking. As the man continued to speak, Wickham gave every indication he was listening, while at the same time planning his strategy for how he would convince his patron that he was worth so much more than the pittance of the living. When Mr. Darcy paused in his words, Wickham was quick to interject.

"You are correct, of course," said he. "Unfortunately, Mr. Darcy, I do not believe I am the best choice to become the parson of Kympton."

The look Mr. Darcy gave him made Wickham uncomfortable, but he weathered it, waiting for the other man to speak. Mr. Darcy obliged him with alacrity.

"I do not know why it would not be suitable. It is a highly sought after living."

"I am sure it is," replied Wickham. A little flattery would not go amiss. "The church is handsome, and while I have never seen the parsonage, I am certain it must be well-appointed and comfortable. There is nothing in the living which is objectionable. It is only that I do not think the life of a parson would suit me."

Wickham was well aware that many gentlemen would become affronted at this point. But he also knew he had Mr. Darcy so much in his power that he would not. As per his expectations, Mr. Darcy nodded slowly.

"It takes a wise man to understand himself as well as you do, George," said Mr. Darcy. "I commend you for understanding yourself to this extent."

George demurred, saying: "It is only the truth, Mr. Darcy. I would no more wish to be unhappy in life than I would to inflict my ill-suited person on those of the parish as their spiritual leader."

"Yes, I can see that," replied Mr. Darcy, seemingly deep in thought. "Then perhaps my promise to your father might be accomplished in another manner."

"Grateful though I am, it is not necessary, Mr. Darcy. Your patronage has given me so much. To accept anything more, when you have treated me like a son all my life, would almost seem like I was grasping."

Wickham paused, eying the other man with satisfaction. Mr. Darcy was still in the midst of some deep thought, though he studied Wickham as his mind worked. Certain his subtle suggestion had not gone unheard, Wickham waited, eager to meet his fate.

"It is no trouble, George, nothing more than fulfilling my promise to your father. Since the church is not an option, the remaining options are the law, the army, or perhaps medicine, should you feel inclined to such a future. Which do you think you would prefer?"

Even now, four years after the event, George Wickham could feel the rage build within him at the memory of Mr. Darcy's unwillingness to bestow upon him his due. Oh, he had never come out and said he wished for an estate, but he had hinted at it as openly as he dared. And yet Mr. Darcy had insisted upon his choosing one of the professions for his future. The disappointment had been almost overwhelming.

The army held no attractions — why would anyone wish to be put in a position where he might have someone shooting at him? Medicine was also an unpalatable option, for Wickham had no desire to listen to others bleat about their ailments. Wickham had no more notion that the law would suit him — anything other than being a gentleman of leisure would most definitely *not* suit him! — but he had finally settled on that. Years of study, though attended to in a cursory fashion, had been followed by Mr. Darcy's efforts to locate him a suitable situation. This had led him to Mortimer and Sons. But George knew he could not sit here, copying contracts forever. Even becoming a full partner had no interest for him. He was meant to be a gentleman. He would accept nothing less.

The problem was he had no idea of how to go about it. Though he had fooled himself into thinking he was worthy of being considered a second son, he now knew that Mr. Darcy would never treat him as such in a way that mattered. Then how could he make his fortune? Marriage was one option, though as a lowly clerk in a law office, there was little likelihood that a woman of means would pay him any attention.

There was always Georgiana Darcy. She was a mousey little thing though handsome enough. Or at least he thought she would be when she attained adulthood. But there was the problem of her brother and her cousin.

Wickham shuddered at the thought of Colonel Fitzwilliam, whom he knew had never liked him. Even marriage to Georgiana might not save him from the man's wrath, though it was possible he might desist should Mr. Darcy accept Wickham as a son. But even then, how far would Georgiana's thirty-thousand pounds take him? Not nearly far enough, George thought, given his habits.

Now Pemberley itself — that was a prize worth obtaining. With such a property, Wickham would never be required to concern himself with his funds again. But the son stood in the way. And George was not foolish enough to believe he could supplant the bastard in his father's eyes.

Perhaps if Darcy had been removed from consideration . . .

Wickham did not know what was to be done. But he had always been a resourceful man. He would not stop until he discovered it. It was his destiny after all.

The days following their initial meeting at church found Elizabeth in the company of Mr. Darcy far more often than she wished. It was Mr. Bingley's fault, though the man was so genial and friendly that it was difficult to blame him for anything. It seemed his intention was to see Mr. Darcy accepted in every home in the neighborhood, and as such, they were much in evidence during those days.

Elizabeth had never been a woman prone to reticence. She had long been known to be one of the liveliest girls in the neighborhood, and her estimation of her courage was not out of proportion with reality, in her mind. Elizabeth was happy to learn her opinion seemed correct, for she did not find herself to be overly shy in his company. That did not mean she was foolish, however, as she was careful to stay near Jane or some other of her acquaintance when in his company. Perhaps her sense of her own courage was filled with fallacy. But Elizabeth did not concern herself with such matters.

One particular case in point happened a little more than a week after first meeting Mr. Darcy at church. Longbourn was situated at such a distance from Meryton—no more than a mile—as to render a walk there exceedingly agreeable, especially when there was nothing to do at home. When the weather was fair, the Bennet sisters could often be found walking thither, sometimes with an errand for their cook or, on other occasions, determined to visit their Aunt Phillips, who lived in the town. They would often look through the various shops Meryton boasted as well, though the number of times they browsed through their favorite merchants far exceeded the changes such places experienced.

On the day in question, the three sisters had met a few acquaintances and had stopped to talk for a few minutes. They had been in this attitude for only a moment or two when Mr. Bingley rode up, accompanied by Mr. Darcy.

"Miss Bennet!" called he, dismounting his horse and leading the animal closer, an act which Mr. Darcy mirrored. "And the other Miss Bennets, Miss Lucas, and Miss Long, of course."

"There is no need to dissemble, Mr. Bingley," teased Elizabeth. "We are all well aware that you only care to see my elder sister."

While Mr. Bingley was quick to blush, Jane looked skyward and then directed a glare at her sister. Elizabeth, however, only grinned, completely unrepentant. It was nothing less than the truth, after all. Then Mr. Bingley proved Elizabeth's statement by addressing Jane, and soon the two were deep in conversation. Mary and Elizabeth exchanged a grin at the sight.

"It seems to me, Miss Elizabeth," said Mr. Darcy, stepping closer to the two ladies, "that you approve of my friend's interest in your sister."

"Who would disapprove?" asked Elizabeth, her wariness for this man forgotten in her desire to challenge him.

"Certainly not I," said Mr. Darcy. The sentiment was offered with promptness with which Elizabeth could find no fault. "It seems to me my friend and your sister are quite well suited. I speak more of the general sense I have received from your family that you all approve of him."

"Indeed, we do, Mr. Darcy," said Elizabeth. "Mr. Bingley has been our neighbor since before my sisters and I can remember and has admired her for nearly as long."

"Then my friend is fortunate. To find a woman he wishes to be his wife is often a difficult thing to do. To accomplish it with so little effort allows him to concentrate more fully on her and will, I suspect, increase his happiness."

Elizabeth was curious in spite of herself. "It seems to me, Mr. Darcy, you speak from experience. Are you, perhaps, in want of a wife and uncertain of where to search for her?"

"To hear my mother speak of it, I *should* be searching for a wife. As to where to search, most of those in my circle would suggest London, amongst the elite."

"But?" prompted Elizabeth when he did not speak further.

Mr. Darcy hesitated, seeming to realize he had been too open in his comments. Not that there was anything improper about such subjects—but Elizabeth had not thought a man who was of a higher level of society and must be acquainted with fortune hunters and their efforts to find wealthy husbands would speak so with a young woman with whom he was only barely acquainted.

"Let us simply say, Miss Elizabeth, that though I have been in society for several years now, I have never met anyone who intrigued me enough to consider her a possible partner. There are many ladies among the first circles who are eligible. But I have never been certain I would find a wife there."

"In that case, Mr. Darcy," said Elizabeth, unable to stop a laugh, "I suggest you try looking in more unlikely places. Meryton, for example, boasts many such ladies who would happily relieve you of your bachelor status. Some may even suit you!"

Then, to show the gentleman that she did not consider herself one of them, she wrapped her arm around Mary's—Mary had been watching them with some amusement—and curtseyed to Mr. Darcy, before informing Jane they would return to Longbourn. Jane immediately agreed and said her farewell to Mr. Bingley, before joining her sisters. Since Elizabeth did not look back, she could not tell, but she had the distinct impression that Mr. Darcy's eyes remained on her person until she was out of his sight.

On another occasion, which occurred only a few days after the first, Mr. Bingley and Mr. Darcy came to Longbourn to call on the Bennet family. Their father was absent that day, having ridden to Meryton to consult with his brother Phillips, leaving the three women to entertain the gentlemen. Or, perhaps it was more accurate to say that Jane amply entertained Mr. Bingley, who had no attention to spare for anyone else in the room, while Mr. Darcy sat with Elizabeth and Mary.

"I must own," observed Mr. Darcy after they had sat for a few moments, "I wonder that my friend has not already made an offer to your sister."

Elizabeth and Mary giggled together. "To own the truth," replied Mary, "we have wondered the same thing."

"It is likely nothing more than Mr. Bingley's desire to ensure he is ready to be a husband," said Elizabeth. "He is yet a young man—only four and twenty. There is no rush."

"There is not," agreed Mr. Darcy. "But then again, I have long known Bingley to be an impulsive sort of fellow. This does not seem to be in character for him."

"When he does propose," said Elizabeth, "I have no doubt he will do so on the impulse of the moment."

"Very likely," agreed Mary. "At present, I suspect he is enjoying the courtship aspect of his relationship with Jane."

"I must own, however, that I am surprised, Mr. Darcy." Elizabeth directed an arch look at the gentleman which he returned with a soft smile.

"How so, Miss Elizabeth?"

"Why, I had not thought you would be particularly interested in your friend's matrimonial prospects. And yet, we have spoken of it twice in as many days."

Mr. Darcy appeared more than a little silly at the observation, but he quickly recovered. "Bingley is such a good friend, I do find myself interested in his concerns. And before you suggest anything else, Miss Elizabeth, the matter of whom he marries and how or when he comes to his decision is not my business. As he is a good friend, I would wish to see him happy. That is the extent of my interest."

"Then you need have no fear, Mr. Darcy. Had I any doubt that Jane would make him happy—and he, her—I should argue against her accepting any overtures he might make."

"Excellent!" said Mr. Darcy. "Then we may leave the subject alone. I have heard you are both great readers, but as yet, I have not seen any evidence of it. Perhaps we could turn our discussion to books?"

Mary laughed. "Though I cannot speak for myself, there is no better way to ensure Lizzy's good opinion than to offer to discuss books with her."

"I am not a great reader, Mary," said Elizabeth, shooting her sister a glare.

"Perhaps I may be the judge of that, Miss Elizabeth," said Darcy. "I have recently had occasion to read a selection of Donne's poetry. Might I ask if you have read it, and if so, would you be willing to share your opinions?"

As it happened, Elizabeth and Mary had both read Donne, as her father possessed various works by the author. The three spent the rest of the visit comparing their opinions, and from thence moving onto other subjects. Mary, while she was as well read as Elizabeth, seemed content to allow Elizabeth and Mr. Darcy to carry the bulk of the conversation. And Elizabeth found herself responding to the gentleman's overtures, for he was both intelligent and insightful. Though she could not have imagined doing so before Mr. Darcy had come to the neighborhood, the half hour conversation was interesting and allowed Elizabeth to forget what had previously happened between them.

When the visiting time had elapsed, Mr. Bingley and Mr. Darcy rose, thanked the Bennet sisters for a delightful visit, and went away. Before he left, Mr. Darcy was quick to bow over Elizabeth and Mary's hands, thanking them for an enjoyable time.

"It is rare to find young ladies with such insights," said he. "I hope to have this opportunity to speak with you repeated in the future."

The gentlemen then departed, leaving the three sisters together. Jane, it appeared, was lost in her own thoughts, focused on Mr. Bingley. As for Elizabeth, she was thinking on the other gentleman, wondering at his behavior. Thus far in his visit, he had not made her uncomfortable in the slightest. The memory of their previous interaction hovered around the back of her mind like an insect buzzing above her head, but it did not usually bother her. On the contrary, she felt like she might be coming to feel something like esteem for the gentleman.

"Well, Lizzy," said Mary, pulling Elizabeth from her thoughts, "it seems Mr. Darcy approves of you."

"We both spoke to him, Mary."

"That may be true. But his focus was reserved for you. Had I been absent, I doubt Mr. Darcy would have noticed or cared."

"Do not tease me, Mary," admonished Elizabeth.

"I do not," replied Mary. Then she fixed Elizabeth with a teasing smile. "Or perhaps I do a little. I know nothing of his admiration, should such a thing exist. But I can say without any doubt that Mr. Darcy does not look on you with disfavor. Quite the opposite, in fact."

Mary then rose and left the room, leaving her elder sisters to their thoughts. While Elizabeth found her own to be a jumble, she realized one thing stood out to her: Mr. Darcy was affecting her like she had not thought he would. And Elizabeth was not certain she wished it.

CHAPTER IX

*D*arcy's increasing interest in Miss Elizabeth Bennet was unmistakable, least of all to Darcy himself. When he had come to Hertfordshire, he had not been certain what to expect. The thought that she would be angry with him because of his behavior on his last visit was not unreasonable. Darcy had half expected her to confront him with it, perhaps with her father and brother in attendance, when he first arrived.

But she had said nothing of it, and while he thought he might have detected a hint of reticence in her manner toward him, it was by no means explicit. To the untrained eye, she treated him the same as she did any of her other acquaintances. Even to those who knew her, Darcy suspected her behavior with him would not be obvious.

When he pondered the subject, Darcy could not quite put his finger on exactly what attracted him to her. It may be because of her obvious intelligence or perhaps her playful attitude, which he had seen directed at himself more than once. Or it may have been because she paid no specific deference other than respect for an acquaintance. Then again, Miss Bingley had given him no such overt deference the last time he had visited, nor did Miss Elizabeth's sisters, and yet he did not find himself madly in love with any of them. The obvious loveliness of her countenance also attracted him, far more than did her elder sister, whom Darcy had heard described as the local beauty. Further thought informed Darcy that perhaps it was all of these considerations combined in one irresistible woman.

Whatever the case, Darcy found himself wishing to be in her company whenever he was out of it. Like a man addicted to opioids, he could not help but wish to drink it in, heedless of what it might do to him. And then Mrs. Bingley announced she had invited the Bennets to dinner that evening. Darcy spent much of the day in anticipation — had he been any more open, Bingley, who was indulging in dreams of his own Bennet sister, might have noticed it.

The Bennets were shown into the sitting-room where the three remaining Bingleys in Darcy's company were awaiting them. Greetings were shared, consisting of those of intimate acquaintances who often met one another. But there was one among the company to whom Darcy had never been introduced formally, whom he found himself interested to meet.

Darcy was a little surprised to see a fifth in their company — the reverend from the church service the previous Sunday, who was introduced as Mr. Collins, a cousin of the family. When the introductions were complete, offered by Mr. Bingley, who had been the elder Bennet's friend since his arrival in the neighborhood, Darcy found himself in company with Mr. Bennet, along with the two Bingley men and Mr. Collins, while the Bennet ladies congregated with Mrs. Bingley on the far side of the room. Darcy was interested to note that while most of the men participated equally in the conversation, Mr. Collins's attention was more often than not fixed upon the ladies.

"I believe I can write to my son with news of your actual existence, Mr. Darcy," said Mr. Bennet. The elder man peered at Darcy from above his teacup, and Darcy suspected he was the object of great amusement. "As my Thomas mentioned before he departed, we have only had Bingley's assurance of his friendship with you, though the tales he told were quite plentiful. I *had* begun to wonder if you were nothing more than the product of his imagination."

The jest was something Darcy could imagine the man's second daughter saying, and he laughed, as he knew was expected. "Oh, I am real, Mr. Bennet. It is only puzzling to me that I did not make your acquaintance the last time I visited."

"You were only here for a matter of two weeks, Darcy," reminded Bingley. "As Bennet's son was away at the time and Mr. Bennet does not enjoy much society, it is not strange you would not have made his acquaintance."

"Bingley has the right of it," said Mr. Bennet. "But that is not important. Of much greater importance is my curiosity as to whether you play chess, young man. For if you do—especially if you play well—then I must entertain the notion that you are a man of some substance."

"I do, indeed, Mr. Bennet," said Darcy. At the same time, Bingley said: "Darcy here was the president of our chess club at Cambridge."

"Was he, indeed?" asked Mr. Bennet.

"From my limited understanding," interjected Bingley's father, "Darcy seems highly competent. He trounced me in very little time when I played him."

"*That* is no great feat, my friend," said Mr. Bennet.

The Bingley men laughed, the matter clearly a well-worn jest between them. "Indeed, it is not," said Mr. Bingley. "I own it myself, though I will confess I am not bothered because of it. I know the moves well enough, but I do not have the ability to plan many moves in advance, which I believe to be an essential part of being skilled at the art."

"It takes an honest man to understand his own limitations," said Mr. Bennet. "I do not think less of you because of it."

"Then you must lack for skillful opponents," said Darcy. "Bingley here is an indifferent player at best."

"There are a few in the neighborhood who play well," said Mr. Bennet, sipping on his tea. "But few who play so well as to provide a challenge. My son, Thomas, is a challenge, albeit not an overly difficult one, as his interest in the game is somewhat limited. Only my Lizzy can beat me regularly, though I will assert that I win as often as she."

"Miss Elizabeth plays chess?" asked Darcy, his eyes finding the woman from across the room. Miss Elizabeth met his eyes and looked at him askance, being too far away to hear their conversation. Darcy smiled and turned his attention back to Mr. Bennet.

"Better than most men of my acquaintance," said Mr. Bennet.

"Elizabeth attempted to teach me the game not long after I came to Longbourn," added Mr. Collins in a quiet and introspective tone. "But I found I have little aptitude."

"We all have different strengths and weaknesses, William," said Mr. Bennet, addressing his cousin with evident fondness. "It is no great tragedy that you do not play. Do not take my jesting as censure."

Mr. Collins smiled and nodded. Then his attention drifted back towards the ladies.

"It takes Miss Elizabeth only a few minutes to best me," said Bingley, his tone rueful. "There are times when she will toy with me, give me the impression that I might have a chance. But usually she is far too ruthless to allow me such hope."

"Aye, that is my Lizzy!" exclaimed Mr. Bennet with a laugh. "Her aggression when playing the game is the one trait which most often causes her downfall. For myself, I tend to be much more defensive and patient."

"Elizabeth is as fearless as any man," said Mr. Collins. Darcy thought it was a bit of an odd comment as it seemed to be apropos of nothing.

"If you mean to challenge me," said Darcy, "it may have been better to stay silent, sir. Now I know what to expect."

"It does not mean I cannot play aggressively, Mr. Darcy," said Bennet. "Only that I find a good defense to be the key to victory."

"Then perhaps we should begin a game, sir," said Darcy. "For I find myself very much intrigued."

"Not tonight, my friends," said Mr. Bingley. "My good wife will not be happy if an impromptu chess tournament began when she is expecting a night of good company."

The men all laughed, Mr. Bennet exclaiming: "I think you have the right of it. Furthermore, I suspect your wife takes as dim a view as mine did concerning Lizzy's ability to play."

"That she does," replied Mr. Bingley.

"Then I shall visit sometime this coming week, if that is agreeable," said Darcy.

"Very well, young man. I look forward to meeting you over a chessboard."

After that, talk turned to other subjects, matters which were common among society such as this. Mr. Bennet and Mr. Bingley spoke of some common issues of concern, in particular about a stream which ran through both of their properties and had apparently caused flooding that spring. Bingley listened intently, asking questions here and there, taking in the experience of the elder men eagerly. Darcy listened himself, nodding at their opinions, learning that the two men were competent in their care of their stewardships. At other times, Bingley spoke to Darcy of various subjects, requesting Darcy's assistance when assessing the needs of a tenant the following day or what Darcy thought of a proposed ride to Luton.

A short time later, the party was called in to dinner, and Darcy continued his study of Mr. Bennet. The man, based on certain comments Bingley had made, was indolent, preferring the comforts of his library to being an active caretaker of his estate or his family's position in local society. Darcy could well understand the lure of a well-stocked bookroom—there were times when he would have cheerfully stayed in Pemberley's library an entire day. But a man also had the responsibility to himself and his descendants to care for his estate and build his family's legacy.

Then again, Mr. Bennet now had an adult son who was engaged in managing the family's interests. After a lifetime of laboring on the estate, it was understandable in some measure that a man would wish to spend his later years in peace. Darcy assisted his father in many ways, but Robert Darcy still firmly held the reins of the family's holdings. Perhaps Mr. Bennet's situation was akin to that shared by himself and his father. Either way, it was not his business, nor was it his place to judge.

As it inevitably must, talk at the dinner table turned to the absent members of the family. As the time approached for their return, Darcy knew he would make the younger Mr. Bennet's acquaintance before long.

"I understand your son traveled with his bride to Ramsgate?" asked Darcy when the couple was mentioned.

"Yes," replied Mr. Bennet. "I have an acquaintance who owns a small property there. As he spends only part of the summer in residence, he was quite pleased to offer it for their use."

"Our letters from our relations have been sparse," said Miss Elizabeth, her tone one of mirth. "Not that we had expected to be inundated by letters. But what we have heard suggests they have quite enjoyed themselves by the sea."

"The ocean is a wondrous thing," agreed Darcy. "I have not experienced Ramsgate, but I have visited Brighton and some cities on the sea further north."

"I have not gone," said Miss Elizabeth, a certain wistfulness evident in her voice. "I should like to."

"Perhaps when Jane is married you shall," said Mr. Bennet. The man turned and winked at his eldest daughter, who colored and looked down at her plate. It did not miss Darcy's notice that Bingley positively beamed. "It is not unusual for a girl to accompany her elder sister on her wedding tour, after all."

"Jane might have gone with Caroline," said Mrs. Bingley. "But she declined the invitation."

"It has always been my understanding," said Jane, "that married couples wish to be alone in each other's company. The house in Ramsgate is not large as I understand. I should have been in the way if I had gone."

"While I commend you for your choice, dearest Sister," said Miss Elizabeth, "I cannot imagine how anyone could think you were a bother."

Miss Bennet threw a smile at her sister, but she did not reply. Since it seemed no one else meant to comment on the matter, Darcy essayed to speak of his own eagerness to meet the younger Mr. Bennet. The man's father gazed at Darcy in amusement, and he thanked Darcy for his sentiments.

"Thomas is eager to make your acquaintance too, sir. He was quite put out with Bingley here for inviting you when he was to be away."

"I am sure, Papa," said Miss Elizabeth, "that Thomas's pique with Mr. Bingley lasted no longer than his first sight of Caroline on his wedding day."

Miss Elizabeth's comment once again provoked laughter among the company, and the subject ran its course. The rest of the meal passed in a similar fashion, though the conversation was more general than specific. Had he not already known, it would have been clear that the two families were great friends and intimates. This extended to the one member of the party other than Darcy who did not bear either the name Bennet or Bingley.

When the meal had been consumed, the ladies departed to the sitting-room while the gentlemen remained in the dining room. A pair of decanters of port were brought in and shared among the five men remaining, though Darcy noted that Mr. Bingley did not provide cigars — in fact, they had been absent since he had arrived. It seemed Mr. Bingley understood Darcy's thoughts, for he spoke on the matter.

"I apologize for the lack of something to smoke, Mr. Darcy. Unfortunately, the smell of burning tobacco does not agree with me."

"It is quite all right, Mr. Bingley," replied Darcy, sitting back with his glass of port. "My father is quite of the same opinion."

"At Longbourn, it was Mrs. Bennet who particularly objected to them," said Mr. Bennet. The gentleman was introspective, lightly moving his glass in circles, causing the liquid inside to flow around, creating a whirlpool in the middle. "Nasty, smelly things, she called them. Said that I would need to have the entire dining room aired out if I dared to smoke them. And a group of men smoking? She would have fled for the hills!"

The four gentlemen who had known the lady laughed at Mr. Bennet's comment, Mr. Bingley shaking his head in amusement. Bingley said nothing, taking a sip from his glass instead. Mr. Collins was the only one who made a response.

"A good woman, Mrs. Bennet. The kindness with which she welcomed me when I came to Longbourn, I shall never forget."

"Yes, she was a good woman." Mr. Bennet paused and smiled. "Perhaps not the most proper specimen, and she often afforded me much amusement. But she kept my home and provided me companionship for more than twenty years. I miss her very much."

Mr. Bennet fell silent, and for some time, he did not say another word. The other gentlemen in the room, apparently sensing the atmosphere becoming a little maudlin, turned the subject to other matters, speaking amongst themselves. For his part, Darcy stayed mostly silent, observing the other men present. It was not long after that Mr. Collins turned to Darcy.

"Mr. Darcy, am I correct in apprehending you are connected to the Fitzwilliam family?"

"I am, sir," replied Darcy, looking at the parson with interest. "May I ask how you know of my family?"

"Of course, sir. You see, I studied at the seminary in the company of a Randall Fitzwilliam, with whom I formed a friendship."

"Cousin Randall," acknowledged Darcy with a nod. "A younger son of my uncle's younger brother. My uncle is the Earl of Matlock."

"That is what I was given to understand. Upon his completion of our studies there, I believe he was destined to receive the living at Rosings Park in Kent. His patron, I believe, is your uncle, Sir Lewis de Bourgh."

"That is correct," replied Darcy. "However, I do not believe he had ascended to the parsonage yet. Mr. Peters is still in possession of the living, though I believe he is getting on in years and means to retire soon."

"So Randall informed me." Mr. Collins paused and seemed in thought for a moment. "Mr. Fitzwilliam is, indeed, a good young man; an excellent example of the nobility, I believe. I still correspond with him regularly." Mr. Collins paused and then said with seeming hesitance: "Your cousin told some rather amusing anecdotes about your aunt, Mr. Darcy."

Darcy could not help but laugh. "Lady Catherine de Bourgh. Yes, Lady Catherine is an interesting woman. I cannot imagine what she might be like if her husband was not there to check her."

"There was some suggestion of a cradle betrothal?"

"So she likes to say," said Darcy, shaking his head. "But though she has attempted to press it on the family, my mother contends that they only spoke of it once, and to her way of telling, it was nothing more than a fantasy — amusing thoughts of what might happen if we suited each other. Lady Catherine does not appreciate it, but my father refuses to even consider a formal betrothal."

Mr. Collins nodded. "I can only wonder what it might be like to be a parson under her patronage. My friend shall soon discover it, though he will not benefit, as I have myself, from another's misfortune."

"I would not necessarily call it misfortune," said Mr. Bennet, rousing himself to speak. "Mr. Taylor was quite elderly and had held the living since my grandfather's time. At times, I wondered if he would ever give it up."

"Of course," said Mr. Collins. "But the fact remains that I have ascended to the incumbency of a living long before most of my fellows. I feel the honor of it exceedingly, I assure you, and intend to do my utmost to fulfill the sacred obligations which have been bestowed upon me and perform my duties to the best of my ability."

Darcy found himself a little surprised by the man's statement, for it smacked a little of subservience, which attitude Darcy had not attributed to him. At the same time, Mr. Bennet caught Darcy's eye, rolling his own and looking at his cousin with evident fondness. It seemed there was a history of which he was not aware, beyond the fact that Mr. Collins had come to the Bennets as a young boy and of his subsequent elevation to the parsonage. But Darcy knew it would not be polite to ask and thus directed the conversation back to a previous statement the man had made.

"Randall will take control of the living before too many years have passed. And just in time too, for I believe he has his eye upon a young woman he means to make the mistress of the parsonage."

Mr. Collins smiled, though Darcy fancied it did not make its way to his eyes. "That has also been a common theme of his letters. I am happy for him — to meet a young woman and have one's feelings returned is the greatest of blessings."

It was an odd statement, to be sure, and Darcy did not know what to make of it. Mr. Bennet, however, seemed to know exactly of what the man spoke. He leaned forward and clasped his shoulder.

"There are plenty of fish in the sea, Son. And the search for one's life mate is not one to undertake lightly. You will find someone with whom to share your life — it is just a matter of time."

The smile Mr. Collins returned to Mr. Bennet seemed more than a little forced, but he did not speak again. After a few more moments of desultory conversation, in which Mr. Collins contributed nothing, the gentlemen arose, making their way toward the sitting-room and the ladies waiting there. It did not miss Darcy's notice that Mr. Bennet walked close to Mr. Collins, speaking to him softly all the way, so much so that the two men stopped as they were walking and stood in the hall for a few moments speaking. Darcy, not wishing to give the impression of eavesdropping, walked around them, though he noticed that Mr. Bennet spoke and Mr. Collins listened, nodding his head on occasion, though his gaze did not rise from the floor.

A few moments after Darcy entered, the matter became clear, for Mr. Bennet entered with Mr. Collins by his side. The young man appeared to have recovered some of his former mood, for he entered with a smile for his cousin. But then Darcy noted a look that passed between Mr. Bennet and his second eldest daughter, and soon after, Miss Elizabeth spoke to Mr. Collins.

"Cousin, will you not come and sit with us?"

A beaming smile lit up Mr. Collins's face and he went eagerly to sit with Miss Elizabeth, who was speaking with her elder sister and Bingley. Soon the four were sharing an animated conversation. Or it was more accurate to say Miss Bennet, Miss Elizabeth, and Bingley were speaking, for Mr. Collins remained mostly quiet. It was the look of adoration bestowed upon Miss Elizabeth which betrayed the truth of the matter.

"I see you have seen it, Mr. Darcy."

The sound of a voice by his side startled Darcy from his study—it had suddenly seemed imperative that he determine Miss Elizabeth's feelings for her cousin. Thus far, he was unable to be certain, though it was clear that she liked him.

"Do not demur. I can see your understanding." Mr. Bennet's own eyes found his daughter and the young man who sat by her side, hopelessly in love with her. "It is not a secret within the community, after all."

"And her feelings?" asked Darcy before he could consider the matter fully.

Mr. Bennet's immediate response was to smile, and Darcy did not miss the smugness inherent in the expression. "Thank you, Mr. Darcy, for confirming your interest."

"That is not it," Darcy was quick to say. "I was merely inquiring whether there was another—or even, I dare say, a third—wedding in the near future of the Bennet family."

It was clear to Darcy that the other man was not deceived in the slightest. Rather than press the issue as Darcy might have expected, instead Mr. Bennet responded to his question.

"I would think it is evident, even to one who has not known her long, that though Lizzy *likes* the young man, she feels nothing more than cousinly affection for him."

Darcy turned and considered the group before him. "Then is it not impolitic of her to draw his attention as she has?"

Belatedly Darcy realized how his question might sound, and he flushed, feeling more than a little uncomfortable speaking to this perceptive man. But again Mr. Bennet confounded him, as he did not become angry at Darcy's comment. Instead he arched an eyebrow and chuckled.

"Do you suggest Lizzy is playing with the gentleman's emotions?"

"Of course not," said Darcy. "It is clear from watching her that is not the case."

"And you would be correct," said Mr. Bennet. "Both Lizzy and William understand the nature of their relationship. Lizzy knows of the young man's feelings, and William knows that while his feelings for her are strong, she does not return them, and he is content to admire her from afar."

"That could be considered a tragedy for him."

Mr. Bennet shrugged. "Perhaps. But I am certain he does not see it that way. A part of his heart will always belong to her, but as time goes on, he will realize that a large measure of what he feels has been driven by infatuation.

"I think highly of my cousin, Mr. Darcy," added Mr. Bennet, his manner more serious. "But it is clear to anyone who cares to look— including William himself—that they do not suit. Thus, he is happy with whatever affection she is willing to grant him, knowing that one day she will marry, and he will too. But they are not for each other, regardless of how much he wishes it might be so."

With an absent nod, Darcy continued to watch the company, noting that Miss Mary had now joined them. Miss Elizabeth was relating some anecdote, her words punctuated by gestures of her hands, as well as what Darcy took to be mimicking whatever person of whom she was speaking. When she delivered the punch line, they all laughed, Mr. Collins as much as any other. Darcy decided that Mr. Bennet was correct—Mr. Collins looked on her with clear admiration, but he did not attempt to turn her attention toward him. He truly was content with whatever he was given, though when she did grant him her attention, he beamed, as pleased as if she were focusing on him to the exclusion of all others.

"Let me also inform you of one more matter, Mr. Darcy," said Mr. Bennet, once again drawing his attention to the gentleman. "My Lizzy — all my daughters, in fact — have dowry enough to enable them to take their own paths in life, even if their brother refused to support them. I care nothing for society or status. They are all free to marry as their hearts dictate. If Lizzy should decide her future lay with my cousin, I would not stand in her way. The same is true should she decide on *any other* man."

Darcy nodded, still distracted. But Bennet was not about to allow him to return to his reverie.

"Now, young man — I have been told you are skilled at chess, and I do long for a challenge. I shall expect your presence at Longbourn tomorrow morning."

"Very well, sir," said Darcy. "I would be happy to."

The rest of the evening was spent in pleasant conversation with Mr. Bennet. And while Darcy might have preferred to be the recipient of some of Miss Elizabeth's attention, he found himself content to watch her from afar. But he would not end like Mr. Collins in this respect — he felt too much for her to remain passive like the other man was.

CHAPTER X

"Check and mate."

While her father gazed at the board for several moments, apparently attempting to find a way out of the trap in which Mr. Darcy had caught him, Elizabeth knew it was fruitless. A moment later, her father saw it too, and he reached out and tipped his king over, accepting his defeat. Then he sat back in his chair and regarded the man across the chessboard from him.

"The tales of your prowess have not been exaggerated, Mr. Darcy. I believe that is now two wins for us each."

"It seems to be so," said Mr. Darcy, his tone brimming with satisfaction.

"Of course, you have not been nearly so proficient with Lizzy. Unless I am mistaken, you have lost both of your matches."

"Your daughter is far more skilled than I had thought," muttered Mr. Darcy, seeming a little annoyed by the fact of his two defeats.

"I did inform you of her skill," said Mr. Bennet, clearly amused. "Then again, perhaps it is merely the fact of having to face a pretty young woman on the opposite ends of the battlefield which has led to your defeats."

Mr. Darcy gaped at Mr. Bennet, which resulted in the elder man guffawing at his own joke. Elizabeth, for her part, was a little annoyed with her father. Many had been the time in the days since the Netherfield dinner that he had teased Mr. Darcy with little innuendos about Elizabeth. It was as if he was attempting to rouse Mr. Darcy's interest in her!

"I assure you, sir," said Mr. Darcy, "I shall not underestimate her again."

"Shall we test the theory?" asked Mr. Bennet lazily. "Bingley appears engrossed in my eldest daughter. I cannot imagine he would be put out should you begin another game."

Across the room, Mr. Bingley, indeed, sat close to Jane, laughing in response to something she said, completely oblivious to the attention they were attracting. A glance at them seemed to confirm to Mr. Darcy what Mr. Bennet had averred, and he turned to Elizabeth, a questioning look on his brow.

"Very well, sir," said Elizabeth. "I am happy to defeat you again, if you wish it."

Mr. Bennet guffawed and quickly gave up his seat for Elizabeth's, so he could watch the game. They set up the board, Mr. Bennet holding the kings in two closed hands. Mr. Darcy indicated for Elizabeth to choose. Mr. Bennet opened his hand, revealing the black king, and Elizabeth gestured to Mr. Darcy to take the first move. His opening move was a standard one, and from there the game was on.

As she played, part of Elizabeth's mind was concentrated on the person of the young man who sat across the table from her. As he concentrated, Mr. Darcy's brow furrowed and his hand clenched and unclenched, a mannerism she had seen from him quite a few times by now. Soon, his hand stretched out to make another move, ceding the next move to Elizabeth.

Her study of the man was a frustrating endeavor as Elizabeth felt she did not have enough information to make a judgment. Mr. Darcy was not the friendliest of men. It seemed to Elizabeth that he was, in fact, quite closed and reserved with most of those in the neighborhood. Only with the Bingleys and the Bennets was he more open, and even then, it was with Elizabeth and Mr. Bennet he was friendly. He was polite enough with both Mary and Jane, but he did not go out of his way to initiate any exchanges with them, as he did with Mr. Bennet himself.

An obvious intelligence hovered behind his eyes, evident in every word he spoke which was always careful and considered. Whether he spoke of literature, the state of the war — usually with Mr. Bennet — his father's estate, or anything else, Elizabeth had the sense he spoke of those things with which he was familiar with confidence. On those subjects with which he was not so familiar, he gave his opinion readily enough, but he couched it as an opinion. Elizabeth had seen so many other men—especially men speaking with a lady—state their opinions as an absolute fact. She did not know if they thought a woman could never contradict them, but there it was. But Mr. Darcy did not talk down to her.

Had she not thought it impossible, Elizabeth might have wondered if he were interested in her. That could not be, of course, for the levels of society they inhabited were so different as to create a gulf so wide it could not be crossed. Furthermore, he did not act with her such as a lover might—Mr. Bingley with her sister, Jane, for example. In fact, though he was always polite when spoke with her, it was never with the eye of a man who admired a woman.

In the back of her mind, the memory of his actions at the assembly four years prior still bothered her. Was that the real Mr. Darcy? Had he changed? Or was he even now lulling her to sleep with his pretty manners and friendship with her father, ready to strike with further improprieties when she least expected it? Though Elizabeth could not see any evidence of such propensities, she could not be certain.

She told herself over and over again to stay clear of him, not to give him any of her attention, leave him to Mr. Bingley and her father. But something always drew her back. Elizabeth did not know what it was. Mr. Darcy was strangely compelling, and Elizabeth was helpless before his appeal.

At least in the company of Papa, he can do nothing, thought she as she watched him concentrating on his next move. His hand reached out tentatively, brushed against his knight, and then jerked back as if stung. Elizabeth watched as he considered for a few moments. Then he stretched out and moved the piece as he had originally intended.

"Excellent," said Elizabeth, moving her queen to the desired location. "Checkmate, Mr. Darcy."

Incredulous, Mr. Darcy examined the board for several moments. The sound of her father's laughter fell over them as Elizabeth sat back in her chair, feeling inordinately pleased with herself. A moment later Mr. Darcy resigned himself and toppled his king.

"A worthy attempt, Mr. Darcy," said Elizabeth, rising to her feet. "But I believe I have won again."

Then with an impish smile, Elizabeth excused herself and departed from the room. The sound of Mr. Bennet's continued chuckles followed her, and as she walked, she risked one more glance behind. Mr. Darcy was watching her, wonder in his eyes and on his countenance. Elizabeth shook her head and turned away—it appeared Mr. Darcy was still unable to understand that she could beat him at his own game.

And so it continued for some days. They saw much of the entire Bingley party, in particular, Mr. Bingley and Mr. Darcy. The Hursts returned to Netherfield soon after and the Bennet sisters called at Netherfield to welcome them. Elizabeth had never been fond of Mrs. Hurst—she had not been well liked in the area in general. But it was the polite thing to do, and the woman did not appear so objectionable as she had in the past. There was also some confirmation of her status as an expectant mother, which predictably put Mrs. Bingley in a jubilant mood.

A few days later, Elizabeth was pleased to receive a visit from Charlotte Lucas, whom she welcomed with eagerness. Charlotte had been away for some days, visiting with a friend at an estate closer to Hatfield. By coincidence, Charlotte's visit overlapped with another visit from Mr. Darcy and Mr. Bingley, who left not long after her arrival. A character as forthright as Charlotte's, who had known Elizabeth for so long, could not fail to tease. The expected inquisition happened as the two ladies walked out to Longbourn's back lawn.

"Has Mr. Darcy visited Longbourn often?" asked she.

"He comes with Mr. Bingley," said Elizabeth. "A shared love of chess has drawn him together with my father."

"Ah," said Charlotte with a knowing grin. "Might I hazard to guess, then, that he has also been drawn together with *you*? Your skills at the game are as good as any, after all."

Elizabeth shook her head, unwilling to allow her friend to draw her in. "Yes, he has played against me. In four matches, I remain undefeated against him."

"If the man was not showing such a promising inclination, I might warn you against such unladylike displays."

Well aware that her friend was jesting, Elizabeth looked heavenward. "Playing chess is not unladylike, Charlotte. There are some men who cannot fathom being bested by a woman, but Mr. Darcy has always been gracious in defeat." Elizabeth paused and giggled. "Of course, the first two and maybe three times, he seemed a little uncomprehending."

"You must own that chess is not a common accomplishment that women claim," said Charlotte. When Elizabeth smiled and did not reply, Charlotte continued: "Regardless, it seems to have done you little harm in his eyes. From what I can see, his admiration has not suffered at all."

"Of what do you speak?" asked Elizabeth.

"Come, Lizzy," said Charlotte. "You must have seen it. Even today in the short time I was in his company, his appreciation for you was evident."

Elizabeth could not help but shake her head with exasperation. "I assure you nothing could be further from the truth."

"Believe that if you will," replied a flippant Charlotte. "But I can see it. Of course, if you marry Mr. Darcy, you shall surely break Mr. Collins's heart."

"Oh, William," said Elizabeth with feeling. "I wish he was not so open. If his hopeless infatuation were not so pathetic, it would almost be amusing."

"That is unkind, Lizzy," said Charlotte. "The young man cannot help his feelings."

"I know he cannot, Charlotte," said Elizabeth with a sigh. "And I have nothing but friendly feelings for Mr. Collins. But I cannot love him, as you know, and if I cannot love him, I will not accept him."

"He knows this, Lizzy," said Charlotte. "I jest with you. When you do become engaged, I am certain Mr. Collins will be one of the first to offer congratulations."

"Yes, he will," said Elizabeth, feeling introspective. "There is not a mean bone in Mr. Collins's body. I only hope he will find someone who respects and loves him as much as he deserves."

"He shall," promised Charlotte. "That person may be closer than you think."

Though Elizabeth did not know what to make of Charlotte's cryptic statement, her friend changed the subject again. "It is fortunate, indeed, Lizzy, that you have no need to marry with any attention to wealth. Your romantic nature might make it difficult to find a man who possesses both a fortune and your heart."

"A few minutes ago, you were trying to convince me that Mr. Darcy would be my future partner in life," said Elizabeth. "If he is to be so, it is my understanding his family is quite wealthy. It seems I may have both, by your estimation."

"How quickly your thoughts move to matrimony!" exclaimed Charlotte. "Perhaps Mr. Darcy is affecting you much more than you might have expected?"

"Oh, Charlotte," said Elizabeth, shaking her head. "I am not unaware of the thrust of your comments. But I must ask you — what of yourself?"

"What *of* me, Lizzy?"

"Your desires for marriage," said Elizabeth. "Your comments concerning marriage used to be plentiful. In fact, I specifically remember you informing me some time ago that happiness in marriage was a matter of chance. It seems unusual for you to suggest that I be guided by my romantic ideas, as you put them."

"Who said I suggested you should be guided by such things?" asked Charlotte, showing Elizabeth an amused grin. "Mr. Darcy's feelings were the focus of what I said. If the gentleman finds himself in love with you, why would you not take advantage of it?"

"Charlotte!" protested Elizabeth.

But Charlotte laughed and patted her hand. "Of course, I jest, Lizzy." When Elizabeth glared at her, Charlotte shrugged. "As for myself, I find I have no particular desire to rush into marriage."

While Elizabeth looked on her friend doubtfully, knowing her age inhibited her ability to marry, she had no notion of how to make that point in a way that was tactful. Charlotte, however, was no simpleton, and she understood what Elizabeth could not say.

"I understand my situation, Lizzy. But I do have a small fortune, and while it is not much, it will sustain me should it come to that. And my brother has informed me many times that I will always have a home at Lucas Lodge. So, there is no reason to be concerned about my future."

This flew in the face of Charlotte's statements, which she had made many times, about not wishing to be a burden on her family. It also did not mesh with Charlotte's opinions, again shared many times, of the estate of marriage, which seemed to have revealed a lack of any good opinion about men in general. Regardless, Elizabeth decided she did not need to push her friend, and she changed the subject.

On Netherfield's grounds a similar discussion was taking place. A matter had arisen with respect to one of the tenants of the estate, and Mr. Bingley had entrusted it to his son's care. As a consequence, Bingley had ridden out with his friend to the tenant farm, some distance to the north of the manor. The matter was minor in the end, and after handling it, Bingley and Darcy turned their horses toward the south, enjoying a more leisurely ride on their return.

Bingley was in a good mood that morning, whistling a happy tune, though Darcy supposed that to call it a tune was generous, indeed.

With the dubious music accompanying the clip clop of the horses' hooves as they rode, Darcy found himself thinking of his time in Hertfordshire, wondering how long he would dare stay. Already he had received a letter from his father suggesting it might be time for him to rejoin the family. Darcy knew his father was not feeling the urgency to remove him from Netherfield just yet, but the longer he stayed the more demanding the letters would become.

"Tell me, Darcy," said Bingley as they rode, "how are you enjoying Hertfordshire?"

"Very much," said Darcy without any hesitation. "In particular, I am anticipating making the acquaintance of your sister's new husband."

"Ah, the Bennets *are* a good family, are they not? My father declares that had he not had Mr. Bennet to assist him when he first came to Netherfield he would have been lost. We are very fortunate, indeed, that such an amiable family was already established nearby."

"I can see that. Mr. Bennet seems to have the needs of his estate quite well in hand."

Bingley laughed. "It is particularly astonishing because Mr. Bennet usually dislikes leaving his study."

"There are worse ways to live one's life than to be a devotee to the written word. The estate does not seem to have suffered much if he is only occasionally lured from his room."

"No, you are correct there. Longbourn has been prosperous since long before my family came to the neighborhood, and it has not suffered under Mr. Bennet's stewardship. Of course, now he has Thomas to assist."

"Has your friend taken on most of the management?" asked Darcy, curious to know if his observations were correct.

"Most of the physical management of the estate, yes," said Bingley. "If a tenant needs to speak with the master, it is usually Thomas, and he oversees repairs, collects rents, inspects the cottages, and deals with tenant disputes. Mr. Bennet is still very much involved with the management from a decision making and budgeting perspective."

"It sounds like an excellent arrangement," said Darcy, wondering if his own father would be amenable to one similar. "The younger man obtains the experience, while the elder still controls the estate, which is, after all, still his property."

"And my father has followed it, though I still do not have as much responsibility as Thomas does."

"You are also younger," said Darcy.

"That is true. I find it agreeable at present, for I am still at the time of life where a little freedom suits me."

"Indeed," replied Darcy. In light of Bingley's words, Darcy considered his own situation, wondered if *he* was obtaining the experience he required. His father had not been lax in teaching him the workings of Pemberley, but he still had a hand in just about every part of it, rather than handing some responsibility to his son.

"Of course," said Bingley, "I find I have little desire to be away from Hertfordshire, and a very good reason to be present."

"Miss Bennet," observed Darcy.

The grin Bingley bestowed upon him was so typical of the man and his usually happy demeanor. "She *is* a veritable angel, is she not?"

"I am sure you think so, Bingley," said Darcy, struggling to keep the wry quality from his voice.

"I do, indeed. Fair, kind, beautiful, accomplished—I have not enough words to express my admiration for her."

Then Bingley proceeded to prove his words to be a lie, for he waxed long and eloquent on the subject of Miss Bennet's perfections. Darcy listened to him with a sort of fond tolerance. While he could readily admit the worth of the lady, for himself he thought it certain he would become bored with her. Now, her younger sister, on the other hand . . . .

"But what of Miss Elizabeth?"

Darcy blinked and looked at his friend, wondering if there was some way Bingley could read his mind. Seeing his confusion, Bingley laughed.

"So I *was* correct," said he with no small measure of self-satisfaction. "I had thought you had some interest in Jane's younger sister."

"It is not possible, Bingley," said Darcy, falling back on his oft-repeated—in his own mind—arguments against Miss Elizabeth. "You know it cannot be so. My parents expect me to make a more advantageous marriage."

"Perhaps your father does," said Bingley. "But having met your mother, I suspect she would be very happy to have Jane's younger sister as a daughter."

There was some truth to what Bingley said, and Darcy did not even try to dispute it. It was all the encouragement Bingley needed.

"It shows a greatness of mind and a superior taste, I would say. Miss Elizabeth is everything a man would want in a wife. She is confident and intelligent and would be a credit to him in whatever she did."

"She could even show his friends a thing or two about chess," said Darcy, a hint of sarcasm coming out in his voice.

"Aye, that she could!" exclaimed Bingley with a laugh. "Her prowess does not seem to have bothered you before now, my friend. Besides, if it is not proper for a young woman to know of the game, then no one needs to know about it. Your skill is sufficient to provide her with a challenge—why would she need to challenge others?"

"Why, indeed?"

"Come, Darcy, confess it—she is a wonderful girl who would make you happy. I have told you about the upcoming assembly, have I not?"

Indeed, it seemed like Bingley had talked of little else these past days. But Darcy's feelings were more difficult to understand, especially considering the events of the last assembly. Thus far she had shown no ill effects due to the last time they met in such circumstances. But in the back of his mind, Darcy nursed the suspicion that she was projecting more strength than she possessed. How would matters proceed if they met at an assembly again?

"I am to dance the first with Miss Bennet," said Bingley, catching Darcy's attention once again.

"You are? You have already secured those sets?"

"If I do not, there are plenty of other men who are happy to do so." Bingley snorted in what sounded suspiciously like disdain. "Miss Bennet is quite popular in the neighborhood. Now it is well known that she is partial to me and I, to her, but should I falter or give any hint of waning interest, several others would step in. There are many who are not happy my sister married Longbourn's heir, to say nothing of my attentions to Jane."

"The Bennets and Bingleys are by far the highest placed families in the district," said Darcy. "The marriages make perfect sense from the perspective of status."

"But others wish to raise their own status. Our obvious preference for each other have largely kept the other families in check. But that will not continue should I falter. Regardless, since I have secured Miss Bennet's, you should see about asking for those sets from Miss Elizabeth."

"And why would I do that?"

"Let us say you want a marriage which has some meaning other than a business transaction."

Darcy looked at Bingley, wondering at his friend's forceful statement. Their roles had usually been reversed, Darcy, taking the lead and Bingley, following. But Darcy was well aware that his friend was not lacking in confidence—rather, Darcy, as the older and more experienced, naturally led while his friend followed. There was no hint of following in Bingley's current manner.

"Having seen you both together," continued Bingley, "I am convinced you would do well with each other. Furthermore, your feelings are clear, though I will own that Miss Elizabeth's are much more opaque. I know your father would not consider it a good marriage for you. But I suspect it would be the making of you."

Bingley guided his horse close to Darcy's and clasped him on the shoulder. "Heed my advice, my friend. A marriage cannot be agreeable if you do not have affection. Do not marry for anything else, regardless of what your father says. He speaks of duty and raising your family's consequence, but in the end, he loves his wife. You should not accept anything less."

Then with a final squeeze of his hand, Bingley kicked his horse into a quicker pace. Darcy watched as his friend moved ahead of him, considering what Bingley had said, and a longing welled up within his breast. Perhaps he could be content in a marriage with a woman of standing and fortune, but one of love with a woman such as Miss Elizabeth would suit him all that much more. Bingley was right. He must see to his own future.

CHAPTER XI

Had Elizabeth considered the matter in advance, she might have been a little intimidated by the thought of once again attending an assembly with Mr. Darcy also present. While she had found herself out of sorts for about three or four events after the one which featured the infamous kiss, she soon scolded herself thoroughly. Simply because one young man behaved inappropriately did not mean they all would. Thus, Elizabeth learned to push her worries to the side and enjoy herself, though she was always careful to refrain from overt forwardness.

But she had not considered it in light of Mr. Darcy's behavior since his return. Not only was the man courteous and proper, but he had made no mention of the event, had made no attempt to impose himself on Elizabeth. Before he came, that was what had worried her the most, that he would attempt to make her an offer which was most improper. His behavior had largely removed that weight from her shoulders, and his intimacy with her father told Elizabeth he could not be contemplating such a step.

When she entered the assembly hall, however, Elizabeth found herself nervous as she had not been since first entering society. She simply had not considered the effect of the man in attendance, though every bit of her told herself she had no cause to worry. Memories of that night plagued her, and the familiar vistas somehow seemed sinister, as if she was trapped in a maze and a ravening beast stalked her.

The Netherfield party entering the room made it all that much worse. Her first glimpse of Mr. Darcy felt like a physical blow. The sight of his eyes fixed on her brought back her insecurities and caused her to doubt his goodness yet again. As he approached in the company of the three Bingleys, Elizabeth found her gaze fixed upon the floor, unable to raise it again. A slight trembling came over her, and she did not know what to do.

"Lizzy!" hissed Jane. "Are you quite well?"

Before Elizabeth could do more than consider answering, Mr. Bingley was at her sister's side, greeting her with his characteristic enthusiasm. Elizabeth found herself oddly fortified by the well-known sound of Mr. Bingley's joviality, though it was not enough to induce her to raise her eyes from the floor.

"I believe this dance belongs to me?" said Mr. Bingley. Elizabeth was startled to hear the music—the Bingleys must have arrived later than she had thought.

Elizabeth felt rather than saw Jane's concerned glance at her, but she could not do anything other than follow Mr. Bingley to the dance floor without making a scene. When Elizabeth heard Mr. Darcy speak, she was shocked once again.

"Miss Elizabeth, might I petition your hand for the first sets?"

The surprise of his application overcame Elizabeth's reticence and she looked up, unable to answer. By her side, she could hear Mary giggling, though the sound seemed to her like it was coming from miles away.

"I did not know the new mode was to keep a supplicant waiting while the dance ran its course."

Mr. Bennet's voice pulled Elizabeth from her frozen state, and she glanced at him to see his amusement. Now that he had her attention, Mr. Bennet favored her with a smile, and gestured at Mr. Darcy.

"Did you mean to dance, my dear? Or would you prefer to keep the young man waiting, possibly forfeiting the ability to dance for the entire evening?"

"Of course, I would be happy to dance with you, Mr. Darcy," Elizabeth found herself saying, though she could not determine whether she had actually meant to speak.

"Excellent!" said Mr. Bennet, even while Elizabeth noticed Mr.

Darcy's piercing look in her direction. Mr. Bennet nodded and went off to speak to one of his acquaintances, while another young man of the neighborhood came to ask for Mary's first set. In this fashion Elizabeth found herself grasping Mr. Darcy's hand and standing in line waiting as the musicians completed the opening notes.

"Are you well, Miss Elizabeth?" asked Mr. Darcy once they had begun to dance.

"Very well," replied Elizabeth by rote.

The doubtful look he cast at her spoke to his disbelief. It was this that galvanized Elizabeth to anger. Was it not this man's fault that she was cast into confusion? Had his improper actions not led to her distrust of men, and of him in particular? Was it not understandable that the return to the place where it would happen would cause her equanimity to be disturbed?

It was one of the most uncomfortable dances Elizabeth had ever shared, and it was evident that Mr. Darcy was similarly affected. Elizabeth found her mood swinging from one end of the spectrum to the other, from confusion and reticence, to anger at the gentleman for putting her in this situation. Gamely Mr. Darcy attempted to engage her in conversation, but Elizabeth found she either could not make herself respond, or had no patience for it, depending on her mood at the moment. Eventually they settled into a sullen silence, Mr. Darcy seemingly confused, while Elizabeth was growing angrier by the minute. The sensation of being released from his company was akin to the condemned being pardoned.

"Lizzy, are you well?"

"Perfectly so," said Elizabeth. The dance having finished, Mr. Darcy had escorted her to the side of dance floor and excused himself. She could see him watching her from the other side of the room, the old suspicions concerning his attentions welling up within her.

"Are you certain?" asked Jane. "I watched you as you danced—I have never seen you so uncomfortable as you were during that dance. Are you certain you are not bothered by Mr. Darcy's presence?"

"Why would that be so?" snapped Elizabeth. Jane appeared taken aback by the vehemence in Elizabeth's voice, but by this time Elizabeth was beyond caring. "It happened four years ago, Jane. Go and dance with Mr. Bingley and enjoy his attentions—I am completely fine."

Elizabeth could see that Jane was hurt by her sudden dismissal, but she did as she was asked. Watching her walk away, Elizabeth's breast filled once again with indignation at the perfidy of Mr. Darcy. Now the man had put her so far out of sorts that she had offended the dearest person in the world!

Enjoyment in the assembly was far from Elizabeth's grasp that evening. Charlotte provided an escape from her thoughts at times when she was not dancing, and while she clearly noted Elizabeth's discomposure, she did not inquire after it, good friend that she was. When Elizabeth danced, as she did every set, her heart was not in it, though she cynically thought that her partners did not notice anything amiss. The longer the evening went on, the more pointless it all became. When she left the floor after the fourth sets, Elizabeth was wondering what the point of it all could be.

Finally, after dancing the fifth with a man of the neighborhood — by the time she left the dance floor, she could not even remember with whom she had danced — Elizabeth was desperate to escape. Moving quickly to avoid any potential partners, she found a chair in an out of the way location and sat with some relief. Perhaps she would go unnoticed there, at least long enough to regain her composure.

Frustration, thy name is Fitzwilliam Darcy.

It was a weak attempt at humor, but Darcy was in no mood for such things. Having been persuaded by Bingley, it had all seemed so easy. Starting that evening, Darcy would begin to show his admiration more openly and would subtly begin wooing the woman who had captured his imagination. Then after a period, he would ask the young woman to marry him.

But tonight, it seemed a different woman was inhabiting the body of the enchanting Miss Elizabeth Bennet. It had started from the first moment of their meeting that evening. In previous days, she had been the same vivacious girl he had known four years before, though matured into a woman of overwhelming appeal. Tonight, nothing had been the same as it had been before.

As the evening wore on, Darcy found that he had no interest in dancing, though he had come that evening with the best of intentions to dance enough to honor his hosts. But with the change that had come over Miss Elizabeth and the resulting confusion it caused, he had little appetite for the activity. Instead, he took to stalking along the edges of the dance floor, avoiding speaking with anyone if he could, and watching Miss Elizabeth as she danced with other men. As he did this, Darcy attempted to tell himself it did not bother him. It was an abject failure.

Darcy wondered if his impulsive action four years before was somehow affecting her that evening, but he did not know how that could be. Since his arrival in the neighborhood, he had detected nothing amiss in her manners. Furthermore, she had said nothing of it, had not confronted him with his behavior when he had first come, like he would have expected. How could it suddenly have changed her, seemingly in the blink of an eye?

All might have been different if Bingley had not accosted him. Whether it would have been for the better or not was not readily apparent. But accost him, Bingley did, and in the heat of the moment, Darcy was not in any mood to hear his friend's words.

"I say, Darcy," said Bingley, stepping up with his usual ebullience. It went without saying that Darcy found his friend's manners incredibly annoying at present. "I thought you had turned over a new leaf, and yet I find you still stalking about the edges of the dance floor in your stupid manner. What has happened?"

"Nothing," said Darcy shortly. "Tonight, I am simply not in humor to dance."

"That is very surprising, indeed," said Bingley, feigning astonishment. Or perhaps it was not so feigned. "By my recollection, you anticipated this evening keenly. In fact, I seem to remember it beginning exactly as you might have wished."

Darcy scowled and looked out over the dance floor, but he could not see the one woman he wished to see at that moment. Miss Elizabeth was not in evidence. Confused, he looked about, wondering where she had gone. She had been dancing not long ago, Darcy had thought.

"Did Miss Elizabeth tire of your society?" Bingley laughed. "Given your apparent mood tonight, I cannot blame her. I have seen behavior this awful from you only a time or two, and usually when you have nothing to do."

"Perhaps I have nothing I wish to do tonight," said Darcy, still scanning the room for Miss Elizabeth. If only Bingley would quit pushing him and just retreat to his partner!

"Then what of the vivacious Miss Elizabeth Bennet, Darcy? I am certain you were eager to spend more time in her company than you have yet managed."

Darcy snorted, a desperate sort of longing coming over him, which he quashed ruthlessly. The disappointment of the night, combining with Bingley's nettling, unsettled Darcy, and he spoke before thinking.

"Miss Elizabeth Bennet." He spoke her name with as much contempt as he possibly could. "A more likely spinster, I have never met."

"Darcy!" barked Bingley, his voice as displeased as Darcy had ever heard him speak. "That is unkind! You may not be in humor to give consequence to deserving young ladies this evening, but I have known the young woman since she was a babe, and I like her very much."

A lump formed in Darcy's throat, and he reached up and massaged his temples. "I apologize, Bingley. Indeed, you are correct. While my temper has worsened throughout the evening that is no reason for incivility."

"I should think not," said Bingley, only partially mollified. "It is beyond my ability to comprehend, Darcy. You were eager for this evening's entertainment—I am sure of it. And yet, after less than half the evening, you have become as irritable as a bear woken from its sleep too early. How can you account for it?"

Just then, Darcy saw Miss Elizabeth Bennet across the room. She was walking quickly, seeking to avoid those around her, as he saw her ignore more than one young lady who attempted to catch her attention. When she came to one of the balconies, she darted a furtive glance about and slipped out to be night air beyond. Her posture betrayed her as distressed, and though Darcy was still not quite certain of the reason for it, he was determined to discover the reason for it.

"Excuse me, Bingley," said Darcy. "There is someone with whom I wish to speak."

Bingley caught Darcy's arm as he attempted to move away. "I shall expect an explanation of what the devil has gotten into you tonight."

"Very well," said Darcy, eager to leave his friend behind. "But it can wait."

With a nod Bingley released him, allowing Darcy to move quickly away. Sir William Lucas attempted to accost Darcy as he walked by, and Darcy halted for a few unwilling moments to speak with the man. But inside he was eager to be away, to join Miss Elizabeth on the balcony. When he was able, he excused himself and walked away. Soon the exit loomed large before him.

The vile words spilling from Mr. Darcy's mouth did not hurt Elizabeth so much as infuriate her. Not long after she had found her little nook, Mr. Darcy had appeared just outside in his erratic prowling about the floor. When Mr. Bingley had come upon him, Elizabeth had thought to warn the man away from attempting to modify the behavior of the detestable Mr. Darcy. But when Mr. Darcy had referred to her the way he had, Elizabeth knew that to speak was to make a scene.

Standing and directing a glare at his back, Elizabeth had stormed away, muttering imprecations as she went. Such was her countenance and fury that at least one man to whom she was known declined to speak to her, though Elizabeth was certain he had intended to ask her for a dance. Mercifully free of any other interference, Elizabeth caught sight of the door to the balcony ringing the assembly hall and slipped through, relieved to be away from everyone.

The light of the moon shone down on the town, bathing it in a soft glow, luminous and peaceful, unlike the emotions roiling in Elizabeth's heart. She stepped to the railing, laying her hands on it, noting the white light shining on her arms, lending her skin an incandescent glow. In the calm light and darkness of the outside world, Elizabeth felt her anger slipping away. Even if she had tried to hold to it, she knew she would not have possessed the means to do so.

Mr. Darcy's words, as disgusting as they had been, were nothing more than the truth. Long had Elizabeth known that matrimony, the state to which all young girls of her status aspired, was not likely to be in her future.

"And whose fault is that?" she demanded to the night sky. "Perhaps it has something to do with my own character. But it has every bit as much to do with Mr. Darcy. He has tainted me, removed me from all possible intimacy with a man forever. How I hate him!"

But even as the quiet words tumbled from Elizabeth's mouth, she knew it was not true. In a most unnerving way, she found herself drawn to the man, attracted to him as she had never been to any other man before. Which was itself a problem. How could she be attracted to a man capable of such perfidy as Mr. Darcy? Did it point to some deficiency of her character, some wantonness staining her very soul?

And what *was* Mr. Darcy? Though she tried, Elizabeth could not make the man out. The same man who spoke to her with such interest unconcealed, who befriended Bingley and spoke with her father with such rationality and interest, was also capable of repulsive words and stealing that which was most precious from young maidens. Who was he?

Her hand trailing along the bannister, Elizabeth strolled along the balcony, her eyes staring unseeing at the town situated beyond those rooms. It may be best for her to flee to London, she thought. Her aunt and uncle would be happy to welcome her there, she knew, though she also suspected they would be full of questions for her. But that was far preferable to continuing to exist under the harsh glare of Mr. Darcy's contempt. And it would remove him from her circle, along with whatever motivated the man. Tomorrow she would send a letter to them, requesting sanctuary. She would depart immediately.

The sound of a soft footstep brought Elizabeth back to her surroundings. She whirled around, one hand pressed against her heart in her shock, only to see the intimidating form of Mr. Darcy outlined in the light of the assembly hall, which escaped through the door still ajar behind him. For a brief moment, all her fears crystallized into that single moment, and she imagined a man with the ruin of a young woman on his mind.

"Miss Elizabeth?" asked Mr. Darcy.

He stepped forward, his countenance appearing in the light of the moon, visible to her wild eyes. The concern in his eyes confused her for a moment, and the fear began to bleed from her like a great wound in her breast.

"Are you frightened of me?"

Those words lit a fire in the very breast which had recently known relief. Elizabeth straightened, her blazing gaze falling on him like a bludgeon. It seemed Mr. Darcy could see the anger in her eyes, for he took an involuntary step back, confusion falling over him. It was all Elizabeth needed to stalk to him, one hand on her hip while the other rose, pointing a finger in the wretched man's face.

"Should I not be frightened of you?" hissed she. "Do you not recognize the place in which we stand, Mr. Darcy? Do you not know what happened the last time we were here? Are you witless, or was the matter so trifling to you that you cannot even remember it?"

Though he had regarded her with concern, now he was staring at her with a gaze so incredulous, she could see the whites around his eyes. But the light of recognition shone within their depths, giving Elizabeth all the courage she needed to continue her tirade.

"I can see you do remember. What have you to say for yourself?"

"Nothing, of course!" snapped Elizabeth, not allowing him to speak. "You took what you wished from a young and gullible girl and departed from these shores, until finally slinking back four years later. And for what? Do you mean to finish what you started? Are am I to be forced to be your mistress, or do you simply wish to have your way with me right here before you leave forever?"

Mr. Darcy did not respond, for he seemed incapable of doing so. Raking her eyes over the man with contempt, Elizabeth shook her head. "You will find me no easy prey, Mr. Darcy. I defy you. If you fight for your unholy desires, know that I shall fight as vehemently as you. I will never give into you.

"You disgust me, sir. Have you no notion of what you have

wrought? Do you not know that a young woman wishes to give the right of her first kiss to her future husband? Do you not know you have robbed me of that privilege? What have you to say for yourself?"

The anger which raged in her breast simmered and roared, and Elizabeth stood there for that single long moment, staring into the eyes of her tormentor. Mr. Darcy, seemingly still astonished by her tirade, did not seem to be capable of responding. At least he was not a man with rape on his mind—Elizabeth was grimly certain that if he had been such a man, he would not have been caught in indecision at such a time. He likely would have proceeded or fled.

But that did not answer what kind of man he was. Elizabeth would not have thought the man a coward, to be intimidated by the sight of an angry woman, and a diminutive one at that. Suddenly Elizabeth was disgusted with it all, eager to be out of his presence.

"The assembly hall is that way," said she, waving her hand at the door behind him. "I wish to be alone, sir. Should you call at Longbourn again, know that I will not receive you. If you wish to maintain your friendship with my father, I shall not stand in your way." A wave of bitterness welled up within her. "I have not informed him of your actions, nor will I do so."

Then Elizabeth turned and made her way back to the bannister, resting her arms on it and staring out into the night. Her gaze, however, rested on nothing. She could not muster such interest in anything. Thus, when the sound of Mr. Darcy's voice reached her, it astonished her anew.

"I am sorry—exceedingly sorry, Miss Elizabeth. I had not meant to steal that which was precious from you, nor was it my intention to frighten you. Whatever you demand in restitution, I shall oblige you."

Turning, Elizabeth gazed at the young man, wondering at the sudden change which had come over him. Mr. Darcy stood there, looking at her, chastened by her words, it seemed. But whatever she had expected him to say next, it was not what came out of his mouth.

"I would also have you consider this: if you were to marry me, your first kiss would have been bestowed on no one but your future husband."

CHAPTER XII

*S*hock bloomed in Miss Elizabeth's eyes. As the glory of her gaze was bestowed on him, Darcy suddenly wished to have her look on him with longing and love, that which had so tormented and teased him during the time of their separation. While the words had issued forth of their own volition, Darcy realized they were the truth. Any thought of his father's displeasure or the expectations of society disappeared in the face of her gaze. A man would do much to have such an exquisite creature as Miss Elizabeth Bennet look on him with love and devotion.

It seemed Darcy had shocked her into silence, for she did not attempt to speak. Instead she looked on him, seemingly attempting to see through the outer man to what lay inside. Mindful of the way she had looked at him when he had first joined her on the balcony, Darcy stepped forward, carefully, slowly, trying, with his every move, to assure her he meant no harm. She tensed at his first motion, wary as a deer which had caught the scent of the hunting wolf. Then he was before her, looking down on her incandescent countenance, marveling in the perfection of her perfect face.

Carefully, Darcy reached down, grasping her hands, clasping them in his own. She looked down at them, her gaze stayed there for a moment, before rising to meet his again. Darcy could determine nothing of her thoughts—she was a closed book, a shuddered window against the light of the outside world. So caught was he by her gaze upon him that Darcy was almost surprised to hear his own voice.

"It seems I must beg your pardon, Miss Elizabeth."

Her stare hardened. "Because I called you out for your behavior?"

"Your words have only provoked it, not made it necessary." Darcy sighed and looked down at their joined hands, noting for the first time how small and delicate they were, but marveling in the strength held within. "Would that I had found an opportunity to apologize when I had first come to Netherfield again. But I foolishly believed you had not been affected by my thoughtless action the last time we met. I determined it would be more detrimental to remind you of it than to leave the matter unintroduced."

"That matter I had put behind me long ago," said Miss Elizabeth. She grimaced and amended: "Or I thought I had. Your return brought back the memory, informing me I was not so indifferent as I had thought."

"I offer my most humble and sincere apologies, Miss Bennet," said Darcy, considering how he had bungled his relationship with this woman in the most egregious manner since making her acquaintance. "When I . . . kissed you the last time I was here, it was an action which had neither forethought nor ill intent. It was not my intention to offend."

A hint of the anger she had shown before swept over her, but this time it was tempered by what he could only call amusement. "Oh?" asked she, a delightful arch of one elegant eyebrow accompanying her words. "So then, I am *not* destined to become a spinster in your estimation."

Darcy gaped at her, then closed his eyes in mortification. Was he never to stop insulting her?

"Might I assume you overheard rather than hearing another's report?"

"That is correct, Mr. Darcy." She gave him an impish smile. "In the future, should you choose to say something derogatory about an acquaintance, you might wish to look about to ensure they are not near enough to overhear."

"I cannot imagine how that came to be," muttered Darcy. "This evening I have been ever aware of your whereabouts, except for those few moments before I uttered those words."

Miss Elizabeth did not reply—she only regarded him with a wry grin. It seemed she had realized his words were not to be taken at face value. But that did not mean she was not due an apology yet again.

"It seems I do nothing but apologize tonight, but I offer you my regrets without reservation. This evening had not gone as I had planned, and I was out of sorts because of it. Still, it was unconscionable for me to say it."

Miss Elizabeth nodded. "Apology accepted, Mr. Darcy." Then she eyed him with evident curiosity. "In what way did the evening disappoint, Mr. Darcy?"

"In your reaction to me tonight." Having no hope but a candid revelation, Darcy determined to do exactly that. If she refused him after this, at least she would understand the true measure of his feelings rather than simply branding him the worst of men. "I had come here with the fond hope of engaging your attention as my friend has engaged your sister."

"I do not understand."

"Have you not seen how I have attended to you since I came?" asked Darcy. "Have you not noticed the way my eyes find you and can rarely be induced to leave you? I do not behave this way with most young ladies of my acquaintance, Miss Bennet. In fact, should you ask Bingley, he would inform you it is usually quite the opposite."

A restless energy came over Darcy, and he allowed her hands to fall while he took to pacing the stone balcony. Within, he was tormented by the thought that she would reject him. But the thought of her acceptance, the joy of having her pledge herself to him, kept him speaking. It would not come today, or any other day in the near future—of this he was certain. But if he only had the hope of her eventual love, he could endure as many weeks of uncertainty as necessary.

"I have hesitated, Miss Elizabeth," confessed Darcy, still working off his agitation. "It has not been due to any lack in you. You are all that is desirable, all anything any rational man would want in a wife."

She gasped at the mention of a wife, but Darcy pressed on.

"But society places certain expectations on any man, and there are certain elements of my family who expect me to make a stupendous marriage to the daughter of an earl, if not a woman of higher standing. I do not wish for such an alliance. Had I ever met any woman of such a standing who interested me, who provoked me as you do, I might have had some interest in her. But to me society is populated by those who think very well of themselves, of those who view marriage as a business transaction for their own gain. For myself, I prefer to find a woman in whom I can place my trust and on whom, bestow my love, hoping for her to reciprocate.

"When we met four years ago, I saw in you the genesis of the woman you would one day be, a woman I knew instinctually could suit me in every way. I did not know it then, though looking back on it now, it is obvious. When I kissed you that night, I was frustrated, looking for a way to stop your infernal teasing."

"Is it your custom, Mr. Darcy, to silence young ladies' teasing by kissing them senseless?"

The note of humor in her voice brought Darcy to a halt. The half-smile with which she regarded him suggested a lightening of her spirit, causing Darcy's to wheel through the sky along with hers. With a quick step, Darcy strode to her again, gratified that she had lost all fear of him. Once again, he grasped her hands and raised them one after the other to his lips.

"Indeed, I have done it but once and then, with a very special young lady. I am mortified that she was hurt by it and distressed that it has caused her to think of me as the worst sort of libertine." Darcy paused, smiled, and decided to risk a little humor. "If I was to kiss you senseless, Miss Elizabeth, it would be much more substantial than what I did."

Delighted, Darcy watched as a fetching blush spread over Miss Elizabeth's cheeks, just visible in the dim light of the moon. The sight of it set an aching in his chest, more evidence he was desperate to have this woman's good opinion. The light also reminded him that he was alone with her. Though it would not cause him an instant's concern should he be required to marry her in the event they were discovered, he did not wish to win her in such a fashion.

"We cannot stay here much longer without risking discovery, Miss Elizabeth," said Darcy. She nodded in agreement. "Before we leave this place, however, I wish you to understand clearly of what my feelings consist. I will not have you go away thinking that I am a rake who toys with the feelings of young ladies. While you might have thought me capable of offering you carte blanche, or other such depravities, I wish you to know that my interest in you is entirely honorable."

"Though I wondered, I never thought you a libertine, Mr. Darcy," said Miss Elizabeth, her voice quiet, though brimming with emotion. "It always seemed like an impetuous action taken without thought."

"It was. But other than the way it induced you to doubt my character, I find I cannot repine my action. I hope for a repeat of it, albeit in more proper circumstances."

Once again Miss Elizabeth blushed. "You do?" was her soft query.

"Very much. But I have learned my lesson. I shall restrain myself until I have the right and your permission for a repeat performance."

"Perhaps we should return to the dance, Mr. Darcy." Though she was outwardly calm, Darcy thought he had heard a little quaver in her voice. He smiled inwardly, pleased at the evidence she was affected by him.

"Before we do," said Darcy, "I should like to obtain permission to call on you. It is not the proper time for a proposal, though I would be willing to offer for you right now if you were ready to receive it. But I wish to show you what kind of man I am. May I call?"

It was the most important question Darcy had ever asked. Though the pause was brief, it seemed eternal to Darcy's senses, as he stood wondering if she would crush his heart forever. It would be no less than he deserved, should she choose to do so. But after that agonizing pause, she relieved his anxiety with two words:

"You may."

Again, Darcy pulled her hands up to his lips. "Thank you, Miss Elizabeth. It is my promise to you that you will never regret extending me this opportunity. Now, perhaps we should return to the ballroom?"

"Of course," said Miss Elizabeth, apparently recovering her wits.

Darcy dropped her hands and motioned for her to precede him into the room. "Please, Miss Elizabeth—if you will go first, I shall follow in a few moments. We should be able to avoid detection in that fashion."

"Thank you, Mr. Darcy," said Miss Elizabeth. Then she was gone.

The evening for Jane Bennet was one of heightened anxiety. As the only person in the world other than Elizabeth who knew of what had happened the last time her sister had attended an assembly with Mr. Darcy present, she thought Elizabeth might feel out of sorts that evening. While Elizabeth had given every indication of good humor, Jane, who knew her sister better than any other, could see the strain.

Something had happened during the first dance, something she could not quite place, but which had affected Elizabeth's equilibrium. Jane, who had been concerned for her sister all evening, had watched Elizabeth, and had noted her withdrawal from Mr. Darcy. In turn, Mr. Darcy had grown more frustrated, and at the end of the dance had spent the rest of the evening stalking about the dance floor. But his eyes had been fixed upon Lizzy all evening.

Now Elizabeth was gone. And what was worse was the absence of Mr. Darcy and the intelligence she received from Mr. Bingley that he had argued with Mr. Darcy.

"Have you seen Lizzy, Mr. Bingley?" asked Jane, hoping she could find someone who could tell her where her sister had gone. Uncharacteristically, Mr. Bingley appeared to be out of sorts himself, though his countenance softened when he beheld her.

"I have not," he replied. "Perhaps she stepped into the card room to speak to your father?"

"Father is sitting in the corner there with Mr. Goulding," said Jane, gesturing toward her father.

Mr. Bingley glanced at the gentlemen and shrugged. "It is also possible she stepped out for a breath of fresh air. I know I certainly find the air in here a little close."

"Mr. Darcy is missing too," said Jane. She bit her lip in frustration over her slip—she certainly did not wish to cast aspersions on Mr. Darcy, not when Lizzy had forced her to promise to keep her confidence.

"For that, we may all be relieved."

Fairly goggling at Mr. Bingley, Jane wondered his tone. It was rare this man whom she admired so much could be induced to say such things, about one of his closest friends too!

"You are at odds with Mr. Darcy?"

Though he remained silent for a moment, Mr. Bingley finally said: "He said something very unkind to me about your sister. Though he apologized after, I am still put out with him. You know how much I esteem Elizabeth."

Fear blossomed in Jane's breast, and she looked about the room in a panic. "Lizzy. Where are you?"

"There she is," said Mr. Bingley. He pointed to the other side of the dance floor to where Lizzy stood, watching the dancers. Though relief flooded through her, Jane was confused, for she was certain her sister had not been there only a moment before.

"I must go and speak with her, Mr. Bingley," said Jane. "Please excuse me."

"Of course," said Mr. Bingley. He appeared on the verge of saying something else but thought better of it. "I shall collect you for the last dance tonight, if it is still agreeable to you."

Feeling unaccountably shy at the request, Jane assented, giving him reason to know that it was her pleasure in as coherent a voice as possible. A grin slipped over Mr. Bingley's features, and he bowed, allowing her to depart. As Jane turned to make her way toward Lizzy, she tamped down on the feeling of euphoria and allowed her concern for Lizzy to hold sway. With these feelings, she approached her sister.

"Lizzy," said Jane, "where have you been?"

If Elizabeth was surprised by Jane's query, she did not show it. She did, however, blush ever so slightly. But she quickly gathered herself and turned a smile on Jane.

"I just stepped outside onto the balcony, Jane."

"Are you unwell?"

"No," replied Elizabeth. She pressed Jane's hands with affection and said: "I merely found it a little hot and required some air. You need not worry for me."

Jane gazed at her sister, wondering if Elizabeth was hiding something from her. It was not in Jane's nature to press her—Elizabeth had always been forthright with her. But still Jane felt a little hesitation, as if she was not being told everything.

"Are you certain?"

"Very certain!" said Elizabeth with a laugh. "Now, has anything of note happened while I was outside? I hope Mr. Collins has not tripped over any lady's feet, for if he has, all those hours of instruction we have rendered were for naught."

"No, Lizzy," said Jane, glancing to where the gentleman was dancing with Charlotte Lucas. "It seems he has taken our instruction well."

"Excellent! I dare say he will never be precisely light on his feet, but he shall at least acquit himself with confidence at any assembly he is asked to attend."

Just then a gentleman from the neighborhood approached Elizabeth and asked for the next dance. While Jane had been speaking with her sister, the previous set had ended, and the next was forming. As Jane's hand was also solicited, she had no choice but to turn her attention away from her concerns for the present. Elizabeth seemed well, and for that Jane was grateful.

Had the matter ended in such a way, she would have been well pleased. But while Jane was dancing, she happened to glance across the room in time to see a tall figure emerge from the door leading to the balcony. It was Mr. Darcy.

It was not in Elizabeth's nature to keep anything from her sister. Indeed, the three Bennet sisters were of such closeness that their shared confidences were extensive, and rarely did they keep personal secrets. In particular, Jane and Elizabeth were each other's confidantes, each sister feeling like she could share anything with the other.

The ballroom was not the place to have a discussion such as the one which would encompass what she had just experienced with Mr. Darcy. It was all so new and so different from what Elizabeth had expected—she was not certain she could share it with anyone, even a most beloved sister.

Thus, when the Bennet family departed from the assembly rooms that night, Elizabeth's heart and mind were full of thoughts of Mr. Darcy. Were she to be honest with herself, Elizabeth was not certain yet what to think of the gentleman. His remarks and actions on the balcony had been so gentle and affectionate, and she was not indifferent to him—had not been, even when she had remained a little fearful of him. The explanation he offered had instilled a sense of relief that she was not required to worry for what he would do next.

No, instead he would pay court to her. She, Elizabeth Bennet, was to receive the attentions of a gentleman who was not only the handsomest she had ever seen but also inhabited a level of society far above what she and her family could boast! Who could understand such a thing?

"It appears, my dear," the sound of Mr. Bennet's voice interrupted her thoughts, "you have made quite a conquest."

When Elizabeth did not immediately respond, Mr. Bennet chuckled, and while Elizabeth could not see his face in the darkness of the carriage, she knew he was grinning widely at her. "At first I thought you had experienced some sort of lovers' spat. But in the end, he seems to have won you over."

"He has, indeed," said Elizabeth softly.

Elizabeth could almost see his grin widening, especially when he continued, speaking to Jane in a lazy tone: "Perhaps you should encourage Bingley to step lively, Jane. I had always thought *you* would be the first of my daughters to obtain a fiancé, and I had anticipated making sport with him when he came to petition for your hand. But if what I am seeing is correct, it seems Darcy might beat him to it."

Jane made a strangled sound, one so curious that all three Bennets looked to her, curious as to its purpose. Of course, they could not see anything in the darkness. When Jane spoke, she did so in a tone which seemed strained.

"I hardly think Mr. Darcy will move so quickly."

"Now, Jane," said Mr. Bennet, laughter in his tone, "there is no need to be missish. Even should Darcy step forward first, I have no doubt

Bingley will secure your hand in a creditable fashion."

"I have no doubt he will," said Jane.

This time, everyone could hear the normal tones of Jane's voice, and Elizabeth put her sister's unusual behavior down to her discomposure due to her father's teasing. She should be well aware of her father's penchant by now, Elizabeth thought, but said nothing out loud.

"That is well, then," said Mr. Bennet. "You should know—and you too, Mary—that I am quite eager to receive any gentleman who petitions my daughters, *and* who is fortunate enough to be accepted by them, for I know they must be worthy, indeed, to secure the consent of any of you. As I am quite at my leisure, you may send them in at any time convenient."

Mr. Bennet chuckled at his own joke, and he fell silent. This was very much the man she had grown up admiring, and Elizabeth shook her head, knowing Mary was likely rolling her eyes while Jane was blushing.

In silence, the family traveled the rest of the way to Longbourn. When the carriage stopped in front of the house, her father stepped down and handed his three daughters down. Then he entered in and, with an affectionate good night for them all, climbed the stairs toward his room. Feeling fatigued herself, Elizabeth followed his example, moving toward the stairs.

"Lizzy," came Jane's quiet voice, "shall we meet in your room to discuss the evening's events?"

Though Elizabeth considered it for a moment, she decided she could not do justice to their little ritual that night. Her mind too full of Mr. Darcy; she would, no doubt, spend the night silent, deep in thought, and since Jane was not of mind to speak much, they would sit in stupid silence the entire evening. Sleep was the best option—they could discuss the assembly the following morning, and, no doubt, Charlotte would come to share their thoughts as well.

"Not tonight, Jane," said Elizabeth at last. "It is best that I seek my bed tonight. Let us speak tomorrow."

Then squeezing her sister's arm, Elizabeth climbed the stairs and, bidding her sisters good night, entered her room. Her maid, Elizabeth had dismissed for the evening upon departing as was her custom— Elizabeth saw no need to insist the poor woman stay awake until they returned, which was always quite late. As a result, Elizabeth divested herself of her dress, donned a simple linen nightgown, and settled herself on the mattress.

But as she might have expected, sleep was long in coming that evening. Instead, she found herself pondering the merits of a handsome, tall young gentleman who declared such exquisite admiration. Such thoughts kept Elizabeth awake long into the evening.

CHAPTER XIII

*D*reams sometimes became reality. Or at least it seemed that way. Not even in the days after she had first been kissed so unexpectedly by Mr. Darcy had Elizabeth thought it likely the gentleman would indicate his interest in her as a marriage partner. At times, she had wondered if he was interested for a less proper reason.

The events of the previous evening had disproved that theory completely, leaving Elizabeth feeling a little light-headed. Everything had changed so quickly, events had taken a turn unlike any she could have expected, leaving her confused and uncertain. All thought of ending a spinster had fled. But in the midst of all this, a hint of excitement had pushed its way into her consciousness. Mr. Darcy was, after all, a handsome man, and by every societal standard, an excellent catch, one far beyond what a woman of her social background could possibly hope to entice. The question for her was, could she love him?

Though Elizabeth had not slept well the previous evening, she found herself awake early the following morning and unable to resume her repose. Fatigue, it seemed, was no remedy, for she was as tired as she could ever remember feeling, yet as wide awake as if she had slept a day straight. Thus, as she could not sleep, a walk seemed like just the thing to tire her — then she could return to the house and avail herself of a nap in the afternoon to restore her strength.

Longbourn's staff were well aware of Elizabeth's habits. While appearing at such an early hour after a night at the assembly hall was perhaps unusual, Longbourn's cook did not bat an eyelash when Elizabeth entered the kitchen, seeking a roll for her walk.

"Aye, Miss Lizzy," said the cook with evident fondness. "I have a number of rolls just out of the oven."

Grateful for her restraint, Elizabeth accepted the bread, which was still warm to the touch, with a word of thanks. Then she departed the house, eager to be by herself for a time. The roll was consumed as she walked, and soon Elizabeth was swinging her arms, taking the path toward Oakham Mount.

While Elizabeth might have expected, and even wished for solitude, it was not to be. The first sign she was not alone brought her up short as the sound of horses' hooves striking the turf caught her attention. Then when she looked around to discover its source, she found herself watching Mr. Darcy as he galloped toward her on the most handsome steed she had ever seen.

At the last moment, Mr. Darcy pulled up his horse and vaulted from the saddle. Quickly he strode to her, executed a handsome bow, and grasped her hand as if he never intended to let go.

"Miss Bennet," said he, a smile like she had rarely seen adorning his features. "So, I was correct!"

"You were, Mr. Darcy? About what, particularly?"

"Your predilection for walking, even after a late night of dancing. I have heard so much talk of your prowess as a walker, that I thought I would seek you out this morning to see if there was any validity to it. It seems there is."

"Yes, I *do* enjoy walking," said Elizabeth, charmed by his manner. "After a late night such as yesterday, I would normally not walk this early. But this morning, I found my eyes opening at a most inconvenient time, and nothing I did succeeded in closing them again."

"I would not wish for your sleep to be interrupted, but I confess I am happy it was so, as I found myself similarly afflicted. It is with great joy I greet you this morning, for I confess I wished to be in your company as soon as I quit it last night."

Feeling unaccountably shy because of this man's open regard, Elizabeth looked to the ground. Thus, when he spoke again, she could hear him, but the sight of him was lost to her embarrassment.

"If I may, Miss Bennet, might I suggest we walk together?"

"Of course," said Elizabeth. "But will it not interrupt your ride?"

"The purpose of my ride was to facilitate my ability to find you. I should like nothing more than to accompany you on your walk."

Elizabeth found that she could not speak, so she nodded her head in agreement. Together they turned and began walking away from her original destination. Walking with Mr. Darcy, alone on the paths near her home was better than going toward a location where most people did not go and would cause less talk if they were observed. As they walked, they carried on a desultory conversation, centering on the banal subjects acceptable for conversation between two people who were, after all, not yet officially courting.

While she walked, Elizabeth paid some attention to their words, but she also considered the man by her side. Any fear she might previously have harbored was now gone, and in its place was a warmth she would not have expected. Her opinion of Mr. Darcy was so incorrect that it was difficult to reconcile it with what she had thought previously. Then again, perhaps it was not so surprising, considering their history. Then a thought crossed Elizabeth's mind.

"Mr. Darcy, I wonder if you would elaborate on something you said last night."

"I would be happy to," said Mr. Darcy. "What would you like to know?"

"You mentioned . . . Well, you suggested that some members of your family would not be happy with your . . . choice . . . of me as a prospective bride. Would it cause much strife if you were to choose me instead of a duchess?"

Mr. Darcy fixed her with a wry smile. "The odds I can secure a duchess are extremely slim. But in answer to your question, yes, there are certain family members who might not appreciate you, at least at the outset."

"Starting with your titled relations, I suspect," said Elizabeth.

"Actually, you would be incorrect with that statement," replied Mr. Darcy. "My uncle, the earl, is not a pretentious man, and his wife and children are much like him, with the possible exception of his eldest daughter." Mr. Darcy grinned. "Rachel has captured a duke as a husband and seems to feel the importance of her position keenly. While I would not expect her to treat you with anything but civility, it is possible she will not wish to forward any intimacy with you.

"The main opposition will come from my father. He is the most class conscious of my family and has begun to suggest it is time I marry, of course, to a woman he considers appropriate."

"Not your mother?" asked Elizabeth.

Mr. Darcy shook his head and said: "Mother's only desire is for me to be happy in life. I am convinced she will love you with little effort. It is, therefore, interesting that the other source of dissent may come from *her* sister, who is everything my mother is not. Luckily her husband is a man who does not subscribe to her feelings and is well practiced in holding her in check."

"She sounds like an interesting woman, Mr. Darcy."

"Interesting is hardly a term I would use to describe Lady Catherine de Bourgh. In fact, she has long insisted there was an agreement between her and my mother that I marry my cousin, even though my mother has told her several times there was not. To hear Lady Catherine speak, the matter was decided with an unbreakable contract. My mother claims it was nothing more than idle speculation."

The possibility of Mr. Darcy being bound to another rolled about in Elizabeth's head, and she attempted to understand how she felt about the notion. Elizabeth found that it did not precisely distress her at present, which told her that whatever she felt for this man, she was not in love with him yet. Any sense of loss she felt was for the possibility of something developing between them, not the actuality of that feeling.

"Then should matters end as you wish, it seems I will need to win over several members of your family."

"I cannot imagine they will be anything but charmed by you," said Mr. Darcy. He did not deny that he wished for something permanent between them, not that Elizabeth had expected him to, given his previous assertions. "Lady Catherine's opinion does not concern me in the slightest, nor should it you."

"And what of your father?" pressed Elizabeth. "Does he not control the inheritance to your estate? Or is it entailed?"

"There is no entailment on Pemberley," replied Mr. Darcy. "While my father might protest, I doubt he would do anything to attempt to disinherit me. Should he attempt to do so, he would need to answer to my mother."

Elizabeth laughed at the notion. "I can readily see it, Mr. Darcy."

"What of you?" said Mr. Darcy, grinning along with her. "Are there relations of yours who will object to the suit of a mere heir of an estate?"

"I cannot imagine it," replied Elizabeth. "The Bennet family has held the estate for several generations, but the family has always been small. Other than my father, my siblings, and a few aunts and uncles,

I do not believe you will be required to win anyone over."

"That is a relief, indeed."

Mr. Darcy's words were a source of merriment for them both, and they let loose their humor. When it had run its course, Elizabeth once again fixed her attention on him, asking him questions about the rest of his family, including his mother and sister and the cousins to whom he was closest. In turn, Mr. Darcy asked about her brother, whom he had not met, as well as of her uncles and aunts. And they spent a pleasant time until Elizabeth returned to Longbourn.

While Elizabeth met with Mr. Darcy once more while walking and daily when the Longbourn and Netherfield parties exchanged calls, an event happened which disrupted these daily meetings. A few days earlier, Mr. Bennet had received a letter from Thomas informing them of the exact timing of their return.

"Are you eager in seeing your brother and your friend?" asked Mr. Bennet of his three daughters. "I must own that I am curious as to how your brother has adjusted to life as a married man."

"I am sure they are very happy together," opined Jane, much to the amusement of the rest of the family. Jane's disposition had always been rather sunny.

"Oh, I dare say you are quite correct, Jane," said Mr. Bennet. "But the presence of another in one's life must be a large adjustment, do you not think?"

"Of course, it must," said Elizabeth. "And your words must be given the weight of experience, as you have lived this exact situation."

"That is true," said Mr. Bennet. In his eyes shone the light of introspection and remembrance, and his daughters knew he was thinking of their mother. "I was shocked," continued he after a brief pause, "when your mother shook me awake our first night together, complaining of my snoring."

The three sisters giggled at the thought of their mother, with her nerves, badgering their father about keeping her awake. Surely it could not have been comfortable for a new bride to speak to her husband in such a way. Then again, Mrs. Bennet had not exactly been a retiring sort of woman and would likely not have concerned herself over waking her husband.

"On the other hand, your mother had a tendency to push her feet against me those first few nights." Mr. Bennet chuckled. "And that is when I discovered that your mother's feet were always ice cold! I practically shot out of the bed the first time she did that, only to have her complain that I was not warming her feet as I ought!"

Again the sisters laughed. It was not precisely the most proper discussion, though to remember their mother with such fondness was a habit they had developed in the time after her death. It made them feel close to her, as if she had not truly left them.

"The point I am trying to make, Jane," said Mr. Bennet, fixing on his eldest daughter, "is that marriage is a commitment to another person, and it is until death do us part. There will always be vexations between two people, for we each have our own way of thinking, our own opinions and habits. At times, a husband or wife might annoy their partner. Though the husband is the head of the family in our society, a man must still learn to live with a wife, to compromise in order to ensure she is happy.

"Even you and your Mr. Bingley, should you make the match we all expect." Mr. Bennet smiled at Jane, who appeared contemplative. "You will not be alike in all respects, though you *are*, each of you, very complying. But you will still need to learn to live together, learn to be happy once you have achieved marriage. Marriage is a first step, not an end game."

"I cannot imagine Thomas and Caroline being anything other than happy with their situation," said Elizabeth.

"I dare say you are correct," said Mr. Bennet. "But I wonder how they have achieved that happiness."

They were not to wait long, for early the afternoon of the third day after the assembly, the carriage rumbled onto Longbourn's drive, pulled by a pair of snorting horses. It stopped in front of the house and its inhabitants soon alighted to the delight of the family members awaiting them. The air resounded with the sounds of excited greetings and laughter, especially as the future master of Longbourn introduced his wife to them with pride and evident happiness.

"To hear you speak, my son," said Mr. Bennet, "one might be excused for thinking that we had never made your bride's acquaintance."

They all laughed again, with Thomas exclaiming: "But you have only spent a few minutes in her company *as my wife*. And with such a wife, one can hardly blame me for espousing a little pride."

"Thomas!" protested the newly minted Mrs. Bennet. "I hardly think it necessary to proclaim my virtues to those who have known me all my life!"

"Is that not what a husband is for?" asked Elizabeth. "By all means, Thomas—she is now under your protection, and thus you must take every opportunity to ensure everyone you meet knows how wonderful she is!"

By this time Caroline was as red as a ripe apple from Longbourn's orchards. Though she attempted to glare at them all, it was clear she was far too happy to be upset with their teasing. The newly arrived were invited into the house, and for the first time, Caroline entered as a resident, to the excitement of her new sisters. As they went, Jane was speaking to her brother and new sister in a manner quite unlike the normally reticent Jane.

"Come in get settled! Caroline, all of your personal effects have been delivered from Netherfield, and your family has been invited to dinner tonight. We expect they will arrive before too long, along with Mr. Darcy."

"Ah, so he *is* real," said Thomas with a laugh.

"Of course, he is," said Caroline. "But I am curious as to his behavior while he has been here. Have there been any developments on that score?"

Elizabeth felt her cheeks heating a little, but Jane spoke up, diverting Caroline. "Mr. Darcy is a good friend to Mr. Bingley and thus must be welcome in our home. As for myself, I do not know what to make of the gentleman."

"I *am* surprised, Jane!" exclaimed Thomas. "From you, that is akin to a scathing denunciation!"

"There is nothing wanting with regard to Mr. Darcy," said Mr. Bennet. "The gentleman can challenge me in chess, which is a point highly in his favor."

By this time, the party had reached the entranceway, and the banter continued, Thomas teasing his father about his chess habits, while the rest of them laughed and talked, several conversations ongoing at once. Curious as to her sister's meaning, Elizabeth looked at Jane, wondering at her words. But Jane was speaking with Caroline in an animated fashion, and Elizabeth allowed the matter to pass.

The newlyweds found their way to their chambers to refresh themselves from their journey, and while they were away, their neighbors arrived. The Bingleys positively exuded eagerness to see Caroline again, but Mr. Darcy, Elizabeth was embarrassed to see, had eyes for no one but her. When Caroline and Thomas returned downstairs, they found Elizabeth in earnest conversation with the gentlemen.

The Bingleys all crowded around them, speaking their congratulations once again while demanding details of their time in

Ramsgate. For a time, the conversations were again loud and unrestrained, as was often the case during such reunions. Then when the immediate curiosity was satisfied, Thomas looked over at Elizabeth and Mr. Darcy, who had largely kept out of the fray. That was all Mr. Darcy required to ask for an introduction, which Elizabeth provided with alacrity.

"I am pleased to make your acquaintance at last, Mr. Darcy," said Thomas. "There have been times when I wondered if you truly existed."

"So I have heard," replied Mr. Darcy. "It is unfortunate we have never crossed paths before."

Elizabeth did not miss Mr. Darcy's almost imperceptible glance toward her, and neither did Thomas. The grin Thomas directed at her provoked a sinking feeling, which was borne out when he turned to Caroline.

"It seems you were correct, my dear."

"Of course, I was," replied Caroline primly.

It was clear Mr. Darcy did not understand. To Elizabeth's relief, neither enlightened him, though they continued to smile as if they knew a secret. Uncertain her relations would not embarrass her, Elizabeth changed the subject.

As dinner parties go, this one was different in the high spirits of the group gathered together. Mrs. Bingley was as happy as Elizabeth had ever seen her, speaking to Mrs. Bennet and obtaining every bit of information she could of their journey. The Bennet sisters also commanded as much of her time as they could, the dream of their family being united finally realized. Bingley was attentive to Jane as usual, which prompted the teasing of his sister and new brother, and even Mr. Bennet was seen to be very happy. The only members of the company who were not quite as enthusiastic about the evening were the Hursts. Mrs. Hurst was not naturally a person given over to merriment, and Mr. Hurst had never been enthusiastic about anything other than his plate, in Elizabeth's experience.

"So, Bingley," said Thomas, directing a lazy smile at his new brother, "one might wonder when you will decide to take that final step with my most reticent sister." Thomas then turned a grin on Jane. "Or do you feel you are still not well enough acquainted with her?"

Mr. Bingley laughed at the irony in Thomas's statement, even as his mother exclaimed: "Nonsense! Why, he has known her all her life! I declare it is high time you ceased keeping the poor girl waiting, Charles!"

"No, I am quite well enough acquainted with Miss Bennet to take the step you suggest, Bennet," replied Mr. Bingley, not at all bothered by the teasing. "But I shall not do so until I am ready and, more importantly, Miss Bennet is ready. It is important to me to know that she feels like she has had a season of courtship."

"Excellent answer, Bingley!" said Thomas. "I dare say you will do well in life when you finally do muster the courage."

"It is not a matter of courage, old man. It is simply a matter of timing."

"And Jane will make an excellent daughter," said Mrs. Bingley. "Your mother and I always dreamed of uniting our families. To know we will have two such ties fills me with such contentment."

Mrs. Bingley turned to Elizabeth and Mary, who were sitting nearby. "If only I had another son, I could perhaps hope to obtain one of you as a daughter as well!"

Louisa Hurst snorted with some disdain, but no one paid her any heed. The response was provided by Mary who said: "I think that perhaps two marriages in the family are quite enough!"

For her part, Elizabeth nodded her agreement. The thought of Mr. Darcy entered her mind, and she glanced at the gentleman to see him earnestly watching her. Feeling a little self-conscious, Elizabeth looked away. Jane was watching her, she noted, but Elizabeth only shook her head at her sister's questioning glance. The matter with Mr. Darcy was still too new, too private to share with anyone, even a most beloved sister.

"It is impossible, regardless," said Mrs. Bingley. "I shall be content with my new son, and hope that I will soon be provided a new daughter." Then she looked from Caroline to Jane and back again. "I also hope that I shall be provided grandchildren before long? My dear friend did not live long enough to welcome grandchildren, so it shall be my duty to provide them with the love of two grandmothers!"

"And spoil them beyond the possibility of redemption!" added Mr. Bennet.

"Of course!" exclaimed Mrs. Bingley to the general laughter of the company. "It *is* the duty of all grandmothers, you see." Then she turned to Louisa. "I am happy we are to *finally* gain a grandchild from you and Hurst. It is high time, for you have been married for more than three years."

Mrs. Hurst as she pinked with embarrassment but did not reply. Privately, Elizabeth thought they might have three children by now if Mr. Hurst had as much interest in his wife as he did the brandy decanter. Even now, the man was sitting on the sofa next to his wife, his head bowed as if asleep. Given her experience with the man, Elizabeth thought it likely he had drunk as much as all the other men combined when the ladies had separated from the gentlemen.

A little later in the evening, Elizabeth found herself next to Caroline while Mr. Darcy, a rarity that evening, was away from Elizabeth, talking with Thomas and her father. Elizabeth had known this moment was coming, for Caroline was almost certain to wish to bask in her accurate prediction. As it was, Elizabeth was not of a mind to protest.

"Well, Lizzy," said she. "It seems to me that Mr. Darcy is quite attentive to you. Are you ready to acknowledge that I had the right of it?"

"More than ready," replied Elizabeth agreeably. "But I do not yet understand my own heart, so any congratulations are premature."

Caroline gave her a long look before reaching out and grasping Elizabeth's hand. "Yes, I should imagine you would wish to confirm your feelings. As he has only been here a few weeks, his admiration must still be new to you."

"It is," said Elizabeth.

"Then there is nothing left to be said. I have known since he visited us four years ago that Mr. Darcy is a good sort of man. The passage of time has not changed that belief, if for nothing more than the fact that he finds you worth his admiration.

"But I shall not push. I am only content with the thought of your ultimate happiness. But I shall not tease much, for I know you must understand the extent of your admiration for him in turn."

"Thank you, Caroline," said Elizabeth. "Should I come to esteem the gentleman enough to allow a deeper connection between us, I shall be certain to let you know."

"I am sure I shall be the *second* to know, then," said Caroline, her eyes shining with laughter. "After all, you will certainly tell Jane before you inform me!"

"Of course," replied Elizabeth with a laugh.

Then Mr. Darcy approached, and Caroline left them together. Elizabeth did not notice her departure, for the gentleman consumed her attention to the exclusion of anything else.

CHAPTER XIV

*H*ad Mrs. Bennet survived, matters would have been easier at Longbourn those initial days after the return of Thomas Bennet with his new bride. Then there would have been no question as to who would act as the estate's mistress.

Sadly, however, Mrs. Bennet had passed away more than a year before, and as a result, Jane had largely taken up the reins of the house, with her younger sisters' assistance. When Caroline entered Longbourn as the heir's wife, there was a period of adjustment for the four Bennet ladies. It was clear from her early actions that she had no wish to step on any toes. It took more forthrightness on Jane's part than Elizabeth thought her sister possessed to resolve the situation.

"What are your plans for the day, Brother?" asked Jane when they sat at breakfast three days after his return.

Thomas eyed his sister, his expression inscrutable. "I thought to visit the Johnson farm, for there is a matter I need to discuss with him." He turned a fond smile on his wife. "While I might wish the honeymoon to last longer, there is work to be done on the estate and life, after all, does go on, regardless of my wishes otherwise."

The elder Mr. Bennet looked on his son with amusement. "Very good, Thomas. We can discuss the matter of Johnson's farm when you return. I think it best that I spend some time with the ledgers this morning."

Thomas nodded and returned to his meal. Elizabeth suspected that both men knew something of the delicate state of affairs between the ladies at present. It was to their credit that they meant to allow them to handle the situation and not become involved.

When breakfast ended, and the gentlemen excused themselves to see to their sundry tasks, Jane suggested the ladies retire to the sitting-room. They all agreed without comment, Elizabeth and Mary with some amusement, and soon they were ensconced in that room. Jane lost no time in raising the subject at that point.

"Caroline," said she, "I believe we should discuss our roles within the house now, so that we all may have clarity."

The look Caroline directed at her new sister suggested wariness. She did not disagree, however, motioning Jane to continue.

"My sisters and I wish to thank you, Caroline," said Jane. "It is clear you have taken great care of our feelings since your return to Hertfordshire. Elizabeth, Mary, and I appreciate your forbearance.

"Having said that, I must ask what you mean by constantly deferring to me when it is clear that the authority must rest with you?"

Caroline fairly gawped at Jane's pointed words, while the two younger ladies giggled at her astonishment. That, of course, did not endear them to her, which she demonstrated with a mock glare. Her displeasure, however, only made them laugh longer.

"Our silly sisters aside," said Caroline with a superior sniff, "I did not wish to assume I might simply enter the house and take over its management with nary a by your leave."

"To push me to the side may not have been the best course," replied Jane, her typical serenity firmly in place, "but this level of caution is not required. Thomas will be the master of the estate one day. As you are his wife, you will be the mistress. I fail to see how there is any ambiguity in these facts."

"There is not, I suppose," replied Caroline slowly.

"Caroline," added Elizabeth. "Jane is not concerned about being supplanted. It is not necessary for you to shoulder the burden alone — we will help you in whatever you require. But I believe Jane is correct; I would never have thought I would see the day when Caroline *Bennet* would give way to such an extent as you have since you arrived. Has marriage to my brother truly changed you so much? Or has he simply addled your wits?"

The teasing tone with which Elizabeth spoke induced them all to laughter though Caroline somehow maintained a scowl as she laughed. When their mirth ran its course, she turned that scowl on Elizabeth.

"It seems to me our younger sister's impertinence requires curbing, dearest Jane. With your assistance, I will attend to it first, as I suspect it is more important than anything else."

"Perhaps you will try," said Elizabeth. "But you will fail. I suggest you retreat from the field before you are required to resign in humiliating defeat."

"It seems you are correct, Caroline," replied Jane. "Decidedly impertinent."

"We must stick together, Lizzy," said Mary. "It appears our elders wish to make improvements to our characters."

"Do not think *you* have escaped our notice, dearest Mary," said Caroline.

When Thomas returned from his visit, he found the ladies ensconced in the sitting-room, sipping tea and speaking of their plans for the room. Mrs. Bennet had not redecorated the main sitting-room in the time she had been the estate's mistress, and as a result, the wallpaper was a little faded in places and the furniture was beginning to show its age. As affectionately as a newlywed man can, he greeted his wife and then his sisters, sitting with them for a few moments, looking on them all with some speculation.

"I see you are already intent upon spending as much of my father's money as you can manage, Caroline," said he.

"It may wait, if you feel that is best," said Caroline, unperturbed by his tease. "But you must own that the room requires updating."

"Oh yes, I suppose that is so," was Thomas's offhand response, though he did not look about the room at all. "There is no reason it may be put off that I can think of, and I am certain my father would agree." Thomas paused a moment, his eyes finding each lady in turn. "Is everything well?"

"Why should it not be?" said Caroline, her question clearly rhetorical.

"Indeed, I have no notion at all," replied Thomas.

While he allowed the subject to drop, the changes in the house soon became clear. The subject was never raised in Elizabeth's hearing, but she did not think he misunderstood what had happened. But as a resolution had been achieved, he appeared content to leave well enough alone.

As the month of August was waning, so too were the warm

summer days, which would soon devolve to the less certain weather of autumn and the rains which came with it. Given the lengthening of the season, the inhabitants of the area were more likely to wish to be out of doors, to store up their fill of the warmth and comfort against the onset of cooler temperatures which were approaching. And as the intimacy between Longbourn and Netherfield continued apace, it was unsurprising the two families were often to be found in each other's company.

One such occasion was the day after the ladies' conversation. Elizabeth suspected the outing was suggested partly as a means by which to throw her into the company of Mr. Darcy—at times Caroline's motives were not precisely hidden. And she hardly needed to bother, for Mr. Darcy and Mr. Bingley came to Longbourn almost every day, or the Bennet ladies visited Netherfield, and Elizabeth had met the gentleman once more during a morning walk. But as she was willing to further understand the gentleman's feelings and determine her own, Elizabeth raised no objection.

The location chosen for their outing was a little glen on the northern edge of Longbourn's boundaries. Oakham Mount stood to the north of the estate along its border with Netherfield, but if one traveled a little to the west and around the foot of that prominence, there was a delightful location, forested with a bubbling brook running through its center. Since it was a little distant to walk, the party set out on horseback, their food baskets for their picnic strapped to the saddles. When they arrived, a location under the extensive branches of a large tree was chosen, their lunch laid out, and consumed amid the laughing conversation of the company.

As Elizabeth's habits were well known to them all, no one was surprised when she rose after their repast and indicated her desire to walk a little along the stream. She did not misunderstand the amused looks of the company when Mr. Darcy indicated his intention to accompany her. In times such as this, however, Elizabeth recognized the benefits of simply ignoring them and set to it with a will.

"Have you come here often?" asked Mr. Darcy as they walked away from the rest of the group.

"It is a little further from Longbourn than I usually roam," replied Elizabeth. "At times I have come on horseback, but I do not ride so often as I walk."

"Georgiana would love it here."

Elizabeth turned a curious look on her companion. "Your sister."

"Yes," replied Mr. Darcy. "My mother, you see, suffered multiple miscarriages. Georgiana is my only sibling and my junior by twelve years. As she was born at a time when my mother had given up hope of another child, she is precious to us all. She is also the youngest of my generation in my extended family by several years."

"What kind of girl is your sister?" Elizabeth directed an arched brow at her companion. "I suspect, considering your own character, that she is confident and poised, yet uneasy in society. Am I correct?"

Mr. Darcy chuckled and shook his head. "You are partially correct, for Georgiana shares the Darcy trait of reticence. In her case, however, it is more shyness. If she did not have my mother to guide her, I might worry that her retiring nature would be her undoing. But my mother is attentive to her difficulties and has done much to soothe her fears. She is still but sixteen, and will not be out for two more years."

"And her interests? Does she share these with you?"

"To some respects. She *is* intelligent though I say it myself. But I think she may enjoy novels too much; as my mother declares there is no harm in them, there is little hope she will desist. Georgiana's favorite pastime is music, particularly the pianoforte. If my mother allowed it, I am certain she would play and sing all day long."

Elizabeth laughed. She stepped up to the stream beside which they walked and bent down, slipping her hand into the water, allowing the flowing liquid to run through her fingers. Then as Mr. Darcy stopped beside her, watching her with a half-smile, Elizabeth experimentally flicked her fingers, spraying water in his direction, though it did not travel half the distance.

"I would suggest you take great care, Miss Bennet," warned he, though his smile never faded. "As it is you who are destined to lose such a battle, it would not be in your best interest to draw me in."

"Surely you are too much of a gentleman to seek to wet me through," said Elizabeth, injecting a measure of shock into her voice.

"Rather, I would be honor-bound to respond," was Mr. Darcy's amused reply. "To refuse such a challenge would be unconscionable."

"Then I suppose it is for the best that I have little desire to provoke a battle." Elizabeth shook off the hand that she had trailed in the water and rose. "As for Miss Darcy, I hope that I am introduced to her one day. She sounds like a delightful girl."

"My dear Miss Bennet," said Mr. Darcy. "I believe your introduction is inevitable. The timing is yet to be decided, but it *shall* happen."

The intensity in Mr. Darcy's countenance and stare was something to which Elizabeth was still becoming accustomed. She did not misunderstand the inference, however, and she blushed and looked away. Since Mr. Darcy did not speak, they continued their walk in comfortable and companionable silence.

Though Elizabeth and Mr. Darcy appeared comfortable in each other's company, one of those watching them was not certain. There was something odd going on, and Jane Bennet did not know what to make of it.

Having been her sister's confidante for many years and knowing Mr. Darcy's actions toward Elizabeth, Jane had long been doubtful of the man. Her natural instinct told her that there was some explanation, but the protective elder sister rejected such possibilities in favor of suspicion. When he had been absent from the neighborhood, it had been easier to allow the first part of her nature to dominate her thinking. Now that he had returned and was paying Elizabeth so much attention, the latter part was gaining strength.

But how could Jane be certain? To her eyes Elizabeth was not distressed in Mr. Darcy's company—quite the opposite, in fact. But Jane had seen enough of Elizabeth's blushes to wonder if the man was sincere in his affections, or merely flattering her for some purpose of his own

The worst part of it was that Elizabeth had not confided in Jane as she always had in the past. Was that not a reason for concern? Jane could not say for certain, but it worried her. Could Mr. Darcy have improper motives? Was he attempting to charm Elizabeth because of those motives? Or had he threatened her somehow to prevent her from speaking to her family?

Surely that last was unlikely. But Jane still worried. She did not know what to do. Her claim she would approach her father should she be excessively concerned flitted in the back of her mind, and she wondered if she should not have done it already. Elizabeth's countenance, which did not seem concerned at all, kept Jane's fear in check. But it did not dispel it.

"Some deep thought seems to have come over you, Miss Bennet."

A blink, and Jane turned to Mr. Bingley, noting his jovial smile, tinged with concern. Jane blushed, for she had been so caught up in concerns for her sister, she had not paid any attention to Mr. Bingley. And here they were walking some distance from their picnic site, yet she had not said a word since they had arisen and walked away!

"Pardon me," said Jane, her cheeks heating from mortification. "I was not attending. It seems I am prone to woolgathering today."

"It is no trouble," replied Mr. Bingley, his good humor completely restored. "The times in which I am introspective are few, but I *do* have them."

Sensing this was an opportunity, Jane turned to Mr. Bingley and said, as casually as she could manage: "You have known Mr. Darcy for some time, have you not, Mr. Bingley?"

"Some years, yes," said Mr. Bingley. "We attended university together—or rather, my first two years overlapped with his last two."

"You seem like close friends," said Jane.

"Yes, we are," replied Mr. Bingley, his voice firm. "There are few friends as dependable as Fitzwilliam Darcy once he admits you to his circle. That he has few whom he calls friend makes it even more of an honor once it has been achieved."

"And you have never known him to be . . . dishonorable?"

Mr. Bingley turned to Jane, a question in his eyes. Then they widened, and he looked over to where Mr. Darcy was escorting Elizabeth along the stream. A grin suffused his countenance, and he turned his attention back to Jane, mirth dancing in his eyes.

"It is obvious to where these questions tend, Miss Bennet. While I would not have you question Darcy's character or his honor, the happiness of a most beloved sister is reason enough to do so, indeed. And you need not worry. Darcy is as good a man as ever breathed. Should he decide on your sister as a prospective bride, Elizabeth will be very well cared for. There is nothing he would not do for her happiness."

Reassured by Mr. Bingley's testimony, Jane glanced again at her sister, noting that Elizabeth appeared to be teasing Mr. Darcy. Surely if he had threatened her, she would not show this uninhibited playfulness. Perhaps her worries were without foundation. At the very least, Thomas was here and would provide an able protector. And so, Jane turned her attention to Mr. Bingley and attempted to put the matter of Mr. Darcy from her mind.

There was another who noted the attentions of Mr. Darcy to Elizabeth Bennet. And unlike Jane, he had no intention of allowing the matter to proceed without some measure of reassurance. The happiness of that good woman was too important a matter to leave it to chance. Thus, after observing them for some days, he finally mustered the courage to bring up the subject with the man in question on Sunday after church.

"Mr. Darcy, I would like to speak with you, if you will spare me a moment."

It was clear that the gentleman was taken aback by this somewhat terse request, but he did not hesitate to give an affirmative response. It was fortunate that Miss Elizabeth was engaged in conversation with Miss Lucas, for he did not know what she might say in response to his interference. As it was, he led Mr. Darcy to the side, out of hearing of any parishioners departing after the church services. When they had reached an out of the way location, Mr. Darcy turned a questioning look on him.

"Yes, Mr. Collins? How may I be of assistance?"

Now that he had the gentleman's full attention, William Collins was not certain what to say. It felt, at once, to be both his duty and an impertinence to ask such questions of a man of the eminence of Mr. Darcy. But the weight of his resolve once again settled over him, and Collins straightened and looked the other man in the eye.

"I would like to know, sir, of your intentions regarding Miss Elizabeth Bennet."

Had he declared his purpose to walk to the moon, Collins did not think Mr. Darcy could have been more surprised. He did not respond for several moments, apparently attempted to discern whether the question had been asked with a seriousness of purpose.

"You wish to know of my intentions toward Miss Elizabeth," repeated Mr. Darcy after a moment of silence.

"Yes," replied Collins firmly. "Let me say that I do not suspect you of ulterior motives, Mr. Darcy. In fact, I possess the highest respect for your position in society, and your character, especially considering others whom I consider highly moral and intelligent people have a good opinion of you.

"But Miss Elizabeth is my cousin, and I am . . . I have the highest opinion of her. I am neither her father nor her guardian. I am nothing more than her cousin. As her cousin, I would not wish for anything untoward to affect her happiness. Therefore, I should like to know if you are serious in your pursuit. Or is she simply a pleasant diversion while you are here?"

Though he appeared bemused, Mr. Darcy was much quicker to answer this time. "I assure you, Mr. Collins, that I too think the best of your cousin. There is nothing more in my interest for her than you see. My intentions are entirely honorable and not the whim of a moment."

Until that moment, Collins had not known he was trembling, but he realized that his shaking was now from emotion, rather than anxiety. It seemed Mr. Darcy realized this also, for he looked on with compassion.

"This is difficult for you, is it not?"

"Nothing less than concern for my cousin prompts me to speak so," said Collins, attempting to hold on to the merest shred of his dignity. "Though you are a man to whom I would never speak in such a fashion, it is imperative that whoever chooses my cousin must understand the worth of the gem they seek. She is the most remarkable young woman I have ever had the good fortune to meet."

Collins had the distinct impression that Mr. Darcy was not misled at all in his attempts to obfuscate. The words he spoke next were proof of his supposition.

"Then you may rest easy, Mr. Collins, for I quite agree with you. At this time, I cannot speak with any surety about the ultimate success of my suit. But if it *is* successful, she will always be treated as a woman of her caliber demands. I give you my word."

"Thank you, Mr. Darcy. Now if you will excuse me."

With a nod, Mr. Darcy turned away and rejoined Miss Elizabeth, who was watching them curiously. When he felt her gaze on him, Collins gave her a smile, hoping she did not see how difficult it was to avoid bursting into tears. As the congregation slowly made their way from the church, Collins avoided her, speaking with other gentlemen, until the crowd finally cleared. Then he made his way slowly toward the altar, sitting on the front pew and gazing at the cross displayed so prominently there.

That this day would come was something William Collins had always known. But that did not make it any easier to bear. Though he had been in love with his cousin since the first moment he had come to Longbourn, he had always known she would never be his. The reality of how soon he expected she would belong to another man was akin to the crushing weight of a quarry full of rocks on his head.

Feeling, rather than seeing someone sitting to his left, Collins turned his head slightly to see his patron sitting beside him. What Mr. Bennet displayed for his benefit was not pity—would never be that. But it was compassion, respect, and the pride of a father for a son, something Collins had never known until he had come to Longbourn.

"It is difficult."

The voice breaking the silence caught Collins off guard though he supposed it should not have. Though he had attempted to keep the matter quiet, hoping to avoid attracting attention, his cousin was as observant a man as Collins had ever met. It was not surprising that he had noticed what had occurred.

"I never thought it would be this excruciating," whispered Collins. "I would never stand in the way of her happiness. But the very thought of her in another man's arms fills me with sorrow such that I wonder how I shall withstand it."

"And yet you shall," said Mr. Bennet. "When Elizabeth marries, you will finally be free to move forward, to find your own happiness. In some ways, her presence at Longbourn has not allowed you to look at life with hope and anticipation."

"She is not engaged yet," said Collins, a half-hearted final attempt to deny what his heart already knew.

"No, she is not," replied Mr. Bennet. "But I believe you know as well as I that it is likely she will be.

"The reason I stayed behind today, William, is to tell you that I am proud of you. In fact, that is an understatement. I have never been prouder of my own children than I am of you at this very moment." Mr. Bennet put his hand on Collins's shoulder and squeezed it gently. "Your presence in my family has always been welcome. It has never been more apparent to me than it is now that I made the correct decision to bring you into our home. You are a good man, William Collins."

"Thank you, Mr. Bennet," said Collins, feeling all the compliment of his mentor's words. Though it did not manifest physically, he felt his backbone firm and his spine straighten. It was for the best that Elizabeth find someone to love her as she deserved to be loved. Mr. Bennet was correct—now Collins could find someone of his own to love and receive her love in return. And he had just the candidate in mind.

"Shall I make your excuses at dinner today?"

Collins turned to face his cousin, and for a moment the offer was appealing. But there was no reason to avoid his family, and every reason to continue in intimacy with his only living relations. And Collins decided he would not avoid them, even on this day.

"That will not be necessary. I shall come at the dinner hour as usual."

With one final squeeze, Mr. Bennet released his shoulder and stood. "You know you are welcome at any time."

"I know," was all Collins said.

With a final smile, Mr. Bennet turned and walked out of the church, leaving Collins to his thoughts. They were brighter, happier than they had been before. And on a certain level, Collins felt freer than he could remember feeling at any time in the past. The future approached, and Collins was eager to discover what lay over the horizon.

CHAPTER XV

Monday morning saw the arrival of a surprising letter addressed to Elizabeth and Mr. Bennet. And while Elizabeth might have been happy in other circumstances to receive the invitation it contained, in this instance she thought it was a matter of poor timing.

"Your uncle asks for your presence in London for a few days, Lizzy," said Mr. Bennet. The family had been sitting down to break their fast when the mail was delivered by the butler, and Mr. Bennet wasted no time in opening it.

"Oh, well . . ." Elizabeth paused, biting back the refusal which had entered her mind in an instant. Instead, she composed herself and asked her father: "What is the reason for Uncle's request?"

"It seems that Mrs. Gardiner has caught a cold, and a bad one at that. Though my brother states she is in no danger, his wife has been bed ridden, and the nurse is struggling to watch the children with no one to manage the house."

An image of Mr. Darcy and the increasing intimacy of his attentions of late entered Elizabeth's mind. But she could not refuse this request from her dear relations, particularly when they had favored her with an invitation to visit the North Country.

"Of course, I shall go," said Elizabeth. "Please write to Uncle and inform him I shall arrive before noon tomorrow." Then Elizabeth turned to Thomas and smiled. "If you and my brother will consent to arrange for the carriage to take me there."

"If that is what you wish," said Thomas with a grin.

But Mr. Bennet only directed a long look at Elizabeth. "Perhaps we could offer to send Mary?"

"I should be happy to go in your stead, Lizzy," said Mary.

"Thank you, Mary, Papa," said Elizabeth, smiling at her father and sister in turn. "But it is no trouble. Aunt and Uncle have always been so kind to us all—I would feel churlish if I were to refuse to help now in their time of need."

It was clear that the family understood why Elizabeth might wish to be in Hertfordshire at that particular moment, but once she made the decision, she would not be moved. Mary continued to assert her willingness to go in her stead, and Mr. Bennet asked her another time or two if she would not reconsider, but Elizabeth stood firm.

Jane's reaction was different, and more than a little surprising to Elizabeth. Through the discussion at the breakfast table, Jane had remained quiet and watchful, not saying a word. When they had retreated from the table, Elizabeth to her room to begin packing a few essential items to take with her to London, Jane followed her.

"Lizzy, I am happy you are to go to London."

"Oh?" asked Elizabeth with a frown her sister did not seem to see. "Why would you be grateful that I am going away?"

For a moment, Jane peered at her, and Elizabeth had the distinct impression there was something she wished to say. "A change of scene and society is always good, is it not?"

Elizabeth was further convinced that Jane had not said what she wished. Though Elizabeth thought of pressing her sister, the needs of preparing for the morrow were in the back of her mind, distracting her. As such, she did not attend her sister as she usually would have.

"In fact," continued Jane when Elizabeth did not respond, "perhaps it is best if you pack for a longer stay. Once you arrive in London, you may find you have no desire to leave it."

Then with a brilliant smile, Jane excused herself, leaving Elizabeth to watch her, confused at her sister's words. Why Jane would think Elizabeth wished to stay in London long she could not fathom. But now was no time to consider it, and Elizabeth pushed it from her thoughts.

Elizabeth's next visitor was even more surprising. Though she had known Caroline all her life, Elizabeth had never been so close to Caroline as Jane. There had been times when Elizabeth found her new sister positively infuriating, for Caroline could, at times, display a hint of arrogance, not to mention disdain for others. She was a good sort of woman, and Elizabeth was happy her brother had been able to obtain Caroline for a wife. But they had never been intimate, which made Caroline's appearance all that much more curious.

"Do you need assistance?" asked Caroline when she entered the room.

"Thank you, but I believe I have it under control," replied Elizabeth with a smile. "It is not as if I shall be gone for weeks. All I require are a few dresses and some other items I do not believe I could do without."

"You mean to return quickly."

"Is there any doubt?" asked Elizabeth. Ignoring the heat rising in her cheeks, Elizabeth continued to fold her dresses. Caroline would not miss the opportunity to tease her, she thought, given how the other woman had done so concerning Mr. Darcy at every opportunity.

"No, I suppose there is not."

Caroline fell silent for several moments while Elizabeth continued her work, and for a time neither spoke. Though she could not help but feel curious as to her new sister's reason for speaking to her, Elizabeth decided she would allow Caroline to make her point, if, indeed, that was her purpose.

"I have always believed you were a good match for Mr. Darcy," said Caroline at length.

A laugh escaped, with which Caroline joined Elizabeth's amusement. "Truly? Given your lack of commentary on the matter, I might never have guessed!"

"You shall not take that tone with me, Elizabeth Bennet," said Caroline in a haughty tone. "As your brother's wife, I am to be respected."

Having seen the other woman's arrogance on occasion, Elizabeth knew Caroline was teasing. As such, she only threw her sister an amused look and continued with her packing. Caroline was not insulted in the slightest.

"Well, perhaps I have mentioned it on occasion. But I have been proven correct, have I not?"

Once again caught in the throes of embarrassment, Elizabeth turned away. Even though Caroline could be insufferable, however, Elizabeth could not but agree.

"It is still early. But it is quite possible you *have*." Then Elizabeth threw Caroline an insolent smirk. "I suppose one must be right occasionally."

"Impudent woman!" cried Caroline, though there was no heat in her voice. "So, you are not immune to the gentleman's charms?"

Elizabeth turned to Caroline and favored her with a pert smile. "You mean to pester me until I confess to it—I see your game. Then I suppose I shall have to own to it and endure your insufferable smugness, for I find I have some measure of attraction for the gentleman."

With a smile, Caroline stepped forward and grasped Elizabeth's hand. "Lizzy," said she, surprising Elizabeth—Caroline rarely called her by her familiar moniker, "all teasing aside, I wish to say that I am very happy for you. While I *am* feeling no little satisfaction at being proven correct, I am more interested in your happiness. He has always seemed like a good man to me, one who would suit you. And I must point out that I think there are few men who would suit you as a bride."

"What do you mean?" asked Elizabeth, frowning at Caroline's inference.

"You are far too outspoken, far too intelligent and not afraid to show it." Caroline smiled, indicating she did not mean to speak in censure. "Do you think every man wishes to have an intelligent wife, one who will contradict and tease him?"

Elizabeth frowned, her thoughts turning inward. "I . . . I suppose I had never thought of it."

"*I* have," said Caroline. "In many ways, you and I are alike. I have found a man who does not object to a wife such as I described in your brother. But at times I have wondered if you will find it as easy to do the same. There is certainly no one in Meryton who fits that description."

"But I have a dowry," said Elizabeth. "Surely on the strength of that alone I would receive attention from eligible gentlemen."

A snort of exasperation was Caroline's response. "Would you wish to be married to such a man?"

"No, I would not," replied Elizabeth, feeling more than a little subdued.

"Of course, you would not. Trapped in marriage with such a man would be akin to a punishment for you. The Elizabeth we all know and love would soon disappear.

"Mr. Darcy is not such a man. It is clear he is attracted to you precisely *because* of those qualities other men would disdain."

"I am not engaged yet," managed Elizabeth weakly.

"Do you doubt your effect on the gentleman?" Caroline smiled and squeezed Elizabeth's hand. "If you have any wits about you at all, you do not. None of us can predict the future, but I shall be very surprised if Mr. Darcy does not offer for you. And I am very happy for you, Elizabeth. We will lose you to a great estate in the north, but none of us will resent the loss of your society if it makes you happy."

Caroline released her hand and moved toward the door. But before she left, she turned back to Elizabeth and regarded her, a wry smile lifting the corners of her lips.

"Do not worry for your Mr. Darcy in your absence. I will ensure the likes of Agatha Goulding does not turn his head."

It was Elizabeth's turn to laugh. "Surely if you believe you are correct concerning his feelings for me, you can have no notion he will abandon me simply because I am gone for a few days."

"Perhaps. But one cannot be too careful."

When Caroline was gone, Elizabeth stood staring at the door for several long moments. It seemed her new sister was correct in her assertions, and now Elizabeth was forced to confront the subject she had never before considered. The brief conversation had prompted Elizabeth to think of Caroline in terms she never had before.

The revelation of Miss Elizabeth's upcoming journey to London caught Darcy off guard, unsure what to make of it. Their unofficial courtship had seemed to be proceeding well, Miss Elizabeth accepting his overtures with pleasure. But now she was to go visit her relations in town, and Darcy wondered if she was doing it to avoid him.

When in company with the rest of the Longbourn family, Darcy could say little, unable to ask the question burning in his mind while they were all there. But Darcy studied her as they spoke, wondering at what she was not saying. Several times someone else in the room directed a comment or a question at him, and Darcy was forced to ask them to repeat their question, so unaware was he of anything else but this woman before him. Thus, it was a relief when Bingley finally suggested a walk out of doors.

"May I escort you, Miss Elizabeth?" Darcy was quick to say, half afraid she would refuse.

Contrary to his fears, however, she readily agreed. Then with Bingley escorting Miss Bennet, the four exited the house, the rest of company declining the invitation. Their destination the rear of the property where the formal gardens stood, Darcy allowed Bingley and her sister to outpace them, eager to speak with her alone. But as they were walking away, Darcy witnessed Miss Bennet look back at them, and though he could not be certain, he thought she looked at him in particular with an expression which could only be termed self-assured.

"It seems you were eager to have a moment alone with me, Mr. Darcy," said Miss Elizabeth, pulling his attention back from his contemplation of her sister.

"I was . . . I mean, yes, I . . ." Unable to form his thoughts into coherent sentences, Darcy paused for a moment, wondering how he might bring up the subject. The sight of her amusement at his expense drew the confusion from Darcy's mind, and he returned the grin.

"Am I not always eager for time alone with you?"

As he had intended, a blush bloomed on her cheeks to his delight. But this young woman was a hardy soul, for she immediately recovered and fixed him with a stern glare. Grinning, Darcy held out his hands in surrender. By now he understood that her journey to London was for some reason other than to escape him, and it made his confidence swell in his breast.

"Hearing of your imminent journey to London was a shock, I will own. But I sense you are called there for some reason other than to escape my society. Am I correct?"

"You are," said Miss Bennet. Her manner turned serious. "A letter came in the post from my uncle, requesting my presence in London. My aunt is ill and requires my assistance. Given all they have done for me and the affection which exists between us, it is a request I cannot refuse."

"That speaks very well to your character, Miss Elizabeth," said Darcy. "You will be a great comfort to her, I am sure."

"That is my hope," replied she. "But I do not believe I shall be gone long. When Mrs. Gardiner is on the mend, I shall return—you may be assured of that."

The echo of a memory entered Darcy's mind, and he frowned, certain he had heard the name "Gardiner" before. But he could not place it, try though he might.

When Darcy focused again on Miss Elizabeth, he thought her color was a little higher than usual. As they walked, she looked out over the gardens, and it took Darcy a moment to realize she was avoiding his gaze.

"I am certain I have heard that name before," said he slowly, and when her cheeks pinked even more, he knew he had guessed correctly.

"Why does the mention of your aunt and uncle embarrass you when I have never made their acquaintance?"

"Have you not?" asked Miss Elizabeth, turning to face him. "The name is familiar to you—can you not place it?"

She was baiting him, Darcy realized. Opening his mouth to speak, Darcy frowned and remained silent, the memory of earlier that summer filling his mind. Then he looked up and stared into her eyes, curious as to her meaning.

"There was a couple who toured Pemberley this summer by that name, I believe. Were they your aunt and uncle?"

"They were," replied Miss Elizabeth.

"But how could you know of that? Did they inform you of the matter?"

Though Miss Elizabeth was silent for a moment, there was never any question of her ultimate reply. A moment later, she said: "Because I was with them, Mr. Darcy."

"You were?" Darcy could not believe his ears. Had he seen Miss Elizabeth that summer, it was quite possible he might not have allowed her to leave without an assurance of seeing her again. In fact, his thoughts had been on her to such an extent that he may have made a fool of himself!

"Yes, I was there, Mr. Darcy. You did not see me, though I most certainly saw you." The question evident in his countenance was enough for her to explain. "If you recall, you greeted my aunt and uncle close to the house. There was also a small grove of trees nearby."

"You were within those trees?"

"I was. Near enough to hear you speak, but concealed enough that you would not see me, even if you had chanced to glance in my direction."

Darcy was aghast. "You wished to avoid me?"

The look she shot at him was pointed and fierce, and Darcy felt ashamed because of it. But it was nothing next to that which he felt when she began to explain her feelings.

"At that moment, I did not know *what* you were, Mr. Darcy. Were you the reticent young man you portrayed during our first dance, or were you a man who ruined young ladies on a whim?

"And before you say anything," said Miss Elizabeth as Darcy opened his mouth to speak, "a young lady may be ruined by much less that what you did the last time you were here. As my sister has sometimes been fond of saying: 'A woman's reputation is no less beautiful than it is fragile.'"

"I had no intention of minimizing the potential effect of my actions," said Darcy, quickly so as to diminish the force of her glare. It did not let up for several more moments though she did finally relent with a sigh.

"So, to answer your question, no, I was not eager to meet you at Pemberley. While I had no wish to visit your family's estate, my aunt, who was raised in the neighborhood, was eager to tour it, and I could not refuse without opening myself to their embarrassing questions." She turned a significant eye on Darcy. "Or revealing certain matters, the accounts of which would soon make their way to my father and my brother."

"Did you confide in no one?" Darcy was not certain he wished the question to be answered, but he felt a certain curiosity whether there had been anyone on whom she could rely.

"Jane knows," replied Miss Elizabeth. "But I have told no other and sworn her to secrecy."

A quick glance across the lawn revealed Bingley walking with Miss Bennet, and a moment's study brought to Darcy's mind for the first time that Miss Bennet was watching them carefully. Now that he thought on it, the young woman had always kept him in sight when he was with her sister. The reason was now clear.

"So, your sister believes I am a rake."

Miss Elizabeth shook her head and glanced over at Miss Bennet. Though she was looking away, Darcy saw the smile on her face, which seemed to reassure Miss Bennet. She did not relax her vigilance, but it seemed she was a little easier, that Bingley commanded more of her attention after that.

"Jane does not possess the capacity to think ill of others," said Miss Elizabeth. "In her opinion, there must be some other explanation for your actions, some extenuating circumstances which precipitated them. You need not concern yourself for my sister's opinion."

While Darcy wondered if Miss Elizabeth were not dismissing her sister too readily, there were other matters to consider at present. When she turned her eyes to him, Darcy could see her glares had been replaced by her usual smiles. Happy though he was at this development, for the first time Darcy truly understood what this woman had suffered due to his actions, and he was shamed by it.

"It is a wonder you did not inform your father," said he, not quite certain what to say. "You could have forced me into a marriage, and none would have gainsaid your right to do so."

That Miss Bennet rolled her eyes in response to his comment was not a surprise. "What would that have accomplished? At that time, I knew only that you were Mr. Bingley's friend. Why should I wish for a husband I did not know, one whose character I suspected? Would I be happy in such a marriage?"

Darcy smiled at the young woman. "Then you are a rare breed, Miss Elizabeth, though I already knew it. Most young ladies of any station would jump at a chance to connect themselves with my family, and I gave you the perfect opportunity to do so."

"Then most young ladies are fools," said Miss Elizabeth, her tone leaving no room for argument. "All the riches in the world are not enough to make up for misery in marriage."

"That presupposes most young women do not wish for riches above all other things," murmured Darcy.

"Then we have established the fact that I am *not* most young ladies."

"And for that I am most grateful," said Darcy. "Given all these things, I am astonished you agreed to allow me this chance, despite the pretty words I spoke to you the night of the last assembly."

Miss Elizabeth stopped and turned to face him. The light of humor was absent from her eyes, replaced by an entirely serious gravity. For a moment, Darcy stilled, wondering if his words had caused her to reconsider her permission.

"Those few moments on the balcony gave me the insight I needed to see your character in a manner I had not previously had the opportunity to see. Your pretty words, as you call them, showed me you were not the man I had spent four years suspecting you were. If I have given you this chance, Mr. Darcy, you should understand it was entirely by your subsequent behavior it was granted."

"Then I am in your debt," said Darcy, taking her hand and bowing over it carefully. "It is my vow that I shall never give you any other reason to doubt me."

"If that is so, then I have made the correct decision."

As their conversation had once again turned playful, Darcy felt easy in grinning at her, and saying: "Then your decision to go to London has not been made out of a desire to avoid me."

"I have already informed you of why I go to London."

They began walking, once again comfortable in each other's company. As they walked, an idea formed in Darcy's mind, and he spoke again, his tone light.

"Do you think you shall be occupied at every moment of the day caring for your aunt and cousins?"

"Without a doubt, sir," said Miss Elizabeth in the same tone. "Doubtlessly I shall work my fingers to the bone, slaving for my relations, the only barrier between my aunt's house and utter chaos."

Darcy laughed alongside this delightful creature, once again wondering at having gained even as much of her favor as he had. "Then you will not be at all averse to receiving a visitor while you are at your uncle's home?"

"A visitor?" asked Miss Elizabeth, turning an arched brow on him.

"It would not be a problem for me to visit London for a few days." Darcy grinned at her. "In fact, I believe there is some pressing business for which I must go to town."

"Then I believe I would be delighted to see you, sir," replied Miss Elizabeth.

"Excellent. I look forward to it."

CHAPTER XVI

Elizabeth's arrival in London the following morning saw the relief of those resident at Gracechurch Street. While Mr. Gardiner was absent at his offices, as Elizabeth might have expected, the house was in chaos, not having a clear direction. Not only was Mrs. Gardiner ill, but the housekeeper, who had been with the Gardiners for several years, was away tending to an ailing relation of her own. Thus, the children's nurse was struggling, attempting to deal with the children and the rest of the house all at once, while the two maids were experiencing their own difficulties, attempting to help the nurse and see to the house at the same time. No one, Elizabeth suspected, was happier to see her than Miss Collingford, the nurse.

"Your aunt is in her room, Miss Bennet," said Miss Collingford upon Elizabeth's arrival, for it was she who answered the door.

"How is she?" asked Elizabeth, setting her bonnet and gloves to the side. "And how are the children?"

"Mrs. Gardiner is not in any danger, I believe," said she, "but she is feeling quite unwell. As for the children, I have checked on them a time or two, and so far they are being well-behaved in the nursery. But I have no doubt they will grow more difficult if I do not attend to them."

"Then that must be your task, Miss Collingford." Elizabeth smiled at the harried young woman. "You have done as well as can be expected. Thank you for your assistance, but I shall deal with the house, so that you may attend to your duties."

With a grateful smile, the nurse curtseyed and fairly ran from the room. The Gardiner children were active and, at times, mischievous, though well behaved—but at that moment, occupying herself with only the youngsters and not worrying about the house must have been a relief for the young woman.

Though Elizabeth wished to visit her aunt and judge her condition for herself, she knew she must take some time to set everything in order. As such, she visited the cook to finalize the menu for the rest of the week, along with any other items the woman wished to mention. They she spoke with the two manservants and the two upstairs maids. It was only once these tasks were concluded that she took herself to her aunt's bedroom.

"Lizzy!" cried Mrs. Gardiner. Or she attempted to exclaim it, for it came out as little more than a croak. The countenance of her dearest aunt shone with perspiration, though the room was not hot, a clear indication she was beset by a fever.

"Oh, Aunt!" exclaimed Elizabeth as she rushed to the bed. "What has happened to you? It has not been that long, and yet you are not the woman I remember from only a few weeks ago."

Mrs. Gardiner smiled in spite of her distress, her voice gravelly when she spoke. "An ague I picked up from somewhere. It is fortunate that neither my children nor my husband have succumbed to it yet."

"Fortunate, indeed," said Elizabeth. "Has the physician come to examine you?"

The snort with which her aunt responded sounded even more guttural due to her condition. "Useless fop," said she. "These gentlemen physicians who will not examine a patient are a useless lot, in my opinion! Mr. Gardiner sent for a surgeon of his acquaintance, and the man was much more thorough. I shall be right as rain in a few days, but until then, he prescribed bed rest."

"Then that is what you shall receive," promised Elizabeth. "I shall manage the house until you are well. There is no need to worry."

"You are a treasure, Lizzy," said Mrs. Gardiner with evident affection. "Then when I begin to recover, we must sit and visit. There have been some intriguing comments in my letters from your family of late, made all the more interesting as you have been derelict yourself in writing."

Her aunt's keen eye, not diminished in any way by her illness, well understood Elizabeth's flush. There was nothing to do but agree. Then, with Elizabeth's encouragement, her aunt lay back against her pillow, and soon her eyes began to droop closed. It seemed the poor woman had kept herself awake by force of will and worry alone. Elizabeth meant to remove that burden from her shoulders.

As was to be expected with the house in a state of disorder—though Elizabeth knew it was his custom regardless—Mr. Gardiner appeared for luncheon. The relief he expressed upon arriving to see it much calmed was expressed in his profuse thanks for Elizabeth's quick arrival. Elizabeth, of course, did not think his gratitude was warranted, and professed herself pleased to assist. There was one matter which she knew must be brought to his attention, and while she did not doubt it would be a matter which would provoke his teasing, she did not shirk from raising it.

"I have reason to believe, Uncle, that I will have a visitor while I am staying with you."

Surprise and curiosity warred for supremacy on her uncle's countenance and he rested his fork, which had been poised near his mouth, on the side of his plate. "A visitor, you say. Tell me, Niece—is this a matter of conjecture, or do you have sure knowledge that some as yet unnamed person will invade my home?"

"Uncle!" exclaimed Elizabeth, laughing at his choice of words. "I do not expect the entirety of the French Army to descend upon your sitting-room!"

"Perhaps not, my dear," said Mr. Gardiner. "But my question remains the same."

"I know he will visit, Uncle. He said he would be in London this week and promised to call on me."

"O ho! Now it is a 'he,' is it? Might I know the name of this mystery gentleman?"

By this time Elizabeth was becoming a little flustered at her uncle's teasing, though she could not quite determine why that should be so. Thus, when she replied, it was by blurting the gentleman's name, rather than calmly stating it.

"Mr. Darcy!"

The fork Mr. Gardiner had taken up again clattered to his plate, and he looked on her with astonishment. "Mr. Darcy?"

"Yes, Uncle," said Elizabeth, drawing in her control and holding to it most firmly. "Mr. Darcy has been staying in Hertfordshire these past weeks visiting the Bingleys."

"He has, has he?" Mr. Gardiner's eyes narrowed. "As I recall, there are currently two Mr. Darcys of which I have knowledge. Both are gentlemen of some standing in society who live at a beautiful estate we saw during our summer tour. Might I ask, Niece, if the gentleman you have promised will soon visit my sitting-room is the younger of these two gentlemen?"

"Of course, you are welcome to ask any questions you like," said Elizabeth, regaining her humor and ability to tease.

Mr. Gardiner's eyes narrowed, prompting Elizabeth's laughter. She held up a hand in surrender and said: "Very well, Uncle. Yes, the Mr. Darcy who will visit is the younger gentleman—the man, I might add, you met when we visited Pemberley."

"Well," said Mr. Gardiner, slumping back in his chair. "This is surely a surprise. Then after all the trouble we have had to get to this point, I also wish to know if he is visiting you with a specific purpose in mind." Elizabeth tried to answer, but her uncle held up his hand. "A gentleman of his position does not visit a woman in this part of town due to mere courtesy. I wish to understand his intentions."

"The gentleman's intentions are the usual ones, Uncle. But I must stress that Mr. Darcy has made no promises, asked nothing of me. Before you think to tease me concerning my *conquest*, as my mother might have put it, Mr. Darcy is not paying court to me."

"Perhaps he is not, Lizzy. But as I said, if he deigns to visit this part of town, his attentions are not of a trivial nature."

"That is correct, sir," whispered Elizabeth.

"Does your father know?"

Elizabeth squirmed a little in her seat and attempted an evasive answer. "Papa has eyes enough to see and wit to understand. There is little doubt he sees what has been happening."

"In other words, Mr. Bennet has no notion that Mr. Darcy is to follow you to town in order to avoid being separated from you." Elizabeth tried to deny it, but Mr. Gardiner only smiled and shook his head. "No, Lizzy. You may protest, but that describes the situation perfectly. There is little doubt your father knows something, but I doubt Mr. Darcy has made his intention to come to town known to him, though when he learns of it, he will understand why.

"It is fortunate, then, that we have heard a little of Mr. Darcy's actions, though the identity of the gentleman was never vouchsafed to us." Mr. Gardiner paused and looked kindly at her. "I suppose the purpose for this conversation is to inquire after my permission."

"Of course," said Elizabeth.

"Then you have it, though I should like to speak to the gentleman myself."

"I believe that may be arranged," replied Elizabeth.

"Good. Then I shall try to arrange it so that I am present when Mr. Darcy comes, though that may be difficult. If I am not home, you may accept him, as long as one of the maids is present as a chaperon. But I would also appreciate your sending Tommy to the warehouse to fetch me — I shall come if I am able."

"I shall, Uncle."

"Excellent!" Mr. Gardiner retrieved his fork and began to eat again. "Then let us not allow this excellent food to go to waste."

"You are returning to London?"

Bingley's voice suggested disbelief, enough to prompt Darcy to laughter. These past days had found Darcy in more of a mood for such merriment, a sentiment he had not really felt in the course of his life. Miss Elizabeth, it seemed, had that effect on him, though from what he had seen of her, the phenomenon was not limited to Darcy himself.

"It is only for a few days, Bingley," replied Darcy. "There are a few matters of business I must look into while I am there. I shall return in no more than a week."

Privately Darcy hoped that the week was enough time for Mrs. Gardiner to recover, for he would be forced to keep his word and return, even if Miss Elizabeth was still required to stay in London. Then again, that may be better, for if he returned together with Miss Elizabeth, it would set tongues wagging in Meryton. Darcy had little concern if he was linked to Miss Elizabeth, a matter which still seemed to have escaped the neighborhood's attention. But he was unsure of her feelings and did not wish her to feel pressured by open gossip.

"I had hoped you would stay for at least two months, my friend," said Bingley.

"Oh, nonsense, Charles!" exclaimed Mrs. Bingley. "Of course, Mr. Darcy must attend to his business. We would not wish to stand in his way of his duties."

"Thank you, Mrs. Bingley," said Darcy, bowing to his host and hostess, who were sitting nearby. "At this time, I would like to thank you for your hospitality. After my business is complete, I shall, of course, return."

"It is no trouble at all, Mr. Darcy," said Mrs. Bingley. "I expect your business will be completed quickly, and you will be brought to us again. Come again at any time, and we shall be happy to have you back."

The knowing grin with which the woman was regarding him suggested Mrs. Bingley knew *exactly* what business was taking him away from them. As the woman did not seem inclined to speak any more on the subject, Darcy allowed it to rest. For Bingley's part, Darcy was certain his friend had not yet made the connection between Miss Elizabeth going to London and his own announcement, though it quite escaped Darcy's understanding how his friend could remain ignorant.

"Very well," said Bingley, though he clearly was still not pleased. "Would you like me to travel with you? If so, I should be happy to oblige you."

As it turned out, Bingley's presence was *not* required, nor wanted, and Darcy was quick to reply. "That is not necessary, Bingley. I dare say you would be much happier here with your friends."

"Very well, then," said Bingley, Darcy thought with some relief. Darcy thought he understood—his attentions to Miss Bennet were growing more pronounced, and as such, London was the last place Bingley wished to be at present.

The next morning—the day after Miss Elizabeth departed for London herself—the Darcy carriage departed from Netherfield. It was an easy journey, no more than four hours. As Darcy was in good humor, the necessity of fitting his long legs into a small vehicle did not bother him as it usually would. There was little doubt many of his friends would have teased him had they known in what direction his thoughts tended, but as it was, he passed the time in pleasant contemplation of the woman in whose company he would soon find himself.

The days after Elizabeth's departure were happy ones for Jane, though she felt the irony of being made happy by her sister's absence. The only matter which was not to her satisfaction was that Mr. Bingley was also absent. But assuming his reason for not attending her was due to some matters of the estate, she found that she could endure his absence. Regardless, Mr. Darcy was in Hertfordshire and Lizzy was in London, and that was a reason to celebrate.

Life was idyllic in those days. The weather remained fine though the calendar showed the approach of the end of September. Many were the times when Jane thought of her sister, thinking that she would love the weather here, frequenting her favorite paths on a daily basis. For Jane's part, she was not nearly the walker her sister was. Jane was happy to stay in the back gardens, to tend to the roses and walk the paths she had known all her life.

The family was happy together. A letter had come from Elizabeth soon after her departure, informing them of her arrival and imparting the information concerning their aunt's condition.

"If Lizzy should have required me to go in her stead, I should have been quite happy to do so," said Mary after her father had read the letter addressed to the family. "But it is good to know that Aunt Gardiner is on the mend."

"Lizzy would not push the responsibility on anyone else," said Thomas, fixing a fond smile on his youngest sister. "Your offer was doomed from the start, Mary, for Lizzy would never have given way."

"Yes, that is so," replied Caroline. "Never let it be said that Elizabeth will not protect those she loves. Then again, the timing of Mr. Gardiner's request *is* unfortunate."

"Actually," replied Mary, "I think a little uncertainty and distance is good. It will certainly do no harm if what I have seen is true."

The rest of the family shared amused grins. The attentions of Mr. Darcy toward Elizabeth had not been missed by anyone in the family. But Jane did not join their merriment, for she had information on the matter which they did not possess.

As the conversation continued, Jane allowed her attention to slip back into that which had dominated her thoughts of late. Not for the first time, Jane wondered if she was right to suspect Mr. Darcy of ulterior motives. It sorely went against the grain for her to think ill of anyone. But Elizabeth was far too important to Jane to treat the matter with anything other than the seriousness it deserved. In the absence of any other information from Elizabeth herself, Jane vowed to remain cautious.

That evening, the family sat down to dinner. It being a family dinner, the seating was allowed to be a little unusual, for though Caroline occupied the mistress's position as was her right, Thomas sat beside her and Mr. Bennet occupied the master's chair. Mr. Bennet, amused as he was by his son's blatant affection for his wife, made no comment, though it could be argued that Thomas should have been next to Mr. Bennet instead.

As they partook of the meal, they spoke of various matters. Thomas and their father discussed some issues of the estate, while Jane and Mary talked of their visit with Charlotte Lucas, who had stopped by Longbourn that morning. It was a family dinner, one which had happened many times over the course of Jane's life. The atmosphere was filled with love and laughter, happiness in the society of those who are dearest.

As dinner drew to a close, Mr. Bennet rose to return to his library as was his wont. But before he departed, he turned and looked directly at Thomas and Caroline, addressing them thus:

"Let me say, Caroline, that I am happy you have fit into our home so seamlessly. I never doubted your competence or desire to please, but you have taken up the reins of the house, and I have not noticed a difference from when my own dear daughters were tasked with the responsibility."

It was not often that Caroline Bennet was rendered abashed, but this appeared to be one of those times. "Thank you, Mr. Bennet. Your words mean much to me."

"You are a good girl." Mr. Bennet paused and grinned at his newest daughter. "But this 'Mr. Bennet' business is nonsense. I understand you refer to your own dear father as Papa, but I would be happy if I could attain the position of Father in your eyes. Mr. Bennet is far too stuffy and implies a distance I would not have between us."

Caroline was recovered from her shyness by now, and she smiled widely, and nodded, acknowledging his request. "Very well, 'Father' it is."

"Then I shall retreat to my library. Should some young man come in a tizzy wishing for the hand of any of my daughters, I shall be at my leisure to receive them."

With a wink, Mr. Bennet left the room, the rest of his family smiling as he passed through the door. The next one to speak was Thomas, who looked at his two sisters and said: "I, on the other hand, am not ready to lose any of my sisters. If you have gentlemen suitors hiding under the sofa, I must ask them to leave."

"For my part," said Mary, laughing at her brother's jest, "I believe there is no reason to worry. For Jane, however . . ."

They all laughed at Jane's embarrassment, and no amount of glaring did any good.

Later, Jane received an unexpected visitor to her room as she was preparing to retire. It was a bittersweet time for her, as it had been ever since her dearest Lizzy had left, for the two young women almost always spent some time in each other's chambers in the evening, speaking of the day or talking of their dearest thoughts and dreams. And yet, should Jane marry Mr. Bingley, as she was increasingly certain would happen before long, such nightly conferences must cease. Thus, it was a decidedly melancholy Jane who granted permission to enter when she heard the knock on the door.

It was Caroline. She appeared uncertain. Rarely having seen her new sister in such an attitude, Jane welcomed her in, looking at her with some concern, until Caroline opened her mouth.

"Jane," said she. "I wish to ask you . . . That is, I must know . . ." Caroline flushed and threw up her hands in frustration. "Oh, I do not know what I wish to say! Or I do know, but it would be much easier if I was speaking to Elizabeth."

"Speaking with Lizzy?" echoed Jane, feeling slightly offended.

"No!" Caroline turned and rushed to Jane's side, grasping her hands and blurting: "That is not what I meant! You are so good, Jane, that I *know* what you will say. But I require honesty. At least, I think I do."

"What is it, Caroline?" asked Jane.

Though Caroline paused for a moment, when she spoke, her words came out in a rush. "Is it true your mother would approve of me?"

"Of course!" exclaimed Jane. "Why do you even ask such a silly thing?"

"I am not silly, Jane!" said Caroline, apparently feeling a little cross. When a giggle escaped Jane's lips at her sister's discomfiture, Caroline's scowl grew that much darker.

"Please, Caroline," said Jane, controlling her mirth, "what has brought this on?"

"Your father's words after dinner," mumbled Caroline. "It is important to me to know that your mother would have approved of me."

It was still a silly worry in Jane's opinion. But she saw that Caroline was serious, and as such, it behooved Jane to take care for her new sister's feelings.

"Let there be no doubt in your mind, Caroline. Of course, my mother would have approved of you. Do you not remember the woman?"

Caroline's lips curled in a smile as Jane intended. "I see you do. Mama wished for the match almost as soon as you came out. There is no doubt she would have approved of you and been proud of the manner in which you have begun to care for her beloved home."

"Thank you, Jane," said Caroline in a soft tone. "I am aware that you think me daft, but I believe I needed to hear that."

Turning to depart as quickly as she entered, Jane watched her sister retreat, though Caroline stopped at the door, turned and looked at her. "I was wrong, Jane. Asking you was perfect—Elizabeth could not have reassured me any better than you have."

Then Caroline departed, leaving Jane feeling warm all over. There was nothing better than having your closest friend as a sister. Then again, perhaps it *was* better to have a close friend become one's *husband*.

The following day saw the return of the Netherfield gentlemen to Longbourn—or at least one of them came, along with his parents. The company was in a fine mood that morning, little knowing matters were about to take a turn for the worst.

As happy as Jane was to see Mr. Bingley, the absence of Mr. Darcy was curious. Then it was alarming. The reason for it soon became clear.

"I should have thought Mr. Darcy would accompany you to Longbourn," said Caroline to her brother. Then her look became sly, and she added: "Then again, perhaps it is not surprising. For there is nothing to draw Mr. Darcy to Longbourn *now*."

The meaning of her words was not lost on anyone, and most of those in the room showed their amusement. For Jane, however, Mr. Darcy's absence *at Longbourn* did not trouble her in the slightest. Quite the opposite.

"If there is nothing to draw him here," said Mr. Bennet, "then I must call myself ill-used. The charms of an old man as a chess opponent must pale in comparison to a pretty young woman, but I had thought Mr. Darcy would make do until my Lizzy returned."

"Perhaps he may have made do," said Mr. Bingley, "but as it happens, he is not here."

"Not here?" asked Jane with a frown. "I do not understand. It is evident he has not accompanied you to Longbourn."

"What I mean is that Darcy is no longer in Hertfordshire," said Mr. Bingley. "In fact, he left for London only the morning after your sister departed. I should imagine he has already been in her company."

A sense of utter horror filled Jane's senses, and she gasped. Mr. Darcy had followed Lizzy to town? The possible implications of the gentleman's actions flooded her mind, and she suddenly could not breathe. Lizzy was in danger, possibly at that very moment!

CHAPTER XVII

Caroline was the first of the company to notice the expression of utter horror which spread over Jane's face. It was so unlike the woman she knew, who could usually be counted on to greet any event in life with calm rationality, that Caroline paused for a moment, unable to speak.

"Jane, dearest, what is wrong?" said Caroline at length, finally finding her tongue.

But Jane did not answer. Her eyes found Caroline's, full panic and distress revealed in them, such as Caroline had never before seen. By this time, others had become aware of the problem.

"Are you ill, Jane?" asked Mary. Reaching out, Mary grasped one of Jane's hands and spoke to her softly. "What is it? Has something happened to distress you?"

"I . . ." managed Jane before trailing off. "I do not know."

Though Caroline was confused at Jane's reply, others were not. In particular, Thomas regarded his sister, suspicion alive on his countenance.

"It seems to me, Jane, you became distressed upon hearing that Darcy is in London. Why could the gentleman's movements be of concern to you?"

Appearing as if she were frozen and unable to move, like the deer caught in the sights of the hunter, Jane only gaped at her brother. A cacophony of voices arose, all wishing to be heard, until a loud voice interrupted them. Mr. Bennet stood and scowled at the company.

"Nothing will be discovered of this matter until we allow Jane to speak." Then turning to his daughter, Mr. Bennet said: "What is this all about, Jane. Thomas's words suggest you fear for Lizzy and that the object of your fear is Mr. Darcy."

"But that is absurd!" exclaimed Mrs. Bingley. "It is obvious that she enjoys his company greatly!"

"While I cannot dispute that, Madam," replied Mr. Bennet, "I do recall some hesitance in Lizzy's manners soon after Mr. Darcy arrived in the neighborhood. Jane? What can you tell us?"

Though Longbourn's eldest daughter was silent for several moments, unable to speak, a peculiar shift in her features and a firmness of her jaw suggested she had come to some decision. Then in a halting, though increasingly confident tone of voice, she began to relate the particulars of her fears.

Caroline listened in silence, though others exclaimed at certain parts of the tale, unable to fathom the tale Jane related to them. Was Darcy a dishonorable man who went about compromising young women? There had never been anything in his behavior which suggested he was capable of such acts. In fact, everything Caroline had seen of him informed her he was a good and upright man, one who had the particular intelligence to understand how much of a gem Caroline's new sister was.

The tale did not take long to relate, concerned as it was with a specific event, but when Jane finished speaking, all was silent for a moment. Thereafter, however, the reactions of the company could not be more disparate. The most vocal among them, however, were her husband and brother, though again, their responses were very different.

"I do not believe it," averred Charles. "Darcy a seducer of women? I have never heard of such a thing."

"I know little of his past, Bingley," said Thomas. His countenance might have been chiseled from stone. "But I do not mean to let this stand. I shall go to London and confront him with it."

Charles's eyes found Thomas and his countenance darkened. "Now wait a moment, Bennet. I cannot believe my friend is any danger to Elizabeth. Have you not watched them these past days?"

"Are you suggesting my sister is lying?" demanded Thomas.

"Of course not!" cried Bingley. "But there must be some misunderstanding. Darcy is not a libertine!"

"Now you sound like Jane," said Caroline, throwing an amused glance at her sister.

It was, unfortunately, an abject failure to diffuse the situation, as Thomas only scowled at her. Into this increasingly tense discussion, Jane's voice tentatively rose again, saying:

"I thought it must be a mistake myself."

"What I wish to know is why Lizzy kept this from us?" Thomas glared at his sister. "Why, for that matter, if you knew of it, did you not speak to me of it?"

"Because Lizzy swore me to silence."

"Surely this is not a matter of which one keeps a confidence!" thundered Thomas.

"Mr. Darcy left soon after. Lizzy thought it unlikely she would meet him again and feared what the damage would be to her reputation should the matter become known."

"Should you not have spoken of it when it became known he would come again?" Thomas was almost growling in frustration at his sister. "It is my duty to protect you all, but I cannot do so if you do not confide in me. Matters such as this may be handled without the facts becoming known to others. You are two of the most sensible girls I have ever met. But in this instant, I must wonder if you are not among the silliest!"

"Perhaps it was because of Elizabeth's fear of this reaction that she stayed silent."

The company well understood Caroline's words, though Thomas glared at her. It achieved Caroline's objective of silencing the argument, at least for the moment, allowing her to use the opportunity to further calm her belligerent husband.

"Let us think of this rationally," said Caroline. "Whatever Mr. Darcy has done in the past—and I do not doubt your account, Jane—I have no indication on Elizabeth's part of any fear of the gentleman. To me, she has seemed easy in his company, especially of late."

Caroline turned to Jane and smiled at her sister. "Is there some reason why you think that Mr. Darcy is an especial danger to your sister at present?"

"Is what I have told you not enough?" demanded Jane.

"That is most unlike you, Jane," interjected Mr. Bennet. "You are more apt to attribute questionable motives to misunderstandings. Why have you become so frightened for your sister in this instance?"

"Does it not seem strange to you all that Mr. Darcy has followed Lizzy to London?" demanded Jane. "Elizabeth has been remarkably closed-mouthed since the gentleman's arrival in Hertfordshire, which is most unlike her. Furthermore, I saw her emerge from a balcony *again* at the last assembly we attended, Mr. Darcy following not long after, and she has not spoken to me since." The indignation propelling Jane's outburst seemed to dissipate, and she wilted. But she managed to make one last comment: "I very much fear that he has made her a most indecent proposal, and she will not tell me, for she fears to upset me."

Thomas's eyes burned with a cold fire, and even Charles seemed to be spoiling for a fight. The elder generation were mostly silent though Mrs. Bingley's countenance suggested doubt. Mary leaned in toward her sister and comforted her, pulling Jane's head to her shoulder and whispering soft words to her.

"Do you suggest Mr. Darcy made Elizabeth an offer of *carte blanche*?" asked Caroline. Though she projected a feeling of calm, inside she was a mass of roiling emotions.

A deepening scowl was Thomas's reply, though he did not speak, likely because he did not trust himself. Jane's head did not rise from Mary's shoulder, though her expression was filled with horror — apparently, she had not considered such a thought

"Surely not," said Mr. Bennet.

"Exactly," said Caroline. "Not only do I not think Mr. Darcy would be so lost to good behavior to offer such a disgusting situation, but I do not think Lizzy would stand for it. Can you imagine her not giving the gentleman a piece of her mind, large enough for him to choke upon it? Would she meekly accept her fate and stay silent to protect us all?"

Caroline's snort informed the rest of the company what she thought of such a suggestion. "Mr. Darcy is a good man — Charles, you have not been deceived in his character. Furthermore, it is apparent he admires Elizabeth. *Admires her!* And Elizabeth has not been reticent or afraid in his company. Quite the opposite."

"I tend to agree with you, Caroline," said Mr. Bennet with a slight smile.

"This cannot be allowed to stand," said Thomas. "We cannot do *nothing*."

"That is not my suggestion, Thomas," said Mr. Bennet. "In fact, I believe there is little to be done but to go to London and confront Mr. Darcy. But we must do it in a matter which does not spawn gossip. Vaulting onto your horse and galloping away to your uncle's home will accomplish just that."

Mr. Bennet's significant look at his son could not be mistaken, and while Thomas scowled, he did not gainsay his father. Furthering the effort to calm him, Caroline took his hand and squeezed it, feeling gratified that he returned the gesture. The look of thanks from Mr. Bennet was as satisfying as his comments concerning her entrance into the house.

"Then I should call for the carriage," said Thomas. "There is no time to lose."

"Tomorrow will be soon enough," said Mr. Bennet. Thomas appeared eager to disagree, but Mr. Bennet shot him a pointed look. "Mr. Gardiner will allow no harm to come to Lizzy. She is safe under his protection."

"That is not guaranteed unless he knows *from what* he is protecting her," snapped Thomas.

"You do your uncle a disservice, Son. There is little impropriety which will escape Edward's notice. There is no danger to your sister at present—I am convinced of it. There is far more danger in rushing off to London to provoke a confrontation. Tomorrow will suffice."

Though he did not like it, Thomas nodded tightly. "Very well. But I shall be among the party that goes to London. I am Lizzy's brother, and I shall not shirk this responsibility."

"And I will accompany you," said Charles. Though he had not spoken much, there was, in his manner, an indignation such that Caroline had rarely seen previously. Her brother was so mild-mannered as to render such outbursts unusual.

"Heaven save us from the fury of a pair of young bucks with protection on their minds," said the elder Mr. Bingley. "I am of mind with Mr. Bennet in this matter. All shall be well."

"We shall go in the Bennet carriage," said Thomas, all but ignoring his father-in-law's comment. "I mean to depart at eight, Bingley. If you mean to join me, then I expect you here a quarter before that hour."

Bingley's tight nod of affirmation spoke to his determination. The rest of the company seemed resigned.

"There are times, Son," said Mr. Bennet, turning to his eldest, "that impatience rules your behavior. Now is not the time to be a hothead—this must be handled in a calm and rational manner." Mr. Bennet's eyes swiveled to Charles. "You are usually more rational than my son when his dander is up. I shall count on you to restrain him."

There was no question of the Bingley party returning to Netherfield that day, so Caroline offered the invitation to stay and dine to her family. But while the decision had been made to go the following day, the discussion of the matter was not over. Little was accomplished that day other than to speak at some length, and there were times when tempers became a little heated because of it.

Throughout the course of the day, it seemed like two camps developed among those present. On one side, Thomas was eager to be off and convinced of Mr. Darcy's perfidy, and he drew Charles along with him, and, at times, even Jane and, to a lesser extent, Mary were pulled into the mayhem. On the other, Mr. Bennet, along with Caroline's parents and Caroline herself, urged calmness and rationality. By the time the hour grew late, the entire company was fatigued by all the debate and ready for dinner. But then Caroline had a thought.

"Mr. Collins is to dine with us today!"

Blurted out as it was in the middle of a lull in the conversation, one not familiar with the gentleman might have thought the comment was apropos of very little. But anyone who was acquainted with Mr. Collins immediately understood the significance.

"This matter must be allowed to rest," said Caroline into the shocked silence. "We all understand Mr. Collins's feelings. I shudder to think of what he might be compelled to do if any hint of these suspicions should reach his ears."

"It may be that my cousin will surprise you," said Mr. Bennet.

But the gentleman did not clarify his statement, falling silent instead. For the next several minutes, the company made several awkward attempts to introduce different topics of conversation into the discussion, with very little success. The matter which had occupied them throughout the day was little inclined to give way to more mundane discussion.

Whether Mr. Collins realized the company was in an odd mood that evening was uncertain. The parson arrived soon after Caroline's exclamation, and he accepted the increase in the company without comment, though she did see him regarding the Bingley party with some interest. For a time, there was little said among them, until Mr. Bennet introduced some matter of the parish and began speaking with Mr. Collins. Then several other conversations began among the others, and while the company never became loud, there was at least the sense of normalcy among them.

As she watched her family, Caroline was struck by a sense of unease. Thomas was still clearly angry, and his conversation with Charles — they had taken themselves to the side of the room, likely to avoid being overheard — was punctuated with clipped hand motions and flashing eyes. To allow Thomas to go to London tomorrow with only Charles for company seemed like a recipe for disaster, especially when his indignation was pulling her brother along in his wake.

"I see you see the same thing as I do."

Startled, Caroline looked up to see Mary regarding her. Caroline had never been close to the youngest Bennet daughter, and while she did not dislike the girl, neither had she much in common with Mary. At times much like her sister, Elizabeth, at times much more serious, Caroline often did not know what to think of her. It seemed Mary was quite serious at that moment and had something to add to the conversation, given her words.

"What, exactly?" asked Caroline. Though she had not meant to be short, the words had been spoken without prior consideration. Mary, however, did not take offense.

"If you will pardon me for saying it," said Mary, "the prospect of your brother and mine traveling to London together to confront Mr. Darcy seems one which is doomed to end badly for all concerned."

"That was my thought as well." Caroline paused while Mary sat beside her, then turned and looked to her new sister curiously. "Do you have a suggestion?"

"If the gentlemen cannot be relied upon, then someone must go with them to ensure their good behavior."

A slow smile spread over Caroline's face as she realized what her sister was suggesting. "I doubt even then they would be restrained."

Mary shrugged. "Perhaps not. But there is a better chance of it than otherwise. They will spend the entire journey working each other up into a greater frenzy, no doubt bringing Lizzy's wrath down on their heads."

The mirth faded from Mary's face and she added: "To tell the truth, I have seen nothing in Lizzy's behavior which suggests that she is afraid of Mr. Darcy or, indeed, that his behavior has been anything other than scrupulously proper. Of course, I refer to *this* visit."

"I cannot disagree," said Caroline.

"Then it falls to us to ensure this situation does not become more uncomfortable for our sister."

The two ladies clasped hands, sealing their agreement. The rest of the time before dinner was spent speaking together in low voices, arranging matters to ensure their sister was protected. Caroline felt better now than she had since Jane had made the shocking revelation. It would all turn out well—of that, Caroline Bennet had faith.

The compulsion to be in Miss Elizabeth Bennet's company was nigh overpowering. Eager though Darcy was, however, he managed to restrain himself. Though he arrived in London the day after Miss Bennet, he allowed the rest of the day to settle himself into the family's Mayfair home, and then spent the next engaged in some small tasks, knowing she was likely still taking the reins of the house in Mrs. Gardiner's convalescence. By the third day, however, he was impatient to see her.

As Mr. Gardiner was her guardian while she was staying with him, Darcy thought it proper to discuss the man's niece with him before calling. As such, he sent his card around the morning of that day. It was a surprise to receive an invitation to dinner in return. Darcy thought about it for several minutes—he was concerned about intruding on the family with Mrs. Gardiner ailing, but the mere existence of the invitation indicated there was no need to worry. Thus, Darcy accepted. While he was made a little more impatient that he would not see Miss Bennet until that evening, knowing he would now see her made his impatience easier to bear.

At the appointed time, Darcy presented himself at the door of what appeared to be a lovely home on Gracechurch Street and was welcomed into the house by a maid. After passing his hat to her, he was directed to Mr. Gardiner's study down the hall. A quick glance in what looked to be the sitting-room as he passed did not reveal the presence of Miss Bennet; as Darcy had suspected, the man wished to speak to him before he was once again admitted to her presence.

"Ah, Mr. Darcy," said Mr. Gardiner, rising from his seat when Darcy opened the door. The older man stepped around his desk, hand extended, which Darcy accepted gratefully. "Please, have a seat. Can I interest you in a brandy?"

"Not at present, I thank you," replied Darcy. "I am grateful you consented to receive me, sir. It must have come as a surprise to hear of me so soon after our meeting at Pemberley."

"Surprise is not the term I might use," replied Mr. Gardiner with a wry smile. "Utter shock might come closer to the truth, but even that seems inadequate."

"I had no notion of it myself."

"But having seen my niece in Hertfordshire, you found yourself helpless before her charms?" The grin with which Mr. Gardiner regarded him betrayed his jesting. "Having long thought much of the charms of *all* my nieces, I can hardly blame you, sir. I assume that the reason for your necessary presence in London is because of hers?"

There was little to be gained from denying it, and Darcy suspected everything to gain from showing Mr. Gardiner how besotted he was with his niece. As such, Darcy decided to be completely open with him.

"The timing of my coming is entirely due to your niece. There were a few matters I saw to when I came to town, but they did were not urgent enough to draw me here otherwise."

Mr. Gardiner laughed. "Excellent! I have always wished for my nieces to attract gentlemen who could not do without them, and I dare say you will do." Then the mirth disappeared, and Mr. Gardiner looked at Darcy with some intensity. "Am I correct in apprehending that you have not neglected to consider your family's reaction to your attentions to my niece?

"There is nothing but a sincere concern in my query, sir," said Mr. Gardiner before Darcy could respond. "Lizzy is a good girl—all of my nieces are—and she is the daughter of a gentleman. Her father, however, is less than half the consequence of yours, and as you can see, she also has ties to trade. It seems this does not bother you—but what of your family?"

"It is a matter I have considered," acknowledged Darcy. "In the end, however, I am content with my decision. Miss Elizabeth will do well in my society, I believe, and while my father and some of my extended family may be disappointed, in the end they will accept her. This is, of course, putting the cart before the horse—I have only just started to pay court to her, and I do not have permission for a formal courtship yet. I have not approached her father."

"Elizabeth's wishes will guide my brother," replied Mr. Gardiner. "Though I do not suppose he will allow the opportunity to sport with you to dissipate without exploiting it."

Darcy laughed. "No, I cannot imagine such a thing."

"Then it is settled. You seem to have my brother's approval, so there is little about which I may complain. As long as there is adequate chaperonage, you may call on Lizzy at any time."

"Thank you, Mr. Gardiner."

"Now, might I interest you in that brandy I suggested?"

"Please," replied Darcy.

At length they were called into the sitting-room where Miss Elizabeth was waiting for their arrival. She arose when they entered, her countenance brightening at the sight of him. For Darcy's part, he could hardly believe his eyes, for though she did not appear to have changed in the short time since he had last seen her, she seemed ever more vibrant, desirable, and beautiful than ever. Perhaps it was nothing more than his perception, or the effect of being separated from her for three days. Perhaps it was not.

"I am enchanted all over again, Miss Bennet," said Darcy stepping forward. He caught her hand up in his and bestowed a kiss on its back for the first time, the thudding of his heart counterpoint to Mr.

Gardiner's snort of amusement. Darcy did not care—he was once again in the company of the best woman in the world.

"It *had* crossed my mind to wonder what had become of you," said Miss Bennet. "Are my attractions so paltry that it takes a man three days to muster up the courage to confront them?"

By her tone one might think she was only teasing, but Darcy was certain it had come about due to her desire to avoid the appearance of embarrassment. Mr. Gardiner laughed at his niece's words, and Miss Bennet arched an eyebrow at him, but Darcy only grinned. Two could play that game after all.

"The only complaint I have concerning your attractions is being overwhelmed by them." Darcy leaned forward and said in a softer tone: "Had I known I would be welcome, I should have come the very hour I arrived in town."

"Perhaps next time you will judge better," replied Miss Bennet.

"Perhaps I will."

In all, it was a pleasant evening. Mrs. Gardiner was still unwell, though apparently on the mend, and did not descend. Thus, Miss Bennet and Mr. Gardiner entertained them. As the evening progressed, however, Darcy noticed that Mr. Gardiner was more engaged in watching them, providing chaperonage as they spoke together about many topics. First on Darcy's mind was when he would be allowed to see Miss Bennet again. It was, therefore, fortunate that the woman herself proposed their next meeting.

"My aunt's housekeeper is to return tomorrow, Mr. Darcy, meaning I shall be more at my leisure. The children have been confined to the house of late, and I thought it would be a treat for them if we were to go to the park tomorrow. Shall you join us on our excursion?"

"Miss Collingford is to join you?" asked her uncle casually. Darcy knew there was nothing casual in the question, for young children could not be appropriate chaperones.

"Of course," replied Elizabeth.

Mr. Gardiner did not reply, instead looking to Darcy, who was of no mind to demur. And, thus, their outing was set for the morrow. While Darcy was of two minds about accompanying children, it would allow him time in Miss Bennet's company.

CHAPTER XVIII

O ne of the perks of possessing a genial and easy temper along with
a gentleman's education was the ability to make friends. When
that was coupled with a handsome countenance, opportunity was
one's constant companion.

On more than one occasion in the past, Fitzwilliam Darcy, the
sanctimonious and detested son of Wickham's patron, had
commented of Wickham's propensity to make friends, without the
ability to keep them. As if Wickham cared what Darcy the prude
thought of him. Friends were all well and good, but Wickham had
never concerned himself with how others perceived him, and if a
friend became offended because of something he did, then so be it. In
the end, the truth of life was that every man needed to look after
himself — especially someone in George Wickham's position.

The situation at the law office was becoming critical. Patterson, that
unimaginative and prejudiced bastard, had been speaking of
Wickham to the partners of late, if the looks he received from Mr.
Mortimer were any indication. Wickham was neither so fast at his
work as any of the clerks, nor so meticulous. There were days when he
simply could not make himself care enough to give any effort to the
work. Cleary, his days at Mortimer and Sons were coming to an end.

What he would do afterwards was a matter of some concern. With no means of keeping himself, Wickham would be forced to return to Pemberley to stay with his patron, and while the thought of living in luxury at that great estate was certainly no hardship, the longer he spent in Mr. Darcy's company, the greater were the chances the old man would discover what Wickham had kept hidden all these years. The house in town was a possibility, but Wickham knew the housekeeper there neither trusted nor liked him, and the butler was little better.

The matter caused him no end of worry as he struggled to complete enough of his tasks to ensure himself continued employment until he decided what was best to be done. It was during these few days that Wickham learned something of interest, which he thought may have the power to change his fortunes.

"The house is occupied?" asked Wickham as he sipped on his ale. The stuff was not the best, but when in distressed circumstances as he was, one must accept what was available.

"Aye, it appears to be so," replied his companion, a man of no consequence whose name Wickham could not even recall. Another benefit of his gentlemanly manners was the ability to obtain information from others in many stations of life. Wickham had always kept a close eye on anything to do with the Darcy family, such that when the house in town was suddenly inhabited at a time it was least expected, the matter would come to his attention.

"Are the whole family in residence?"

"I cannot say," replied the man. He gestured with his mug, which was now empty, and Wickham, flashing him a winsome smile, motioned to the barmaid to refill it. A little ale was effective in loosening many a man's tongue, a strategy Wickham had often found reason to employ.

"I was told nothing more than that the house is occupied again," said the man, his tankard once again full. Then he laughed, a guttural grating sound, which put Wickham's teeth on edge. "The news has gone through several others, so I do not even know if it is true."

"If it had been a more detailed rumor, I might agree," said Wickham thoughtfully. "As it is, a simple rumor such as Darcy house having an occupant suggests truth."

"Maybe," said the man, raising his mug again.

"Thank you for the information," said Wickham, rising to his feet. He dropped a couple of coins on the table to pay for the drinks and sauntered out of the tavern, pausing to pinch the bottom of one of the barmaids on his way out. The way the woman eyed him suggested willingness, should Wickham expend the effort.

But now was not the time for such things. It was not a common occurrence for the Darcy family to be in residence in their London home at this time of year. If his godfather *was* in residence, it would behoove Wickham to make his obeisance to the gentleman in hope of guiding Mr. Darcy to the proper conclusion about Wickham's future. If it was another member of the family, there was a chance Wickham might be able to profit from it. Either way, it would behoove Wickham to discover the truth of the matter, for then he could plan to take advantage of it.

"Why have you decided you wish to go, Caroline? I am well able to handle this matter with your brother's assistance."

"It is precisely because of your ability to *handle* this matter that I believe I should come." Caroline motioned to Jane who stood nearby, also dressed in her traveling clothes. "Jane agrees with me."

Thomas gazed at his wife, apparently attempting to determine if she was telling him the truth. As eager as he had been to set out for London, Caroline knew he was not taking this delay with any measure of appreciation. Charles appeared as impatient to be off as her husband if his shuffling from foot to foot was any indication.

The final member of the immediate family, Mary, stood by, watching with amusement. While it had initially been their plan for Caroline to insert herself into the proposed journey to London, Jane had caught wind of their designs and insisted she be included. Mary, though it was clear she wished to be in London herself, recognized the need for someone to stay behind and manage the house. Furthermore, Jane, being the patient member of the family, was better suited to assist in restraining the gentlemen, though privately Caroline was not certain she possessed the ruthless determination she thought would be required. Either way, Mary was to stay and Caroline and Jane, to go — if they could convince her pigheaded husband.

"Perhaps they wish to be of assistance to Elizabeth," said Charles when Thomas did not immediately respond. "If Darcy has hurt her in any way, she will require the understanding of a woman."

Caroline scowled at her obtuse brother. "It is difficult to comprehend your reaction to this, Charles. A matter of four days ago, Mr. Darcy was the best man of your acquaintance, a man who could do no wrong. And now you suspect him of willingly attempting to hurt Elizabeth."

While Charles had the good grace to appear abashed, Thomas was not affected in the slightest. While he did not speak, he regarded them, and if she did not know him better, Caroline might have wondered if he was attempting to determine if they would seek to prevent him from seeking retribution.

"I believe it would be advisable to include them," rumbled Mr. Bennet's voice.

As one, the company turned to regard the patriarch. It was clear Mr. Bennet felt nothing but amusement over the confrontation playing out before him. The sardonic smile with which he regarded his eldest did not in any way please Thomas, who scowled back at him.

"I might wonder why you do not show more concern for your daughter, sir."

If Mr. Bennet was perturbed at all by his son's statement, it did not show in the widening of his grin. "I merely accept your good wife's interpretation of matters," said Mr. Bennet with a wink at Caroline. "There has been nothing in Darcy's manners which suggest the kind of depravity of which you now seem to have convicted him. Whatever you will find in London will not be what you fear, for Mr. Gardiner would never allow it.

"Take your wife, Thomas, and take Jane too. They will provide a check on your thirst for vengeance. A man who brings his wife to a confrontation is not looking for a fight."

Thomas considered the matter for a few moments before he nodded slowly. "Though I have not the confidence you possess, I have no objection to taking Caroline." A smile lit up his face and Thomas turned to her. "Since you three ladies appear to have planned this between you, I assume you have prepared your trunks accordingly?"

"Of course," replied Caroline, Jane nodding in agreement.

"Very well." Then Thomas glared at them all. "But know this: should I find that Darcy has harmed my sister, no amount of feminine restraint will prevent me from extracting vengeance from his hide. Am I clear?"

What any of them might have said in response would forever remain a mystery, for at that moment the person none of them wished to see entered the room. For a moment, no one could speak, as they all turned to see Mr. Collins, watching them, his stern countenance indicating he had heard something of their discussion. Curiously, however, Mr. Bennet did not appear distressed, though the rest of the company watched the gentleman with horror.

"What is this of Elizabeth?" asked Mr. Collins. "You suspect someone of hurting her?"

"Indeed, they do," said Mr. Bennet, sitting back in his chair, amusement written upon his brow. "Or at least the gentlemen do."

"Mr. Darcy?" demanded Mr. Collins.

At first no one wished to answer his question, but at length, and after much shuffling of feet and glances at each other, Caroline essayed to speak up for the company. She told him, in as brief and soothing a manner as possible, what they had learned of Mr. Darcy's actions from four years ago. Mr. Collins listened with a calmness none of them would have attributed to him. When Caroline finished speaking, the man was silent for several moments, apparently processing what he had been told. And the most curious of all was Mr. Bennet, who watched Mr. Collins as if expecting the man to provide him no end of mirth.

"It *was* improper of Mr. Darcy to have acted in such a manner," said Mr. Collins at length. "But I am surprised you have not seen the truth, Thomas. At least, given what you said, I assume you suspect the gentleman of ulterior motives?"

"I do not see how one could not," said Thomas, though in a tone much less confident than it had been previously. "What, in your estimation, is the truth?"

Mr. Collins shrugged. "I should have thought it obvious to a man who is similarly afflicted, Cousin. Mr. Darcy clearly loves our Elizabeth very much. The actions of a man of four years ago reveal an impulsivity I should not have expected from him, but if he truly meant harm, he could have done it then or any other time in between. The admiration with which he now looks on her cannot be mistaken."

It was clear neither of the younger gentlemen were capable of responding to Mr. Collins's assertions, while Mr. Bennet grinned and uttered a soft "Well done, Mr. Collins" at his cousin. The three women were all astonished that Mr. Collins was accepting this matter with such rationality, given the feelings he had always espoused for Elizabeth.

"You make very good points, Cousin," said Jane, stepping toward him. "It is now left to me to be ashamed that I ever suspected Mr. Darcy, for I am sure we will find Lizzy very well and perhaps even a little annoyed with us when we go to London.

"I *am* curious, however. How do you know this? And what of your feelings for Lizzy?"

"There has never been any indication that my cousin returns my feelings, Jane," said Mr. Collins. "I have long accepted this, though I will own that it has been difficult at times."

Mr. Collins's eyes flicked to where Mr. Bennet sat, and the elder gentleman gave him an encouraging nod. Standing straighter, Mr. Collins's eyes once again found Jane's. "As for the other, it is clear in everything Mr. Darcy does. Why, I myself spoke to him about it after church Sunday last. Mr. Darcy confirmed his interest in Elizabeth without disguise. There is no other interpretation to be had than that he admires her and in a manner which is most proper. In my opinion, Mr. Darcy has repented of his actions and now displays his respect and love for her in the most unabashed fashion. To her loving family, Elizabeth's happiness must be of paramount importance — whatever you do or say, do not forget this fact."

It was a statement so passionate and simple that the rest of the company was caught by Mr. Collins's instinctive understanding. Even Caroline, who had supported the notion of Mr. Darcy's proper interest in Elizabeth, had never put it in so succinct a manner.

"Again, I am embarrassed to have thought otherwise," said Jane. "If I had been a more rational creature, none of this would be happening."

"You show your care for a most beloved sister," replied Mr. Collins. "There is nothing wanting in such clear affection."

"It seems to me," said Mr. Bennet, speaking to them all, "that Mr. Collins's advice is most reasonable. I am happy you revealed the matter to us, Jane, for it is something we should know. I wish we had known it all along. But do not rush to judgment and do not hurry to convict. Mr. Darcy may yet prove himself the besotted suitor, rather than the depraved despoiler of young ladies."

Thomas scowled at his father for speaking so, but Mr. Bennet was not apologetic in any way. Finally, Thomas glanced away, nodding in agreement.

"Then we should depart," came Charles's diffident voice. "We are already a quarter hour past our time."

The statement provoked them to action, and soon the travelers were seen to the carriage by those who were to stay behind. The trunks, little though there were of them, had already been loaded, and the party soon departed. Caroline had been concerned she and Jane would be forced to quell the anger of the gentlemen all the way to the Gardiner townhouse. But Mr. Collins's assertions appeared to have been taken to heart. At least Charles appeared introspective as he peered out the window, occasionally speaking in low tones with Jane. As for Thomas . . .

"All will be well, Husband," said she, grasping Thomas's hand in hers. He would be the difficult one, being naturally more aggressive than Charles. Elizabeth was also his sister, and as such, the protective instinct he felt toward her was immense—though Charles was attached to Elizabeth in much the same way, his was not so close as that of a sibling by blood.

"I hope so, Caroline," said Thomas, squeezing her hand in response. "I very much hope so."

Seeing Mr. Darcy the next day was a revelation, in more ways than one. If Elizabeth were to be honest with herself, she had felt a certain nervousness, one which she had not truly felt in Mr. Darcy's presence before. Even during those days when she had most suspected he might have ulterior motives for seeking her out, Elizabeth had been wary, but never had she been so nervous as she found herself as she waited for him to appear that morning. A few moments of thought did not reveal the reason, but she suspected it was because he had never specifically called on *her*, though he had called at Longbourn aplenty. But this time, it was the avowed purpose of Elizabeth's company which drew him, and while that may have been true in the past, it had never been explicitly stated.

Elizabeth was not a vain woman. Many mornings she had scandalized her maid with a simple knot to tie her hair back, or an old day dress, when more appropriate, flattering options were available. This morning, however, she had surprised her maid—and herself—by taking more than half an hour with her toilette. And while Elizabeth had never considered herself a beauty, the way Mr. Darcy had looked at her the previous day informed her that the gentleman appreciated her looks a great deal.

Whether her efforts were a success, Elizabeth could not quite determine, for Mr. Darcy seemed no more or less appreciative when he arrived. "Miss Bennet," said he, bowing over her hand, "you are a vision. How happy I am to see you today."

"Are you certain you will not regret agreeing to accompany us?" asked she archly. "My cousins, though well-behaved, are rambunctious at times. Will you feel quite safe with us?"

"Quite safe, I believe. My sister is, as you must remember, twelve years my junior. As such, I have experience in dealing with children."

"We shall see how you bear up," replied Elizabeth.

The children were brought in and introduced to the gentleman. The eldest, Jessica, who was ten, gave Mr. Darcy a creditable curtsey, and the boys, Steven and Jeremy, varying degrees of proper bows. The youngest child, a girl of three by the name of Sarah, only ran to Elizabeth, insisting on being carried. When she was ensconced in Elizabeth's arms, Sarah stuck her thumb in her mouth and began sucking it, refusing to do anything other than study Mr. Darcy.

Soon the children were outfitted for their walk, and they exited the house, making their way down the street toward the nearby park, Miss Collingford moving ahead with the elder children while Elizabeth walked behind with Mr. Darcy, still holding Sarah in her arms. It was a pleasant day, even to one who was accustomed to walking much further than the short distance to the park. All might have been carefree, had Elizabeth not noted that Mr. Darcy kept glancing at her, his expression unreadable. It did not appear to be in censure, but Elizabeth, still uncertain as to the gentleman at times, could not imagine what he meant by it. Finally, she determined to ask.

"What is it, Mr. Darcy?" asked she, turning her head to meet his eyes. Sarah protested the action, as it brought her closer to the unknown gentleman, but Elizabeth was not about to give up her question. "Is there something the matter with my appearance?'

Mr. Darcy groaned. "It appears you have caught me, Miss Bennet." He paused and looked away. "Perhaps it might be best to drop the subject?"

By now Elizabeth was grinning, thinking she had caught him in some improper thoughts. It was so rare that a lady possessed an advantage over a gentleman that she was not about to give it up without a fight.

"Nay, Mr. Darcy, I insist on knowing the meaning of your looks."

Caught by surprise, Mr. Darcy's head whipped around, his surprised eyes meeting hers. "Are you certain you wish to know? It may cause you some discomfort."

Elizabeth giggled and arched her brow. "By my estimation, you have been causing me discomfort of some kind since our meeting. You have been caught, and you must now confess. I insist upon it."

"Very well," replied Mr. Darcy. Turning to her, Elizabeth noticed an amusement had appeared in his grin, and she wondered at the wisdom of forcing him to confess. "You see, Miss Elizabeth, there are few images as powerful to a man interested in a woman as the sight of that woman with a child on her hip."

Mr. Darcy looked down at Sarah and gave her a cross-eyed look, which prompted a giggle from the young girl.

"Seeing you with Miss Sarah," continued he, looking back up at

Elizabeth, "has given me an image to keep in mind, one which informs me what you might look like with *our* child on your hip. It is most tantalizing."

Rendered speechless, Elizabeth gawked at the gentleman who appeared pleased at having discomfited her. It was the sight of his enjoyment which saved her from excessive embarrassment.

"It seems to me, Mr. Darcy," said she in a frosty tone, "that you are always having improper thoughts for me. I wonder if you have ever had any which are *proper*."

"At times, I wonder myself," replied Mr. Darcy. "But at least you must have no doubt as to my interest. I *will* make you my wife. If there exists any way of convincing you, I will do it."

It was fortunate for Elizabeth's equilibrium that they soon arrived at the park. These little demonstrations of Mr. Darcy's regard were thrilling, but they were also a little disconcerting. How should she respond to his overtures? Throwing herself into his arms was impossible though a portion of Elizabeth's brain urged her to do just that. In the end, she decided to ignore it, though there was no ignoring the man himself.

The children, eager to run and burn off energy, set to it with a will when they reached the grassy surface. Even Jessica, who tried to appear grown and mature, chased after her brothers and was chased in her turn. Sarah, seeing her siblings at their play, wriggled free, and for some moments, the four children ran with abandon.

Then the children remembered the toys they brought and clamored for Elizabeth to release them. From a bag Miss Collingford carried, two kites were produced and quickly assembled. As the day held a hint of wind, without being too blustery, it was deemed the perfect day for the flying of kites. The string was soon unraveled and the kites, prepared.

Mr. Darcy then took the lead, showing he had indulged in the same activity many times as a child, showing the boys how the kite should be positioned and hoisted up into the air. It took a few tries, but soon the kites were flying, the two boys standing with a careful grip on the end of their strings, while Jessica waited beside them for her turn. Sarah, never having seen them before, stayed in Miss Collingford's arms, but Elizabeth realized she never took her eyes from the flying objects over her head.

"Pull against the string, Steven," instructed Mr. Darcy, keeping a close eye on the boy.

"Mine does not want to fly," said Jeremy, drawing the gentleman's attention back to him.

"A little more wind would actually be best," said Mr. Darcy to the boy. "But today will do. Follow me, and we will urge it higher into the air."

That said, Mr. Darcy took off jogging, urging the boys to follow him, which they did with alacrity, Jessica trailing along behind them. True to the gentleman's promise, the kites soared higher in the air, firmly caught in the grip of the current which did not blow nearer the earth.

The children took turns, their disagreements expertly negotiated by Mr. Darcy to ensure fairness, and all had fun. And as she watched them, Elizabeth was struck by how natural Mr. Darcy's manners were when he played with them, how he watched and instructed and nurtured their understanding. The feeling of respect and regard for this man rose within her breast, and Elizabeth thought she understood something of the feelings he related of seeing her with Sarah. Should she accept him, would they someday engage in similar activities with their own children? The thought made Elizabeth feel warm all over.

When their time at the park had elapsed, Elizabeth was surprised that the children did not complain about their return to the house, as they often had before. Apparently, the benefits of using their seemingly boundless wells of energy had its uses. The kites were once again stowed in the bag Miss Collingford carried, and soon they were on their way from the park. As they passed the entrance, however, they came upon a bench, upon which sat an elderly woman, who smiled at them as they passed.

"Such a wonderful, handsome family you are," said she. A look into her eyes showed they were slightly rheumy, suggesting that she could not quite make out their faces. "I cannot ever remember seeing one more handsome. Thank you for giving an old woman such entertainment, for I have watched you as you played."

"Thank you," said Mr. Darcy smoothly, though the look he cast at Elizabeth spoke volumes. "Do you require assistance returning to your home?"

"Oh, no," replied the woman. "I am quite well, for I live just down the street. See to your family, sir. I shall hope to see you here again."

Elizabeth could feel her face burning in mortification, though underneath she felt more than a hint of exhilaration. For Mr. Darcy's part, though he continued to glance at her, he did not speak again, which was a merciful reprieve for Elizabeth's sensibilities. Miss Collingford, walking ahead of them, seemed amused, if the shaking of her shoulders was any indication. But the woman did not say anything, so Elizabeth decided it would be best to remain silent herself.

Their return to the house was greeted with a surprise, for a familiar carriage was drawn up before the Gardiners' front door. "Papa?" asked Elizabeth, shocked at seeing it standing there.

"This is your father's carriage?"

"It is," replied Elizabeth. "But I cannot imagine what might have brought him here without any word."

They gained the house with haste, putting the children in the care of the nurse while Elizabeth hurried to the sitting-room, all manner of bad news alive in her mind. When she opened the door, she was doubly surprised to see Jane and Caroline sitting together on a sofa, while Mr. Bingley stood by the mantle and Thomas paced the floor in front of them.

The two parties looked on each other with astonishment at the sight of the other, and for a moment nothing was said. Then Thomas broke the silence, stepping forward and directing a scowl at Mr. Darcy.

"Remove yourself from my sister's person and explain yourself, sir."

CHAPTER XIX

"*I* beg your pardon?"

It was a reflexive response, one given without thought in the shock of the moment. In the back of his mind, however, a voice told Darcy his past actions with respect to Miss Elizabeth Bennet were about to come home to roost. Though he had harbored some hope the matter would never be known to anyone else, it seemed that hope had been in vain.

"Are you hard of hearing, Mr. Darcy?" hissed Bennet, his countenance most unpleasant. "Step away from my sister."

Without waiting for a response, Bennet turned his attention to his sister and grasped her hand gently, but firmly, and pulled her away. Darcy felt instantly bereft of her presence.

"Lizzy, come and sit with your sisters," said Bennet, his tone such that it could not be disobeyed. At least, if one was not a young woman of the stubbornness of Miss Elizabeth Bennet.

"But, Thomas—"

"Not now, Lizzy." While Mr. Bennet's tone was not harsh, it was firm. "There is a matter of which we must speak. I must insist upon it."

The look Miss Elizabeth gave her brother was not pleased in the slightest, but she allowed herself to be led to the sofa. Miss Bennet and

Mrs. Bennet rose to greet her, embracing her and ensuring themselves of her wellbeing before settling her between them. The arrangement was a blatant attempt to ensure she was protected, and while Darcy did not note anything of censure in either woman's countenance, it was clear their sister's peace of mind was their primary concern.

"Thomas," said Bingley, approaching his brother and laying a hand on his arm. "Remember of what we spoke in the carriage. This is not a time to lose your temper and do or say something you may regret."

"Trust me, Bingley," was Bennet's only response.

Then he turned to Mr. Darcy, his mouth set in a firm line. A pause ensued, suggesting he was either considering his words or forcing himself to refrain from voicing whatever angry thoughts rolled around in his mind. In the end, knowing to what this interview would relate, Darcy decided it was best to take the initiative.

"Given your arrival and your obvious anger, might I infer that you have heard of what happened between myself and Miss Elizabeth the night of our first meeting?"

"You may," snapped Bennet. "Though I do not know what possessed Jane to keep it from us—nor why Elizabeth would insist upon silence—the matter is now known to us. I trust you understand what you might have done to Elizabeth's reputation had your actions become known."

"Thomas—" protested Miss Elizabeth again, but this time it was Darcy who interrupted her.

"There is every reason for me to answer your brother's question, Miss Elizabeth. I behaved abominably—his response is not unreasonable." Then turning to Bennet, Darcy said: "I am well aware of the potential consequences of my actions, sir."

"Are you?" Bennet glared at him with the heat of a bonfire. "Lizzy may have been seen to be compromised, our family might have suffered. She was a girl of naught but sixteen! You call yourself a gentleman, and yet you importuned her so abominably?"

"I can offer no defense for my actions," said Darcy. "While I do not attempt to defend myself, if the matter had become known at any time, I would have fulfilled my obligations as a gentleman."

"Which is why I did not *want* it to become known," said Miss Elizabeth. She turned to look at Jane. "You knew my wishes, Jane. Why did you bring the matter up now, of all times?"

"Did I not inform you I would speak to Papa if I was concerned for your safety?" Miss Elizabeth was taken aback, but Miss Bennet did not allow her to speak again. "I was worried, Lizzy! It seemed to me you were easier with Mr. Darcy, but you did not speak to me. Then I saw you and Mr. Darcy emerging from the same balcony at the last assembly, and you came to London and Mr. Darcy followed after. What was I to think?"

Miss Elizabeth's mouth worked, but no sound came out. Then she gave a little cry and embraced her sister. "Oh, Jane, I am so sorry! It never crossed my mind to think of your feelings. I was not certain of my own, so I stayed silent!"

"You owe me no apology, Sister dearest. But I am curious what has happened, and why Mr. Darcy followed you to London."

"The reason I followed your sister to London, Miss Bennet," said Darcy, "is due to my regard for her. Though I have made a hash of everything, I have come to the realization that your sister is the best of women." Darcy smiled at Elizabeth, who returned it from the circle of her sister's arms. "It is my intention to court her and win her for my wife."

It seemed Darcy had managed to provoke Bennet's respect, for the man looked at him, a sense of appraisal about him. Bingley, who had remained silent, did not respond verbally, but he nodded at Darcy, clearly pleased with what he was hearing.

"See, Thomas," said Mrs. Bennet, gazing at her husband with fond exasperation, "I told you how it would be. Did I not say from the start that Mr. Darcy admired our Lizzy?"

"Perhaps you did," replied Bennet. "But we could not remain idle when Jane informed us of these matters."

"Of course, you could not. But now that we have Mr. Darcy's assurances of his intentions, coupled with the clear evidence that Elizabeth has not been harmed in any way, shall we not take a less confrontational approach?"

It was clear that the man in Bennet wished to further display his displeasure and ensure his intention to protect his sister was well understood. But he subsided with a curt nod and found a nearby chair. Darcy had not mistaken the man's actions, and as such, could not say he had not understood. But as Darcy had vowed to himself that he would spend the rest of his life atoning for his lack of judgment, he decided it did not signify.

"You thought because of Mr. Darcy's following me to town that he had come to . . . what exactly, Jane?"

The crimson of Miss Bennet's countenance told Darcy exactly what she had suspected. That such a lady as she, who had always been spoken of in the most glowing terms by both Bingley and Miss

Elizabeth, should harbor such thoughts must have been difficult to bear.

"There is little I can say in my defense," said she. "It is clear that I read the situation all wrong, and for that, I apologize."

"No apology is necessary, Jane," said Miss Elizabeth, "for it is my fault for not speaking of my new understanding of Mr. Darcy's character."

The way Miss Elizabeth's eyes rested on Darcy brought him the greatest of pleasure. The gesture was not missed by Mrs. Bennet, who laughed and exclaimed: "For you to have come to such an understanding, the gentleman must have been *most* persuasive."

"That is hardly an appropriate comment, given the situation," said Bennet. The wide smile his wife returned suggested she was not at all chastened by his words. "What I would like to know," said Bennet, directing his attention back to Darcy and his sister, "is how this all came about."

Thus, it fell to the two in question to relate what had happened between them these past few days. Darcy, being the naturally more reticent, allowed Miss Elizabeth to carry the bulk of the response, though he added his own thoughts when he felt it necessary. Their conversation on the balcony, along with an explanation of their growing attachment since, was offered, and Darcy was gratified to see that it was being accepted. Perhaps he had not completely redeemed himself, but it seemed it was now possible.

"It appears as if Father was correct," said Bennet with a shaken head. "Not to mention Collins."

Miss Elizabeth gasped. "William knows of what happened between us?"

"Yes, he does," replied Bennet, this time looking at his sister with open amusement. "He came upon us as we were discussing the matter this morning. I feel no compunction in pointing out that I was shocked at his response."

"As were we all," said his wife *sotto voce*.

Clearly mystified, Miss Elizabeth demanded to know of what they spoke. It was Bingley who responded.

"Your cousin was Darcy's staunchest supporter, Miss Elizabeth. When the matter was made known to him, he acknowledged Darcy's improper behavior, but he nevertheless refused to be moved in his opinion of his trustworthiness. None of us could account for it."

As he listened to his friend's account, a grin spread over Darcy's face, sufficient to draw the attention of more than one of the company.

"It is, perhaps, not so surprising to me as it was to all of you."

Darcy laughed when more than one countenance became flinty, demanding he explain himself. "On Sunday last, Mr. Collins detained me after church, insisting he had seen my interest in his cousin and demanding I confirm my intentions were honorable. When I gave him that assurance, he was most gracious in his thanks and allowed me to depart without further words."

"That is what Father was on about!" exclaimed Bennet. "He knew of the conversation between you and insisted Collins would not be a problem."

"From all I am hearing," said Darcy slowly, "might I assume Mr. Collins possesses a partiality for Miss Elizabeth? Mr. Bennet alluded to it, but he was not explicit as to the details."

The mirth his comment provoked must be the result of inside knowledge of the situation. Miss Elizabeth glared at her relations and undertook the task of explaining the family's history with the gentleman, particularly concerning his feelings for Elizabeth herself. As he had stated to them all, Darcy did not find the knowledge that Mr. Collins was partial to Miss Elizabeth a surprise—Darcy himself had fallen under her spell immediately, and she, a girl of only sixteen!

"It seems to me," drawled Bingley as Miss Elizabeth's explanation concluded, "my friend is relieved he shall not be required to vie with Mr. Collins for Miss Elizabeth's favor. And well he might, for I have no notion who would emerge the victor in such a competition."

The jest struck the rest of the company as highly amusing, and they released their mirth as might be expected in such a situation. Darcy attempted a glare at Bingley, but it was ineffectual, to say the least.

"According to my father," said Bennet, "it seems unlikely Collins will be a problem." He turned to look at Miss Elizabeth. "That should come as a relief to you, Sister. I know how the matter has concerned you."

"There is nothing the matter with William," said Miss Elizabeth, a fond note in her voice. "He is perfectly amiable. But I have long known we would not suit. While he may never have confessed it, I am certain he understands this as well."

"That is all very well," said Bennet, turning back to Darcy. "It seems you have begun to make amends, sir, and for that I am grateful. I had no desire to call you out, though I would have done it if I had not been satisfied."

"Then let us all be grateful," replied Darcy. "Many outcomes are possible when one is engaged in a duel, whether the combatants intend excessive harm or not."

Bennet grunted and spoke again. "What I am most concerned about is your family. We all understand you are of a far more elevated level of society, and I am concerned Lizzy will face censure when your relations learn of your attentions to her. Can you give me some assurance that she will be protected?"

Darcy was warmed by her brother's concern, even while he was exasperated at being asked this question yet again.

"This is the third time I have been asked that question, Bennet," said Darcy, glancing at Miss Elizabeth. "The first time was by your sister and the second, your uncle. It seems you have the impression my family is naught but a collection of elitists, disdaining all those who do not inhabit the same sphere."

"It is a valid concern," protested Bennet.

"Perhaps it is," replied Darcy. "But let me answer once again, so there may be no misunderstanding. My uncle is an earl, yes, but he is quite unpretentious, and his family is largely the same. This includes my mother. I am convinced my sister will love Miss Elizabeth, grateful to have a sister of her own.

"The only one who will protest my choice is my father, who does espouse some hopes for my future. While my father will not like my choice, he will not disparage your sister, and in the end, he will accept it."

"I have met Darcy's family," added Bingley helpfully. "It is as Darcy stated. His cousin Colonel Fitzwilliam is among the best of men, and his uncle was welcoming to me when I met him."

"A friend is much different from a potential wife," observed Bennet.

"Please allow me my understanding of this matter," said Darcy. "There is much less likelihood of my uncle protesting than my father. In the end, it matters little, for if she will have me, my choice is made."

Bennet regarded him with appraisal for several moments before he nodded slowly. "Very well, then. I will respect my sister's choice, and I expect you to do so as well. If she decides against you, you must desist."

"Of course," said Darcy, though the thought caused his stomach to tie into knots.

"Furthermore," said Bennet, his tone even sterner, "the improprieties of the past will not be repeated. Every interaction must be conducted with the utmost decorum."

The man's stern gaze found Miss Elizabeth. "That goes for you too,

Lizzy. I know your character, and I would not presume to suppose you would act improperly. But I well know the temptations of growing desire and regard. Please do not give your poor elder brother grey hair before his time."

While they laughed, no one was inclined to tease him. As it was, Darcy agreed with him wholeheartedly. He did not miss the fact that her brother was not convinced—neither of his intentions nor of his general worth as a gentleman. Eager as he was to have good relations with this man in the future, Darcy knew he would be required to prove himself.

Mr. Gardiner returned to his house that evening to find there were more occupants than there were when he left it that morning. His expressed surprise was short-lived, for he was happy to see his family.

"Mrs. Gardiner is on the mend," replied he when asked. "It will not be much longer, I suspect, before she will join us after dinner for the evening, though her full recovery will take a little longer." Mr. Gardiner paused and peered at them all, a slight frown showing his thoughts. "It *is* curious you are here now when I had no word whatsoever of your coming."

Though his meaning was clearly understood, Elizabeth had pleaded with them all to keep the matter from Mr. Gardiner's attention. Already feeling more than a little shame due to her lack of trust in her family, she did not wish Mr. Gardiner to be distrustful of Mr. Darcy when the men were clearly becoming friends.

"It was a whim, Gardiner, and nothing more," said Thomas smoothly. "Caroline and I do not mean to impose upon your hospitality for long, as we mean to return to Hertfordshire tomorrow. If you are amenable to hosting Jane for a few days, she has decided she wishes to stay with Lizzy."

"Of course," said Mr. Gardiner. Elizabeth suspected her uncle realized he was not being told everything, but he did not seem inclined to push the matter. "Jane is always welcome to stay, and I dare say Elizabeth might like the assistance, though, as I said, I suspect my wife will be back on her feet soon. But what of you, Bingley?"

"It is my intention to stay as well," replied Mr. Bingley. "But I shall not trespass on your kindness—I can simply retire to the family townhouse while I am here."

"There is no need to open your townhouse, Bingley," said Mr. Darcy. "You are more than welcome to stay with me at my house."

"That is kind of you, Darcy," said Mr. Bingley. "I shall take you up on the offer."

Soon after, the company was called to the dining room. Mr. Gardiner invited them in, a wryness in his voice which spoke to his bemusement at having all the extra guests for dinner. They were a merry party, their host not having seen his nephew and new niece since their recent wedding. As such, he was eager to hear of their adventures in Ramsgate, such as they were, and the newlyweds were not at all averse to sharing the accounts of their doings.

As was common in such situations, particularly when she had heard these tales before, Elizabeth allowed her attention to wander. It would have been no surprise to any of them to learn that her thoughts turned to the gentleman sitting next to her as was his right as the highest ranked of the gentleman visitors present.

It seemed to Elizabeth that Mr. Darcy was taking pains to come to know her brother, who in turn appeared willing to allow the gentleman the benefit of the doubt. Strange though it was, for she had thought them well on their way toward friendly relations when they had lately become acquainted, now it seemed they were each careful around the other. Whether this was because of Mr. Darcy's caution or any distrust Thomas still harbored, Elizabeth could not say. Regardless, she was grateful they were taking such care to get on with each other, for she knew it was for her sake.

Every word which passed from Mr. Darcy's mouth, Elizabeth heard, and she was thrilled at the gentleman's intelligence. Even more, however, she was happy to be the recipient of his deference, for it was clear that she was the most important person in the room to the gentleman. And was that not what every woman wished? To be of utmost significance to the gentleman who paid her the compliment of his attentions? It made her feel warm inside; Elizabeth could not determine if this feeling was love, but she was more kindly disposed toward the gentleman than ever before.

"I wish to offer you my apologies," said Jane when they had retired to the parlor after dinner. Though Elizabeth had not attempted to sit aloof from the other members of the family, she found herself alone with Jane, situated on a pair of chairs slightly separated from the rest.

"If anyone deserves to apologize," said Elizabeth, "I believe it would be me. I should have told you of my changed opinion of Mr. Darcy and his attempts to make amends."

"Perhaps you should have," said Jane. "But no one should be forced to share the innermost contents of their heart if they wish to keep it private. I . . ." Jane paused, gathering her composure. "I saw what was happening between you, but I misinterpreted it, as I still suspected Mr. Darcy."

"It is understandable, Jane. Had I taken you into my confidence again, none of this would have happened."

"Perchance it would not have." Jane paused and shook her head in frustration. "It is not my way to be suspicious of others, as you well know. You have often told me to take care of others until I know of their motives. But watching Mr. Darcy with as much suspicion as I did is not like me. It went sorely against the grain."

"Jane," said Elizabeth, looking her sister in the eye and forcing her to do the same. "I do not wish you to change, for you are exactly how you should be. A little suspicion is good, of course, and your suspicions of Mr. Darcy were just, for I did not give you a reason to discard them. I repeat: there is nothing for which you must apologize. Your care of me was, as always, exceptional. In the future, I shall attempt to avoid taking your feelings for granted."

It was apparent Jane was still not reconciled to her behavior. Elizabeth, wishing her sister to forget the past, embraced her and held her close. "Let us leave this disagreeable subject, Jane, for I do not wish to cast blame."

"I agree. But there is one large problem with Mr. Darcy's interest in you, Lizzy."

Elizabeth pulled back and looked at her sister with curiosity, noting that Jane wore a teasing smile, one which was more often seen on Elizabeth's own countenance. Apparently, her desire to tease Elizabeth was strong, for she took Elizabeth's questioning glance as an invitation to continue.

"The problem is Mr. Darcy's estate is in Derbyshire. When you marry, you shall be situated at such a distance as to make frequent visits difficult. I am not ready to lose you to the north, Sister."

"Then perhaps you will not be required to," said Elizabeth with a blush. "I am not engaged."

"From what I see, dearest Lizzy," said Jane, leaning in close to kiss her forehead, "I suspect that condition will not persist for long."

At that moment Elizabeth caught sight of Mr. Darcy watching them from across the room. The tender smile he gave her caused her breath to catch in her throat. Perchance Jane was correct. Elizabeth was coming to believe she wished for such an eventuality to come to pass.

CHAPTER XX

"Can you not make these nags of yours go any faster?"

The coachman on the driver's seat scowled back at Wickham, and his answer was uncompromising. "If you think you can walk there faster, you are welcome to try it."

Wickham just waved the man on, not eager to get into a debate with an utter dullard. After two days riding post from London, he was tired and grumpy, and the only thing that kept him going was the thought of the mayhem which would ensue when he arrived. The very thought of it put a smile on Wickham's face, one he had not had in quite some time.

Perhaps it had been a precipitous move to announce his intention to leave Mortimer and Sons, but it had likely turned out for the best. Not only was Wickham unable to withstand another moment in the sanctimonious Mr. Patterson's company without planting a facer on him, but his time had been limited, regardless.

"Leaving, are you?" Patterson had said when Wickham told him his decision. "You certainly possess a flair for timing, Wickham. I would not have thought you had it in you."

"Timing?" had been Wickham's response. "Do you speak of something in particular?"

The question had prompted Patterson's laughter. "Let us simply say that your performance has been abysmal, and the consensus was that you are not suited for the law." The man then looked at Wickham with some appraisal, saying: "Have you found another position?"

"Let us simply say that certain other opportunities have come to my attention," said Wickham, echoing Patterson's turn of phrase, "which render this position redundant."

"Then we shall leave it at that, for I do not desire to know more. You know where your desk and the door are—when you have gathered your personal effects, you may leave. I will return with your pay. Then our association may be at an end."

As it was, Wickham had little to gather, never having considered that dingy little office anything other than the prison it was. When, a few moments later, Patterson returned with his remaining pay, Wickham tipped his cap and stepped quickly from the room, hoping fervently he never had occasion to see it again. And as he walked down the street, the coins jingling in his pocket, there was a bounce in his step, regardless of the sorry state of his finances. There were new opportunities on the horizon, ones he felt certain would bear fruit.

As the carriage rumbled on down the road leading to Pemberley, he considered the opportunity that now presented itself, the temptation to rub his hands in anticipation nigh overpowering. The news that Darcy had been resident in the family home in London had been positively providential. For not only had Wickham discovered what his former friend was doing, but with whom.

If the knowledge of Darcy's presence had been providential, what he had learned next was no less than a gift from God. Though difficult, Wickham had managed to obtain a little time to himself when offering to deliver an important folder of papers to a client. When that had been completed, Wickham had hurried over to Darcy's house, just in time to see the man himself leaving in the Darcy carriage. The quick hail of a hackney had provided the means to follow him across town to his destination.

There, Wickham had witnessed Darcy in the company of a young woman and a group of children. A young woman! Had Wickham not seen it for himself, he would not have thought the man had it in him. A cold fish such as Darcy was destined to make a marriage to some heiress even colder than himself, such that the begetting of heirs would have been a serious problem. That the woman was comely and apparently lively, from what Wickham could see, had made the matter even more surprising. As it was, the time Wickham spent watching them had almost resulted in his being dismissed from his position that very afternoon.

Sensing a possibility for profit, Wickham had asked into the young woman and had been disappointed to discover that she was, indeed, a gentleman's daughter from some estate in Hertfordshire. Her father's status was not exceptional, though their property was respectable enough, from what Wickham had gleaned. But certainly not high enough for his patron, who expected his son to make a spectacular match, one of no less consequence than what he had managed himself.

But the most delicious aspect of it all was what he had discovered after. It was the final piece of the puzzle to a circumstance which had the potential to pay handsome dividends.

"The uncle is a man of trade?" asked Wickham of his investigator, the incredulous note in his voice making it go ever higher.

"A Mr. Gardiner by name," said the man he had hired to look into their situations. In truth, Wickham did not truly possess the means for such an expense and Mr. Sykes, as he called himself, was rough and dirty and of suspect dependability. But Wickham *needed* that information and was willing to do whatever it took to gain it.

"The business is a prosperous one," grunted Sykes. "He makes several thousand a year, by all accounts."

"And this Miss Bennet," said Wickham. "What are her circumstances?"

Sykes shrugged and scratched himself under his coat. "The daughter of a gentleman for certain. Beyond that I cannot tell you much. Stays with him periodically, decent dowry, her father has an estate in Hertfordshire." Sykes grinned, the gaps between his missing teeth and the smell of his fetid breath making Wickham queasy. "She is worth plucking for a gentleman in your position. You could live the high life!"

While Wickham might, under other circumstances, have considered it, in this case the information was of much more worth to him than the girl. Stealing the girl Darcy was mooning over would fire a satisfying dart right at his heart, and if her dowry was as substantial as he suspected, it would carry Wickham far. But there was the bigger picture to consider, and Wickham thought there were several ways the information could be used.

"I can help you along, if you like."

Wickham turned to look at the man, noting the light of insanity shining in his eyes. This man was the dregs of society, a leach who preyed on others for nothing more than a copper. Fortunately, he was not the sort with whom Wickham usually associated, and he had no intention of continuing to do so since their business was complete.

"The matter requires a gentle touch," said Wickham. "I shall not require your services any longer. Here is something for your trouble."

Coins exchanged hands and Sykes departed, though not without a reproachful look. No doubt the man wished to kidnap the young woman for Wickham and have the first chance at her, something Wickham would not allow. While he was uncertain exactly how his plans would mature, Wickham was not about to allow a dirty ruffian like Sykes to take what was rightfully his.

Cresting a rise in the road, Wickham could see Pemberley lying in the valley before him, the waters of the lake which lay in front of her doors sparkling like a curtain of rippling diamonds. Eagerly, Wickham gazed down upon the estate, able to feel the power of the place, the great wealth which drove it. It was said that one should not covet that which was possessed by one's neighbor. But perhaps those who penned such philosophies had not been brought up in the shadows of such riches. Pemberley was a symbol of all the wealth in the world held by comparatively few men. Wickham was determined to obtain some of that wealth for himself.

The entrance soon loomed before him, and as Wickham looked on, the figure of the elder Mr. Darcy appeared. The old man's countenance was unreadable, but Wickham thought surely he must be annoyed by Wickham's sudden appearance and, even more, the fact that he had left the position the man himself had procured. At once Wickham fell into the role he had perfected over the years, one of pleasant amiability, coupled with just a hint of humor, which he knew would garner Mr. Darcy's favor with little effort on Wickham's part.

"Wickham," greeted Mr. Darcy as he stepped down from the coach. "I was surprised to receive your letter. I thought the position was a good one for you."

"There was nothing wrong with the position, sir," said Wickham in his usually easy tone. "It is merely that it did not suit me. It was best for all concerned for me to resign."

Mr. Darcy grunted as he led the way up the stairs and into the interior of the house. As Wickham looked about the great edifice, unchanged from the last time he had seen it, he had the sense of coming home. Yes, this visit might prove to be profitable, indeed.

"Perhaps I shall write to them. If you have been treated in any way insufficiently, Mortimer shall not escape my wrath."

"It is best to let the matter rest," said Wickham. "Our parting was mutual, and I do not regret it."

"Then what of your occupation? You must have something with which to support yourself."

"There are a few situations I have my eye on," replied Wickham, the lie coming easily. "I am not concerned, Mr. Darcy. Do not worry for me, for I shall be well."

The look his patron bestowed upon him was piercing, and Wickham was instantly made uncomfortable by it. As the man's favorite, he had rarely looked upon him in such a fashion.

"Then should you not be in London seeing about obtaining one of them?"

Not until you see reason, thought Wickham viciously. Out loud he said: "There is some time yet." Pausing, Wickham directed a winsome smile at his patron. "I hope you will not be disappointed with me if I wished to visit with you for a short time. You are all like family to me — the only family with which I am blessed."

That last bit of flattery did the trick, for Mr. Darcy's countenance softened and he slapped Wickham on the back. "Of course, Wickham. You know you are welcome here at any time you are at liberty to visit."

"Thank you, sir," replied Wickham.

Mr. Darcy handed him to the care of Harper, Pemberley's butler, and he was conveyed to the room he usually occupied when in residence. It was not in the family apartments as Wickham would have preferred, but it was near the end of the guest wing nearby, allowing him the illusion of membership into the Pemberley family. As they walked, the butler scowled when he thought Wickham was not looking, and Wickham knew he would face the same disapproval from Reynolds, the family's long-time housekeeper. Both had been with the family long enough to remember some of Wickham's escapades with the maids and his disagreements with the heir. Wickham did not care for their disapproval — let them glare. He had no interest in maids at present, for he could not be turned from his goal.

When the family gathered for dinner, Wickham joined them, using every ounce of his charm he could muster. Lady Anne, though polite, had always been rather distant from him, and Georgiana, though shy and yet a young girl, had always seen him as something of an older brother. They both greeted him with restraint, after which he paid his compliments and then attempted to charm them. Success, in their cases, was not necessary, though the prospect of Georgiana's dowry still played in the back of his head. Perhaps he could find some way to be alone with her to begin undoing whatever her brother had assuredly told her of him. It would be slow going, but in the end it may very well be worth it.

For a time, conversation at the dinner table was almost banal in nature, which suited Wickham's purpose quite well. The news he had come to share would have much more impact if delivered in the face of such trivial concerns. Mr. Darcy spoke of some repairs he was making to one of the tenant cottages, while his wife mentioned some tasks she was undertaking to assist the family. Though Wickham was impatient to share what he knew, he controlled himself, forcing himself to wait for the right moment.

"I received a letter from William this morning," said Georgiana. Behind his mask of polite interest Wickham was smirking with glee, for the girl had provided him with the perfect opportunity.

"Does he say when he will return?" asked Mr. Darcy bluntly. "He has already stayed with that Bingley fellow for more than a month."

"There is no mention of returning," replied the girl. "In fact, I believe he is quite enjoying himself in Hertfordshire."

Mr. Darcy huffed in annoyance and returned to his meal. Wickham, knowing the moment had arrived, turned to look at Georgiana with feigned confusion.

"Darcy is in Hertfordshire? That is odd, for I have heard he has been seen in London of late."

"London?" asked Mr. Darcy hopefully. Then the man frowned. "I cannot imagine what he might be doing there at this time of year."

"Perhaps he has followed the woman he is courting there. It is my understanding she is staying with her uncle at present."

"Courting?" demanded Mr. Darcy. His fork clattered to his plate, and his eyes fixed on Wickham, intensity radiating in their depths. "What do you mean? Fitzwilliam is not courting anyone."

Wickham looked at the man with shock. "But the rumors are all over London at present. I have not spoken with him myself, of course, but it is my understanding that the girl is from Hertfordshire, likely the same neighborhood in which he has been staying these past weeks."

The slamming of Mr. Darcy's fist against the table startled them all. "I knew it was a mistake to allow intimacy with that Bingley fellow! How dare William lose his mind to the man's sister?"

Though Wickham had only met Bingley once, he had the distinct impression of a young man easily manipulated and dull in the extreme. This was a new angle of which he had not known. As the argument raged on about him, Wickham considered the matter, wondering if it was something he could use to modify his plans for maximum effect.

"Mr. Bingley's sister has recently married, Robert," said Mrs. Darcy. The woman shot a glance at Wickham as if intending to let him know she was not misled by his attempts at obfuscation. "It cannot be his sister."

"Do you know anything of this woman?" snapped Mr. Darcy.

"Not much," replied Wickham, feigning thought. "Her name is Barnet, or something like that, but I know nothing more of her." Then Wickham paused and said: "Though, I suppose I *have* heard something about an uncle in town—it must be the uncle with whom she is staying. He is quite successful there as I understand."

It appeared Mr. Darcy did not miss the inference at all, for his lip curled with disgust. "If William is considering allying us with so unsuitable relations, we must go and talk some sense into him. We should prepare to depart tomorrow morning."

"Let us not reach erroneous conclusions on so little information," cautioned Mrs. Darcy.

"That is exactly why I mean to discover the truth for myself. I would never have thought it of my son, but if it is as I suspect, we must act quickly."

"Robert," said Lady Anne, affection and exasperation coloring her tone, "we do not even know if Fitzwilliam will be in London much longer. It is possible he may return to Hertfordshire before we can make our way there."

"Then I shall send him an express," replied Mr. Darcy. "But we *shall* join him. This cannot be allowed to continue."

Once again Wickham remained silent, knowing his work had been completed. At present there was nothing left to do though he would make certain to stoke Mr. Darcy's anger when the opportunity presented itself. So far, everything was proceeding as he had designed. Wickham could not wait to embark on the next phase of his plan.

There was something off about George Wickham's tale, though Lady Anne Darcy could not quite determine what it was. But the smugness in his countenance suggested an unstated motive, which, knowing the man involved, had to do with personal gain. Unfortunately, George Wickham was quite a blind spot to Robert Darcy, so there was little use in speaking to him of it.

After dinner, Lady Anne and Georgiana took turns amusing the men with songs on the pianoforte until it was time to retire. Not liking the look on the man's face as he watched her only daughter, Lady Anne decided to stay close to her. This became doubly important when her husband left them to speak to Mr. Harper concerning their potential departure within the next few days.

"That was wonderful, Miss Darcy," said Wickham, clapping when Georgiana finished playing her last piece. "You have become more talented by leaps and bounds since the last time I saw you."

"Thank you, Mr. Wickham," said Georgiana.

"Are you to travel with us when we depart?" asked he. "You must be eager to see your brother again."

"I am eager," said Georgiana. "I have not seen William for some time now, and I should like to know the woman he is courting." Georgiana smiled at Lady Anne, who returned it in full measure to her beautiful daughter. "Perhaps someday soon I shall have a sister."

"Perhaps you shall," said Lady Anne before Wickham could speak, no doubt intending to poison her daughter against this young woman before they could even become acquainted. "Now, Mr. Wickham, if you will excuse us, I believe Georgiana and I should retire to our chambers."

"Allow me to escort you," said Mr. Wickham with an entirely unwarranted level of gallantry.

"No, that is not necessary," said Lady Anne, directing a pointed look at the man. "Having lived here for the past thirty years, I am quite capable of finding my way upstairs."

Wickham laughed at her jest, but the way his eyes glittered suggested displeasure. There was little Lady Anne wished to see more than this man's back departing Pemberley. For the present, she would have to content herself with taking her daughter from his presence.

"Mama," said Georgiana as they climbed the stairs, Mr. Wickham having left to find Robert, no doubt to continue to ply his trade. "Am I the only one who sees a . . . falseness in Mr. Wickham's manners?"

"No, my dear," replied Lady Anne, pleased with her daughter's discernment, "I believe there are few who do not see it."

"Papa seems to enjoy his company."

"He does," replied Lady Anne. "I have never been able to fathom the relationship. I suppose part of it stems from his sense of indebtedness to Mr. Wickham's father, who served faithfully for many years."

"But Papa paid Mr. Wickham well. Why should he feel indebted?"

"That is, indeed, the question, my dear."

Georgiana shook her head. "Despite Mr. Wickham's presence, I do not mean to allow him to ruin my anticipation for seeing William again. And I hope to meet his lady, for I do so wish to have a sister of my own."

"I know you do, dear heart," replied Lady Anne, kissing her daughter's forehead. "Now, let us see what we might bring with us when your brother replies. I have a feeling we will not soon return to Pemberley."

Upon receiving his son and daughter-in-law back at Longbourn, Bennet listened to their account of what happened in London with some amusement. Thomas was a good man and would someday be a good master of the estate—he already was, given how much of the management of Longbourn he had already assumed. But he still had a tendency to rush to judgment, colored by a hint of belligerence. Further maturity would temper those traits, Bennet thought, as would the knowledge that his righteous crusade against Darcy was stymied by his sister's feelings for the man, not to mention Darcy's own attempts at redemption.

"It is as I told you," said Mr. Collins. In addition to Bennet himself, Mary and Mr. Collins had joined them, eager to hear of what had happened in London. "There was little doubt in my mind that Mr. Darcy is entirely trustworthy."

Thomas directed a sour look at Collins, which affected the parson not at all. "Yes, you did—I acknowledge it readily. But I am not prepared yet to offer the man full pardon. He *did*, after all, compromise Lizzy when she was but sixteen years of age. Though she has taken it into her head to fancy him, I will require more from him before I am at ease."

Mr. Collins's wave of dismissal seemed to irritate Thomas. "Do you think nothing, Cousin, of Darcy's behavior when he importuned her four years ago? Is that not reason enough for suspicion?"

"I dare say it is," said Mr. Collins. "But I am more concerned with what kind of man he is *now*. Since he attempted no more with her, it seems obvious to me he acted impulsively." Collins grew contemplative and said in a quieter tone: "And I well understand her appeal."

"Would *you* behave as he has?"

"I should like to think I would not. But that is not the point."

"In this situation," said Mr. Bennet, directing a pointed look at his son, "I am afraid I will have to side with my cousin."

When Thomas scowled, Bennet continued in a more conciliatory tone. "I am no happier than you that this happened to Lizzy, Thomas. But we must also remember no harm has come to her because of it. Her reputation was not damaged. Furthermore, having taken the measure of Mr. Darcy, I am confident in saying he is, in general, a good sort of man."

"And he seems desperately in love with our Elizabeth," said Caroline with a grin at her husband. "You must own that shows taste and judgment."

"There is also the matter of Lizzy's feelings on the matter," said Mary with exaggerated slowness. "Can you imagine her reaction if you continue to give Mr. Darcy the short shrift?"

"I am more concerned for my sister's wellbeing than provoking her ire."

"Ah, then perhaps you should obtain a greater respect for Lizzy's temper," said Bennet, winking at his daughter with amusement. When Thomas's scowl remained, Bennet turned to his son with more gravity. "The important fact to remember, Son, is that Lizzy has forgiven Mr. Darcy. What is more, she has forgiven him to the extent that she is now accepting his attentions as a prospective husband. I trust my daughter's judgment."

Finally Thomas's glower relaxed, and he put out his hand in a gesture of surrender, while he rubbed his temples with the other. "Let it not be said that I do not trust Lizzy's judgment, for I do. When they return to Longbourn, I shall do my utmost to welcome them both and see Darcy as a friend and suitor to my sister. But do not expect me to forget what has happened between them so quickly."

"That will be enough, Thomas," said Caroline. "Your desire to protect your sister is admirable, but I am convinced Mr. Darcy is a good man."

Thomas and Caroline continued to speak in low tones, and Bennet watched them. Perhaps it was the greater experience which had given him perspective, but he had never been as incensed about the kiss as his son had been. Though Bennet had thought of the matter at length since learning of it, he had come to the conclusion that Elizabeth had remained unharmed, and if she had gained a little caution among men because of it, that could not be considered a detriment.

CHAPTER XXI

"*A*re you certain, Aunt?" asked Elizabeth for what was likely the third time. "If you wish it, I am quite happy to forgo this evening's entertainment and stay to care for you."

"Lizzy!" said her aunt with a laugh. "I am quite on the mend, so there is no need to concern yourself for me. Nurse has the children in hand, and all is well."

"But with Uncle away, do you not require my assistance?"

"Would you assist me in reading my book?" Mrs. Gardiner brandished the book in her hand, forcing it under Elizabeth's nose. "I am quite well, Lizzy, and do not anticipate being required to do anything tonight. My husband has assured me he will not be late. As such, you should go with your sister and the gentlemen and attend your amusement. I shall be quite well here."

"It may be best to listen to our aunt, Lizzy," said Jane, who was standing nearby, watching them with amusement. "If you anger her needlessly, she may be at greater risk for a relapse."

Mrs. Gardiner shot Jane a playful scowl. "That is enough from you both. Go and enjoy yourselves and do not concern yourself with me."

"Very well, Aunt Gardiner," said Elizabeth. She leaned forward to kiss the other woman's cheek, and then she and Jane excused themselves.

"If I did not already know better," said Jane in a teasing tone, "I might have thought you wished to avoid our outing this evening. What would Mr. Darcy think?"

"Be silent, Jane, or I shall tell Mr. Bingley you fancy Samuel Lucas."

"Do your worst," said Jane, her tone entirely too smug. "I have little doubt Mr. Bingley would not be taken in for a moment."

"Come, Jane," said Elizabeth. "Let us make our final preparations. I would not wish to keep your Mr. Bingley waiting."

The two girls entered Elizabeth's room and assisted each other, ensuring buttons were fastened and hair was tied properly. Soon they felt themselves ready and descended the stairs to wait in the sitting-room for the imminent arrival of the gentlemen. Mrs. Gardiner was, indeed, on the mend, such that they would be returning to Longbourn within the next few days.

The evening's entertainment was to be a small ball given by an acquaintance of Mr. Darcy, one he had discovered only two days before when he had looked through the cards and invitations his family had received at their London home. While it was clear to Elizabeth that Mr. Darcy was not normally eager for society, it seemed he wished to dance with her and erase the memory of their previous dances together. It was not in Elizabeth's nature, however, to allow the opportunity to pass without a teasing comment.

"Are you certain you wish me to meet your friends?" Elizabeth had said when the invitation was given to them. "Do you not fear that I shall run for the nearest balcony should you lead me to the dance floor?"

"I believe I shall take that chance, Miss Elizabeth," had been his reply. "This time, I have hope there will be a different outcome."

"Then I believe Jane and I would be happy to attend."

The invitation had also been extended to her uncle—her aunt's recovery still too new to allow her attendance—but Mr. Gardiner was quite busy at his business at present. Thus, Jane and Elizabeth had accepted, to be escorted to the evening by the gentlemen. And thus they were engaged in waiting for their gentlemen callers to escort them to the ball that evening. In previous years, they had attended other society functions in London, but as the Bennets were not members of the first circles, Elizabeth suspected it would be far beyond anything they had ever seen before.

Within moments of their entrance to the sitting-room, the doorbell rang, and the ladies heard the gentleman enter into the vestibule where they were met by the housekeeper and guided within. Mr. Darcy entered with Mr. Bingley, and though Elizabeth had always thought her sister was a lucky woman to be the focus of such a handsome man as Mr. Bingley, tonight her attention was all for Mr. Darcy. He was dressed in a dark suit, finely cut and tailored, a green waistcoat completing his ensemble. Elizabeth was pleased to note that the color of his waistcoat closely approximated that of her own dress, which was made out of a pale green silk.

"How beautiful you look tonight, Miss Elizabeth," said Mr. Darcy, bowing and taking her hand. Rather than bow over it, he bestowed a lingering kiss, only the second time he had ever done so. Elizabeth felt her stomach overturn, a fluttering appearing therein, which she knew would likely stay with her the entire night.

"That is a lovely waistcoat, sir," said Elizabeth, in part to hide her reaction to his presence. "How fortunate you had one available."

"Shall I impart a secret to you, Miss Bennet?" At Elizabeth's nod, Mr. Darcy continued, saying: "I am not certain I have ever seen this particular garment before, let alone worn it. When I described your dress to Snell, he produced this as though he had conjured it by magic. I still cannot account for it as I am normally not partial to light colors."

"Shall you be embarrassed by it?" teased Elizabeth. "Perhaps it might have been better should you have stayed with your sober blacks or other dark blues."

"This evening I shall be happy to endure it, Miss Elizabeth." Mr. Darcy leaned forward and continued in softer tones: "No one seeing us together will misinterpret my interest in you."

Elizabeth blushed, and Mr. Darcy smiled with some satisfaction. Before she could find a reproachful or witty reply, Mr. Bingley suggested it was time to depart. They gathered their wraps together and made their way from the house, entering the carriage for the journey to their destination. As Gracechurch Street was far distant from even those neighborhoods where lower members of society made their abodes, the journey was longer than usual.

The conversation was effortless and interesting, much of it consisting of the nature of the gentlemen's acquaintance with their host for the night. He was a school friend of Mr. Darcy's, though a few years his elder. It seemed like Bingley had made the gentleman's acquaintance through Mr. Darcy's auspices, though he too confirmed he was well known to their hosts. When they arrived, they were introduced to Mr. and Mrs. Connors, finding him a genial man and her a friendly though slightly shy sort of woman.

"Please enjoy yourselves, Miss Bennet, Miss Elizabeth," said Mrs. Connors. "We are happy to have you with us this evening."

Thanking their hostess, the Bennet sisters made their way into the ballroom with their escorts, chatting happily. The ballroom was decked with finery, glowing candles thoughtfully placed to provide enough light, yet leave the revelers free of dripping wax. As they walked, Elizabeth noted they caught the eyes of more than one of the attendees and watched as several young gentlemen caught sight of Jane.

"This should be interesting," said she as an aside to Mr. Darcy.

The gentleman looked at her, his curious interest all the invitation she needed to continue. "Jane tends to receive an inordinate amount of attention when she attends functions in London. I have no doubt Mr. Bingley will have his hands full fending off the more amorous members of the company tonight."

Mr. Darcy regarded her with a grin. "And will I not be required to stake my own claim?"

"While I have never wanted for admirers, I am clearly not Jane's equal." He frowned, but Elizabeth just smiled softly. "In truth, I am content with that. Jane must always worry if a man is interested in her or enamored with her beauty, though I suppose, given Mr. Bingley's longstanding admiration, it is not a matter on which she must think much. If a man pays *me* attention, it is easier to divine his interest is in me."

"I think you devalue yourself too much, Miss Elizabeth," said Mr. Darcy. "You are a handsome young woman."

"Flattery, my dear sir, will get you everywhere."

Mr. Darcy released a guffaw at her jest, and Elizabeth grinned in response. When, a few moments later, a young man approached Jane, soliciting a dance, Elizabeth shot Mr. Darcy a grin, reminding him with her eyes how she had warned him. A few moments later, a young man approached her for the same reason, and she was forced to restrain a rolling of her eyes when Mr. Darcy returned her expressive look.

"I am sorry, Mr. Hardwick," said Elizabeth to the young man to whom Mr. Darcy had introduced her. "Mr. Darcy has my first sets. But I would be happy to dance the second with you."

Mr. Hardwick's eyes passed between Elizabeth and Mr. Darcy for a moment, and he smiled. "Then perhaps I might have the supper set?"

"Sorry, old man," said Mr. Darcy, his tone all self satisfaction. "I am afraid I have also claimed those dances too."

A rueful smile lit up Mr. Hardwick's face. "In that case, I shall be happy to accept your second sets, Miss Bennet." He paused and turned to Darcy. "The next time we meet, you shall have to tell me where you found her. If the other young ladies there are as handsome as she, it must be a truly spectacular neighborhood."

"She *has* another sister," drawled Mr. Darcy.

Mr. Hardwick laughed. "Then I am eager to hear of her. Pay me a visit when you can spare the time and tell me all about the enchanting Miss Elizabeth's sister."

Then Mr. Hardwick bowed and stepped away, still chuckling to himself. Elizabeth turned to Mr. Darcy, eyebrow arched. "Are you already trying to marry my sister off, sir?"

"Nothing of the kind, Miss Elizabeth," replied Mr. Darcy. "But I have observed a certain similarity between you and Miss Mary. Perhaps she would suit him."

Elizabeth shook her head, amused at his temerity. "I believe my father would agree that Mary is too young to be pursued by a gentleman."

"So Hardwick will be forced to wait," said Mr. Darcy with a shrug. "There are worse things than to be patient to obtain the hand of a woman who suits you. Having waited four years to be reunited with you, I am well aware of it."

"For shame, sir," said Elizabeth. "When last we met, you had no notion we would suit. We only spent part of one evening together, which ended badly, I might add. There is no way you can seriously state that you were pining for me all those years."

"Pining, no," replied Mr. Darcy. "But I will assert that I thought of you often, and it is only after I won the right to court you that I realized what I longed for." Mr. Darcy stepped close, looking down on her with his serious gaze, his breath tickling her cheek. "And I am determined I shall not allow you to escape, Miss Elizabeth. Take heed, for I rarely am denied that which I truly want."

Elizabeth could not speak, and she decided it was perhaps best she did not. There was something in Mr. Darcy's voice, some depth of passion she had never detected before. The man's admiration had become an established fact, but for the first time Elizabeth began to see just what that admiration and passion might portend for their future. The mere thought almost caused her to break out in goosebumps.

Throughout the evening, Elizabeth was much in company with Mr. Darcy, usually with her sister and Mr. Bingley. Every time a gentleman would approach for an introduction and an invitation to dance, Mr. Darcy would gaze at her with his laughing eyes, his expression suggesting he had predicted the exact sequence of events. And when more than one gentleman asked for those dances he had already secured, his satisfaction would become all that much more evident.

When he was not annoying her with his smugness, they shared many conversations, where she learned much of him. Conversely, she told him more of herself and her family, not holding back anything which he wished to know.

"My reticence is a family trait," said Mr. Darcy at one point in the evening. "My father is similarly afflicted, and I have heard my grandfather was much the same." Mr. Darcy paused and smiled. "The Fitzwilliam family, on the other hand, is quite the jovial bunch, with a few notable exceptions."

"Oh?" asked Elizabeth, interested to hear of his relations

"My uncle and his family are all amiable," replied Mr. Darcy. "But my mother is a little quieter than her brother, and my Aunt Catherine, of whom I have already spoken, is more dictatorial than jovial. It is fortunate she has married a man of strong character, for she would rule him if he was not. Georgiana is much like me though she is much shier. We are hopeful she will gradually come out of her cocoon, for she will be coming out in another two years."

"It is difficult for a young girl of a reticent nature to feel successful in society," said Elizabeth.

"And you have firsthand knowledge of this?" asked Mr. Darcy, flashing her a wry smile. "I should have thought not, since I have seen nothing of reticence in your character."

"I have, at times, been reticent," replied Elizabeth. "But no, mostly I am as you describe. I was more thinking of Jane."

Mr. Darcy's eyes found Jane across the room where she was speaking with Mr. Bingley and another gentleman to whom Elizabeth had not been introduced. Then he turned back to Elizabeth and said:

"Though Miss Bennet is quiet, I had not thought her lacking in confidence."

"No, Jane is confident enough. But she was not as a young girl, particularly since she is the oldest daughter and the first to come out into society. And she was much too young, being only fifteen."

"That *is* quite young," observed Mr. Darcy. "But you were only sixteen yourself, as I recall."

"True. But I also possessed more self-sufficiency at that age than Jane. I was also able to lean on her as my elder sister, *and* I only attended Meryton events until I was eighteen."

"Your sister began attending events in London at fifteen?"

Elizabeth nodded, laughing softly at the startled look he was giving her. "When you visited before, you never met my mother, did you?"

"Met her, no," replied he. "There is some recollection of seeing her the night of the assembly, but I do not think we were introduced."

"It is not surprising at all that you would remember her, for she was difficult to forget. Mama was of a nervous disposition, and even though Longbourn is not entailed and there is an heir, she often acted like we were all destined to be thrown out of our home when my father passes. Her disposition was naturally born to some extent, but it was also exacerbated by a family tragedy.

"Oh?" asked Mr. Darcy, his attention fully on her.

"There was another son between Thomas and Jane," replied Elizabeth. "My brother Richard passed not long after his fourth birthday from a sudden illness that swept through the neighborhood. According to my father, we almost lost Jane to it, though Thomas was unaffected. As Jane was too young, she does not have any memories of him, though Thomas does. He will not talk about his brother, however.

"After that event, my mother became convinced that my sisters and I must marry to obtain the protection of a husband, for if Thomas also were lost to us, there would be no one to see to our care."

"Longbourn is not entailed, is it?"

"That is it, Mr. Darcy," said Elizabeth. "There was an entail on the property many years ago, but when the terms of the last entail were fulfilled, the master at the time decided against enacting another. So even if Thomas should have succumbed to some illness, my father could simply have left the estate to Jane, thereby providing for all of us. There are also our dowries to consider, and they are not insubstantial.

"My father does not like London and will not often be induced to come here. When he discovered that my mother had allowed Jane into society in London, he immediately came and retrieved them, after which he had a long conversation with my mother concerning what was proper and what was not when they returned home. It is entirely possible my mother never truly understood why we should not be introduced that young, but she obeyed my father's edicts after that."

"Then you have not had much experience in London."

"On the contrary," said Elizabeth, "as my brother grew into his position as heir to the estate, he took on the responsibility of escorting us in London. Now that he and Caroline are married, I expect they shall spend much more time here, for Caroline is fond of society."

Matters turned to other subjects then, and the evening passed in a pleasant fashion. Elizabeth, as she was often known to boast, was rarely required to sit out for a set. Mr. Darcy, should he have chosen it, would not have had any difficulty securing partners himself. But when he was not dancing, he seemed content to watch her, though he did dance once with Jane, and once with another young lady.

Not knowing yet whether to abuse him for his unsociable behavior, Elizabeth instead contented herself with a few mild teases, suggesting he might find agreeable partners if he would only take his eyes off her. That, of course, rebounded on Elizabeth with alacrity, for Mr. Darcy's smoldering look was followed by a quick rejoinder.

"Why should I look anywhere other than at the most pleasing sight present tonight?"

Choosing not to respond, Elizabeth only gave him a tremulous smile and changed the subject. They were to return to Hertfordshire in the next few days, and, therefore, the scrutiny would be a thing of the past. But Mr. Darcy had been so overt in his admiration that evening that Elizabeth was certain rumors were already flying. Though few people of consequence were in London at present, his attentions to her would surely be known soon, which would eventually bring the attention of his family. Given what she had heard of his father, in particular, Elizabeth did not know how to feel about it.

While Elizabeth was concerned with the possibility of Mr. Darcy's father becoming aware of their growing association, little did she suspect he already knew. The two gentlemen returned to Darcy house that evening after the ball, both dwelling on happy thoughts of their preferred Bennet lady. When they stepped through the door, however, they were met by the butler who had a letter in his hand.

"This arrived express tonight, Mr. Darcy," said Gates, hand extended. "It is from the master."

Concerned, Darcy accepted the letter and thanked Gates, dismissing him for the evening once their coats had been taken. The missive was thin, comprised of only one sheet, addressed to Darcy in his father's neat hand. There were no other markings to give him any indication of what it might contain.

"I hope your family is all well, Darcy," said Bingley, pulling Darcy from his study of the letter.

"It is more curious that my father knew to write to me in London," said Darcy. "It is addressed to this house."

Bingley frowned. "You did not inform him you were coming to

London for a short time?"

"There did not seem to be a need," replied Darcy with a shrug. "My stay was only to coincide with Miss Elizabeth's, and she did not expect to be here long."

The frown turned to a grin. "It seems to me you are being quite transparent, old man. It might have served you better had you been more open when we were in Hertfordshire. Then I might not have come rushing across the countryside with her brother and sisters to take you to task."

"If I was more open in general, that might be easier," replied Darcy absently.

"Will you open it?" prompted Bingley, pointing at the letter. "Unless you are somehow able to read it from the outside."

Darcy shook his head and motioned his friend to follow. "Perhaps it is best to open it in privacy. If it is a matter of delicacy, I would not wish the servants to overhear."

There was no need for his friend to point out there were no servants in evidence, not at this time of the night. In a house like his father's, there were always at least a footman or two on duty throughout the night. The servants at Darcy residences were well compensated and expected to be circumspect when speaking of the family's business, but one could never be too careful.

As was his custom, Darcy had dismissed Snell for the evening, well able to see to his own disrobing, so his sitting-room was deserted when he stepped into it. Lighting a few candles to enable him to read properly was the work of a moment, and Darcy lost no time in opening the missive soon thereafter. The contents shocked him exceedingly.

"What is it, Darcy?"

"It seems my father has some unknown method of keeping track of me," said Darcy, looking up at his friend, bewildered by what he was reading. "He has already learned of Miss Elizabeth."

"I thought your father knew nothing of the Bennet family."

"That is precisely what I thought," said Darcy. "Though he does not refer to her by name, he declares his knowledge of me 'losing my head to some country miss' and warns me against doing anything rash until he arrives."

"That is odd. We have not been seen in company with the Bennet sisters until this evening. The only time we have been with them and not at Gracechurch Street was when we went to the park with them."

"It is possible we might have been seen," said Darcy slowly. "But I do not think most of those to whom I am known frequent that area of town." Darcy caught Bingley's raised eyebrow, and he shook his head with annoyance. "I do not censure the Gardiners, Bingley. They are good people. I only spoke the truth—many of the first circles would rather die than have it known they sullied themselves by going into Cheapside, and I would hardly think most of the second circles have connections with those in that neighborhood either."

"That is true, I suppose," said Bingley, frowning. "What do you mean to do? If your father is traveling to London, he may very well arrive and discover you no longer in residence. We are to return to Hertfordshire the day after tomorrow."

"Then I shall have to wait in town, I suppose," said Darcy. "Though the very thought vexes me greatly." Darcy glanced down at the letter again. "My father does not even say when he will arrive, though given the urgency of his manner of expressing himself, I cannot imagine he means to tarry in the north."

"Invite him to Netherfield," suggested Bingley.

Turning to his friend, Darcy regarded him as if he had two heads. "I am not sure that is wise. There is little in this letter which suggests he will be well-behaved should he stay at your estate."

"Darcy, I believe you are too harsh on your father. Remember, I have stayed at Pemberley, and he was perfectly polite."

"Though perhaps not precisely welcoming," said Darcy.

Bingley shrugged. "It is of little matter. I am convinced of your father's civility, even if my family is not as high as he prefers. Furthermore, it will be of benefit to have your father stay with us is to show him that we are not savages. He can see you with Miss Elizabeth, witness your connection, feel your happiness. In the face of such proof of future felicity, how can he not accept her?"

Sensible though Bingley's suggestion was, Darcy still felt a frisson of unease. While Mr. Darcy *had* been perfectly polite to Bingley when he had stayed with them, Bingley had not been there to witness the continual attempts to induce Darcy to sever the friendship. Mr. Darcy was not precisely an elitist, but he was firm in his opinions that there was little to be gained by encouraging friendships with those of a lesser station.

"Come, Darcy," urged Bingley, "it will be for the best. Respond to your father's express with one of your own and invite him to Netherfield. In fact, ask him to bring your mother and sister too. My parents would be pleased to make their acquaintance."

Darcy nodded slowly. "Do you not need to solicit your parents' permission first?'

"Not at all. They will be happy to receive your family, I am sure."

There was nothing left but to accede to his friend's suggestion. Though Darcy's misgivings concerning the scheme were not laid to rest, he did not wish to linger in London, waiting for his father to arrive to try to argue him away from Miss Elizabeth. Perhaps Mr. Darcy would be better behaved if he was staying with the Bingleys in Hertfordshire. At the very least, Darcy would not be required to give up Miss Elizabeth's company while he waited.

Thus, Darcy wrote a quick letter, inviting his family to Netherfield. It was sent out by express the following morning.

CHAPTER XXII

*E*lizabeth had not thought she would feel so concerned at the thought of meeting Mr. Darcy's parents. While she had known it was inevitable if he carried his courtship through to its natural conclusion, Elizabeth was in no hurry to expedite that meeting. In fact, given her tumultuous history with the gentleman, she rather thought she would prefer to take this matter of their courtship slowly, accomplishing such intimidating matters as meeting the elder Mr. Darcy at some point in the future. Preferably the distant future.

But Mr. Darcy's communication the day of their return to Hertfordshire came as a complete surprise, and it worried her. The sympathy Mr. Darcy displayed to her feelings was welcome, but as her father was not at all an intimidating man, she was not certain he understood.

"Oh," was all Elizabeth could say when the communication had been made. It seemed—to Elizabeth, at least—that a whole host of feelings could be summed up in that one word.

"I apologize for this surprise, Miss Elizabeth," said Mr. Darcy, his manner suggesting he was being quite sincere. "How my father discovered our courting I cannot imagine."

Elizabeth frowned. "Did you mean to keep the matter from him

230 🦢 Jann Rowland

until we were married? Or until we were engaged as it would be a fait accompli?"

"No!" exclaimed Mr. Darcy. "I beg you do not misconstrue my words for meanings I do not intend. There is *nothing* which will prevent me from offering for you except you yourself. I am neither ashamed of my feelings for you, nor am I ashamed of *you*.

"It was my thought we could quietly court here in Hertfordshire for some weeks before I reveal the news to my family. I *know* my father, and I am well aware of his opinions and wishes. Your comfort was foremost in my thoughts."

"Will he be angry?" asked Elizabeth, now becoming alarmed for another reason.

"It seems I am making a mess of this business," said Mr. Darcy woefully, as Bingley laughed by his side.

"Indeed, you are," said Mr. Bingley, clapping his friend on the back. "Perhaps you should allow me, Darcy."

Mr. Darcy gestured to Mr. Bingley to proceed, an almost desperate quality in his motions. Though still concerned, Elizabeth was charmed. It seemed the ever-unflappable Mr. Darcy was capable of being quite discomposed.

"Miss Elizabeth," said Mr. Bingley, leaning forward and favoring her with a soft smile, "what my friend is trying—and failing miserably—to say is that his father *is* a traditional man, and as such, has certain expectations for his son's future marriage partner."

"This I already understand, Mr. Bingley," said Elizabeth, beginning to become a little impatient.

"I am sure you do," replied Mr. Bingley with a wide grin. "What he has not been able to say coherently is that while his father *is* a traditional man, he is not an ogre. It is possible that he might disapprove of you in general, but he will not treat you as inferior, nor will he be unkind. Though I was aware of his opinion concerning me when I stayed with them, he was not unkind, and I do not believe he had anything against me in particular."

"No, he did not," said Mr. Darcy. "His disapproval was that I had befriended one he considered inappropriate. The Bingleys *are* newly landed. My apologies, my friend."

"I am not offended," replied Mr. Bingley with a shrug. "It is nothing less than the truth."

"But will his disapproval not be worse with me?" asked Elizabeth. "Mr. Bingley is only your friend—I am being considered for the position of his only son's wife."

"You are more than being considered, Miss Elizabeth," said Mr. Darcy. His look caused Elizabeth's insides to flip over. It was like she was melting under the force of his love.

"Lizzy," said Jane, her tone slightly admonishing. "The Lizzy I know lets no one intimidate her. If you show Mr. Darcy your quality, just by being the courageous Lizzy I have always known, I have no doubt Mr. Darcy's father will have no choice but to love you."

"I agree," said Mr. Darcy. "Please, Miss Elizabeth—I ask you to trust me in this matter. He will take some convincing, but in the end, he will be won over."

Though still uncertain, her courage bolstered by their words, she nodded, determined to put her fears behind her. Jane patted her hand, and Elizabeth grasped Jane's in return. The subject was then dropped though Elizabeth did not forget it.

The rest of the journey was passed in quiet conversation, with nothing of substance discussed, though at times it seemed every word which passed between Elizabeth and Mr. Darcy was fraught with emotion. As the summer was waning, giving way to autumn, the weather was still fine, and the miles flew by. Soon, the carriage passed through Meryton, taking the path towards Lucas Lodge, then Longbourn beyond.

When the sight of her beloved home wove into the view through the trees, Elizabeth considered the building. Though she had always loved this scene, something in Elizabeth's own heart had shifted. It was difficult to understand what made her feel this way, though she thought it had to do with the man sitting on the other carriage bench. While Longbourn was still her home, it would not always be, and for the first time in Elizabeth's life, she knew that time was quickly approaching.

Shaking herself of these thoughts, Elizabeth allowed herself to be handed down from their conveyance when the carriage stopped with a gentle lurch. Those faces she had known all her life were gathered there waiting for her, and Elizabeth greeted them with laughter and love. Thomas and Caroline, she had parted from only days earlier, and though separation from her father and sister Mary was only a little longer, she greeted them as if they had been sundered for months.

It was quickly evident that Mr. Darcy was more than a little nervous at his reception, but Mr. Bennet quickly moved to put him at ease. He stepped forward and offered his hand, first to Mr. Bingley and then to Mr. Darcy.

"Thank you both for bringing my daughters home safely." Mr.

Bennet laughed and added: "Hopefully you will both one day understand, but a man's daughters are his most beloved treasures. And then despite all this, you must watch them cleave to another man when they become old enough. It is a wonderful, but excruciating, feeling."

Mr. Bingley laughed at Mr. Bennet's words, but while Mr. Darcy did also, his was of a more hesitant quality. Elizabeth was watching him, and thus she saw how he gathered himself, squared his shoulders, and addressed Elizabeth's father.

"I believe, Mr. Bennet, that I must have a conversation with you. Would it be acceptable to ask for a moment of your time now?"

"It seems to me, Mr. Darcy," said Mr. Bennet, "that it may be best to defer it to another day. I am eager to speak with my daughters, and you are all tired and dusty from the road."

That Mr. Darcy was nonplussed was evident, but he was also relieved. Elizabeth's perceptive father also noted this fact, as he laughed and clapped Mr. Darcy on the back. "Yes, I believe it is better to wait to canvass such weighty subjects. Let us discuss it the next time you visit. Can I assume it will be as early as tomorrow?"

"I have no wish to stay away longer," said Mr. Darcy. "And I doubt Bingley would allow me to, regardless."

"Then come and be welcome. I wish you a safe journey to Netherfield though it is only three miles distant."

These words exchanged, the two gentlemen once again boarded the carriage, and soon it was off, Elizabeth and Jane watching as it disappeared from Longbourn's drive and out through the village. It left her feeling bereft, more evidence she was coming to esteem Mr. Darcy highly.

"Come, my dears," said Mr. Bennet. "Let us go into the house. Surely you can do without your young men for a few hours."

"Yes, Papa," said Jane, turning to follow her father.

The family filed into the house. But as Elizabeth entered those well-known halls, rested her eyes on scenes beloved and precious to her, she wondered if this was the last time she would ever return to her home as a resident of it.

The reception at Netherfield was as happy as the one they had received at Longbourn. As their last child still living at home, Darcy knew the Bingleys cherished the return of their only son, though one of their daughters was situated only three miles distant.

Together, he and Bingley accepted their welcome and then excused themselves to return to their rooms in order to change and wash. And though he was not anticipating it, Darcy knew the communication regarding the coming of his parents must be made to his hosts.

The family was gathered to afternoon tea soon after, the hot liquid soothing the travelers' throats and putting them to rights again. Then Bingley made the communication to his parents.

"Of course, Mr. and Mrs. Darcy are welcome to stay at Netherfield at any time," said Mrs. Bingley. The woman's excitement at the prospect of such guests seemed genuine interest, but also contained a certain level of awe Darcy knew he did not provoke himself. Whether it was because he was yet a young man or because his mother was the daughter of an earl, he did not know. Mrs. Bingley was well enough behaved that Darcy did not think his family would see anything untoward or grasping in her excitement.

"I would be pleased to make their acquaintance," added Mr. Bingley.

Whereas Mrs. Bingley had been all excited enthusiasm, Darcy thought he caught a hint of hesitance in the elder man's manners. Nothing further was said during their tea, but when Mr. Bingley invited the younger men to his study, Darcy was certain he would discover the truth of his feelings. It turned out that Darcy was completely correct in this assessment.

"Have a seat," said Mr. Bingley, waving negligently to a pair of chairs before his desk. Sitting behind it in his own chair, Mr. Bingley regarded them thoughtfully, though his eyes were on Darcy more often than he looked at his son. "The result of my son's hasty journey to London I shall not raise, as it seems to have been resolved. But this matter of your parents strikes me as curious, and I wished to ask you about it."

Mr. Bingley sat back and waved his hand, forestalling Darcy's reply. "Of course, I know nothing to suggest the matter is anything other than what you have told me. And, I would assure you, I do not suspect your parents of any untoward behavior. I am well aware they are much higher in society than the position my family can boast, but from Charles's account, there was nothing in their welcome to him which suggested anything other than perfect civility."

A nod was Darcy's response, as he sensed the man had more to say. In truth, he was relieved, for he had grown tired of defending his parents' supposed tendency to look down on others beneath them in society.

"What more concerns me," continued Mr. Bingley, "is that your father might have heard of your recent attentions to Miss Elizabeth, though I cannot imagine how he might have learned of the matter."

Darcy sighed and sat back in his own chair. "That appears to be his reason for wishing to join us, though I am at as much of a loss as you to explain how he discovered it."

"You *did* intend to inform him?"

"Yes," replied Darcy, "though I had thought to wait until I was more secure in Miss Elizabeth's regard. I know he has much higher hopes for my future wife than Miss Elizabeth."

Mr. Bingley regarded him for a moment and then nodded, his manner still thoughtful. "Perhaps it is best he discovers it now, rather than later, when you are committed to offering for her. It will give him time to become accustomed to the situation."

"That is one way to consider it," said Darcy with a grimace. "But I might have wished my father would not have the power to frighten her away from me."

A laugh was Mr. Bingley's response, joined by his son. "That girl is not one to be frightened away by anyone, Mr. Darcy. If she decides it is you, she wants, I cannot see anything your father might say that would change her mind." Mr. Bingley paused and sobered. "I am curious of one thing, however, though you may, of course, refuse to answer if you will. Will your father be angry enough at your choice to resort to disinheriting you?"

While Darcy's first thought was that it was unlikely, he paused for a moment to consider Mr. Bingley's question. "I do not think so," said he at length. "I have no brother he can promote in my place. While it is possible he could make my sister his heir, I doubt he would carry it so far. Furthermore, my mother would strenuously oppose such a measure."

"Very well," said Mr. Bingley. "Nothing more than sincere concern provokes me to raise this subject. If your father was to take a drastic step such as removing your inheritance, you would need to choose how to act. My friend has provided his daughters with excellent dowries, but your consequence would be much diminished."

"It would," acknowledged Darcy, "but I own some other investments through my mother's family, perhaps enough to purchase a small estate where we could live. I would not be in a position to offer her anything equal to Pemberley, but we would be comfortable."

"The Bennets are good people," said Bingley. "Miss Elizabeth would not bat an eyelash in such a situation. She would be content with whatever you were able to give her as long as she felt strongly enough to accept you."

"Indeed," said the elder Bingley. "In that case, I suggest you confirm the invitation to your parents. I assume you did not give final confirmation pending my wife's approval?"

"Yes, sir," replied Darcy. "If I may have a bit of paper and a pen, I shall do it directly." Then Darcy turned to his friend. "Would you care for a ride into Meryton? I would prefer to send my letter express."

"Of course, my friend," replied Bingley. "I am at your disposal."

"Well, Lizzy, it appears you have managed to wrap that young man around your finger tighter than a matron wraps her dress around her ample person."

The company smiled at Mr. Bennet's jest, though some — such as Mr. Collins — did so fleetingly. That did not serve to temper Mr. Bennet's wit.

"With the power you now possess at your disposal, I might wonder if you mean to use it." Mr. Bennet winked at Jane. "Both my eldest daughters seem to have wealthy gentlemen willing to do anything for them, and that is not a power to be trifled with.

"Then again, a gentleman's affections can sometimes be akin to fleeting breaths of wind on an otherwise calm day. Perhaps you should make the best use of their current infatuation, lest those other interests begin to crowd out their interest in young ladies. Your mother would have advised you to secure them as soon as may be. Then you may be in a position to throw Mary in the paths of other rich men."

"Oh, Papa Bennet!" said Caroline. "How you do carry on."

Mr. Bennet grinned at her and continued, completely unaffected. "Then again, I have heard it said that a young lady likes nothing more than to be crossed in love. Should you wish to induce your gentlemen to jilt you, I suspect they would do so in a highly creditable manner."

"There is little that can be done to pull them away from my sisters," said Mary, though she was grinning at her father's teasing. "I wonder how I shall cope here alone under the authority of my brother's wife."

"That is enough from you, missy," said Caroline rather primly. "We shall get along well enough, I am certain. As for Mr. Darcy and my brother, I cannot be more delighted that they show signs of such constancy."

"Indeed," said Mr. Bennet, his attention once again fixed on Elizabeth. "And despite what we all — or *some* of us," Mr. Bennet glanced at Thomas who was watching all with a longsuffering air, "thought, it seems it was Mr. Collins who possessed the sagacity to see that Mr. Darcy meant no harm to our Lizzy."

"If you will recall, I had no doubts either," said Caroline. Mr. Collins just looked self-satisfied, though he did not say anything.

"Nor I," said Mary, looking to her brother.

"His actions still remain open to interpretation," said Thomas. When the rest of the family looked on him as one, he gestured with his hands, a sign of surrender. "Very well, it does appear he has nothing but honorable intentions for Elizabeth. But I will not lower my guard."

"The proprieties must be observed," said Mr. Collins.

"Indeed, they must," said Mr. Bennet, "though these young lovers still find ways to have their own way." Then he turned a more serious eye on Elizabeth. "I was not happy to learn what happened between you, Lizzy, and even less that you did not trust me enough to take me into your confidence. But I do understand why you did not."

"I apologize, Papa," replied Elizabeth. "At the time, I had no intention of being bound to Mr. Darcy to restore my reputation. And you know how Mama would have reacted to it."

"Yes, well, we could have kept it from your mother." Mr. Bennet paused. "In the future, Elizabeth, I want you to feel like you can come to me with anything. Do not carry the weight of the world on your shoulders, for your family is ready and willing to carry it with you."

"Thank you, Papa," said Elizabeth. "I shall remember that."

The conversation turned then, focusing more on their relations in London, Elizabeth informing her family of Mrs. Gardiner's recovery and the recent antics of the children. Mr. Bennet, Elizabeth knew, esteemed his brother by marriage highly, and he commented more than once that he had known Elizabeth would be safe at Gracechurch Street. With their aunt's recovery, the situation was returning to normal there, and Elizabeth knew they would almost certainly come to Longbourn, as they did every year, to spend Christmas with the Bennets.

Whether Elizabeth would remain a single woman until that time, she could not determine. Given the gentleman's ardency, she thought it likely he might propose long before then, but Elizabeth's acceptance was not yet determined. That Mr. Gardiner got on so well with Mr. Darcy was a surprise, but one which spoke well to the gentleman's character, when one accounted for his position in society. All these things led Elizabeth to espouse a warmer regard for the gentleman than she would have thought possible only a few short weeks ago.

Later in the evening, Elizabeth sat down to a game of chess with her father while the rest of her family were involved in their own concerns, reading or speaking quietly, or in Mary's case, playing quietly on the pianoforte. At the start of their game, both players were locked in concentration and little was said between them. Then, after a time, Mr. Bennet addressed her.

"Please tell me the truth, Lizzy. Did you ever feel in danger from Mr. Darcy?"

Elizabeth considered the question for several moments before she replied. "Not physically in danger. I was wary of the man and questioned his motives and his future plans, but I never felt unsafe in his presence, even when he acted so inappropriately. I saw him at Pemberley, you understand."

"Oh?" asked Mr. Bennet without moving his eyes from the chessboard.

"Aunt Gardiner insisted on touring the grounds of his father's estate. We were told the family was from home, but Mr. Darcy returned that day to see to some business. But while he spoke briefly with my aunt and uncle, I was concealed in a strand of trees. He did not see me."

Mr. Bennet looked up. "And yet you told me you were not afraid of him?"

While his tone was not precisely accusatory, there was a challenge inherent in his question. Elizabeth replied quickly to forestall his ire.

"I *was* wary of him. I had not seen him in almost four years, and you know what happened at our last parting. But he has never acted in a way which would make me *fear* him."

Though he continued to regard her for several more moments, soon Mr. Bennet nodded and turned his attention back to the game. "It is not every young lady who will forgive a gentleman such behavior." After a few more moments of ostensibly studying the board, Mr. Bennet chuckled. "Then again, perhaps it is every maiden's dream to provoke such a depth of feeling in a young man that he forgets all propriety and declares himself madly in love with her."

"It certainly has its charms, Papa."

They laughed quietly together over the board. "Well, I must inform you, Lizzy, that I have always liked the young man. Intelligence, kindness, thoughtfulness, and an undying regard for a young woman are not always bound up together in one young man, though many young men give the appearance of it when in the first throes of infatuation. Now that you are past the first great test, I suspect you will do very well together."

"I suspect we might, Papa."

"Then perchance you should simply accept him when he walks in the door tomorrow. Throw yourself on him, return his kiss from four years ago, and beg him to take you to Gretna right at that moment."

"Papa!" exclaimed Elizabeth in embarrassment. Though she knew Mr. Bennet to be jesting, the thought of such actions made her feel decidedly warm.

"Ah, very good," said Mr. Bennet with some satisfaction as Elizabeth made her move. "Check and mate, my dear."

Elizabeth looked at the board with astonishment, seeing he was absolutely correct. Then she looked up at him, vexed with him for his subterfuge. Mr. Bennet only grinned and rose to his feet.

"You always did play carelessly when your emotions were excited. Perhaps I shall not share this little tidbit with Mr. Darcy. It would be much more amusing to allow him to discover it on his own."

Mr. Bennet kissed her cheek and announced his attention to retire to his bookroom, leaving Elizabeth watching him as he left. Looking down at the board again, she noted her mistake. If her father thought she would be duped using such arts again, he would be quite disappointed.

CHAPTER XXIII

*J*acob Fitzwilliam, Earl of Matlock was a man who was acutely aware of his position in society. Jealous of his family's honor, Lord Matlock demanded the best of behavior from his family, eager that their name remained unsullied, unlike that of so many other nobles.

But the knowledge of his position did not lead to false pride or arrogance. The privilege in which he lived was, after all, a mere accident of birth, having the good fortune to be born into such circumstances. Though Lord Matlock demanded the best from his family, he never lost sight of the truly important things in life, and he did not look down on those less fortunate than he was himself.

All possessed qualities which contributed to society, when directed properly, from the lowliest scullery maid to the prince regent himself. One thing his second son had learned during his time in the army, toiling amid war and hardship, was that any man, whether born high or low, could display a superior form of nobility to that of the most powerful duke. It was a lesson Lord Matlock could not have taught his son so well himself, though he knew Anthony was a good boy, one who had proven himself time and time again. His other son and his daughters were of similar characters, though it was true his eldest daughter could be a trial at times.

With such an outlook on life, Matlock had always thought it ironic that those beneath him by society's standard were themselves far more arrogant and impressed with their position in life. Take his sister, Lady Catherine de Bourgh, for example. Now there was a lady who could benefit from a month spent as a scullery maid. Her husband, Sir Lewis, was of a like mind with Matlock, and he controlled his wife's excesses admirably. Lady Catherine had always been a trial on them all, and Matlock himself was eager to avoid her wherever possible, even though he enjoyed Sir Lewis's company.

It was another of his relations who was testing Matlock's ability to hold in his vexation at present. There were few better men than Robert Darcy, and the man had made his dear sister, Anne, a very good husband. Darcy was affable with his tenants and servants, diligent in the management of his estate, brought up his children to be creditable members of society, and though reserved, was as firm a friend as any man could ever want. But he was also a proud man, one who took a great deal of satisfaction in his family history—which was much longer and more prestigious than Matlock's own, to own the truth. This made him inflexible, particularly with respect to those with whom his family associated. Considering such truths, his continued support of George Wickham, against all the evidence of the boy's worthlessness, was something Matlock could not explain.

"I cannot imagine what the boy is thinking!" exclaimed Darcy for perhaps the tenth time since he had invaded Matlock's study, his animated hand gestures punctuating his words.

"First," said Matlock, directing a severe look at his brother-in-law—not that the man noticed it, "at present you have nothing more than the unsubstantiated report from your godson. It would be best if you waited until you spoke with your son to form an opinion."

Darcy scowled at him, but at least he stopped his infernal pacing. "I know you have been poisoned against Wickham by your son and mine, but I have never found him to be anything other than trustworthy."

It was a discussion which had played out many times, and Matlock was in no mood to revisit it. "If you recall, Darcy, I did not question Wickham's character—only his report. My opinion of him is not at issue. For all I know he is telling the absolute truth as he knows it. But the existence of rumors is not enough to substantiate anything. London is always rife with rumors—this you know."

"Not usually at this time of year," snapped Darcy. "With most prominent families seeking their estates, there is usually little enough occurring there. If there are rumors there at this time of year, there must be something behind them."

"Or it is something Wickham heard and saw fit to inform you of for reasons of his own." Matlock waved his hand in dismissal when Darcy turned to him, his annoyance clear. "No, Darcy, I will say nothing against the lad. But I would urge you to remember that Wickham and Fitzwilliam do *not* get on at all, and given the enmity between them, you must acknowledge his reasons for quitting his position and rushing to inform you are suspect, at best."

Darcy frowned. "Wickham did not rush to inform me. In fact, he had been at Pemberley for hours before he made it known. Wickham did not even bring up the subject himself — as I recall Georgiana did. Or Anne."

"Surely you do not believe that," said Matlock. "Whoever brought it up, the fact remains that Wickham rushed to Pemberley, leaving a position you had selected for him, and informed you of Fitzwilliam's supposed activities when another allowed him the opening to do so. Do you not think he was waiting for the opportunity, knowing sooner or later one of you would speak of your son?"

"Perhaps he was. Wickham knows my concerns — if he did come to Pemberley specifically to bring the information to me, I find myself very much in his debt."

Matlock shook his head. His brother's devotion to that bounder was aggravating at times, as he often favored the boy over his own son. Having heard enough of the exploits of George Wickham from his own younger son as well as Darcy's, Matlock had no trust in anything he said or did. Over the years, Matlock had ensured his daughters were kept well away from Wickham's influence and had even spoken firmly to Wickham on one occasion when he had made suggestive statements to Charity, Matlock's youngest daughter. The man was all glib insincerity, claiming Charity misunderstood him. Of course, Matlock had not believed him for an instant, but he was as slippery as a snake. The present concern was Georgiana, for she was now sixteen and of an age where a bounder such as Wickham might consider her his prey.

"Whatever you do, I suggest you approach your son with delicacy," said Matlock. "As I said, you do not truly know the situation, regardless of whatever Wickham has said. And if Fitzwilliam *has* found a woman to admire, what of it?"

Darcy whirled on him, aghast. "Do the standards of society mean nothing? Fitzwilliam can aspire to marry the daughter of an earl, or perhaps even a duke! At the very least, a woman who has been brought up in the same sphere *must* be his choice."

"As long as she is a gentlewoman, she is his equal in society, though perhaps not in consequence."

"I will not allow it!" snapped Darcy. "It *cannot* be allowed. Fitzwilliam needs to marry a woman who will raise our consequence in society, and any acquaintance of his friend *Bingley* cannot be acceptable."

"If you will forgive my bluntness," said Matlock, "he is a man full grown, capable of deciding what he wants in a wife."

"I can disown him."

A long silence ensued, tense and uncomfortable. Matlock ignored it, gazing at his brother, trying to decipher his determination in this matter. Fitzwilliam possessed the ability to be a great master of the estate when his time came and had become a truly good man in his own right. Surely his father would not overlook all of that.

"I hope you are jesting, Darcy. If it *is* a jest, it is in very poor taste."

Darcy laughed, though it was particularly mirthless. He sank down in a nearby chair and put his chin in his hand, staring morosely at something only he could see.

"Perhaps I am. Perhaps not." Then he chuckled again. "In a moment of madness, I even thought to disown him and make Wickham my heir in his stead."

"Now *that* is madness," growled Matlock. "Surely you cannot be contemplating such an action. For all your going on about expectations and your son's choice of an unsuitable woman, Wickham is nothing more than the son of a steward. Good heavens, Darcy, what are you thinking?"

"It was a stray thought, nothing more." Darcy paused and attempted to smile. "I would never consider making Wickham my heir."

"I hope you do not. If you persisted with such madness, you know I would have no choice but to oppose you."

"I know," replied Darcy with a nod. "And I should not blame you.

"The thought has occurred to me that I could disinherit Fitzwilliam and make Georgiana my heir, but I would not do that either unless there was no other choice. Regardless of my opinion about his choice of a wife, Fitzwilliam is my heir, my blood, and I would not leave my family's legacy to any other. He is everything I could ever have wished for in a son, and I know Pemberley will be in good hands when I am gone."

"It is heartening to hear you acknowledge that. For a moment, I thought you had forgotten it."

"No, I have not. That is why I am at a loss to understand how he could have forgotten himself in this manner. I thought I had taught him better."

Matlock considered his brother for a moment and then said: "Have you considered the possibility that she might be suitable?"

Looking up, Darcy's expression invited clarification. Matlock was only too happy to oblige. "You know nothing of this woman—even Wickham has said he only knows her name."

"He knows she is connected to trade!" snapped Darcy.

"Even that is suspect," soothed Matlock. "Regardless, if the connection is an uncle, he can be safely kept out of sight. Furthermore, Darcy, you know that tradesmen are becoming more accepted and wealthier. In time, they may even exceed the influence we landowners possess."

Though he appeared to little like it, Darcy nodded.

"More to the point, this woman must be a gentlewoman—I doubt Fitzwilliam would consider her if she is not. Let us say she has a dowry of fifteen thousand and is a member of the second circles. Further, let us say she is an intelligent girl, one engaging and comfortable in society. Would you be willing to alienate your son, even if such a woman were to be a benefit to him?"

It was to Darcy's credit that he did not respond with a statement to the effect that such a woman could not be anything other than a detriment to the Darcy family. It was clear he still did not appreciate the notion of such a woman joining his family, but Matlock thought he had at least induced his brother to consider the matter in a more rational way.

"It may be that I have no choice but to accept her," said Darcy after a moment's thought. "But I hope you will excuse me if I attempt to persuade him. I would wish my grandson and the future master of my family's legacy to come from more acceptable stock."

Matlock knew he was not about to gain any more concessions from his brother, so he did not even make the attempt. "No, I will not blame you. But I would advise you to take care. If Fitzwilliam truly loves this girl, you may push him away. You do not wish to alienate your son."

When Darcy left Matlock's study a short time later, he was thoughtful. It was all Matlock could ask for.

The footsteps of the footman receded down the hall, allowing George

Wickham to breathe a sigh of relief. Though he might have succeeded in explaining his presence outside the earl's study door to Mr. Darcy, the earl himself was a different matter. Whereas Mr. Darcy enjoyed his company and did not hear anything against him, Lord Matlock had always listened to the words of his nephew and son. Charming him had been as difficult as stopping the tide.

When the footman was gone, Wickham heard another sound—the footsteps of his patron, moving away from his position of concealment. Wickham risked a glance around the corner, noting Mr. Darcy's retreating form until he turned a corner, and when he was gone, Wickham took the opportunity to make his own escape.

Not knowing what to think of the conversation he had overheard, Wickham found himself in a part of the house which would not result in uncomfortable questions and slowed his pace, walking deep in thought. Though his heart had soared when Mr. Darcy suggested disinheriting his prig of a son and making Wickham his heir, even then Wickham had known it was unlikely the man would follow through with it. Mr. Darcy had been obligingly easy to flatter into being Wickham's firmest supporter, but he was, at heart, still a proud man, his reaction to his son's reported courtship evidence of that fact. Making Wickham his heir was an impossibility. Much as Wickham wished it to be different, he was the son of a steward, and nothing would change that.

The question was, could he use the knowledge he now possessed for his own gain? In the end, Wickham thought it was possible Mr. Darcy might be induced to disinherit his son if he was pushed to it. If he did so, Wickham had no doubt Georgiana would assume the position of his heir, likely with the stipulation her future husband take her name to preserve it for future generations. Could Wickham resign his name in order to gain the great wealth of Pemberley?

The mere thought caused Wickham to chuckle under his breath. There was very little Wickham would *not* do to become a rich man himself. He had no particular attachment to his name, it being in no way prestigious or having done him any good in his life. Besides, gaining the Darcy name, being in a position to thumb his nose at Darcy that he, Wickham, was to inherit the estate would be a most delicious revenge.

The sound of a pianoforte reached through Wickham's ruminations and he paused, listening. While both Lady Anne and Lady Susan were accomplished pianists, Wickham was certain it was Georgiana Darcy who was the current author of the music floating through the halls. A grin suffused Wickham's face—perhaps the time to begin charming the girl was now.

The music room at Snowlock was situated in such a way that the pianoforte was on the other side of the room, the musician's back to the door. Silently, Wickham opened the door, a quick look about confirming that she was alone in the room. Then he slipped inside, leaving the door ajar to give the appearance of propriety—appearance was everything at present.

For a few moments, Wickham listened to the girl play. As his understanding of music—and interest—was rudimentary, he was not certain what she was playing. One of the great composers, no doubt. But Wickham could easily see that she was quite talented, notwithstanding her tender years. When she finally finished what she was playing with a flourish, he took the opportunity to take the first steps to ingratiating himself into her affections.

"Marvelous, Miss Darcy," said he, clapping. "Absolutely marvelous."

It was to some disappointment that Wickham watched the girl as she turned, apparently unsurprised by his presence. She was a mousey sort of girl, shy and reticent, and he had thought he might provoke her to fright, which he could use as a pretext to comfort her.

"Mr. Wickham," said she with perfect civility. "Thank you, sir. I have been practicing this piece for some time."

"Simply breathtaking, my dear," said Wickham. "I do not think I have ever heard such a wonderful rendition of Mozart in my entire life."

Miss Darcy smiled at Wickham, and he had the distinct impression she was laughing at him. "That was Bach, Mr. Wickham."

Though Wickham was not at all versed in music, he thought he was familiar with all the principle composers—or at least their names. Bach was a name with which he was unfamiliar. Miss Darcy appeared to realize his confusion, for she nodded and said:

"Bach was a German composer who died many years before Herr Mozart, Mr. Wickham. It is unfortunate his music is not well-known today, for it is quite impressive, do you not think?"

"Impressive, indeed," said Mr. Wickham, pushing his mistake to the side. "Have you any other pieces you could play for me? I find myself highly desiring to hear you continue to play."

"Oh, there are many others I could play, Mr. Wickham. But as my mother is now here, I believe we are to walk in the gardens for a time."

Startled, Wickham, turned his head, noting that Lady Anne had, indeed, entered the room and was watching him with what could only be termed distrust. But Wickham was not one to allow surprise to pierce his mask of amiability. Thus, he bowed to his patron's wife.

"Lady Anne. I am certain you must be quite proud of your daughter. Her skill is nothing less than exquisite."

"*We* are very proud of her, Mr. Wickham," said Lady Anne, a clear reference to her husband. "Now, if you will excuse us."

"Of course," said Wickham smoothly. "I would not dream of keeping you from your exercise. I hope you enjoy yourselves."

"Thank you," said Lady Anne, before guiding her daughter from the room.

When the door closed behind them, Wickham stood there for some time, looking at it, considering. Lady Anne had been as immune to his charm as Lord Matlock had been, which made Wickham's task all that much more difficult. The woman was watchful over her little daughter, and Wickham doubted he would find it easy to maneuver around the mother hen.

But it mattered little. There was plenty of time still. The first step was to convince Mr. Darcy of the merits of disowning his son. When that had been accomplished, he would have plenty of time to complete the wooing of the man's daughter.

"I do not trust Mr. Wickham, Mama," said Georgiana Darcy as she exited the house with her mother.

"A wise stance, Georgiana," said Lady Anne. She turned and looked at her daughter. "What did he say?"

"Nothing in particular," said Georgiana with a shrug. "He complimented me on my playing." Georgiana paused and giggled. "He mistook Bach for Mozart."

"As you know, Bach is not at all popular," said Lady Anne, distracted by her thoughts.

"Perhaps he is not," replied Georgiana with a hint of exasperation. "But their styles are so different that even if Mr. Wickham did not know I was playing Bach, he should not have thought it to be Mozart. Handel, perhaps, but Mozart?"

Lady Anne turned a smile on her only daughter. "It has never seemed to me that Mr. Wickham cared much for music. I doubt he knows Vivaldi from Beethoven."

"That much is evident."

"He is planning something," said Lady Anne, still considering her husband's unwanted protégé.

"Is he not always engaged in some stratagem? William does not trust him at all."

"As he informed us himself when we were last in his company," said Lady Anne. "This may be nothing more than Mr. Wickham's usual practice of flattery for gain. But I want you to take care with him, Georgiana. He lusts after riches and would undoubtedly find your dowry an irresistible temptation."

"There is no need to worry for me, Mama," declared Georgiana. "William's word is more than enough for me to be on my guard in Mr. Wickham's company. He will not charm me."

"That is good," replied Lady Anne. "But remember that a man such as Mr. Wickham may not be content with simply attempting to woo you. Under no circumstances are you to be alone with him—a maid should attend you at all times, at the very least."

"I understand, Mama."

With her daughter's agreement, Lady Anne allowed the subject to drop. But she continued to think of it for some time, worrying the matter of George Wickham over in her mind as they continued to walk. Whatever the man planned, she would not allow him to succeed, and as her husband would hear nothing against Mr. Wickham, it was her responsibility to ensure he was watched carefully.

While Darcy was becoming fatigued at being constantly asked questions concerning his father's likely reaction to his intentions with respect to Miss Elizabeth, he kept his countenance neutral. Mr. Bennet, whom Darcy had grown to esteem greatly, deserved to know the answer to his questions. When the assurance had been given and accepted, Mr. Bennet sat back in his chair, his scrutiny not comfortable in the slightest. Knowing he deserved the man's hesitance and more, Darcy remained quiet, waiting for him to speak.

"The other matter which we must canvass is, I suppose, this business between you and Elizabeth from your first visit to the neighborhood." Mr. Bennet paused and considered Darcy closely. "If I was concerned at all about your character, I would run you off the estate at once. Do not allow my retiring nature to mislead you, young man, for I love my daughters very much!"

"That was never in question, Mr. Bennet," said Darcy, eschewing any further comment.

"As it is," replied Bennet, "I can readily see the esteem Lizzy holds for you, and it is quite similar to my own. While I would prefer you had acted properly, I can see where a man's sense might be overcome

248 *> Jann Rowland

by the reality of a beautiful young girl teasing him."

"I am not happy with my own behavior, Mr. Bennet," said Darcy quietly. "When I examine my own memories, however, I can only say that it was nothing less than the impulse of the moment."

Mr. Bennet chuckled and shook his head. "It seems it was, sir. I trust there will be no more impulses of that nature? Now that you are courting my daughter, the time for such things is in the future. It may be closer than you think."

"That is my fervent wish, Mr. Bennet," replied Darcy with a smile. "Having raised her, you can be in no doubt as to the extent of the enticement your daughter offers. But as to improper displays, I pledge to you that they shall not occur. I shall behave with perfect gentlemanly compartment."

"Excellent!" said Mr. Bennet. "I shall count on it. Now, I should appreciate your dispensing with this 'Mr. Bennet' nonsense. I suspect I shall be gaining you as a son-in-law, and in such a situation, I shall not countenance formality. Bennet will do excellently if you please."

Smiling, Darcy gave his assent and requested the same as Mr. Bennet. It was an auspicious start, and far more than he deserved — of this Darcy was well aware. If the younger Mr. Bennet still looked on him with wariness, Darcy knew he deserved that as well. In the future, his behavior would speak for itself, proving to the man he wished would be his future brother of his trustworthy nature.

They left Mr. Bennet's study soon after, joining the other members of the family and Bingley, who had accompanied him from Netherfield and was situated with the eldest Miss Bennet. Then Darcy found himself in the enchanting Miss Elizabeth Bennet's company again, and his attention could not be spared for anyone else.

CHAPTER XXIV

$\mathcal{F}$oreboding. It was a premonition of utter disquiet that spread through Darcy when the carriage carrying his family was sighted approaching Netherfield's manor.

But there was nothing to be done. The invitation had been offered and accepted, and while Darcy was not convinced his father would not offend his friends, the die had now been cast. The Bingleys were good people, and hopefully his father's innate sense of politeness would prevent him from making a poor impression.

"You appear as if you fear the approach of the French army, Darcy," said Bingley in his ear. "Do not concern yourself, for I am certain all shall be well."

Though he was not certain Bingley had the right of it—and his friend was altogether too prone to expecting the best—Darcy quelled his nervousness. It was the family's largest and most expensive carriage, and Darcy could not help but wonder if his father had chosen it because it would impress his hosts with the extent of the Darcy family's prosperity. Then the carriage stopped, the footmen opened the door, and Darcy witnessed a sight which changed his disquiet to rage.

"Mr. Darcy," said Bingley, as the only one of the Bingley family with whom they were acquainted, "welcome to Netherfield! And Lady Anne and Miss Darcy too!"

The fourth member of the party stood just behind Darcy's father, looking about with interest, not to mention the hint of avarice which was always present. Then he caught sight of Darcy and smirked, sending Darcy's anger spiraling ever higher. Insensible to the anger the man's presence had provoked, Mr. Darcy allowed the introduction to be completed between his family and the Bingleys — the Hursts were also present — and then turned to introduce the other member of the party.

"Please allow me to introduce my protégé, George Wickham."

Darcy could not determine if Mr. Bingley had known of Wickham's inclusion in the party in advance, for he welcomed them all with equal amiability, inviting the travelers into the house. Mrs. Bingley offered them some refreshment after they were shown to their rooms, to which Darcy's parents agreed with alacrity.

"Thank you, Mrs. Bingley. It has been a long journey. An opportunity to refresh ourselves would be welcome, indeed."

When the family had made their way above stairs, Darcy lost no time in speaking to Mr. Bingley and his son. "I apologize, Mr. Bingley, but were you aware of the inclusion of Mr. Wickham in my father's party?"

"Only last night," replied Bingley's father. "Your father sent me a letter, informing me of his presence in their party. Is there some problem?"

Incensed that his father would see fit to impose Wickham on the Bingleys when he was not even part of the family, Darcy remained silent for several moments, taking care to master his pique. The dilemma was what to do on the matter. It would reflect poorly on his father if he informed them exactly what kind of man Wickham was, but he did not wish to leave the Bingleys unarmed against the machinations of his detested former friend. At least Miss Bingley was now married, as was Mrs. Hurst — neither could be a target of Wickham's schemes, though Darcy knew Wickham was not above wooing a married woman. The Bennet sisters were another matter altogether as they were all handsome, possessed impressive dowries, and were connected with Darcy himself. At least they did not reside at Netherfield.

In the end, Darcy decided to give them an oblique warning to avoid shaming his father. "I have not associated with Mr. Wickham for some years. To be honest, the last I heard of him, Wickham was in the employment of a law firm in London. I am shocked to see him here."

"Is there something deficient in him?" asked Mr. Bingley. The man was as serious as Darcy had ever seen him, and he knew it was not wise to keep what he knew from his knowledge.

"My father will hear nothing against him," said Darcy, trying to put the other man on his guard with as much tact as he possessed, "but he has not had the opportunity to see George Wickham in unguarded moments as I have. Wickham will be on his best behavior with my father present, but that does not mean he should be trusted."

It seemed Mr. Bingley heard what Darcy did not say and understood the reason for it. Rather than become angry or press further, the gentleman reached out and squeezed Darcy's shoulder.

"Seeing your father favor another man cannot be easy — I begin to understand some of the friction between you. I will have a word with the butler and housekeeper and have a discreet watch maintained on Mr. Wickham."

Then the elder gentleman turned and departed, leaving Darcy alone with Bingley. While in normal circumstances Bingley deferred to Darcy, in this instance his concern for what he was seeing overrode that tendency.

"Now that my father has left us, shall you not inform me of what you know of Wickham? I know you and Fitzwilliam have made some uncomplimentary comments about the man in the past, but this is a little more serious than a simple rivalry."

"Wickham? A rival?" Darcy snorted with utter disdain. "Perhaps if you were to sit at the gaming tables with him. Otherwise, the only competition for him exists in the worst of humanity, for I certainly do not consider him a challenge.

"He is a gamester," said Darcy, holding up his hand when Bingley would have spoken again. "When we were at Cambridge, he had little interest in his studies and much in every manner of vice known to man. To this day, I have little understanding how he managed to graduate, for I never saw him so much as open a book. The shopkeepers in Meryton should be warned to avoid extending credit, and you should speak with the housekeeper and insist she watch over the maids. While he might not attempt to seduce one with my father in residence, he is not above trifling with them. And when he is eventually introduced to the Bennets, you may wish to ensure he is not left in their company alone."

"That is not a flattering picture you paint of the man."

"If you doubt me, ask Fitzwilliam. His response will be much less complimentary and much more colorful."

Bingley shook his head. "Thank you, Darcy. I will second my father's words to the housekeeper." Then Bingley left, muttering to himself.

"Are you telling tales again, Darcy?"

"That would suggest I am relating falsehoods," said Darcy, turning to glare at his nemesis, who was descending the stairs from the upper level of the house. "When I speak of you, there is no need to embellish, for the truth will more than suffice."

A snort was Wickham's reply, and his eyes raked disdainfully over Darcy. Given the speed at which he had once again descended, Darcy thought it certain he had not changed and had only given the barest attention to making himself presentable. The only times when Wickham ignored such things—for he was vain, attempting to show himself an impeccably groomed gentleman at all times—was when he thought presenting himself with alacrity was more important. Or when he thought he could torment Darcy.

"What is this I hear of you courting a young lady?" sneered Wickham. "I had not thought you had it in you, old boy. Then again, I assume there *must* be some woman in this world who is as dull as you. It *is* astonishing, however, you have managed to find her."

"And I am equally astonished to see you here, Wickham," taunted Darcy in return. "Did your employers finally have enough of your affected manners and throw you out? If that is the case, it is not surprising you would return to Pemberley to leech off my family."

It seemed they were having two different conversations, for Wickham ignored him and continued in the vein of his previous statements. "I cannot wait to be introduced to the woman who captured the elusive Fitzwilliam Darcy. Of course, it may be better for you if she remained unknown to me. You know as well as I that no woman would continue to favor you when I am nearby."

Darcy smiled at his nemesis, and Wickham eyed him warily because of it. "Just remember, Wickham—I know exactly what you are. If you presume to step one foot out of line while you are here, not even my father will save you." Darcy stepped close and hissed in his ear: "And stay clear of Miss Elizabeth. Depend upon it: I shall be relating to her *exactly* what manner of man you are at the first opportunity."

"I see you two are already in fine form."

Stepping back, Darcy noted the approach of his father, followed by his mother and sister. Mr. Darcy was peering at them, exasperation evident in his countenance and manner. When he reached the bottom of the stairs, he put himself between them and glared at each in turn.

"As we are now guests, I would remind you both your conflict cannot be allowed to continue. I will not have you staining the family's name with this pointless contention. Cease it now, I say!"

"Of course, Mr. Darcy," said Wickham smoothly. "For your sake, I shall endeavor to forget Darcy's offenses directed at me."

For his part, Darcy shook his head. "If you would have harmony between us, I suggest you send him back to whatever hole he inhabited in London. If you will not, then keep him from speaking to me and suppress his usual proclivities. Then I shall be pleased."

"Can you not bury your enmity as Wickham does?" asked Mr. Darcy with a rueful shake of his head.

"It is a mark of your blindness with respect to this snake that you think *anything* he says is sincere," retorted Darcy.

How the situation might have escalated Darcy did not know. It had been apparent to him for some years that it was pointless to discuss Wickham with his father as Mr. Darcy would not hear. It was, perhaps, unwise to speak in such a manner to his father, but the sight of Wickham angered Darcy, and he knew he was not always rational when angry. It was for this reason he had always striven for calm before speaking.

In this instance, however, his mother chose to intervene. "I believe it is best to refrain from further argument. Our hosts await us."

Though it was clear Mr. Darcy wished to say something more, he nodded curtly to his wife's words and motioned Darcy to show them to the sitting-room. It did not escape Darcy's notice that Wickham was watching him, self-satisfaction clear for all to see. But Darcy ignored him. When he offered his arm to Georgiana before the libertine could, he proceeded toward the sitting-room with his sister on his arm, noting with fierce satisfaction that Wickham was forced to walk by himself.

The Bingley family proved themselves to be genial and welcoming — or at least those who bore the Bingley name did. Hurst was, as usual, uncommunicative, saying little, concentrating his attention on the refreshments Mrs. Bingley had ordered. Mrs. Hurst was a little more open, but Darcy thought he detected a hint of avarice in her manner, though he did not know how the woman thought she could profit from a distant acquaintance with his family.

The elder Bingleys were, however, gracious and welcoming, and Bingley was his usual garrulous self. There was some brief conversation, especially between Mrs. Bingley and Lady Anne, who spoke of some domestic matters, Georgiana sitting with them. Darcy's father spoke primarily with Mr. Bingley and his son, and while he appeared to listen to them closely and speak with perfect civility, Darcy, who knew his father, noted he appeared to be more than a little aloof and proud. For Wickham's part, he sat and observed, a pose more troubling than had he attempted to charm them all.

"I understand you have owned this estate for many years, Mr. Bingley," said Mr. Darcy after they had been sitting together for some time.

"Yes, before the turn of the century," replied Mr. Bingley. "The former owners were to immigrate to the Americas, allowing me to purchase at a good price."

"Do you primarily produce wheat, or do you engage in crop rotation?"

The next several moments were spent talking of estate matters, and Darcy was pleased that Mr. Bingley proved himself capable of speaking intelligently concerning the typical concerns of gentlemen everywhere. His father seemed to see this as his manner became a little less aloof and a little more interested the longer they spoke. Then the conversation turned, and Darcy felt his good humor dissipate because of it.

"Since you have lived in this neighborhood for many years, I must assume you are familiar with the families nearby."

"Of course," was Mr. Bingley's simple reply.

"What can you tell me of them?"

The attempt to learn more of the Bennets was transparent, but Mr. Bingley responded regardless. "The people are worthy. There is a preponderance of smaller estates, but they are good people, nonetheless. The only other family who are of our level of consequence are the Bennets, and we have been close to that family since we moved here. My youngest daughter is, you understand, recently married to the Bennet heir."

"Yes," said Mr. Darcy with a short nod, "I had heard that. Please accept my congratulations."

"Caroline is happy," interjected Mrs. Bingley. "We had long expected their union, and it would have occurred sooner, had it not been for Mrs. Bennet's unfortunate passing. There is also reason to suppose our own son, Charles, will be united to the Bennets' eldest daughter, Jane, before long." Mrs. Bingley favored her son with a warm smile—Bingley appeared a little silly, seemingly immersed in a recollection of Miss Bennet's manifold attractions. "Their inclination is plain for anyone of any wit to see."

"I have not yet proposed to Miss Bennet," said Bingley, shaking off his introspection.

"Perhaps not, Charles," said Mrs. Bingley. "But we all anticipate it, regardless."

"The Bennets have other children?" asked Mr. Darcy.

"Two more daughters," supplied Mr. Bingley. "Elizabeth is the elder, Mary the younger. Both are good girls, lively and poised, though Elizabeth is the more open. Neither are a match for Jane, who is widely considered the most beautiful lady in the district, but both are lovely ladies in their own rights."

What his father hoped to learn from his discussion of the Bennet ladies, Darcy could not be certain. It may be that he doubted Darcy's ability to speak of them with anything resembling impartiality, and Darcy supposed he was likely correct. The conversation persisted for some time, the Bingleys extoling the virtues of the Bennets, while Mr. Darcy subtly attempted to draw out more information.

At length, however, the Bingleys invited their guests to return to their rooms to rest before dinner, and the company dispersed. Had Darcy had any thought to the contrary he might have been disappointed, but knowing his father, he was aware that Mr. Darcy would wish to speak further of the reason that drew them to Hertfordshire. In this, he was not disappointed.

"The rooms to which we have been assigned have a sitting-room attached," said he as soon as they were out in the hall. "Let us make use of it for a family conference."

Darcy nodded and led his family up the stairs. When they reached the door, he stepped aside, allowing his mother to lead the way with Georgiana, though she stopped and ran her hand along her son's arm in a gesture of affection. Then Darcy had all the pleasure of seeing his father enter the room without a second thought, not sparing a glance for Wickham. It was clear that, whatever his pretensions, Wickham was *not* a member of the family, not that he appreciated the evidence before his eyes.

With a smirk, Darcy entered the room and closed the door on the scoundrel, relishing the anger with which Wickham regarded them. When the door closed, he turned to look at his family — his mother and Georgiana had seated themselves on a sofa, while Mr. Darcy remained standing. It was his father who drew his gaze.

"I am sure you can be at no loss as to the reason for our journey here, Fitzwilliam."

"Even had your letter not betrayed the reason," said Darcy, "I could hardly have misinterpreted it. I will own I am uncertain of how you learned of the matter, and I cannot say what you mean to do about it."

"Do not speak to me in such a way!" snapped his father. "The manner of our learning of the situation does not signify. While I thought I had instilled into you a sense of your own worth, it seems I was mistaken. How can you consider bringing such infamy on this family? Do you not remember yourself, your family, your very heritage?"

"None of these would be ruined if I were to aspire to a connection with Miss Bennet. You do not know her, Father—I would appreciate it if you would not lower yourself to disparage her without making her acquaintance."

Darcy's words provoked such a stony expression that he wondered if his father would manage to respond without completely losing his temper. Even so, he could not have predicted what his father was to say next.

"Do you not know I thought of disowning you?"

"You would cut me off for following my heart?" said Darcy, his anger growing as he regarded the man who had raised him.

"That is enough," said Lady Anne, rising and stepping between their increasingly tense confrontation. "Though the thought crossed your mind, you and I know you would never do disown our son. It does no good to speak of it and will only increase the tension between you."

"I wish to meet Miss Elizabeth," said Georgiana softly. She darted a look in Darcy's direction, her smile widening when she saw his affection, and continued: "If my brother has chosen her, I cannot imagine she is not everything lovely."

"It is possible she *is* a lovely young woman," said Mr. Darcy, in a tone which suggested his daughter should not gainsay him. "But that is not the point. There is little chance she is suitable, having been raised in this neighborhood. I heard what your friend's father said—these Bennets, for whom you appear to have lost your head, are naught but modest gentry."

"And yet Miss Elizabeth is perfect," said Darcy. "She may not possess the highest of connections or a dowry to rival that of the daughter of a duke, but she is capable of anything to which she sets her mind, and her dowry is respectable."

"Tell us of her, Fitzwilliam," said his mother. The glance at her husband which accompanied her words was enough to quell Mr. Darcy's objections for the moment. He was no happier than before, but at least he had ceased his open objections.

"As I said, she is a lovely girl." Darcy paused, thinking about the woman who held his heart, all the qualities that endeared her to him running through his mind. "Miss Elizabeth is calm and poised, lively in company, and sings like an angel. She is happy, her manners genuine, and she can speak of matters of substance, unlike what I have often seen among the heiresses of the ton. Furthermore, she can debate Shakespeare or Milton, plays chess with sufficient skill to best me with regularity, and shows compassion, caring, love, and charity with ease and without artifice. If you only knew her, you would agree she could not be more suitable if she was the daughter of the prince regent himself!"

"She sounds lovely," said Georgiana with a shy smile, Lady Anne agreeing with her daughter.

But Mr. Darcy was not amused. "So far I have not heard you say anything of her *suitability*, Fitzwilliam. She may be the most intelligent lady in the world, but if she lacks those attributes which make her acceptable to society, she remains unsuitable. What are her connections, her dowry, her position in society?"

"Irrelevant, in my opinion," rejoined Darcy. His father's countenance darkened, but he appeared to be trying to master his anger. At Lady Anne's pleading look, Darcy capitulated. "As I said, Miss Elizabeth's family is gentry and have been for many generations. The estate is a good one, the house fine, if nothing to Pemberley. I suspect the estate takes in something in excess of five thousand a year, and it is managed prudently and with all the most modern techniques by Mr. Bennet and his heir.

"As for their connections in town, I will own I do not know the extent of any relations. They have an uncle—related to the late Mrs. Bennet, I believe—who is not only very successful, but possesses connections to men of wealth himself. They are, themselves, of the second circles, well respected, and with no stain of anything untoward attached to them. Mr. Bennet's heir is, as I believe Bingley's father mentioned, married to the Bingleys' youngest daughter."

Darcy turned a pointed glare at his father. "There is, in short, nothing with which to reproach them, unless you count being separate from the worst elements of our society detrimental."

"Except that they are not of our circles," growled Mr. Darcy. "And it sounds, unless I miss my guess, like this uncle in town is in trade."

"The Gardiners are respectable," said Darcy. "Mr. Gardiner is a good man who would not be out of place in any society in which he chooses to move. The only difference is he is a far better man than most of them."

"But she is not of the proper lineage and position to be the future mistress of Pemberley!" cried Mr. Darcy. "What must I say to induce your understanding?"

"You cannot," said Darcy. "In my eyes she is perfect. It is my hope you will someday see her worth."

"I am anticipating meeting this paragon," said Lady Anne, again glancing at her husband. "There is no issue with making her acquaintance."

While he scowled yet again, it seemed to Darcy his father was fatigued by their argument, though he was not foolish enough to believe he had given in. Mr. Darcy threw himself in a nearby chair, sitting there with his chin held moodily in one hand. For a moment, he did not say anything.

"I suppose we must meet this woman," said he at length, turning to face his son. "But at present I shall promise nothing more than to reserve judgment."

"That will suffice," said Darcy. "All I wish is for you to meet her and remain open to her qualities. I have every confidence in Miss Elizabeth's ability to win even you over, Father."

"We shall see," said Mr. Darcy, standing. "For now, I believe I shall take Mr. Bingley's advice and rest before dinner."

When he was gone into the bedroom, Darcy turned to his mother and sister, giving them a wry smile he was not certain was not sickly and wan. "Thank you for your support, Mother."

Lady Anne's affection shone forth in the smile with which she favored him. "I trust you, Fitzwilliam. There is no thought in my mind you might favor an unsuitable woman."

"Of course not," said Darcy. "I am curious, however, about Wickham's presence. Was he not in town?"

"Mr. Wickham arrived at Pemberley about a week ago," said Lady Anne. "It was he who brought word of this young lady to us in Derbyshire."

Surprised, Darcy could only stare at his mother. "Then I know not how he might have learned of it."

"You were not seen in town with her? Gossip spreads quickly in London."

"It does," replied Darcy. "But we were very discrete and were only in town for a few days. Miss Elizabeth's presence was requested as her aunt had fallen ill. We attended one ball, but as Bingley and I escorted the Bennet sisters, I do not think I gave the appearance of favoring her over any other young lady."

Lady Anne regarded him with a fond smile. "It does not surprise me you do not think so. But as my son, I am well aware of your ways, and I suspect a single look at you together would have set tongues to wagging. Perhaps Wickham heard of it. The man is a born schemer."

"Father's express arrived the day of the ball," said Darcy with a shaken head. "That evening could not be what informed Wickham of my activities. I have always suspected he has some means of keeping track of the family — this seems to prove my supposition."

"Perhaps it does. But there is nothing to be done about it now. Regardless, Georgiana and I are fatigued as well. We shall see you at dinner."

Lady Anne extended her hand to her daughter, and Georgiana followed her into her own bedchamber, though Georgiana smiled expressively at Darcy as she was led away. Georgiana would, Darcy thought, love Miss Elizabeth, and the presence of a woman her own age and as confident as Miss Elizabeth in her life would benefit her.

As Darcy let himself out of his parents' sitting-room, his mind kept replaying the confrontation with his father, and from thence to the question of how Wickham had learned of Miss Elizabeth. It was fortunate the libertine was nowhere in evidence at that moment, for Darcy did not think himself capable of withstanding Wickham's glib tongue without planting a facer on him. And while he was not certain of how Wickham had obtained his information, he did not think it was because of gossip.

Regardless, Darcy decided it did not signify. The more pressing matter was the protection of Miss Elizabeth from Wickham's depredations. For Darcy had little doubt Wickham would take any opportunity to hurt him through Miss Elizabeth. Vigilance was required.

CHAPTER XXV

"Relax, Lizzy. There is nothing of which you need fear."
Though Elizabeth had not thought her nervousness was that pronounced, the looks in the faces of her family—which ranged from concerned to amused—told her otherwise. Caroline, who had spoken, reached out her hand, grasping Elizabeth's, and squeezing. By her other side, Jane was watching with sympathy.

"There is no need to fear, perhaps," said Elizabeth. "But I hardly think my worries are without foundation."

Sitting not far from the four ladies—for Mary was also nearby, ostensibly with a book in hand, though Elizabeth did not think she had turned many pages—the two gentlemen watched, Mr. Bennet showing his own interest, while Thomas's feelings were unreadable. Mr. Bennet gave Elizabeth a fortifying smile before turning back to his newspaper.

"When Mr. Darcy comes, you will see his father is not so fearsome," said Caroline. "If nothing else, he will accept you for his son's sake."

"Why, thank you Caroline," replied Elizabeth, injecting all the sarcasm she felt into her voice. When Caroline's smile widened, Elizabeth huffed with exasperation. "It is not as if you have any frame of reference, *dearest* Sister. Your marriage was anticipated long before it occurred, and your husband's father was in favor of the match."

A snort from behind Mr. Bennet's paper drew Elizabeth's gaze, but as he did not lower his paper, Elizabeth was unable to show her father her displeasure. Elizabeth decided to ignore him.

"This is an interesting picture, is it not?" said Jane, her countenance a mask of pure innocence. "If Elizabeth was indifferent to Mr. Darcy, her nerves would not be as noticeable, I should think."

"It *does* suggest feelings our sister has not yet acknowledged, does it not?" added Mary in a teasing tone.

"Perhaps we should encourage her to be more explicit," said Caroline.

When faced with three sisters all intent upon teasing her, Elizabeth did the only thing she could: she laughed. While her brother looked on her as if she had lost her mind, Elizabeth could not help herself, and the release of tension felt marvelous. Of course, her sisters were drawn along with her, their mirth lasting for several moments. When it had run its course, Elizabeth directed a look of mock severity at them all.

"Is it not I who is supposed to be the tease?"

"And it is only fair we return it when we can," said Caroline, Jane and Mary nodding and grinning widely.

"Now answer the question, dear," said Jane. "Are you more welcoming of Mr. Darcy's attentions? Do you love him?"

"Love?" asked Elizabeth softly, testing the word on the tip of her tongue, trying to determine how it felt when she said it aloud. "This has all happened too quickly to be love, I think."

"But you are not indifferent to him," pressed Jane.

"That seems impossible, Jane," replied Elizabeth. "Mr. Darcy is, I believe, a good sort of man, possessing all the qualities which render him a desirable prospect."

"His wealth is fabulous," said Caroline, grinning.

"He is handsome, too," chirped Mary.

"And you must not forget how he speaks with our Elizabeth on her level," giggled Jane. "As far as I am aware, our father is the only other one who does so."

"He is perfect!" declared all three girls at once, prompting them all to laughter. This time, Mr. Bennet lowered his paper and laughed along with them, and even Thomas showed them an indulgent grin.

The sound of the door chime startled them to silence, and Elizabeth's nerves returned as if they had never left. Mr. Hill was, at that very moment, no doubt greeting their guests and leading them to the sitting-room—the dreaded meeting was upon her!

"Just remember, Lizzy," said Jane, her whisper for Elizabeth's ears alone, "show these people Lizzy Bennet, my sister, and everything will be well. If you do that, I doubt they can resist you."

As the door opened, Elizabeth flashed a smile at her sister, Jane's words of encouragement bolstering her courage more than anything else had that morning. Then Mr. Hill was leading their company into the room, the Bingleys accompanying the Darcys, and Elizabeth's attention was caught by the demands of the moment.

Mr. Darcy stepped forward and performed the office of introducing his family to the Bennet family's acquaintance, and Elizabeth obtained her first impressions of the family. The girl, Georgiana, was tall and pretty, blond and blue-eyed, but possessing what Elizabeth suspected was a shy demeanor. She was the very image of the older woman, Lady Anne Darcy. But where the girl was reticent, Lady Anne was confident and forward, greeting the family with excellent manners and gracious interest.

As for Mr. Darcy, the elder, he was a tall man, much like his son, and also like his wife and daughter, his son resembled him closely. There was a little grey on his head, mostly around the temples, though it was also sprinkled through his hair. His jaw was squarer than Fitzwilliam Darcy's, and his eyes burned with an icy cold fire. Those eyes rested upon Elizabeth, inspecting, judging, and unless Elizabeth missed her guess, she was found wanting.

There was one other member of the party, a handsome man with wavy blond hair and shocking blue eyes. When Mr. Darcy introduced him, his manner was such to make it appear an afterthought, which brought a scowl from the elder Darcy, though the blond man smiled in what seemed to be amusement. He was introduced as a Mr. Wickham and greeted them with an effortless charm. After, however, he sat largely silent, observing them all and, in particular, Elizabeth, unless she missed her guess.

In her capacity of the estate's mistress, Caroline welcomed their visitors, inviting them to sit while she sent for tea and cakes. For the first few moments, the elder Mr. Darcy was silent, seemingly weighing what he was seeing. The residents of Netherfield and those of Longbourn carried much of the conversation, speaking of matters of the neighborhood common in such gatherings. The younger Mr. Darcy—Elizabeth idly wondered what she should call the younger man, since the elder was indisputably "Mr. Darcy"—sat beside Elizabeth in seeming defiance of his father's contempt, asking her quiet queries of how she was, which Elizabeth answered with an absence of thought.

Then Elizabeth's father struck up a conversation with Mr. Darcy's father, speaking of their journey from the north. It seemed Mr. Darcy recognized her father as an intelligent man, for he conversed with him with nothing less than perfect civility.

"You have a good property here, it seems," observed Mr. Darcy. "Has it been in your family long?"

"Ten generations," replied Mr. Bennet.

Mr. Darcy seemed impressed.

"A distant ancestor provided a service for the Crown," continued Mr. Bennet, "and was rewarded with a small plot of land immediately around the house. Subsequent masters of the estate made additional purchases and expanded the house and property to what it is now." Mr. Bennet smiled with fondness at his family's legacy. "I have continued in my ancestors' footsteps, adding a pair of fields on the northern edge of the estate. I hope my son will continue the tradition."

"A concern for the master of any estate," said Mr. Darcy, his tone ever so slightly friendlier. "My family has a similar history with our lands."

Mr. Bennet nodded. "Given what your son has told us, I dare say Longbourn is nothing to Pemberley. But it is a good estate, and we are fond of it."

"Surely ten generations of a family must spawn many connections."

"Indeed, it does," said Mr. Bennet, understanding the thrust of Mr. Darcy's comment. "Our family has been a rather small one for the past few generations—my own children aside. But we do have cousins in Surrey, Norfolk, Wiltshire, and a few other locations. There are none of them noteworthy or possessing any fame, but they are good people, nonetheless. I imagine it must be the same for you, sir."

"The Darcy family has been much like yours," replied Mr. Darcy. "Small for several generations. Most of our connections of late appear to be those families into which the Darcy family has married, as the closest Darcy cousins we have are several generations removed."

"Such as your noble connections," said Mr. Bennet, nodding in Lady Anne's direction. "If my late wife was still with us, she would be impressed with the rank of those who grace our sitting-room."

"Your late wife was not of the same level of society?" asked Mr. Darcy. Elizabeth imagined a fox pouncing on a fat hare. By her side, Mr. Darcy tensed.

"A few generations removed," replied Mr. Bennet, not offended by Mr. Darcy's questions. "My wife's great grandfather was a gentleman, and his son became a solicitor, passing his business down to *his* son. As the present Mr. Gardiner had no interest in the law and a head for business, the practice was passed down to the husband of my wife's eldest sister."

Mr. Bennet chuckled. "The landed Gardiners have not had much to do with my wife's family until she married me, and even now hold my brother-in-law at arms' length. Not that he is unhappy with their distance—I believe his income is now greater than his distant relations', and he intends to one day purchase an estate. I believe *his* wife would prefer to purchase in *your* neighborhood, sir, for she was raised as the parson's daughter in Lambton."

Mr. Bennet laughed. "I imagine if you were to ask them, they would be reluctant to speak of such matters. The Gardiners have no wish to publish their connections to improve their lot, though they have much better relations with Mrs. Gardiner's family, than with her husband's."

"Is her family from Lambton's neighborhood?" asked the elder Mr. Darcy, seeming curious in spite of himself.

"They are," confirmed Mr. Bennet. "Her maiden name is Plumber."

"Ah, yes. I am familiar with the Plumbers. They are good people." Mr. Darcy paused. "Do you produce much of the same as Mr. Bingley's estate?"

As the gentlemen began to talk of estate matters, Elizabeth looked to her suitor, seeing subtle signs he had relaxed, if only a little, though it was clear he kept a close eye on Mr. Wickham. When he saw her scrutiny, he gave her an affectionate smile, and turned back to attend the conversation between his father and hers. Their conversation attracted the other gentlemen, who drifted over to listen and give their opinions.

"Now, this will not do," said Lady Anne with a laugh. "If you gentlemen must speak of estate matters, that is your prerogative. But if you will, I should like to speak with Miss Elizabeth to become better acquainted with her."

With a shy smile at the great lady, Elizabeth nodded her willingness to accede to the plan. Mr. Darcy did not object—he seemed more at ease with Elizabeth in his mother's care and away from his father. The elder man did not reveal his opinion, though his eyes followed Elizabeth as she moved across the room. As it was, she was the only lady who moved—Caroline, Jane, and Mary, along with Mrs. Bingley, stayed together, content to allow Elizabeth to come to know her suitor's mother.

"Thank you for indulging me, Miss Elizabeth," said Lady Anne when Elizabeth was seated beside her. "Georgiana and I are both happy to make your acquaintance today. My son has spoken highly of you."

At that moment, Elizabeth's eyes met Mr. Darcy's from across the room, and she was warmed by his regard. Then she turned back to Lady Anne, noting the woman had seen the exchange. Whether she was amused or pleased, Elizabeth could not be certain. But she was certain the lady was not disapproving—in that, she was quite different from her husband, whose questions had bordered on impertinent. It was a curious dichotomy, considering Lady Anne was the daughter of an earl, whereas Mr. Darcy was naught but a gentleman.

"I hope you do not consider me impertinent, Miss Elizabeth, but we would like to come to know you better."

"Of course, Lady Anne," replied Elizabeth automatically. "What would you like to know?"

"Oh dear, that will not do!" said Lady Anne with a laugh. "You make it sound like an inquisition. It is most certainly not—I hope when we speak, our conversation will be easy. That is a much better way to come to know another, do you not agree?"

"Yes, I do," said Elizabeth, feeling even more relieved.

"Do you play the pianoforte?" blurted Miss Darcy. The girl colored at her sudden question, and even more when her mother laughed. But she did not relent, gazing at Elizabeth with a palpable interest.

"I do," replied Elizabeth, "though I do not think I can count myself a true proficient. But I enjoy it. If you wish to become acquainted with someone who is an enthusiast, you should approach my sister, Mary."

"Will Mary wish to play with me?" asked Georgiana shyly.

"We all will," replied Elizabeth, already charmed by this girl. "There seems a dearth of talented pianists in this neighborhood, which leaves our musical conversations somewhat lacking at times."

"Oh, that will not do!" exclaimed Miss Darcy. "Music is my favorite subject."

Lady Anne Darcy smiled fondly at her daughter. "Indeed, it is—so much so that at times we despair of inducing you to speak of anything else!"

When they laughed, Elizabeth laughed along with them, already feeling at ease. It seemed pretention was not a family trait—even for Mr. Darcy the elder, for though he did not approve of her, she thought it was more a consciousness of his family position, rather than self-importance. Then again, the two were interlocked, one often leading to the other.

The thought of the elder man drew Elizabeth's eyes to where he stood, conversing with the other gentlemen, and she found his eyes upon her. Rather than looking away, however, Mr. Darcy continued to gaze at her, whether in absence of thought or some other reason, Elizabeth could not say. Not one to allow herself to be intimidated, Elizabeth held his gaze for several moments before turning back. It was then she realized that Lady Anne had not missed their exchange.

"My husband is not disapproving of you, my dear," said Lady Anne. Then she smiled and added in a rueful tone: "Well, not of you in particular. The Darcy family is old, and they have become accustomed to the best of everything, including marriage connections for their children. Do you know that my family's noble status was the only reason my husband's father approved of me?"

"Truly?" asked Elizabeth, surprised to hear it.

"The Fitzwilliam family does not have nearly the history of the Darcys. We were ennobled only five generations ago and had not been landowners for long before that. Next to the Darcy family, which has held Pemberley's lands since the time of William the conqueror, we are mere babes in arms."

Lady Anne paused and smiled at her husband. "The Darcy family has refused titles more than once, though they have always been among the most loyal families to the crown. In some ways, I am certain my father-in-law considered the Fitzwilliams to be upstarts, opportunists who jumped at the chance to gain noble status when the Darcys had always spurned such things."

Lady Anne shook her head. "In some ways, he might have been correct, though we Fitzwilliams can be a proud lot ourselves. It is for this reason my husband pauses when confronted with you as a potential bride for our son. He married an earl's daughter, after all, while his father did the same. There are noble brides littered throughout the Darcy family tree, and even the daughter of a duke or two."

"With such illustrious heritage, it is of no surprise he would disapprove," said Elizabeth, feeling more than inadequate.

"For my part," continued Lady Anne, "I am much more concerned with my son's happiness. While my husband and I made a love match, he would have been content in a society marriage to a woman who brought him nothing but wealth and connections. Fitzwilliam is not the same, for he possesses a softer side, one which craves a meeting of the minds with his future wife. It is a trait my husband has often struggled to display, even with his own wife.

"Now, enough of this," said the lady. "I said I wish to know more of you. Speaking of my family's peculiarities will not accomplish it. Let us speak of other matters."

The visit was, in Elizabeth's opinion, a successful one. Mr. Darcy, for his part, remained with the other gentlemen, and while Elizabeth often felt the weight of his gaze upon her, he made little effort to speak directly with her, contenting himself with watching and contemplating. Since Elizabeth did not quite know what to make of him, she was content to leave it at that for the present. And while it might be supposed that the younger gentleman would prefer to be in Elizabeth's company, he kept to his father's side.

Of Mr. Wickham, Elizabeth was able to gain the least insight. She did not know anything of the man, which led her to believe she should reserve judgment—if he was with the Darcys, she assumed he must be a good man at the very least. But it seemed to Elizabeth that Mr. Wickham watched her as much as the elder Mr. Darcy, and once or twice, she thought she saw her suitor glaring at the man, which just as often provoked an insolent sneer in response.

Elizabeth found herself becoming fast friends with the Darcy ladies. While they spoke of music for some time, as was Miss Darcy's preference, they also canvassed many subjects, including literature, fashion, care of an estate's tenants, Elizabeth's friends and many other things besides. Everything both ladies uttered was said with intelligence and honesty, and Elizabeth found herself liking them very much. As the visit continued, her sisters and Mrs. Bingley drifted over to join the conversation, and eventually they were all involved.

When the time of the visit had elapsed, the visitors rose to depart, and Caroline exerted herself to invite the entire party for dinner. Mrs. Bingley, as the mistress of the manor at which they were staying, accepted with pleasure, embracing her daughter with affectionate pride. It was during this time that Lady Anne once again approached Elizabeth and grasped her hands, gazing at her with fondness.

"It was wonderful coming to know you, Miss Elizabeth. I hope the opportunities to further deepen our friendship will be plentiful."

"As do I," replied Elizabeth, feeling shy. "Tomorrow we shall return the favor and visit Netherfield. I look forward to it."

Lady Anne's smile gained a wry quality. "I believe you will do, my dear. In fact, I do not think my son could have chosen better."

The confusion Elizabeth felt must have been noticeable, for Lady Anne chuckled and said: "I know my son, Miss Elizabeth. Fitzwilliam is reticent and is considered by some to be entirely devoid of feeling.

But I know better. If the way he has looked at you the entire time of our visit has not informed me, the simple knowledge of his seeking you out would inform me of his feelings."

Lady Anne kissed Elizabeth's cheek. "I always knew that once he began to show interest in a woman, he would do so with his whole heart. It is a fact which my husband does not wish to acknowledge yet, but I know my son loves you. Mark my words—you will be my daughter someday."

Then with a final squeeze of her hands, Lady Anne left Elizabeth feeling quite light-headed. It did not last long, however, for as the visitors began to leave, Elizabeth turned to walk Mr. Darcy to the door. While they were thus engaged, a short and serious conversation ensued.

"I hope you liked my mother and sister."

"I liked them very much, indeed," replied Elizabeth, knowing the man could easily see her delight. "In the future, I hope to learn more of you, sir, for I am certain they have many stories they could share with me."

Mr. Darcy grinned, but then the smile ran away from his face. Halting, he watched the others of the party as they moved toward Longbourn's entrance, and when he deemed sufficient distance had been achieved, he turned to her, his mien as serious as Elizabeth had ever seen.

"Before I leave, I cannot go without warning you concerning Mr. Wickham."

"Mr. Wickham?" echoed Elizabeth, surprised. "I do not understand."

"And I do not have time to explain the matter in full. But I wish you to be aware that he is not as he seems. Wickham is adept at showing a charming front before the world, but at heart, he is lacking in character and vicious in his propensities."

Elizabeth gasped. "Are my sisters in danger?"

"At present, I do not believe so. As maintaining my father's good opinion is paramount in his mind, most of his propensities will be kept under good regulation for the moment. Or as much as he is capable.

"I more particularly wish you to be aware that he has been known to say some unsavory things about me and would consider it a triumph if he was able to change your opinion of me. As he has always been jealous of me, I doubt his forked tongue will remain in his mouth. He is also . . . rather free with his favors, though again, my father's presence will mute such tendencies."

"May I inform my sisters?"

"Please do," replied Mr. Darcy. "I would not have them taken unaware, for they possess enough dowry to tempt Wickham, whose goal in life has always been wealth in whatever manner he can obtain it. If he can ever manage it, he will put aside all pretense of restraint."

"Thank you for this warning." Elizabeth's eyes slid toward the entrance hall where the entire party had disappeared. "I will take care in his presence."

"Good," said Mr. Darcy.

They continued on their way toward the front door and found the others waiting for them there. Most all were grinning at this display of tardiness though Mr. Darcy did not appear happy at all. Elizabeth's eyes sought out Mr. Wickham in particular, and while he maintained a passive demeanor, Elizabeth was certain his eyes flashed in anger at the sight of Mr. Darcy. Clearly this was a man to watch with great care.

"Until next time, Miss Elizabeth," said Mr. Darcy, as he bowed and kissed her hand.

The rest of the company said their farewells, and soon the visitors had entered their carriages for the return journey to Netherfield. Elizabeth entered the house with her family.

"Well, it seems you have won over at least part of the Darcy family, Lizzy," teased Caroline as soon as they were within again. "Lady Anne appears ready to welcome you with open arms, and I dare say Miss Darcy would be happy if your wedding was tomorrow."

The rest of the company laughed at Caroline's sally. But while she expected Elizabeth to blush, there were other matters on her mind, the principal subject being the warning Mr. Darcy had just given her.

"Let us retire to the sitting-room," said Elizabeth. "For I have a communication I would make to you—something Mr. Darcy told me before he departed."

Sensing her sober mood, the family acquiesced without hesitation. And thus, Elizabeth informed them of the scant information she had learned. Though she still did not know what to make of it herself, she thought the gentlemen of her family would be asking for further details when next they were in Mr. Darcy's company.

CHAPTER XXVI

*T*hroughout the carriage ride back to Netherfield, Darcy watched
Wickham. It took no great insight to see that his former friend
was eager to let loose his wit, to see if he could provoke a
response in Darcy with the hope that his father would censure him.
Wickham had obviously seen the short tête-à-tête which had
proceeded between Darcy and Miss Elizabeth, and he would be a fool
if he did not know the reason for it—this would make him more bitter
than usual.

But what Wickham did not stop to consider was that Darcy was not
the same as he had been when they were younger. When they had been
boys, Wickham's taunting would have led to a fight, and he had
managed to ensure Darcy received a reprimand from his father on
more than one occasion. Even during their time at university, his ways
had resulted in fisticuffs more than once.

Now, however, Darcy was a man full grown, one who could fend
for himself, could take whatever Wickham chose to deliver and return
blow for blow in a metaphorical sense. The opinion of his father had
long ceased to be a source of worry for Darcy. Simply put, if his father
should happen upon them trading words, it did not matter to Darcy
what his father thought of it. The time when Darcy allowed Wickham

to do as he would without repercussion had come and gone.

Those in the Darcy carriage were largely silent, most thinking of what had just taken place. His father was clearly caught up in thoughts of Miss Elizabeth, and while Darcy hoped he approved, Darcy would be satisfied if he was nothing more than resigned. As for his mother and sister, Darcy was certain they had enjoyed meeting Miss Elizabeth. There was no fear of their disapproval. This, his mother made clear when the carriage stopped in front of Netherfield, and the party descended.

"Please walk with me for a moment, Fitzwilliam." As Georgiana walked into the house with her father, Darcy noted Wickham sneering at them before he turned to follow his only friend in the family.

"When I heard of your attentions to a young woman, I was not certain what to think."

Darcy could not help but frown. "Were you concerned I would be taken in, or that I would choose an unsuitable woman?"

"Many in our society *would* consider Miss Bennet unsuitable," replied his mother with a smile. "Your father is not alone in his views."

Not wishing to speak more on his father's views at present, Darcy nodded, waiting for his mother to speak again.

"It is not that I thought you would choose an unsuitable woman. It is more that I wondered if you knew exactly for what you were searching."

"I do not understand."

"Come to the back garden," said Lady Anne, guiding him around the corner of the house. "It is not every day a mother is able to secure her son's escort, and I am loath to give up your company."

Agreeing without delay, Darcy led them around to the back, his mind still mulling over his mother's words. As for Lady Anne, she seemed to be taking more joy in the day than Darcy had any attention for. It was, indeed, a beautiful autumn day, the twittering song of the sky's denizens filling his ears, accompanied by a warmth in the air and the brightly shining sun. But all these passed Darcy by with nothing more than a cursory thought. Too many other considerations clattered for attention in his mind, leaving little room for such frivolities.

Netherfield's back gardens were not nearly as extensive at Pemberley's, and the season had rendered them devoid of color. But it was a calm, tranquil spot, perfect for quiet conversation and family communion. Darcy had not been in his mother's company much of late. He had always found her to be a calming influence as her rational manner countered his father's more austere character.

"Let us sit on this bench," said Lady Anne, gesturing toward a stone bench which sat amid several lively bushes, which in the summer would contain a plethora of beautiful roses.

Darcy guided her to the indicated location and saw her seated before he settled in beside her. Given the manner in which she had interacted with Miss Elizabeth, he thought she would not say anything to give him alarm. But the defensive nature of his interactions with his father since his arrival made him wary.

"It is evident to me," began his mother, "you have not been happy in society since you entered it. Balls do not interest you, you avoid dancing as much as possible, and you do not converse with the young ladies in town enough to ever find a wife among their number."

"I . . ." Darcy paused, wondering what he should say. His mother's encouraging smile prompted him to continue without fear of offending her. "Society has little interest for me. While I have always been aware of my need to marry and my duty to uphold the Darcy position in society, I have often observed that many young ladies are raised with all the proper accomplishments, but little substance."

The grin his mother gave him showed her agreement. "That is why we have not sent Georgiana to a finishing school. She will be made into an image of the accepted woman of the day—it is one with which I do not agree. I should much prefer to make her into a proper woman myself."

"And you have a wonderful touch with her," said Darcy.

"Thank you, Fitzwilliam. I have high hopes for Georgiana.

"In reference to what we were discussing, your disinclination for society and opinion of society women caused me to wonder if you knew what you wanted in a wife. For if all young ladies are not suited to you, where could you find a woman who is?"

"Perhaps it is an overstatement to say *all* ladies are unsuitable. Of course, I cannot refute your statement, for I have never found one myself."

Lady Anne gave a delighted laugh and patted Darcy's arm. "In Miss Bennet, you seem to have overcome this deficiency."

"She is nothing like society ladies."

"No. And that is to her credit, to be sure. She is a breath of fresh air. Had you looked at every society girl to come out in the next twenty years, I do not think you could have found a woman more suited to you. I am happy for you, Fitzwilliam. I cannot imagine you being anything other than pleased with Miss Elizabeth as a bride."

Darcy beamed. "Thank you, Mother. Will you help me convince

Father?"

"It should not be required," replied Lady Anne. "Your father is a reasonable man, though he is often a severe one. In time, he will see how good Miss Elizabeth is for you, that there is nothing wanting in her. She may not possess the kind of dowry the daughter of an earl might, but it is respectable, and if she lacks connections, she more than makes up for it in character."

The conversation went on for a few more moments, but Darcy's thoughts were consumed with gratitude for his mother's support. Soon after, Lady Anne indicated her desire to find Georgiana, and Darcy escorted her inside. There was no one else in evidence, leading Darcy to wonder where his father had gone. Thinking he might be with Mr. Bingley in his study, Darcy's steps began to take him there, before he came upon a most unwelcome intrusion.

"Well, I must hand it to you, Darcy, loathe though I am to do so." Wickham flashed an unpleasant grin. "Then again, I suppose it must be a compliment to myself, for we always did have a similar taste in women."

"Similar taste in women?" asked Darcy, his tone deriding his unwelcome companion. "If you recall, I do not frequent brothels, Wickham. The women *you* find agreeable would never be found in the places I frequent."

"Charming, as always, Darcy. If I have certain needs, what is it to you how I choose to meet them? Either way, we are not so different in our tastes as you think."

"There is nothing I wish to hear from you, Wickham."

Darcy moved to walk past the libertine, but Wickham turned and walked along with him.

"Take Miss Elizabeth Bennet, for example."

Abruptly, Darcy stopped and turned a glare on Wickham. One might think it was sufficient warning to desist, but Wickham had never possessed the knowledge of when he might push too far.

"I had no idea you could not only choose such an exquisite woman, let alone possess the knowledge of what to do with her when you found her. It seems I was wrong in my estimation of you." Wickham paused and laughed, an unpleasant cackle of glee. "Of course, it remains to be seen if you manage to carry your so-called courtship to its proper conclusion. There is little doubt in my mind you will make a botch of it. You always were inept in the art of making love to a woman."

"Now that I have found a woman worthy of my love, I find I am quite adept at it. Perhaps you should mind your manners—Miss Elizabeth already knows what manner of man you are, and soon her family will know too. Your tricks will not work here, Wickham, for I will see everyone warned."

Wickham huffed in disdainful unconcern. "If you think the people of this town will prefer you to me, you appear to have picked up a certain delusion, Darcy. The only reason any of them will ever pay you any attention is because of your status and future wealth."

"Or perhaps because I will not rob them blind the moment they turn their backs."

"Then again," said Wickham, ignoring Darcy's insults, "I doubt your father will ever allow you to marry the girl. It is not as if she is a suitable match for the great Darcy of Pemberley." Wickham gave him a dark grin. "Perhaps you can make her your mistress once you have married some colorless woman of the ton? You had best do so quickly as I will if you do not."

"Bastard!" growled Darcy as he clenched his fists at his sides.

"Can you not abide each other's company for even a few minutes?"

It was his father's voice that saved Wickham from a pummeling, such as he had not received since they were boys. As it was, Wickham directed an insolent smirk at Darcy before turning an aggrieved look in his patron's direction. For perhaps the first time Darcy could remember, his father did not even notice.

"We are guests at present, and I will not have you two behaving like a pair of ruffians. If you cannot abide each other's presence, do not be in the same room as the other."

While Darcy only nodded, it was clear his former companion did not appreciate his share of Mr. Darcy's set down. But Mr. Darcy was not watching his protégé. Instead, his attention was fixed upon Darcy himself.

"If you will excuse us, Wickham, I must speak with my son."

"Of course, Mr. Darcy," said Wickham, his grin showing how certain he was that Mr. Darcy wished to make his disapproval of Miss Elizabeth known. It was of no concern to Darcy what his father's opinion might be—he was not about to give Miss Elizabeth up.

Without a second glance at Wickham, his father motioned Darcy to proceed him down the hall, and Darcy acquiesced, but not before he noted a look of pure poison Wickham was throwing at them both. It seemed Wickham was not as confident as he appeared.

Netherfield's library was situated not far from where his father had interrupted the confrontation, so Darcy led them there, knowing they could expect reasonable privacy. The sound of the pianoforte reached their ears, telling Darcy his sister was in the music room, likely in the company of his mother, and possibly Mrs. Bingley. While he did not know the location of the Hursts or Mr. Bingley, he was confident they would remain undisturbed.

"I am sure you can guess my reason for wishing to speak with you," said Darcy's father as soon as they had entered.

"It seems rather obvious," replied Darcy. "Is there something else you wish to know of Miss Elizabeth, or did you wish to speak directly of your opinion?"

The way his father looked at him told Darcy he was trying to decide if Darcy was being insolent. As Darcy continued to look at his father, betraying nothing, he must have come to the correct conclusion. Darcy had no interest in disrespect to his father. But he would not allow his father's disrespect toward Miss Elizabeth either.

"While I am certain questions of the girl will arise at other times, at present I need know nothing more."

Mr. Darcy paused, clasping his hands behind his back as he so often did, and peered at nothing, his thoughts clearly inward. Knowing it was his father's means of marshaling his arguments, Darcy remained patient, waiting, preparing himself for a disagreement.

"I am certain you must apprehend," said Mr. Darcy after a few moments' pause, "Miss Elizabeth is not what I wished for your future bride."

"That was never in question," replied Darcy.

The pacing ceased, and Mr. Darcy turned to peer at him. "But you are determined to follow through with this madness."

"Have you ever thought that I do not consider it madness?"

"That much is evident," was his father's short reply. "At present, I am attempting to determine whether this imprudence is naturally born or if I have somehow been negligent in your education."

"Father," said Darcy, speaking in a slow and measured tone to ensure his father understood he was considering the situation in a rational manner, "perhaps my definition of what is good for me is different from your own."

His father's eyes rested on him, judging. "Explain."

"It is simply that I do not value connections to the same extent as you do, nor am I enamored with society. Do we not have so many connections that we can hardly take a step in London without tripping over one of them? And I know you do not care for the majority of those to whom we can claim as part of our circle."

When Mr. Darcy did not reply, Darcy continued: "There is no way you or anyone else can claim that Miss Bennet is in any way unsuited for the role I mean her to assume. She is intelligent and poised and will bring honor to our family. She is not deficient in any way."

"Well, she *did* seem to be a good sort of girl," grumbled Mr. Darcy. "And perhaps what you say about the state of our position in society is true. But I must remind you that it will one day be your duty to uphold our position in society."

"Though I am not fond of London, I understand my responsibilities," replied Darcy. "But if you will forgive me, Father, I would point out that it is *I* who must live with the woman I choose as my wife. I will be required to sire an heir, to converse with her, to be her husband. To be perfectly frank, I am far more interested in choosing my bride with a mind to ensure my own happiness, rather than the family's dynastic expectations. Our position in society will not be damaged by Miss Elizabeth. In fact, I am convinced it will be enhanced."

It was several moments before his father responded to Darcy's impassioned speech. In that time, Darcy watched him, alert for any indication of what his father might be thinking. But Robert Darcy was as inscrutable as always.

"There appears to be little choice," said his father at length, his words accompanied with a sigh of resignation. "In some ways — though not the ways I would wish — you are much as I am: stubborn, willful, and unwilling to bend when you believe you are in the right.

"As I have said, I would have wished for more in your future wife, but *my* wishes would have been for those material advantages. You have chosen to value those assets which are not readily apparent. While I cannot say you are correct, I also cannot state the opposite. It is possible, though I assume you have already apprehended this fact, a marriage born in love will not bring the happiness you expect. But I have my experience with your mother and do not blame you for wishing for your own meeting of minds.

"Thus, I will support you should you ultimately choose Miss Elizabeth." His father paused, a wryness unusual in his character evident in the upturn of his lips. "In the end, I do not doubt you will do as you wish, my support or not. I only ask you take care to be certain you know what you are about before you propose. While a society marriage may be bad enough, marrying a woman you *think* you love with the expectation of a life of happiness will lead to a lifetime of misery if you are wrong."

"Thank you, Father," said Darcy, feeling choked up by his father's words. Rarely had he heard his father speak so much; Robert Darcy was a man who did not believe that every silence must be filled by a voice. What was more, Darcy had not expected his father to be resigned so quickly.

But while he had given his approval, Darcy could sense that his father was yet anything but accepting. A single nod was his father's response, after which he excused himself, leaving Darcy alone in the room. Miss Elizabeth would still need to convince him of her suitability. At least Darcy had the hope now that it was possible. He had feared his father would dig in his heels and never relent.

Something momentous had happened that day. It was easy for one so close to the two principals to notice. What it was, Lady Anne Darcy could not say, though she had her suspicions.

A glance at Fitzwilliam at dinner that evening informed her that her son was more comfortable now than he had been at any time since their arrival. Fitzwilliam sat with Georgiana and the younger Mr. Bingley and spoke, if not with animation—for it was not his way—at least with ease. And though his father sat nearby, speaking with the elder Bingley, none of the tension which had characterized their interactions since their arrival—and to some extent for some years now—was absent.

Had her husband bent his stiff neck concerning the matter of Miss Elizabeth Bennet? It was possible, for he was not nearly so prejudiced as he often displayed. For a moment, Lady Anne considered the relative merits of approaching her son—for her husband could be remarkably close-mouthed when he desired—to learn the truth. After a little reflection, she decided to allow him to inform her of the matter when he saw fit. For now, she was more than happy to enjoy the easier relationship between the two most important men in her life.

The other issue she could see was the matter of George Wickham. That the young man had come to them intending to foment discord between father and son, Anne did not doubt. Though she had not known the extent of Wickham's true character until Fitzwilliam had informed her, she had always seen his jealousy, his efforts to make himself appear better than her son. Perhaps this episode would result in Wickham showing his true colors to her husband.

She also did not misunderstand the looks Wickham was giving her only daughter. Georgiana's dowry was more than enough temptation for a man like Wickham. Lady Anne knew her daughter would not give George Wickham any encouragement, but there was still the matter of his becoming desperate enough to force the issue. Was it possible to break the hold the young man had on her husband?

"I would like to announce," said Mrs. Bingley, drawing Lady Anne away from her thoughts, "I have decided I should like to hold a ball at Netherfield in honor of our guests, if that is agreeable to you all."

While Lady Anne had no objection, she looked to the men in her family, knowing that Fitzwilliam and Robert were not fond of dancing. It was, therefore, difficult to stifle her laughter when she noted that Fitzwilliam appeared eager, the reason for which was a mystery to no one. Robert, she thought, noticed it too, though he appeared more resigned than anything. Curious, Lady Anne watched her husband.

"That is a lovely idea, Mrs. Bingley," said Lady Anne, turning a warm smile on her hostess. "As there is so much romance in the air, I would imagine a ball would be agreeable, even to our menfolk."

The sudden embarrassment in her son delighted Anne as did Mrs. Bingley's rapid nod of her head. "Yes, that is exactly it! By that time," continued she, turning to look at her son, "I hope we may be in a position to announce an engagement."

"Perchance we shall," said the younger Bingley, "though I believe Darcy might be in a position to propose to his Miss Bennet before me."

"The only reason for that," jibed her son in return, "is that you have dragged your heels these past years. Had you worked more quickly, you would already be married to your Miss Bennet."

Instead of offense, it was clear Mr. Bingley was excessively diverted by Fitzwilliam's quip, as was most of the company. The talk thereafter centered on the notion of hosting a ball and what might be done to prepare for it. The men added little when it came to discussions of arrangements, and Anne found herself agreeing to help her hostess organize it. It was no trouble for her part, as Anne suspected it may turn into an engagement ball, even if *Mr. Bingley* did not propose.

It was later that evening when they had retired to their rooms that Anne learned the truth of the events of that day. Her husband was also less than happy about the amusement Mrs. Bingley had proposed at dinner.

"Must you encourage them in such a manner?"

Though laughter bubbled up at the sound of her husband's plaintive manner of speaking, Anne feigned ignorance. "Of what do you speak?"

"This . . . ball Mrs. Bingley wishes to hold." Robert grunted with annoyance. "There is still hope Fitzwilliam will come to his senses, but that will not happen if he is continually urged to give in to his infatuation for the girl."

"Oh?" asked Lady Anne. "This signals a change in your previous unbending opinion. Has making her acquaintance won you over?"

Robert's sour look spoke volumes. "There did not seem to be much of a choice. I am not convinced of the wisdom of elevating the girl, but seeing him so determined, I had no option but to give him my support. At the same time, I did ask him to ensure he knows what he is about — though it is a faint hope, it will be no hope at all if everyone about him continues to extol the girl's virtues."

"The girl is Miss Elizabeth Bennet, Robert," said Anne. Sensing he needed her support, Lady Anne approached her husband and laid a hand on his arm. "I understand your hesitance, Robert, but I believe it best you become accustomed to referring to her by name, for there is no doubt in my mind she will one day be our daughter.

"And to be frank, I do not think Fitzwilliam could find a better woman in the home of the Duke of Devonshire himself! Please give her all the benefit of her character, Robert, for she is truly a gem. I am happy Fitzwilliam has found her."

While it took no great insight to see Robert's disagreement, he nodded and allowed the subject to drop. Anne was under no illusion that he had overcome his objections, but as long as he did not continue to voice them, it was enough. They prepared to retire, and when the candles had been snuffed, Anne settled in unfashionably beside her husband, like she had most of the nights of their marriage. Not for the first time, she thought with amusement how the ton would gasp and look in horror if they knew how unfashionable the Darcys of Pemberley were.

Before sleep took her, a thought occurred to Anne, and she voiced it without thinking. "Georgiana is becoming a lovely young woman. It will not be much longer before she will be in society — can you imagine the swath she will cut among the young men?"

Robert groaned. "Do not remind me."

In the cover of darkness, Anne smirked. Georgiana was the light in Robert's eyes. While he knew she would one day leave for her own home, the thought was hard, as it must be for any parent who cared for a daughter. But Anne could use that, for it was about time Robert learned a few truths.

"She is already receiving attention when she leaves the house. Why, I saw one young gentleman looking at her with obvious appreciation at the last inn we stayed at on our journey here."

"Georgiana is naught but sixteen," replied Robert. "I will not tolerate anyone playing with her affections."

"And yet she will have admirers. Some closer than you think."

Robert did not respond, and Anne was content with her work that evening. While Robert might not notice it immediately, she had planted the seed of the possible attraction young men would begin to show for her daughter. If Wickham continued his charming ways — and Anne had no reason to suppose he would not — he would draw Robert's attention. Regardless of his fondness for the boy, Anne knew he would not countenance any admiration for Georgiana on Wickham's part. Perhaps he might even see what Wickham truly was.

Chapter XXVII

$\mathcal{A}$utumn in Hertfordshire was a risky proposition at best. At times, the residents were treated with warm winds, beautiful sunlight, the vivid colors the trees assumed when readying themselves to shed their summer glory, and a lessening of the summer heat. But autumn could also be fickle, with wind and rain, the appearance of muddy paths and grey, dreary days, with the promise of winter looming on the horizon.

The autumn of Elizabeth's courtship with Mr. Darcy saw a mixture of the two extremes and very little consistency, for it seemed that one day might be bright and warm, while the next saw the patter of rain against the window and the roiling of clouds above.

In other circumstances, Elizabeth thought she would consider the weather with considerable annoyance. Walking had ever been a favorite pastime, so much so that she often indulged three of four times a week. Being denied such escapes more days than not—for even if a day dawned sunny, if it had rained the previous day, the paths would not be fit for her to walk—would be more than she could bear.

But Mr. Darcy removed that concern. Though the gentleman did not venture forth to Longbourn—or the Bennets to Netherfield—on a daily basis, they were in each other's company more than they were without it. As Elizabeth was coming to esteem the man more as time passed, she began to crave his presence. That Lady Anne and Georgiana were quickly growing in Elizabeth's affections rendered them a welcome presence also. Mr. Darcy was not nearly so agreeable, but as he had made no objections, Elizabeth decided to endure his scrutiny and respond whenever he deigned to speak to her.

On one occasion, not long after first meeting the Darcy family, Elizabeth had an occasion to learn from her suitor what had passed between him and his father. Elizabeth was heartened as a result.

"His support means much to you," observed Elizabeth when Mr. Darcy informed her of the conversation.

"It does," was Mr. Darcy's simple reply. "There have been times when I have disagreed with my father. When I was young, he was perfect to me in every way, and I looked up to him, wishing to become just like him. Though I now see him with the eyes of an adult, I understand he is a good man who is worthy of emulating."

"It is a mark of the passage from child to adult that we realize our parents are not perfect. That you can still esteem him as a flawed but good man shows you have learned this lesson."

Mr. Darcy smiled and leaned forward. "There *is* one who is perfect — perfect for me, at least."

The jest prompted Elizabeth's laughter. "I hope you are not too disappointed when you realize I am as imperfect as anyone else."

"Ah, but recall I qualified my statement by saying you are perfect *for me*," replied Mr. Darcy, fixing her with a special smile Elizabeth thought was for her alone. "No one will ever convince me otherwise."

A powerful feeling welled up within Elizabeth's breast. "I am beginning to believe the reverse might be true as well, sir."

Delight glowed in Mr. Darcy's countenance. The moment, it seemed, was too flawless for words, and Mr. Darcy did not attempt to say that which could not be said. But they stayed in each other's company for some time after, saying little and feeling much.

Soon after that day, the Netherfield party returned to Longbourn for the promised dinner. It was a merry party which gathered, their mirth flowing freely in the warmth of their regard for one another. Elizabeth sat with Mr. Darcy as usual, but their attention was focused on other members of the party, particularly Jane and Mr. Bingley, who stood near. It appeared Mr. Darcy had been teasing Mr. Bingley of late, for his wit was unleashed again that evening, though Mr. Bingley accepted it all with nary a hint of annoyance.

"I rather wonder at this interesting dichotomy of our changed natures, Bingley. As long as I have known you, impulsivity has been a hallmark of your character."

"So it has, my friend," replied Mr. Bingley.

"Then it seems as if you are not living up to your reputation. By my count you have known Miss Bennet for two and twenty years—" Mr. Darcy looked at Jane who nodded, a giggle unlike Jane's usual manners escaping "—but you have yet to propose to her."

"All in good time," replied an unruffled Mr. Bingley. "I merely wait for the right opportunity." Mr. Bingley eyed his friend, his brow furrowed as if in thought. "It seems you are changed too, old man. The measured, careful Darcy I always thought I knew has been replaced with this facsimile of a man who leaps without looking."

"I am merely impatient, my friend. I should have thought you would be too."

"It is a trait our mother shared," observed Mary.

The sisters shared a wistful smile while Mr. Darcy looked on with interest. When the others in the room began to speak of other matters, he leaned toward Elizabeth.

"You were close to your mother?"

"Actually, it is Jane who was closest to our mother, though she was excessively proud of the heir she produced." Elizabeth smiled in fond remembrance. "Jane is most like Mama in looks, you understand, and being her eldest and prettiest daughter, neither Mary nor I could compare."

"Then your mother was afflicted by poor eyesight?" asked Mr. Darcy. The grin he directed at her betrayed his jesting, though there was a core of sincerity deep in his manner. "To think you inferior to your sister shows a remarkable inability to see properly."

"Though I thank you for your words, sir, I have no illusions as to the truth of the matter."

Mr. Darcy regarded her, softly smiling for several moments, then said: "Tell me of your mother."

"Mama was . . . a force all unto herself," said Elizabeth. "While she was not a stranger to proper behavior, her excitable nature often led her to forget it. Mama's father was not a gentleman, as you know, and as his own wife passed away quite young, he often did not know how to raise his daughters."

"And yet she raised three fine daughters."

Elizabeth favored the gentleman with a smile. "Thank you for saying so, Mr. Darcy. Mama had help in this respect as my father insisted on a governess. She had her own trials in behaving properly, but she was a loving mother, unstinting in her displays of affection for us all."

"Mrs. Bennet was a wonderful woman," said Mr. Collins, who was sitting nearby. "The welcome I received when I came to this house after my father's death was warm and inviting, and she treated me like I was one of her own children. I am grateful to both Mr. Bennet and his late wife, for I should have been forced to shift for myself otherwise."

"It was my mother's pleasure to welcome you, Mr. Collins," said Elizabeth, smiling at the awkward young man. "She had a protective instinct which she extended to anyone within reach of her influence, and in you she saw a boy, eager to please and possessing so much potential. It is well known to us all that she was very proud of what you have become."

The beaming smile that was Mr. Collins's reply showed his appreciation. Then Mr. Collins turned to Mary and allowed Elizabeth her relative privacy with Mr. Darcy.

"One regret I have," said Elizabeth, "is that my mother's early passing did not allow her to realize her greatest dream in her lifetime."

"Oh?" asked Mr. Darcy. "And what was that?"

"The marriage of all her daughters," said Elizabeth with a laugh. "Mama always said it was a woman's primary duty to see her daughters disposed of in respectable marriages. We all knew that Jane would marry Mr. Bingley, and Mama anticipated it, intending to plan a celebration such as this neighborhood has never seen. It would have been a sight to behold."

"She would be proud of you," replied Mr. Darcy. "It is clear your sister is on the cusp of a proposal from my friend, and you must know I will do the same at the first indication it will be accepted."

"Then it is well I am the sensible one of us," said Elizabeth, shyly lowering her eyes to the floor. "There is no need to rush, Mr. Darcy. There is plenty of time, and I would prefer to know more of you before taking such a step."

"That is why I have not proposed yet. But I will. Of that you may rest assured."

Had Elizabeth any doubt concerning the matter, his heartfelt declaration would have put it to rest. The feeling of being cherished fell over Elizabeth, and she smiled with as much poise as she could imagine. At that moment, however, she rather felt like soaring over the trees like an eagle in flight or bursting into tears, overwhelmed by it all—she did not know which. In the end, she contented herself with smiling at Mr. Darcy and leaning toward him. Their confidences

safety, should my concerns become truth. It is elsewhere that worries me."

Mr. Darcy considered what he had heard, his eyes now fixed on Wickham rather than his son. In time, he spoke, and Mr. Bennet, knowing it was his move, allowed him time to think rather than pressing him.

"I have much on which to think, Mr. Bennet. Though I am convinced of Wickham's goodness, I shall consider your words. Perhaps it is time Wickham returned to his profession."

"That would likely be for the best. A man must be engaged in his life's work, after all. If Mr. Wickham wishes to take a wife, he will need to improve his situation, and I assume he cannot remain a clerk forever."

The absent nod from Mr. Darcy was all he was to receive. Bennet was happy with the result of the conversation, for at least he had induced the other man to think. Another pair of eyes watching Mr. Wickham could only help.

CHAPTER XXVIII

$\mathcal{M}$r. Bennet was not the only member of the Bennet family to notice Mr. Wickham's apparent aversion for Darcy and how it encompassed Elizabeth. And he did not like what he saw in the slightest.

It was strange. The knowledge of Darcy's actions with respect to Lizzy had come to light not that long ago, and Thomas Bennet had returned to Hertfordshire determined to watch the gentleman to ensure his good behavior and satisfy himself of the man's worthiness. When Thomas considered the matter further, he realized it was not all this new threat posed by Mr. Wickham driving the change in his opinion of Darcy. The man had been perfectly well behaved, respectful, thoughtful, and, perhaps most importantly, clearly showed himself to be besotted with Elizabeth. While that was no guarantee, it was promising to say the least.

The question was, what to do with Mr. Wickham. Had Thomas thought his father remained ignorant of the man's behavior, he might have approached him about barring Wickham from Longbourn, but Mr. Bennet watched Wickham as closely as Thomas did himself. And there was the matter of the discussion he had witnessed between his father and Mr. Darcy at Longbourn, which resulted in closer scrutiny from the elder Darcy.

It seemed there was nothing to do at present, and as Thomas suspected Wickham would not be daft enough to attempt to hurt Elizabeth and ruin his standing with the man who provided him whatever standing he had, he settled on remaining watchful. That did not mean he was above taunting the man on those occasions when he had the opportunity. One such presented itself a few days after the dinner at Longbourn.

Thomas had always thought Hertfordshire had been particularly blessed with respect to its variety of wildlife, even though the countryside had been largely tamed. Had he been inclined, he thought the hunting would have been quite fine. As it was, the only hunting in which Thomas indulged was pheasant, which was fortunate, indeed, as he was fond of Cook's recipe.

On the day in question, a group of the younger gentlemen gathered together to shoot on Longbourn's land, and of their number was Mr. Wickham. While he might have wondered if it was wise to hand a rifle to a man who obviously hated Darcy with such passion, Darcy had no seeming reservations. With an eye on Wickham, Thomas went about his hunting, bagging several birds himself. What he saw of Wickham amused him to no end.

When Wickham had missed yet again, marking at least three quarters of an hour without a successful shot, Thomas turned to Darcy, who was nearby, and said: "Either your *friend* lacks practice, or he is simply the worst shot I have ever seen."

Darcy understood Thomas's sarcasm at once, for he shook his head and glared in Wickham's direction. "If I was ever senseless enough to call Wickham a friend, you would be correct in despising me."

Nodding agreeably, Thomas did not speak, waiting for his companion to respond. Darcy's grimace presaged his reply.

"There are few who shoot as poorly as Wickham. Though I might have wished it to be different, Wickham was given most of the training available to young gentlemen, but he only applied himself when he found the subject interesting. Or thought it might benefit him in some way. Shooting was never his forte, and when he saw I was a better shot, he lost interest."

"Most gentleman can shoot," replied Thomas. "Given how much he obviously likes to maintain the illusion of that status, I might have thought he would attend to it."

Darcy shrugged. "One might think so. But I cannot say I have ever understood how Wickham thinks." A pause ensued after which Darcy grimaced. "Then again, I understand far too much of what he thinks. Jealousy is a defining characteristic as is his lust for riches. You might think it is hypocritical for me, a wealthy man, to speak of another's desire for money, but there it is."

"I think no such thing, Darcy," said Thomas. "Some of us are born into more privileged situations than others. It is not the wealth that makes the man, but what he does with it."

A tight nod formed Darcy's response. "I cannot agree more. But Wickham could never see that. In his mind, wealth is a means by which he need never work to earn his keep and spend his life in idleness and dissipation."

"Yet your father enjoys his company."

"He does," replied Darcy with a sigh. "We Darcys are usually not possessed of lively manners, being more reticent and awkward in society. My father is amused by Wickham's ability to make him laugh. Though I have often attempted to inform my father of Wickham's true character, he calls it jealousy, dismissing my words without consideration. Why he believes I might have reason to feel envy for Wickham, I cannot say."

"His manners?" asked Thomas. "Or your father's attention?"

"It is possible. But I have only spoken against Wickham in truth, never because of any feelings of envy. I should much rather be a man unable to be at ease in society than a man of little moral fiber."

"True. I commend you for it." Thomas considered the matter before he voiced his try worry. "My concern in this matter is Lizzy. The times we have been in company, I have seen the way Mr. Wickham looks at you. Should he decide to act, my sister might be a path to you."

Darcy frowned. "I have never known him to be violent. Wickham is much more adept at getting what he wants through his charming manners and guile."

"While that may be true, I urge you to remain watchful. The jealousy and hatred he displays for you may make him irrational."

Though Darcy did not reply, Thomas noted his eyes on Wickham, considering, searching. Knowing Mr. Darcy was always wary of Wickham helped, but he knew extra vigilance would not go amiss.

After some more time had passed in which Thomas had continued to watch the unwelcome member of the party, he saw an opportunity to approach Wickham and deliver a warning he knew was overdue. Wickham had not, to the best of Thomas's knowledge, hit a single bird, and after a time his rifle had gone unused, as he chatted with other members of the company, leaning on his weapon as if it were a crutch.

But when Samuel Lucas, with whom he had been speaking, raised his weapon to his shoulder to aim at a pair of birds taking wing, Wickham moved off. Thomas seized the opportunity.

"It seems as if you are having difficulty with your weapon," said Thomas as he stood next to Wickham. "Are the sights perhaps a little off?"

Wickham turned to him, his countenance expressionless, though the glittering of his eyes suggested he knew Bennet was mocking him. "It is unlikely," said he, his brevity suggesting he had little interest in exchanging words.

"Oh?" asked Thomas. "I have never seen a rifle which does not require an adjustment on occasion."

"I did not deny that," replied Wickham. "This weapon is Mr. Darcy's, and I am certain he takes excellent care of it."

"Then how do you account for your lack of success?"

An insouciant shrug was followed with a short: "There has not been much opportunity to practice. Of late, my residence has been in London. There is little chance to shoot there."

"Ah, that must be it."

Mr. Wickham frowned at Thomas's mocking tone. But he did not say anything, leaving Thomas to make the next comment.

"Should your residence not be in London again soon? As a man of the law, I might have thought you would be engaged in your work. Yet, you have been here for two weeks without any sign of returning to your place."

When Wickham turned on him, Thomas noted his eyes burned with a cold fire. It was precisely the reaction Thomas might have predicted and feared. When provoked, this was a dangerous man.

"What you refer to as my place is at Mr. Darcy's side. Though I shall return to my profession at some time, do not presume to guess my worth to my patron."

"It seems to me you overestimate your worth." Thomas directed a thin smile at the man he was quickly coming to suspect was a danger to them all. "If you were of as much worth as you seem to believe, do you not believe Mr. Darcy might have done more for you?"

Thomas sniffed with disdain. "He has done much more for you than most gentlemen would, including educating you, seeing to your employment, favoring you with his attentions. But he has not seen fit to gift you with what you truly desire, has he?"

Standing up straight, Wickham stepped close and hissed: "Do not speak of what you do not understand. I will not be questioned by the likes of you."

"The likes of me?" said Thomas, his voice laced with derision. "I am your superior in all ways, worm. I am a gentleman where you are nothing more than the son of a steward jumped up in his own pride. Do not attempt to compare yourself to anyone in this company."

A feral grin lit up Wickham's face. "Spoken with true conceit. I might almost think you close friends with Darcy. He, too, has nothing but contempt for those he deems are lower in importance."

"Oh, no," said Thomas. "In fact, I have never spoken to another in such a way in all my life. Only you, who seem to believe the world owes you everything on a silver platter.

"Regardless, I do not wish to speak of such matters. The only reason I have approached you is to issue a warning."

"A warning?" mocked Wickham. "So, the gentleman thinks he has fangs?"

"Someday, Mr. Wickham, your patron will no longer protect you, for he will know you for what you are. But I care not. Do not importune my sisters, sir. I know what you are and will not allow you to attempt your wiles with them."

"I have no interest in your insipid sisters."

With that final snarl, Wickham turned and left, giving Thomas a wide berth for the rest of the day, such as it was. Thomas continued to watch him, noting Darcy did so as well. He had made an enemy that day. A truly dangerous man, indeed.

The warning Thomas Bennet had left ringing in his ears stayed with Darcy, whispering to him of where Wickham's enmity might lead. Once Darcy might have dismissed his concerns as mere paranoia, for Wickham was a soft man, one who was too invested in his vices to summon the will to act with violent intent. What was more, he had always seemed something of a coward to Darcy, given the many instances he had run to Darcy's father every time there was a disagreement. Now, he was not so sure.

Those fears which had heightened in the days following the shooting party burst into a certainty that Wickham had some devilry planned. And it occurred only two days after Bennet had warned him.

While his father had given his reluctant blessing to Darcy's pursuit of Miss Elizabeth, he was not happy about it. Nor was he above attempting to change Darcy's mind. It was not often much more than a little comment here, or an observation there, but it was clear to Darcy he was attempting to sow some uncertainty in the hope his son would reconsider. The effort was wasted, for Darcy knew what he wanted and had no intention of yielding. But the comments wore on him, driving him out of his father's company on more than one occasion.

One such day, Darcy retreated to the stables, had his horse saddled, and rode out onto the estate. As the thought of his father's stubbornness flew through his mind, Darcy did not pay attention to where he was going, allowing the horse his head to gallop as he pleased. Thus, he found himself not far from the western border of the estate, where he came across Wickham.

A scowl marred his features as he considered what he might be doing, astride one of his father's horses so far distant from the house. Having no desire to exchange words with his father's detested protégé, Darcy decided to leave without the argument which would inevitably erupt should he greet Wickham. Then his eyes followed Wickham's and saw what he was looking at out on the neighboring estate.

Darcy saw red.

Without a second thought, Darcy wheeled his horse and charged forward. The beast's hooves thundered against the turf, catching Wickham's attention. The woman on the other side of the divide was far enough distant that she did not hear, for she did not glance in his direction. Then Darcy pulled his horse to a halt in front of his father's favorite.

"What are you doing?"

"What does it seem like I am doing?" taunted Wickham. "Merely out for a morning exercise. Your father has given his permission to use his horses."

"I do not doubt he has," spat Darcy. "As always, you are more than willing to impose upon his generosity. But I was referring to your spying on the woman I am courting."

Wickham laughed, a jeering sound. "So what if I was? Did I not already acknowledge she is a lovely woman? What man does not wish to watch a beautiful woman even if it must be from afar?"

"This will be the only warning you ever receive, cur, so I suggest you take it seriously. Do not stalk Miss Elizabeth's footsteps. If I find you have been following her, even innocently, I will take it from your hide."

"Charming, as always," said Wickham. "There is no way you can believe I wish her harm, though I still think she would prefer me. As it is, you may have her. I have no doubt she has been poisoned against me, regardless."

If Wickham had not spurred his horse into motion, Darcy might have finally planted that facer on his smirking countenance as he had longed to do for many years. As it was, while he thought of going after Wickham, Darcy thought better of it. There were other, more pressing matters to consider at present.

The fence between the two properties was surpassed with one great leap of his mount, allowing Darcy to set off in the direction he had last seen Miss Elizabeth walking. It was toward the manor house, unless he was mistaken, likely a mile or two distant. After a few minutes, he caught sight of her, proving luck was on his side that morning. The smile with which she greeted him was a common occurrence by now though a welcome one.

"Miss Elizabeth," said Darcy, leaping from his horse and bowing over her hand in one motion. "How fortunate I am to find you today, as even one day out of your company is difficult to bear."

The clear, bell-like laughter she released was a balm to Darcy's troubled soul, and he grinned along with her. "I dare say we, neither of us, will expire from longing should we not meet, sir."

"Perchance not. But it certainly feels that way."

"In that case, I shall allow you to escort me to Longbourn."

"Your wish is my command, my lady," said Darcy, extending his arm.

As they walked, Darcy found himself entranced by her enchanting voice while they spoke on many subjects. If he was truthful, Darcy would acknowledge that he did not add much to the conversation, though it had long been a pattern between them for her to speak more than he, which was nothing more than a function of their characters. For some time, he allowed her to speak of her doings, having no requirement to feign interest, content to listen to her voice. After some time, however, she made a comment with respect to that morning which drew Darcy's interest and provided him a reminder of why he had sought her out.

"You are returning from a visit to one of the tenants?"

"Yes. The Campbells tend the land in the northeast of the estate, and Mrs. Campbell has recently given birth to her second daughter. I visited this morning with a basket of treats for her older children and a few items which will enhance their table."

"That is good of you, Miss Elizabeth. Being engaged in the care of your tenants is a duty for every lady of an estate."

Miss Elizabeth flashed him a modest, yet pleased smile. "My sisters and I are all engaged in caring for the tenants, Mr. Darcy. Caroline is not yet well known to them all, but she is growing into her position.

What I do is no great thing, nothing particularly laudatory at all."

"In my opinion, Miss Elizabeth, any service undertaken for the betterment of another is something to applaud."

Again, she was pleased, but Darcy, sensing the moment had come, halted and turned toward her, prompting her to startle. A smile reached his lips, telling her all was well, but it soon faded in favor of the serious matter he wished to discuss with her.

"Do you usually walk when you visit your tenants?"

Miss Elizabeth seemed surprised, but she recovered quickly. "At times I do. As you know, I do love to walk. But I will also ride at times when the fancy strikes me."

"And you have no escort?"

"I have never needed one."

The pointed comment informed Darcy she was beginning to wonder at his questioning. Darcy forced himself to come to the point, for he had belatedly realized he sounded as if he did not trust her.

"I apologize for my questions, Miss Elizabeth, but I am concerned. You see, I just came across Wickham watching you from the Netherfield side of the border between your estates."

"Mr. Wickham?" asked Miss Elizabeth with a frown. "I do not know why he would be interested in my doings."

"Nor do I," replied Darcy. "Though I have never known him to be anything other than lazy and entitled, I am concerned. His hatred for me is to an extent that I cannot predict his actions with respect to you."

Amid widening eyes, Miss Elizabeth gasped: "You believe he means me harm?"

"I cannot say," said Darcy, grasping her hand in a gesture of comfort. "As I have said, I have never known him to possess violent tendencies, but I have also never seen him so angry. The hatred he possesses for me has become all consuming, I believe, and I do not know what that will drive him to do. Your duties on the estate are of utmost importance, and I by no means ask you to suspend them. But I would be much more secure if you would take care. The escort of a footman would not go amiss."

As independent as she was, Darcy was not sure she would agree to the restriction at all. But she proved her good sense by nodding to acknowledge his concerns.

"It has never been my practice to take an escort, but I see the sense in your suggestion. In the future, I will ensure I am escorted when I leave the house."

"Thank you, Miss Elizabeth," said Darcy, raising her hand to his lips. "I believe that is the sensible decision."

Soon the house rose before them, and Darcy farewelled her, content she would now be safe, though he stayed there until she reached the house, unable to depart without ensuring it himself. When she had disappeared into the manor, Darcy turned his mount and began to make his way back toward Netherfield. For a moment, he toyed with the idea of approaching his father, but Mr. Darcy had proven time and time again that he would not hear anything Darcy said which contradicted his view of Wickham. It would be better to continue to watch the man and take action when required. If Wickham attempted to harm a hair on Miss Elizabeth's head, he would soon regret it.

"Ah, Wickham. There you are."

The glower which had adorned Wickham's countenance since the confrontation with Mr. Darcy's son was instantly replaced, and he forced down the murderous anger. It was a habit with which Wickham was well acquainted. It would not do to allow a man as prudish as Mr. Darcy to see anything he did not like.

"I had just gone out for a ride, Mr. Darcy," was Wickham's smooth reply. "Is there something I can do to help you?"

Wickham did not quite like the look with which Mr. Darcy regarded him. It spoke to knowledge, or possibly understanding, though precisely what it might presage, Wickham could not say.

"Let us step into the library."

Gritting his teeth, Wickham followed his benefactor, not liking the tone of command. Oh, to be free, to be independent and not beholden on anyone else! But even if he was to achieve his own freedom by way of his machinations, Wickham knew he would still be required to deal with Mr. Darcy. A man could dream, but reality must be acknowledged.

When they had reached the safety of the library, Wickham stood silently, waiting for Mr. Darcy to speak. Again, the feeling of being judged did not sit well with him. There was nothing to be done, however, so he ignored it.

"I have been thinking," said Mr. Darcy at length. "Though I value your company and support, and especially your warning about Fitzwilliam's intentions, I am concerned."

"Of what, sir?' asked Wickham. "The support I provide, I give eagerly."

"That much is evident. But I have realized my selfishness in keeping you here. Naturally, you must wish to return to town to continue to pursue your profession, and I have been preventing you from doing that."

"It is nothing," attempted Wickham, a sudden panic rising within his breast, but Mr. Darcy was already shaking him off.

"Of course, it is. As always, you put your ties to my family over your own interests, and I do appreciate it. But the longer you stay here, the more delayed your own rise in the law profession. I do not wish to be the reason why you are not successful in your chosen field."

Dismayed, Wickham could not even find the words to reply. Then the rage he had so recently suppressed returned, filling his ears with a roaring sound, occluding the edges of his vision as if fire was licking around the corners of his eyes. Darcy! He must have spoken to his father and complained! And Mr. Darcy had agreed to send him away, even though Wickham thought his influence with the old man far exceeded the son's!

"To that end," said Mr. Darcy, ignorant of the fury running through Wickham's veins, "I have contacted a few acquaintances in town to begin the process of finding another position for you. If all goes well, I should hear back next week, and a position should result within the month."

"As always, I am undone by your generosity," said Wickham, thinking furiously. "But I think it best that I stay with you and assist you in extracting your son from this predicament. It is in my mind that Miss Elizabeth is not all she seems—I would not wish to leave your son prey to such a woman as she."

"What do you mean?" asked Mr. Darcy, a frown descending.

"At present, I do not know," said Wickham, as if reluctantly confessing to failure. "She appears to be everything lovely and amiable, but there is something about her . . . Well, I should not speak in such a way of a lady."

"Please, Wickham. I value your opinion."

The desire to smile at the man's continued vulnerability to manipulation warred with his anger. As it was, Wickham was adept at showing what he wished, and he kept his countenance worried.

"You have noticed Miss Elizabeth is lively and open, have you not?" Mr. Darcy's nod confirmed the obvious statement, but it was curt, unlike the man's usual manner with him. "It seems to me," continued Wickham, "the lady is a bit of a flirt, for she will bestow her attentions upon anyone who sees fit to give her any notice."

Mr. Darcy frowned. "I have not noticed that."

"Have you spoken much with her?"

"Have you?"

"More than you have, I would wager," replied Wickham. "There may be nothing at all. Having said that, something about her strikes me as strange. I should like to observe her more, speak with her to learn what I can. You must acknowledge that I, being more of her age, am in a better position to determine anything untoward about her."

"It is possible, I suppose," said Mr. Darcy, with far less interest than Wickham might have expected. "That you consider my son's wellbeing is surprising, considering his antipathy toward you."

A false smile came easily over Wickham's face. "The memory of our closeness when we were young has stayed with me. Though he has seen fit to disapprove of me, I cannot forget it."

Mr. Darcy clasped his shoulder and smiled. "Thank you, Wickham. When in company, I will observe her for any hint of your suspicions. As to your future, I am determined to be of use. I will inform you should anything arise."

With those final words, the man left the room, leaving Wickham fuming behind him. Wickham was well aware Mr. Darcy would find no great opinion of him among the law firms in London, as he had no doubt Patterson had been voluble in his condemnation. That sort of word tended to spread among the fraternity quickly. Should Mr. Darcy learn of his exploits in London, Wickham had little doubt it would not reflect well on him, even leading the gentleman to question him closely.

It was clear there was much work to be done and little time to do it. Wickham set his shoulders and departed from the library, determined to do what needed to be done.

CHAPTER XXIX

$\mathcal{E}$lizabeth could not explain the happiness she felt as the Bennet family departed for Lucas Lodge. It was something freeing, something which allowed her emotions to soar with the knowledge she was loved by a good man. That she had not seen Charlotte in some time only added to the pleasure of an evening in the company of dear friends.

"Well, Lizzy," greeted Charlotte when the Bennets were shown into Lucas Lodge. "I have always known you to be a cheerful sort of girl, but you positively glow tonight. Could your new sister have been correct in asserting Mr. Darcy's interest?"

Flushing, Elizabeth fixed her friend with a hard stare, warning of retribution should she continue to tease. Charlotte, however, proved herself unintimidated when she laughed and embraced Elizabeth with affection.

"There is something about those who like to tease which does not allow them to be teased in return. It may be prudent for you to become accustomed to it, my dear Lizzy, for I cannot imagine you will escape."

"If you choose to provoke me, I shall have no recourse but to endure," replied a laughing Elizabeth. "But do not expect to be unscathed in return."

It was an odd statement, and Elizabeth could not quite make out her friend's meaning. But Charlotte fixed Elizabeth with a grin and moved to greet the rest of the Bennet family, which included her brother and sisters, father, and Mr. Collins, who had attended with them. For a few moments, Elizabeth watched her friend, trying to puzzle out the meaning of her statement. As it was impossible, she shrugged it off, intending to speak to Charlotte at a later date.

The Bennet family was, as usual, among the first families to arrive, a custom begun by their mother, especially in the days after her daughters had begun to reach a marriageable age, in hopes of showing them off in order to marry them to eligible men. It was a habit they had kept, and particularly so in this instance because the Bennets were close friends with the Lucases. Sir William, the patriarch of the family, greeted Elizabeth with pleasure, to which Elizabeth responded. He was a jovial man, though a little simple, and while his tendency to be impressed with his knighthood could be a little tiresome, he was, in essentials, a good man.

When the party from Netherfield arrived, Elizabeth was aware of it instantly, and while she had known the Bingleys for all her life, she only had eyes for one member of the group. Watching as he greeted their hosts, Elizabeth waited patiently as Mr. Darcy made his way toward her, his purpose clear to anyone who cared to look. The indulgence of the company, the looks she received, even the way some few glared at her with envy, passed Elizabeth by with nary a second thought. And soon he was standing before her.

"Good evening, Miss Elizabeth. How happy I am to see you tonight."

"As am I to see you, sir."

Mr. Darcy reached down to grasp her hand. "Come. It has been torture today, not being in your company until this evening. If you will, I should like to keep your company to myself for a time."

"I am at your disposal," replied Elizabeth, coming along willingly as he led her to an unoccupied corner. There they stayed for some time, lost in the beauty of each other's presence.

As the evening progressed, Darcy began to wonder if it were possible to expire due to all the exquisite sensations coursing through him. Miss

Elizabeth Bennet was incandescent—there was no other way to describe her. The force of her presence had struck him like a speeding carriage, pulling him as the proverbial moth to the flame, and he was helpless before her. Those few precious moments they stood together, speaking in quiet voices, were bread from heaven, wings to his soaring soul.

Now, as they had separated for a time, Darcy watched her as she moved among society, noting her effortless manners and ability to elicit a smile here, a laugh there. Had he once thought himself able to resist her charms? The notion seemed utter absurdity now when confronted with the reality of her present desirability. There was no more chance of his refusing to love her than there was of him taking wing and flying to the moon.

Such open manners often bought other attention, however, though Darcy learned to accept it as her due rather than descend into jealousy. More than once did he catch the longing looks of men of the neighborhood, watched as she spoke and laughed with them, her animated replies provoking sighs of pleasure or regret. But every time she moved from one conversation to the next, her eyes would find his, and she would grin or lift one elegant eyebrow, a silent challenge to him for standing and looking at her, unable to move under the force of her gaze. Darcy did his best to mingle, to speak with these people who were so dear to her with interest and civility. But it was difficult when he was so transfixed by the sight of her.

As the evening progressed, Darcy found himself watching another more and more, and he was no more pleased by the distraction than he was about the other's presence. Darcy had seen similar behavior in George Wickham in the past, but whereas Wickham's manners were calculated, his words often flattering and contrived to provoke approval, Miss Elizabeth was effortless and open, with nothing of cunning. But as Wickham stayed away, Darcy decided there was little to be gained from confronting him.

Eventually when Miss Elizabeth made her way to Lady Anne and Darcy's sister—who was being allowed to attend this evening under the supervision of her mother—Darcy drifted closer to hear what they were saying and join in with their conversation. In the days since their arrival, the Bennet sisters had taken Georgiana under their wings and welcomed her. Darcy had never seen his sister as open as she was becoming with the Bennets. To a shy girl, such attention from ladies all older than she was a beautiful gift for her confidence. Miss Elizabeth took every opportunity to build it further.

"There will soon be a call for music, Georgiana," said Miss Elizabeth, already extended the privilege of referring to his sister by her Christian name. "From what I have heard of your playing, I dare say you could outshine us all. Shall you not perform for us?"

A look of such horror came over his sister's face that Miss Elizabeth laughed and patted her hand, even as Georgiana exclaimed. "Play? In front of all these people?"

"It will be expected when you come out, dear," said Lady Anne, directing a wry smile at Miss Elizabeth. "There is nothing amiss with your talents — only your confidence."

Though his sister gaped between the two women, Miss Elizabeth embraced her with one arm. "Of course, we shall not insist upon it, dearest. Perhaps it would be beneficial if you were to begin playing for small groups of friends in order to increase your comfort. By the time you come out, I am sure you will be a sensation."

"I thank you for the compliments," replied Georgiana, her pleasure still colored by the dismay she had earlier felt. "But what of you? Shall you delight the company tonight?"

"It will be impossible for me to decline," replied Miss Elizabeth. "My friend, Charlotte, is always searching for opportunities for me to exhibit, and none of my protests deter her in the slightest. As we are in her home, I will be subject to her whims and shall be forced to display my poor talents for all the company."

"There seems to be more than a hint of self-deprecation in the air," observed Lady Anne. "We have heard you play, Miss Elizabeth, and it is quite fine, indeed."

"Should my vanity have taken a musical turn," said Miss Elizabeth, laughing, "I should thank you very much. But I know my own talents. I flatter myself that I am proficient, at least, but not in any uncommon way. If you wish to hear those who are truly talented, then we should ask Caroline and Mary to play, for they both far outstrip my poor efforts."

"Do not allow her to protest with false modesty," said Darcy, stepping into the conversation. "If we asked them, I am certain both Miss Mary and Mrs. Bennet would insist that Miss Elizabeth is at least their equal."

"They might," agreed Miss Elizabeth. "But anyone listening to us will agree with me on this matter."

"Surely you are overly modest," said Georgiana. "My brother has said your playing has given him more pleasure than anything else he has ever heard, and he always tells the truth."

Miss Elizabeth's glorious eyes found him, amusement lighting her countenance. "When have you heard me play, Mr. Darcy? I do not recall playing at any event since your arrival."

Forcing embarrassment to the side, Darcy smiled — he had no desire to inform her he had listened outside the door of Longbourn's music room on more than one instance. Instead, he confessed to a less embarrassing: "There have been occasions when I have heard you practice at Longbourn."

Darcy could see that Miss Elizabeth did not quite believe him, but he was grateful when she turned back to his sister. "Shall we play together? If you play a duet, you share the attention, it easier to endure."

Georgiana was so horrified by the suggestion that Elizabeth reached out and patted her hand. "Not today, Georgiana. But in the future after we have practiced together."

A shy smile was Georgiana's response. "I believe I would like that."

The ensuing conversation was carried entirely by Miss Elizabeth and Georgiana, though it was clear to Darcy his mother was following closely. A hint of jealousy of his own relations made itself known, but Darcy, realizing it was more than a little silly, contented himself with watching and listening, glorying in every arch statement which drew out Georgiana's laughter, or in appreciating the intelligence which made up Elizabeth's opinions. Though they had been friends before, Darcy could see his sister opening herself further, their friendship becoming ever firmer. Miss Elizabeth would be good for his sister, of that he had no doubt.

True to Miss Elizabeth's prediction, Miss Lucas arrived not long after to cajole her into playing for the company. The look she bestowed on Darcy was a wry one, containing all the satisfaction of having foretold her friend's actions. Then she protested, albeit playfully.

"Should you not go and importune Caroline or Mary? They like to exhibit their talents. And so would Penelope Long, I am sure."

"But none of them are my particular friend, Lizzy," said Miss Lucas. "And though they play well, none sing as you do. Come, Lizzy — you cannot refuse."

Miss Elizabeth laughed at her friend. "I do not remember the last time I was *allowed* to refuse!"

"And you shall not be this time," was Miss Lucas's smirking reply.

Darcy's earlier assertion was then proven when the lady sat down to entertain the company. Darcy had heard many superior artists — his sister being one of them, he thought. But Miss Bennet's voice was akin to that of an angel, for her song was effortless, her voice climbing the register, each note as sweet and clear as the one before. The company listened, and Darcy thought this scene must have been repeated many times before, for there were few who were not giving this exquisite woman all the attention they possessed.

"I must confess, my son," said his mother, as she stepped to his side, "I had not thought to find such a jewel in a small neighborhood such as this. It is now no longer a mystery how you were captivated so quickly."

"It was when I visited Bingley four years ago that I first made her acquaintance," replied Darcy with an absence of thought.

"Oh?" asked Lady Anne, looking to him with interest unfeigned. "What was she like as a young girl?"

"As vibrant and magnetic as she is now. But she was not so polished then and had a tendency to speak without cessation." Darcy paused, smiling at the memory of Miss Elizabeth as she had been then, their last interaction no longer possessing the power to mortify him. "It was evident even then she would be a special woman."

"Then I am surprised you resisted her as long as you did." Lady Anne smiled and, rising on the tips of her toes, kissed his cheek. "Do not concern yourself for your father, Fitzwilliam. When he sees what I have seen, witnesses your affinity for her, he will not make any further protest."

Darcy nodded, though he did not speak. When Lady Anne moved away to rejoin Georgiana, Darcy stayed where he was, his vantage perfect for viewing the countenance of the fair performer. And view her he did, his eyes drinking in the sight of her as he contemplated the good fortune which had led him to her.

The trouble started soon after.

"That was exceptional, Miss Bennet!"

The sound of his most hated enemy's voice brought Darcy from his reverie, and he was shocked to see Wickham approaching Miss Elizabeth with a bow. Before he could move, Wickham had grasped her hand, bowing over it, his intention to kiss it thwarted by Miss Elizabeth's hasty reclamation of her appendage. Her retreat seemed to affect him not a jot, however, for Wickham fixed her with an unctuous smile and continued to speak.

"Rarely have I heard anything which gives me more pleasure! Why, other than the possible exception of Miss Georgiana Darcy, my patron's daughter, I dare say you are the most talented performer I have ever witnessed."

"Thank you, Mr. Wickham," said Miss Elizabeth, her manner all hesitation. "But I know it was nothing special."

"Please allow me my differing opinion." Wickham leaned forward as if to impart a secret though Darcy could see his eyes flicking to her décolletage. "And handsome too. Had I any notion Hertfordshire boasted such beauty, I should have come here long ago."

"We are a simple society, Mr. Wickham," said Miss Elizabeth, regaining her composure. "There are many other neighborhoods like this one, I am sure."

"Perhaps," replied the libertine. "Regardless, as the woman my patron's son is all but courting, I think I should like to come to know you. Shall we?"

With Wickham's motion toward the side of the room, Darcy was prompted to action. Only a few feet separated them, which allowed him to reach Miss Elizabeth's side before Wickham could attempt to spirit her away. With a smile—that she returned in a dazzling fashion—Darcy captured her hand and placed it in the crook of his arm. It could be called rude, but Darcy spared not a glance for Wickham, instead guiding Miss Elizabeth away from his father's protégé and to a place a little to the side where they could speak openly.

"After ignoring me since your family's arrival, Mr. Wickham chose a curious time to unleash his charm."

Darcy shot Miss Elizabeth a glance and was heartened when she grinned at him, seemingly unconcerned with Wickham's action. A rueful smile was all he could muster.

"Come now, Mr. Darcy," continued she, her tone slightly censorious, "his manners are obviously practiced. Surely you do not believe my head to be turned at such blatant flattery."

"Not at all," said Darcy. "I am more concerned for your wellbeing, for Wickham is not a man to be trusted."

"There is little he can do in such company as this. Do not be concerned for me, for I shall be well."

It was good advice, and Darcy was well aware of her resilience. Despite that, however, as the evening wore on, he found himself becoming more concerned, for it seemed like every time his back was turned, Wickham made, straight as an arrow, for Miss Elizabeth's side. And every time he approached to take her away from the wretched man's attentions, he received nothing more than an insouciant grin and a knowing look. When he asked after what Wickham wanted, Miss Elizabeth merely shrugged her shoulders.

"Mr. Wickham has had little to say to me, other than to speak of himself," said she. "I might consider him to be Adonis himself, given how much he loves to refer to his exploits. As to what he hopes to accomplish, I am not certain. He can hardly suppose himself to be the superior man between you." A wink was followed by a laugh and a hand on his arm. "And I do not refer to your position in society or wealth."

Regardless of the seriousness of the situation, Darcy found himself grinning in response. "So, you do not find him my superior in society? His manners have often drawn praise though his ability to keep the friends he makes has ever been uncertain."

"It may be that he is more at ease in society," agreed Elizabeth. "As I said, his manners are artful, and I suspect there is not much substance to him. Nothing at all like you."

"Thank you, my dear," said Mr. Darcy, raising her hand to his lips. "Coming from you, it means everything to me."

Miss Elizabeth put her hand, recently lowered from his mouth, on his arm, and stepped forward as close as she had ever dared. "There is no other man like you, Mr. Darcy. I feel fortunate you have persuaded me of your goodness, for I would have it no other way."

The words stayed with him for some time. After the apology, Darcy had not been certain he would be successful in persuading her. To feel her affection and bask in the warmth of her smiles and regard was more than he dared hope. It would not be long now—Darcy doubted he could hold himself in check.

But Wickham persisted, and after a few more times of chasing him away from Miss Elizabeth's side, Darcy's patience was at an end. The gentleman in Darcy would not allow him to make a scene in the home of one of the prominent men of the neighborhood. But that did not mean he would not take action.

"If you know what is good for you," said Darcy the last time he pulled Wickham away from Miss Elizabeth, "you will leave Miss Elizabeth strictly alone. I have no more patience for this game."

"What is the matter, Fitzy?" jeered Wickham. "Are you afraid Miss Elizabeth will like me better?"

Darcy barked a derisive laugh. "No, Wickham, I do not fear that at all. But I know your ways, and I am aware of your proclivities. I will not permit you toying with her affections or whatever other depravity you intend. Back off!"

Punctuating his demand with a pointed finger at Wickham's chest, Darcy escorted Miss Elizabeth to the side of her brother and asked her to stay with him. Bennet's nod told Darcy he had witnessed what was happening that evening—she would be safe with him until Darcy returned, and for the rest of the evening, as Darcy had no intention of leaving her side again. But first Darcy mean to have a word with the one person in the room who could exert some form of control over Wickham.

Robert Darcy saw his approach, the grim set to his mouth indicating his understanding of the situation. The severity of it, however, Darcy was certain his father did not know—Darcy lost little time in explaining it to him.

"I suggest you control your toady, Father," hissed Darcy, taking care to ensure they were not overheard, though he knew many of the company were already aware of it.

The elder Darcy frowned at his tone. "Do not speak to me in such a way. I am your father."

"Yes, you are," replied Darcy. "But you also insist on keeping that leech among us when he does not deserve to wipe our boots." Darcy stepped closer, speaking with deadly determination. "I have no wish to insult you, Father. If you choose to associate with Wickham that is your business. However, if he continues to importune the woman who will soon become my fiancée, I shall beat him to a pulp. I suggest you rein him in."

Eyes wide with shock, his father stared at him, uncertain which of Darcy's assertions he should respond to first. When he did not immediately speak, Darcy decided he did not wish to speak of the matter anymore.

"There are several others—most notably Bingley and Miss Elizabeth's brother—who would be eager to assist me. Control him, Father, if you do not wish him to meet such a fate."

Then Darcy nodded and stepped way. Soon he was by Miss Elizabeth's side again, a location he did not intend to vacate for the rest of the evening.

"Wickham!" said Mr. Darcy when he had reached his protégé's side. "What do you think you are doing?"

"Why, enjoying the company," said Wickham, his tone all that was congenial and friendly. A subtle undertone provoked Darcy to wonder if he was being mocked, but he pushed the thought to the side.

"I am speaking of Fitzwilliam's lady," said Darcy, trying to inform Wickham he was in no mood to be put off by Wickham's insouciance. "Do you not know you are provoking my son to anger?"

312 ~☙ *Jann Rowland*

"While I do not wish to anger him," replied Wickham, "I am determined to learn the truth of Miss Elizabeth Bennet."

Taken aback, Darcy directed a questioning look at his former steward's son. "To what do you refer?"

"Do you not consider her odd?" asked Wickham. "Look at her and see how she makes love to them all. She is perhaps the biggest flirt I have ever seen."

Darcy turned to the side of the room where his son was standing beside Miss Elizabeth like a guardian angel, and he noted how she was speaking to one of the neighborhood men with evident animation. The whole group of them—perhaps seven or eight, including his son—laughed at whatever she said, and more than one set of eyes rested on her in appreciation.

"I think you overstate the matter," said Darcy, turning back to the conversation. "And even if she is, what is it to you? She *is* playful, but her behavior does not breach propriety."

"Because, Mr. Darcy," said Wickham with exaggerated patience, "I would spare your son from the machinations of a temptress, if I could. I know he has no love for me, but I still feel loyalty to him for the friendship we once shared."

Darcy regarded his godson and shook his head. "It is apparent to me that we must obtain your next situation as soon as may be."

The amiable countenance Wickham usually supported was gone in the blink of an eye, the mask of an inscrutable man replacing it. Had Darcy not been watching Wickham, he might have missed it—instead thoughts he had never considered before began to worm their way into his consciousness.

"Do you not see how you are angering my son?" asked Darcy, shunting those thoughts to the side for the moment. "It would be best if you did not create difficulty for yourself, Wickham, as I cannot predict Fitzwilliam's actions should he deem your behavior too forward."

"I have no fear for anything he might do." It sounded like so much bravado. "Even if he should make an attempt, I should think it a small price to pay for rescuing him from a most unpleasant connection."

"That is not for you to decide," said Darcy firmly. "For my sake, stay away from Miss Elizabeth for the rest of the evening. I would not wish to make a scene."

"Of course," replied Wickham. "I have no desire to cause trouble in this house. But let me ask you one question, Mr. Darcy."

"Very well."

"If you do not think Miss Elizabeth is a brazen flirt, why do you think she holds Collins in her thrall?"

"The parson?" asked Darcy, confused.

"Her cousin," confirmed Wickham. "Surely you have seen how the man positively moons over her. I have heard in the village that Mr. Collins has been in love with her for many years, but she strings him along and teases him, though she has no intention of gratifying his desires. No, her sights are set rather higher."

Having said this, Wickham bowed and moved away, leaving Darcy to his thoughts. Though he had not thought on the matter any great deal, Darcy *had* noticed the young man's seeming infatuation with Miss Elizabeth. At present, he was standing in company with her, Fitzwilliam, the other two Bennet sisters and some others of the neighborhood. And while he thought Wickham might be overstating the matter, there seemed to be something of truth to his words.

For the rest of the evening Darcy watched her, wondering if this was something he could use to pry his son away from her. But more than that, Darcy questioned whether he even wished to.

CHAPTER XXX

$\mathcal{T}$ ime was running out. Though determined to discredit his detested rival and set himself up in his place, Wickham knew he would have to do something, and soon. Within days, Mr. Darcy would receive reports back from London concerning his conduct there, and the uncomfortable questions would follow. Ever confident of his ability to talk his way out of difficulty with the gentleman, Wickham still knew his standing would suffer. If there was ever a time to act, it was now.

In the days following the party at Lucas Lodge, Wickham focused on his plans, perhaps more than he had ever focused on anything before. The first prong of attack was his continued attempts to charm Georgiana Darcy. That, however, Wickham was forced to acknowledge as a monumental failure, and it was all because of the actions of Lady Anne Darcy. Simply put, the girl could never be found out of her mother's company. It was as if she was a mother bear, never more than a few feet from her cub, ready to lash out if anyone stepped between them. This was made evident by an exchange between them one day at Netherfield.

It had seemed perfect. Though the young heiress had avoided him and stayed with her mother, Wickham, quite by chance, had found her walking the halls of Netherfield unaccompanied. Eager to once again subject her to his charms, he bowed and approached her, showing her the winsome smile which never failed to dazzle his chosen conquests.

"Miss Darcy," said he. "How are you this fine day?"

"Very well, Mr. Wickham," said Miss Darcy. The smile she bestowed upon him stopped him for a moment, for it had a wry quality he could not quite like.

The moment passed, however, and Wickham proceeded, confident of his success. "It appears to me this little holiday in Hertfordshire has not affected your routine. Your dedication to your education is inspiring, my dear, for there are not many who would continue with such diligence as you."

"Thank you," replied she with a little curtsey and a giggle. "Your approval is positively inspiring."

Again, Wickham paused, for it sounded almost like she was mocking him. Shaking it off, he extended his arm to her. "We have not spent much time speaking of late, and I miss the times we spent together when you were a girl. Shall we sit down together?"

"Ah, Georgiana—there you are."

Stifling a curse, Wickham whirled to see Lady Anne smirking at him. A glance back at the mousey girl showed her shared connection with the elder lady, for their expressions were identical. Wickham almost scowled.

"Georgiana, dear, please wait in the music room for me. I must speak with Mr. Wickham."

With another giggle, Miss Darcy curtseyed and entered the room behind her mother, a skip in her step which deepened Wickham's inclination to glower. But then the lady stepped forward a little, regarding him, a pensive frown bestowed upon him. As women went, Lady Anne was as handsome as any Wickham had met, despite her more than fifty years. Wickham might have attempted to bed her, had she not been his patron's wife.

"How may I help you, Mrs. Darcy?" asked Wickham when she did not immediately speak. The reference to her husband's name was intentional.

Lady Anne delivered a faint smile, which Wickham did not like at all, and said: "Let us dispense with the servility, shall we, Mr. Wickham? I am well acquainted with what you want, and I have no intention of allowing it."

"I am not certain to what you refer," replied Wickham, feigning astonishment.

"Oh, I am quite sure you are," rejoined she. "As long as you are living under the same roof as my daughter, I will be in her company. I suggest you find some other heiress to seduce, for you will not succeed with her.

"Furthermore," said she, speaking over his protests, "you should consider what my husband would think of you attempting to seduce his daughter. While Robert finds you amusing for some reason I cannot understand, he is quite traditional and will not accept even a hint of improper behavior with our daughter. Do not test his resolve, for you will not like the result."

Then Lady Anne turned away, without further acknowledgement, and disappeared into the music room, Wickham watching her with flinty eyes as she did so. A part of him was frustrated, but he knew he could bide his time with the younger Darcy. Discrediting the brother was the far more pressing concern, regardless.

With that quest, Wickham thought he had more success. Every chance he had, Wickham was speaking in Mr. Darcy's ear, filling him with his observations of Miss Elizabeth, and as the man was already disposed to disapprove of her, Wickham thought his words were growing in fertile ground. That Darcy's attentions to Miss Elizabeth were growing ever more ardent was a circumstance which suited Wickham's designs. Wickham did not approach her much though he did on occasion. Not only did that provoke the younger Darcy to greater belligerence, but the elder Darcy still looked on him with suspicion.

"There she is again," said Wickham during a morning visit a few days later. "I begin to feel sympathy for Collins, though he truly is a dull specimen."

Mr. Darcy, though he noted Wickham's words, said nothing. Wickham continued to regard the woman with distaste, his chin jutting out at her as she spoke with Mr. Collins, her eyes sparkling with delight. For his part, Collins appeared as silly in his adoration as he ever had.

"I wonder if she has yet given him a taste of what she is hiding under her dress." Wickham's eyes darted to the side to see how his patron was taking his words. "It would not be surprising—I suspect there are many men hereabouts who have sampled her charms."

"Silence, Wickham!" hissed Mr. Darcy. "Do you think you will remain in this house should you be overheard?"

"I offer my apologies," was Wickham's smooth reply, though not meaning a hint of it. "Perhaps I was overstating the matter. But she *is* a flirt—that you must confess."

"I know nothing of the sort."

The man's short statement was belied by the frown he directed at Miss Bennet. Though Wickham knew he had not convinced Mr. Darcy in any way, still his calculated words had sown further seeds of disquiet in the elder gentleman. He turned away, unwilling to show Mr. Darcy a smug grin of satisfaction—how much in life would have been different had he not been able to secure such a man who doted on his every word?

"You claim she is a flirt," said Mr. Darcy.

"Her brazen overtures are evident to anyone who cares to look," replied Wickham.

"Then why has she not attempted to work her wiles on you? From everything I have seen, she tends to withdraw from you when you approach her."

With an uncaring shrug, Wickham said: "That does not concern me, for I do not wish to associate with a woman such as she. Her retreat I put down to her knowledge that I can see what she is about. It is understandable she would have no wish to put herself in my company when I may expose her." Wickham turned to Mr. Darcy. "I suspect it is for that reason she also avoids you."

"There is a much simpler explanation for that," replied Mr. Darcy. Wickham turned to look at him. "It is because *I* have not been welcoming to her, and she has undoubtedly learned of my disapproval from my son."

"That may play a part in it," allowed Wickham. "But it is more than just that. But do not take my word for it, Mr. Darcy. I am certain you are as adept at spotting her inconsistencies as I."

Even this bit of flattery did not affect the gentleman as much as Wickham might have thought. Though he had never considered the possibility, it seemed Mr. Darcy might be becoming more resistant to his manners. It seemed more drastic action might be required. As they sat there, watching Darcy and his doxy, the hate flowering in Wickham's mind grew and strengthened. And one way or another, he was determined to ensure he received his due.

As this intrigue was surrounding Darcy, he did his level best to avoid being affected by it. After a few more days and threats, Wickham finally desisted, though he continued to watch Elizabeth. Those in Darcy's circle, particularly Bingley and Bennet, who most loved her, watched Wickham along with him, Bingley even suggesting a solution.

"My father is also concerned for Wickham's behavior. It would not take much persuasion to insist on Wickham's removal from the house. Then he would have no choice but to return to London."

The thought of the row which would ensue with his father should that happen caused Darcy to grimace. It may yet be required, but for the moment, Darcy thought Wickham had been sufficiently cowed.

"As long as we remain vigilant, there should be little to worry. Of course, your father may do as he chooses, and if he prefers Wickham to leave, I will do nothing but applaud. But I will not ask it of him at present."

Bingley nodded. "Then we shall all watch over Elizabeth. And do not think she is incapable of defending herself. Should Wickham attempt anything untoward, he will discover how capable she is."

On a certain day, Darcy and Bingley made their way toward Longbourn, talking and laughing, their high spirits affecting even their mounts, who pranced along, seemingly eager to gallop. To anyone who knew him, Charles Bingley was possessed of an irrepressible temper and enough cheerfulness for ten men. It seemed something auspicious was in the air that day, and had Darcy not been contemplating a similar action, he might have envied his friend.

The sense of expectation seemed to intrude on the senses of the family that greeted them at Longbourn. Mrs. Bennet made them feel welcome with an order for tea as they sat down with the family. As comfortable as he was with this family by now, Darcy spoke with the two Bennet men at length, noting that the younger man was now friendly and open, unlike his behavior upon their return from London. Though Darcy could not imagine thanking Wickham for anything, Bennet's acceptance was almost certainly hastened by Wickham's actions.

"The rest of your family have been a fixture in my sitting-room of late, Darcy," said the elder Mr. Bennet. "I am surprised they have not accompanied you today."

"Mother indicated a need for Georgiana to attend her studies. My father and Mr. Bingley were discussing a matter of the estate."

"And you took the opportunity to depart while they were occupied," said Mr. Bennet, observing Darcy over his teacup. Darcy did not respond, for that was exactly what they had done. "I suppose without the support of his patron, Mr. Wickham would not feel comfortable following you."

"There are few places in the neighborhood Wickham would feel welcome without my father's presence."

Mr. Bennet nodded absently. "He seems well contained, then. Shall he return to London soon? A man in his position cannot ignore his profession long."

"It is possible. My father has mentioned his efforts to find a new position for his godson. How long that search will consume, I cannot say. I hope he will leave soon."

A nod was Mr. Bennet's response, and their talk was turned to other matters. Before long, Darcy found himself once again in Miss Elizabeth's company, her father having ceded his, and they sat for some time in that attitude, speaking softly.

It seemed Bingley was not to be denied, for it was some few minutes later that he spoke up, looking at Miss Bennet with obvious intent. "The day outside is quite fine for November. Shall we not walk out, Miss Bennet? Darcy? Miss Elizabeth?"

"I have no objections," said Miss Elizabeth, as her sister nodded, unable to speak because of emotion. Darcy gazed at her fondly—he had become quite attached to this mild creature, and he hoped that she would soon be his sister.

"Mary, shall you walk out with them?" asked Mrs. Bennet, a sly smile on her two sisters.

Miss Mary, however, demurred. "There is no need for me to accompany them. I am sure they can provide chaperonage for each other. It would be my preference to stay and play for a while."

The sound of Mr. Bennet snorting from behind his cup was heard by everyone and acknowledged by no one. The open grin Mrs. Bennet showed the company informed them all of her opinion, as was the affectionate smile Thomas Bennet bestowed on his sisters.

"That is an excellent idea, Mary dear," said Mrs. Bennet. "Would you like some company?"

It was astonishing to Darcy how quickly the room cleared after that, and he wondered if a little of the late Mrs. Bennet's matchmaking tendencies had been absorbed by her family. Mrs. Bennet and Miss Mary soon departed to the music room, and the Bennet men excused themselves to look after some estate business, leaving the two couples in each other's company. Bingley shot a look at Darcy, which he confirmed with a nod, and soon the ladies were donning their outerwear for their walk.

It is a commonly understood truth that couples make poor chaperones. Once out of doors, Darcy found he had little attention to spare for Bingley and Miss Bennet, for Miss Elizabeth consumed all of his focus. They walked for a time in the back gardens before choosing at random one of the paths which led around the park. By this time, Bingley and his lady had disappeared, leaving them quite alone. It was quite a contrast to the one occasion, foremost in his mind, when they had engaged in similar activities, just before Miss Elizabeth had gone to London. Then, Miss Bennet had been determined to keep him in her sight!

Shaking himself free of Miss Bennet, Darcy looked to his own Miss Bennet, noting how her bonnet covered her face as she walked beside him, revealing only her profile. What a lovely woman he had found! There could be no man so fortunate as he, for no woman could possibly combine a handsome countenance with such a keen mind and playful disposition. It would undoubtedly lead to argument when they were married, but Darcy would not have it any other way—there could be nothing like having an intelligent, passionate wife to share his life!

The thought of marriage filled Darcy's mind, every hint of his ruminations focused on his need for her, on how he must find a way to make her his. The receptive hints she had been giving as his attentions grew more ardent, and though he had thought to wait, a sudden impatience overtook him. Stopping in the middle of the path, Darcy turned her to him, taking her hand, noting the arch look she was giving him. The curve of her lips told Darcy she had been expecting this. Expecting it! All doubt was washed away by that knowing look, allowing Darcy to proceed with confidence.

"Miss Elizabeth," said he, "it seems like I will forever be required to stay on my toes, for you seem to anticipate me at every turn."

"Forever?" asked she with an arch of her brow. "That seems like an awfully long time, Mr. Darcy."

"It is, indeed," was his sage reply. "But it is exactly how long I would wish to have you in my life. I have never been an eloquent man, as you have had occasion to see for yourself. But I am an honest one. The regard I felt for you as I considered what happened between us during our separation is nothing compared to what I feel for you now. There is little doubt you are the most incredible woman of my acquaintance, and I would be eternally happy if you would consent to marry me."

"Well," said Miss Elizabeth, "if it be for your eternal gratitude, then I suppose I shall be required to accept." Then she paused and laughed, catching his hand in her own and pressing a kiss against it. "Perhaps you do not know, but my sister, Jane, and I, have always pledged to marry for love alone. I find, Mr. Darcy, that my heart is quite full of you, the best man I know. There is nothing that would make me happier than to become your wife forever."

It might be supposed that a lover, having been accepted, would wish to keep the woman of his affection to himself for as long as he was able. Darcy, having endured the uncertainty of her initial distrust and the actions of his father's protégé, was eager to secure consent. Thus, after sharing a few intimate moments with the woman he loved, he pulled her toward the house, both of them laughing all the way.

When they had gained Longbourn's front hall, he whispered to her of his intentions, grinning when she informed him she would go to her sisters, and stepped quickly to the master's study. Given how the gentleman had regarded them that morning, Darcy was amused to see how the man had anticipated him. Consent was quickly given after which Mr. Bennet welcomed him to the family.

"Though I shall lose my daughter to the north, I am happy to say I predicted it all from the beginning. It was clear as soon as you came that you would be unable to resist her charms!"

"Such a thought would be blasphemous!" replied Darcy, laughing along with his host. "And do not think of it as losing a daughter, for we shall visit often. As fond of her family as she is, I suspect Elizabeth will demand it."

"That she will!" said Mr. Bennet. "But I have one condition, young man. I have heard, though you have been reticent on the subject yourself, that you have a splendid library at your estate. I hope I shall be invited to sample it in the near future."

"Of course," replied Darcy. "And you should further be aware that both my father and my uncle are excellent chess players. We shall have a tournament when you visit."

"I shall anticipate it keenly."

Their conversation was interrupted when the door to Mr. Bennet's study was unceremoniously yanked open and Bingley darted into the room. The flushed nature of his countenance coupled with his heavy breathing suggested he had rushed back to Longbourn, likely pulling Miss Bennet along behind him. The notion struck Darcy as rather amusing, and he burst into laughter, joined at once by Mr. Bennet.

"This is certainly an auspicious day," said the gentleman as Bingley looked on them both, wondering if they were mad. "It is not every day *any* man receives two gentlemen in his study for the same purpose. If you will excuse me, Darcy, it seems I must give up another of my daughters."

"Certainly," replied Darcy, rising to his feet. Approaching Bingley, he caught his soon to be brother's hand and grasped it in a firm grip, Bingley's smile growing delighted as he did so. "It seems I have beaten you to it, my friend. Though I have often been termed deliberate and careful, it seems in this instance I have been more impulsive even than you!"

"We have changed places, indeed, my friend," replied Bingley with a grin. "But you may gloat later. For now, I believe I require a moment of my neighbor's time."

With another slap on his friend's back, Darcy left the study. There was a young lady in the house, likely receiving the congratulations of her beloved sisters, and offering her elder sister the same. At that moment, Darcy found himself impatient to be in her company once again.

"Well, it seems like your son is happy, at least. I only hope it lasts."

"Pardon me, Wickham?" asked Robert Darcy. "Why do you say that?"

It might be supposed Wickham actually rolled his eyes at Darcy's statement, but as he had turned back to look at the scene before them, he could not be certain. That he did not look on Fitzwilliam with anything resembling friendship was becoming more evident all the time, regardless of Wickham's attempts to obfuscate.

"Come, Mr. Darcy," said he, "I am sure you can see it as well as I do. Had *I* been in your son's position, Miss Elizabeth would have accepted *my* proposal just as readily."

This recitation did not quite fit Darcy's feelings. "Surely you overstate the matter, Wickham. Though I cannot guess the depth of her feelings, it is clear she feels *something* for my son. Her interest in him is not solely motivated by reasons of prudence, or even mercenary."

Though Wickham did not scowl, Darcy thought it was a near thing. For the moment, he could not pay much attention to his protégé, for his focus was on Fitzwilliam in its entirety. His wife and daughter, it seemed, could not be happier with Fitzwilliam's choice. Georgiana, in particular, exclaimed her expectations of having a future sister to love and to receive her sister's love turn.

It was difficult to confess, but Darcy could not help but note his son's happiness. Fitzwilliam had always been a serious boy, and he had grown to be a man with the proper amount of gravity, respect for his situation and family, and diligence to his duty, all as Darcy demanded. Before this fascination with the Bennet girl, there had been little to criticize with respect to either his conduct or his opinions. Oh, he had befriended the Bingley boy, heedless of all the drawbacks to his friendship, but Darcy had never considered his friend to be deficient in manners or understanding. Quite the contrary.

Though it seemed like it was a matter which was already decided, Darcy thought he would make one more attempt to appeal to Fitzwilliam's better nature. Not that he was certain any longer that the boy was not correct in singling the girl out for his attentions. Be that as it may, the Darcy in him, steeped in centuries of family tradition and pride, demanded this final attempt.

It seemed that Fitzwilliam well understood his purpose, for later that day, when Darcy found him alone, he was treated to a knowing look, accompanied by a smirk. Though Darcy did not care for his son's manner, he was aware he had no choice but to endure it. The chances were small—infinitesimal, to be honest—of his convincing his son, even without angering him.

"It is obvious you understand my purpose," said Darcy without preamble. "Thus, I shall not sport with your intelligence by means of obfuscation. I am willing to acknowledge Miss Elizabeth's attractions, and I can see how you have been captivated by them. But I must ask: are you certain of what you are about?"

"Utterly convinced," was his son's reply with nary a pause to give Darcy an option to attack. "She is the woman for me—I shall have no other."

Darcy paused, wondering how far he should push. His son returned his look without expression, perhaps expecting a fight, perhaps not. A sense of fatigue washed over Darcy. This continual fighting with his son was difficult to endure, particularly when they had usually been aligned when he was younger.

"It is difficult," said Darcy, putting his hands behind his back and taking a few steps forward. "I have always expected you to make a stupendous match, for you are a Darcy, with centuries of ancestors who have done likewise."

"I *am* making a stupendous match," replied Fitzwilliam. Darcy frowned at the interruption, but his son was already speaking again. "Miss Elizabeth will add to our family's legacy, Father—not detract from it. She is a special woman. I feel fortunate she has accepted me. Her character is such that she can do anything she chooses, yet she feels like I am a worthy risk to ensure her happiness."

For a moment Darcy considered expressing his disbelief in his son's suggestion of Miss Bennet as their superior, though he knew there was a hint of hyperbole in his son's words. At the same time, he considered bringing up the possibility of withholding his blessing, or even disinheritance.

There was little point in doing so, however, so he desisted. It would be nothing more than a bluff, and Darcy was well aware Fitzwilliam would call him on it. Furthermore, he had told his son he would be supportive if he made his choice in a rational manner. It seemed Fitzwilliam had done that though there was an obvious element of affection in his choice. As Darcy had chosen his own wife with his heart in mind, he could not fault his son for acting in a similar manner, though Darcy personally did not approve.

Therefore, Darcy did the only thing he could. "Then there is nothing more to say. I hope your choice is the correct one, but you have made it now, regardless."

"Thank you, Father," said Fitzwilliam. "I appreciate your acceptance in this matter."

Darcy nodded and clasped his son's shoulder, a gesture of support. Then he turned and departed, seeking to find his wife. Anne would know what to say to make him feel better about it.

CHAPTER XXXI

"*I* cannot be happier for you both."

A broad smile accompanied Caroline's words, filling Elizabeth with affection for this woman to whom she had, at times, struggled to feel close.

"It *is* unfortunate, to be sure," continued she, "that you will be leaving this house so soon after I have entered it. I am certain your late mother would agree with me."

"No doubt," replied Elizabeth with a laugh.

"Mama would be even more despondent because you are going to the north," said Jane. "You know she always hoped her daughters would settle nearby."

"Perchance she would," replied Elizabeth. "But she would not begrudge me my happiness."

"Of course, she would not," replied Caroline, catching Elizabeth in an affectionate embrace. "Her enthusiasm for the match would be boundless!"

"Do you not think she would rejoice at your going?" asked Mary with a sly glance alighting on Elizabeth. "She always did say you were her greatest trial as a child."

Elizabeth laughed along with her sisters at the tease. "You never could keep your skirts clean!" exclaimed Jane. "And the number of times you ripped your frock climbing trees, I thought Mama would expire from mortification!"

They all joined Elizabeth in laughter, after which Caroline gathered them both close, holding their hands and looking at Jane and Elizabeth in turn. "All jesting aside, I am very happy for you both. Your young men will make you happy."

Jane and Elizabeth shared a glance. "I am certain they shall," was Jane's fervent reply.

The engagement of one daughter would have sent Mrs. Bennet into a tizzy. The engagement of both would have sent the entire family fleeing in terror. As it was, though Jane and Elizabeth were not subjected to a multitude of visits such as they would have been had their mother been alive to show them to the neighborhood, Caroline made a worthy substitute. Morning engagements during those days were plentiful, and Elizabeth found herself in more sitting-rooms, drinking more tea and accepting more congratulations than she thought she might have in a lifetime! If *some* of those neighborhood ladies with whom Elizabeth did not feel herself at all close sounded insincere in their congratulations, Elizabeth did not allow it to bother her.

Knowing Mr. Darcy was not at all fond of society, Elizabeth was appreciative of his forbearance, for he allowed no hint of frustration or impatience to escape while he was subjected to the inquest of the neighborhood. While it was true that many looked on both Elizabeth and Jane with envy, many more considered them to be the neighborhood's own, and their engagements to be a point of pride—particularly Elizabeth's, the surprise that it was.

What was the largest surprise to Elizabeth was the reaction of Mr. Darcy's father. The gentleman had, by her fiancé's admission, made one last attempt to persuade his son against the match, but his congratulations to Elizabeth were all that was cordial.

"Miss Elizabeth," said he the first time she saw him after her engagement. "Please allow me to congratulate you on your engagement to my son." The older gentleman smiled and nodded. "Though I will own to a certain partiality of opinion, I consider Fitzwilliam to be a fine man, one whom any woman in the kingdom would feel fortunate to secure."

"You will receive no argument from me," replied Elizabeth, bemused by his sudden acceptance. "William is quite the best man of my acquaintance."

"William, is it?" asked Mr. Darcy, turning a curious look on his son. "To the best of my knowledge, no one has ever shortened my son's name."

"Most of my friends call me Darcy," said her fiancé. "And everyone in the family calls me Fitzwilliam. For Elizabeth, I wish to be less formal than my usual moniker allows."

Behind them, Lady Anne was laughing, her reaction a clear indication that she was not offended that Elizabeth would not use her family name — the name she had given to her son — to address him. Mr. Darcy considered the matter for a few moments before he nodded.

"That is understandable." The gentleman paused, looking uncomfortable, and then seemed to come to a decision. "I also wish to extend my apologies, Miss Elizabeth. Am I correct in apprehending my son has informed you of my feelings concerning your courtship?"

Though Elizabeth felt her cheeks heat a little, she looked back bravely at the father of the man she was to marry. "He has."

Mr. Darcy gave her a tight nod. "Please be aware it was never my intention to presume that you are, in any way, lacking. My concerns were for the family's expectations for my son. You are, I suspect, aware that he was capable of aspiring to marry the daughter of a noble, if he so chose."

"Yes, I am well aware of it," replied Elizabeth, while William rolled his eyes at his father.

"It is a different path my son has chosen, and I cannot say he has chosen incorrectly. For my part, I hope we can put any past disagreements behind us and come together as a family."

It was a half-hearted effort at best, but Elizabeth was not at all inclined to reject the olive branch offered. Instead, she leaned forward and put her hand on the gentleman's arm, saying: "Of course, Mr. Darcy. As I am to marry your son, I wish to have good relations with all of his family. If there is anything to forgive, for myself, it is all forgiven." "Good," replied Mr. Darcy.

The one member of the party who was not accepting of Elizabeth was Mr. Wickham, though Elizabeth knew William would not consider that man to be associated with him. Though he was not there on the first occasion that Elizabeth met with the Darcy family, she met him several subsequent times. That he was not happy was clear to Elizabeth, though she could not determine why he should disapprove of her as a bride. What was it to him? He was nothing more than a greedy man riding on the coattails of a wealthy patron. As he did not approach, Elizabeth put him from her mind.

* * *

The seed of hate which had long been nourished in Wickham's mind was now full flower, and encompassed within his ire was the young lady to whom Darcy had proposed. His own campaign to discredit his rival was turning to ashes around his feet, as Mr. Darcy, who he had been so certain would never accept the young woman, betrayed Wickham and did nothing about it. And Lady Anne, true to her word, spent every waking moment with Georgiana, watching him always when he was nearby, ensuring she was a shield between them. The unfairness of it all made Wickham want to scream out his frustration.

Doggedly determined to realize his own dreams, Wickham kept at Mr. Darcy, continuing to malign his son's name, along with that of the little tart for whom he had offered. But the more he spoke, the less Mr. Darcy seemed to listen, and a few times Wickham even caught a look of annoyance on the man's countenance. On one occasion he even pushed back.

"Wickham, I believe this line of conversation has been exhausted."

Cut off, as he was, Wickham stared at his patron, wondering that it had come to this. Mr. Darcy apparently considered this enough reason to continue.

"The identity of my son's bride is not your concern—I must wonder why you speak of it at all."

"For nothing more than concern for *him*," cried Wickham.

The huff which comprised Mr. Darcy's response told Wickham how far his influence over the gentleman had fallen. "It seems unlikely you care so much, considering your estrangement from Fitzwilliam which has been of several years' duration. Please do not insult my intelligence by claiming such altruistic motivations when your disdain for her is clear to see."

Wickham opened his mouth to protest, but it died in his throat unspoken, for Mr. Darcy's scowl allowed no argument. Though Wickham would never use such a term to describe himself, he sulked for the rest of the afternoon.

The matter came to a head the day before the ball Mrs. Bingley had planned. While the woman's originally stated purpose for the ball had been to honor the Darcys, it took no great discernment to determine the recent engagements had taken precedence. Wickham watched the preparations, dissatisfied by the way matters had turned out, particularly when he had gone to Pemberley with such high hopes. Surely there must be some way to still exert some control over events, but he found himself unable to determine how it might be done. And the smirking visage of Fitzwilliam Darcy, seemingly understanding how Wickham felt and reveling in his supposed victory, filled Wickham with the urge to lash out.

Finally, having had enough of the preparations, Wickham let himself from the sitting-room, certain he was not storming away in a fury. As he walked, his mind worked the problem over and over, trying to find some crevice he could pry open, some weakness he had not yet considered. But it was all dross. There seemed to be nothing to be done. That was when the summons to attend Mr. Darcy in the library arrived.

"The library is little used, as none of my family are much for reading," the elder Bingley had said when Mr. Darcy had inquired soon after arriving. "If you please, I would think that room would be perfect for you to conduct whatever business which needs your attention during your stay."

Mr. Darcy had thanked Mr. Bingley, and from that time forward, he could be found there most mornings. More than once, Wickham had attempted to induce the gentleman to see his point of view, his failure leading him to an irrational detestation of the room. In recent mornings, he had avoided it, as the sight of his patron filled him with the urge to lash out, and if anything of Mr. Darcy's patronage was to be salvaged, that would not do.

So involved in his disappointments was he that Wickham did not immediately see the grim set to Mr. Darcy's countenance. He entered with a greeting, not knowing how curt it sounded, and approached the small desk Mr. Darcy had taken to using. Mr. Darcy indicated a chair nearby, and Wickham allowed himself to fall into it gracelessly, akin to a rag doll discarded by a child, he thought without humor. It was then he noted Mr. Darcy's severe countenance and uncompromising glare.

"How may I help you, Mr. Darcy?" asked Wickham in a belated attempt at appearing as cheerful as ever.

"You may help me by explaining this," spat Mr. Darcy, throwing a few sheets of paper on the desk.

Wickham did not know what the letters contained, but he could guess. The mood of his patron was one Wickham had never seen before—or at least he had never seen it directed at himself. It would take all of his wits to charm himself out of this one, it seemed.

"This is a letter I received from Mr. Mortimer, when I asked after your time there."

Mr. Darcy paused, reaching for some other letters which were meticulously sorted on his desk, dropping a sheaf of them on the table beside the letter from his erstwhile and detested employer. Then he glared at Wickham.

"These are from several other law firms in the city. I had written to my own solicitor asking him for assistance in finding you another position. Though he complied, he informed me he was not certain anyone else in town would accept you, as your reputation, gained while working for Mortimer, had become exceedingly bad. Every other firm to which I wrote replied with similar tidings.

"At first I wondered what had happened and gave it little credence. I know you, I assured them. I know your character, trust in your diligence, your industrious nature."

The sound of Mr. Darcy's fist hitting the table prompted Wickham to jump in his chair. "When the evidence became too great to ignore, I wrote to Mr. Mortimer to hear his account. Do you know what he said in reply?"

"I can imagine," snarled Wickham, knowing this was his only opportunity to extract himself from this situation. "Patterson, Mortimer's head clerk, never liked me. He has done his best to blacken my name."

"He has?" Mr. Darcy's tone was all disbelief and fury. "Let us see what he says, shall we?" Retrieving the letter, Mr. Darcy perused it. "Mr. Wickham is slothful, lazy, and sloppy in his work. Several times his work had to be given to another clerk to correct it, as an unacceptable number of errors were found. At times Mr. Wickham arrived at work late, and on at least three occasions, came bleary-eyed and top-heavy, or recovering from that state. At least twice, he offered to deliver papers to another law firm and was not seen for several hours after. He is the most indifferent man of the law I have ever had the misfortune to know!"

The letter was cast aside, and Mr. Darcy leaned forward, looking at him, fire raging in his eyes. "Are you attempting to inform me that a respected solicitor and a clerk with years of experience and impeccable integrity are attempting to besmirch your character without reason?

"Before you answer," continued Mr. Darcy, not allowing Wickham to speak, "let me warn you that I have met Mr. Mortimer and hold him in the highest respect. Though I use Danforth's firm for my legal needs, it is not because of any lack in Mortimer. You should also know that Mr. Patterson has been employed by Mortimer for many years and has the full trust of Mortimer and all his sons. Now, what have you to say for yourself?"

The emotions playing across Wickham's face told Darcy more than the man's words ever could, and he began to feel like a fool. This man had played him for years, his sibilant whispers turning him against his own son. For a moment Darcy wondered how he could have been so blind.

Then he realized he had *wanted* to be blind. The memory of the elder Wickham, the faithful and industrious man he had been, had colored Darcy's view of the younger man to the extent he would not even consider what he was told by his son. It had all been his own doing, his reward the strained relations he shared with Fitzwilliam. Now his eyes were open, he vowed it would be different. Robert Darcy would no longer take Wickham's side—there was little character in his steward's son.

"It appears there is little I *can* say," replied Wickham. The resentment in his voice was clear in Darcy's ears. The boy was beyond caring. "Have I not already been convicted?"

Darcy was not amused. "If you had any means of defending yourself, I assume you would use it. So, tell me now," Mr. Darcy leaned forward in his chair yet again, "have I been mistaken all these years? Fitzwilliam, Anthony, even James all tried to inform me of your true nature, but I vouched for you, educated you, saw to your employment in a most advantageous position. Tell me the truth, Wickham. Have my son and nephews been telling me the truth?"

"I am who I have always been," rasped Wickham, the strain of holding his temper easily seen. "I am the one you have always favored, even more than your own son." Wickham laughed, harsh and cold. "If I am not a perfect man, then neither is your son, or any other man. This *position* you have boasted of securing me is a mere pittance, an insult! I deserved so much more! And yet you sit there and question me on the words of men unknown to you. Unknown to me!"

"So this is what this is all about," said Darcy, seeing clearly for the first time. "You are aware, are you not, Wickham, that many a wealthy man's second son has accepted a church living with gratitude? You are not even my son—and yet you wanted more than Kympton? What sort of audacity is this?"

"Have you not always treated me as a second son?" demanded Wickham. "And the Darcys are far wealthier than most families. I am well aware you own several estates—the way you favored me, what was I supposed to think?"

"Then let me disabuse you of whatever notions you have kept in your head these years. If you *were* a second son, one of the estates would have been yours. But you are not. You are my former steward's son and nothing more. My acquaintances all told me I was making a mistake in giving you as much as I did, and now I see the truth of their assertions. To any man in your situation, the Kympton living would have been an annual income such as it would have taken them five years or more to earn otherwise, and then only if they were fortunate. And yet you spurned it, wanting more."

Darcy stood, looking down at his protégé with disgust. The boy's greed was now fully open to him, and Darcy did not like what he saw. It was time to let him fend for himself, to make his own way in the world. Darcy had given him advantages no one in his situation could have gotten any other way. Whether Wickham made use of them and made something of his life was now his own business.

"I have found a law firm in town who will accept you on my recommendation," said Darcy. "But you should be aware they know of what is being said of you and will give you little benefit of the doubt should you test their patience.

"This is the last assistance you will receive from the Darcy family, for I am cutting ties with you."

Wickham gasped, but Darcy fixed him with a cold glare. "Mr. Bingley has agreed to allow you to stay until Thursday so you may attend the ball, though I begin to wonder if you should not be sent on your way today. Be that as it may, prepare to depart from Netherfield on Thursday and report to your new employer Monday next. I suggest you take this opportunity, Wickham, for if you ruin it, the life I envisioned for you will be out of reach.

"One final piece of advice," said Darcy as he gestured for Wickham to leave. "Do not approach my daughter, for my wife has informed me of her suspicions. Furthermore, I suggest you leave Miss Elizabeth strictly alone. She will not be an avenue for you to revenge yourself on my son. I have given you every advantage to assist you to make a good life for yourself. It is now up to you to seize the opportunity."

Without a word, Wickham rose and stormed from the room, the sound of the door slamming behind him echoing throughout the house. Sighing with regret, Darcy sank down on his chair and rested his chin in his hand. It seemed he would be required to make his lack of discernment up to his son. Hopefully Fitzwilliam would accept his offer to repair their damaged relationship.

The fall of George Wickham was satisfying to one who had seen his depravities for years but been unable to do anything concerning them due to his father's support. When Robert Darcy came to his son to apologize for not believing him, for the briefest of moments, Darcy thought to rebuff it. The mere thought of doing so informed him of how damaged his relationship with his sire had become, not only because of the fiasco with Wickham but also over his courtship with Miss Bennet. Mr. Darcy had given his blessing, though reluctantly, to their marriage, removing that obstacle. That he was clearly contrite regarding Wickham was of equal consequence.

"I wish you had believed me, Father, without the testimony of the law firm." Darcy paused and sighed. "But I am well aware of how silver-tongued Wickham can be, for I have witnessed it time and again at university and other sundry places."

"The past is impossible for me to undo," was his father's quiet reply. "An apology is all I have to offer, which I do without reservation."

"And I thank you for it, Father." Darcy stepped to his father and clasped his hand. "I wish to return to what we were when I was younger, before Wickham increasingly came between us. It will be difficult, but I do not wish to continue to be at odds."

The first true smile he had seen from his father in some time warmed Darcy's heart. "I wish it too, Son. Let us begin anew. I shall also make the attempt with your future bride."

And make the attempt he did, though it was easy for Darcy to see the awkwardness of his effort. Elizabeth, wonderful woman she was, accepted his father's overtures, her amiable character setting him as much at ease as she could. It would take time. But now Darcy had something he had not mustered before—hope.

Unfortunately—or fortunately, depending on one's perspective— Wickham could not manage to stay in the house without causing some trouble. That Elizabeth would be discomposed by the libertine was not something Darcy could tolerate. But privately, he could not help but view the matter with satisfaction, for they would all be made safer by his early removal.

It was nothing, really. A look, nothing more. But it was a look which vowed vengeance, which stood for all the misdeeds Wickham had committed over the years, the daughters with whom he had trifled, the shopkeepers he had defrauded. It happened when Elizabeth visited with her sisters that afternoon the very same day. It happened almost the moment Elizabeth entered the room.

"It seems the blinders have been removed," said Elizabeth

moments after they had begun speaking. At first, Darcy did not know to what she referred.

"Mr. Wickham," said Elizabeth, nodding in his direction. "He has not taken his eyes from us since I arrived. Where his previous looks have been shuttered, keeping his true feelings from the world, the loathing he directs on us now would set us afire if he possessed the ability."

When Darcy turned, it was easy to note that Elizabeth was entirely correct. In an instant, white-hot ire settled over him, and he clenched his fists. But he might not have bothered, for his father and Mr. Bingley, had already seen it. They were not slow to act.

"I apologize, Darcy, but it seems your protégé cannot be trusted," said Mr. Bingley. "If he cannot behave himself enough to avoid looking on a girl who was raised with my own children with such loathing, I am afraid he must leave my house immediately.

"Wickham is no longer any charge of mine," said his father in response. "It seems you must depart earlier than planned, Wickham. Go to your room and gather your things. You can still be on the afternoon post to London, where you can return to your lodgings and prepare for your Monday appointment with your new employer."

"I no longer have lodgings," replied Wickham, his tone far more sullen than Darcy had ever heard from him. "I let them go when I departed for Pemberley."

The hard look Mr. Darcy gave him made Wickham squirm. "More evidence you intended to grasp for everything you could." Mr. Darcy paused and sighed. "I shall give you enough money to stay in an inn for a few days. But you will be required to let lodgings of your own quickly, for I will not continue to support you."

Wickham gave his former patron a tight nod. "There is a woman known to me who lets out rooms in a house she owns. I shall go to her."

"Good," said Mr. Darcy. "Now, Wickham, I believe it would be best if you departed."

Wickham turned to leave the room, but as he left, he cast one more glance at Darcy. Forever after, Darcy was unable to determine what the man meant by it. There seemed to be an element of regret in it, though whether it presaged his remorse for not being successful in his schemes or some other unhappiness, Darcy was not certain. In the end, it did not matter. It was his fervent desire to never again meet George Wickham.

Chapter XXXII

$\mathscr{A}$s the first notes of the first dance drifted over the assembled, Elizabeth stepped forward, accepting William's hand, and moved around him in concordance with the steps of the dance. On her fiancé's countenance rested a slight smile, the one she knew graced his face when he was considering her virtues. So much had begun in distrust and suspicion that ending in this happy place was nigh unfathomable to Elizabeth. But here they were. Elizabeth could not be happier.

To either side of them, other couples were included—Mr. Bingley and Jane, along with Thomas and Caroline, Mr. and Mrs. Darcy and Mr. and Mrs. Bingley. All stood up for this first set, and while Elizabeth knew the older members likely would not dance again, their show of support for the engaged couples was a treasured blessing. Even Mr. Darcy's mien had softened, and with Mr. Wickham's absence, the man appeared lighter, as if his protégé had somehow affected his mood.

Another couple had taken to the dance floor, and Elizabeth looked curiously at them. But Mr. Collins and Charlotte seemed oblivious to any scrutiny as they spoke together in low tones which did not reach Elizabeth's ears. Even Mr. Bennet had stood up with his youngest daughter, Mary, who laughed as her father guided her around the

336 ~~ *Jann Rowland*

floor. Mr. Bennet almost certainly would not dance again, but his effort in this instance was gratifying. And dear Georgiana, who had become as close to Elizabeth as a sister, was standing by the side of the floor, watching the activity. Though still young, her parents had decreed she could attend, but she would retire after dinner and only dance with a select few close acquaintances. Fitzwilliam would dance the next with her and her father the one after. The excitement in her eyes was palpable as she waited impatiently for her turn to come.

"Am I not enough to hold your attention, Elizabeth?"

Hearing the voice of her beloved interrupting her thoughts, Elizabeth found him with her eyes, her slight smile matching his. Or at least it did until his grin widened to cover his whole countenance.

"If so, it is a terrible thing, indeed," continued he. "It does not bode well for our future felicity if you forget me when I am standing in front of you."

"I do say, Mr. Darcy," said Elizabeth playfully, "I am not certain from whence this teasing manner of yours has appeared. Teasing is *my* province as I recall."

"It seems to me I have learned from the best, my dear," replied William. "You cannot expect to go through life without receiving a taste of your own medicine. Particularly when I best you at chess — then the wit shall flow long!"

Elizabeth laughed at his conceit. "Is that so? By my count, you have yet to best me, sir. It is nothing more than conceit to boast when you have not yet triumphed."

"Eventually I shall, dearest Elizabeth," replied William.

"Perhaps. But it may be best to save your boasting for when that eventuality comes to pass."

Mr. Darcy did nothing more than grin at her as he moved past her in the dance. Elizabeth watched his graceful motion, reflecting on how fortunate she was to have attracted such a man as he. Should societal norms allow it, Elizabeth was convinced she would like nothing more than to dance every dance with him. As it was, she was happy to know the first, supper, and last sets of the evening were his.

When the dance was completed, Elizabeth joined her fiancé and the other members of her party at the side of the floor, laughter flowing between them without reserve. When the music began again, Elizabeth allowed the elder Mr. Darcy to take her hand, leading her to the floor. The gentleman's request to partner her for the second had taken Elizabeth by surprise, though she had been more than willing to allow him the dances.

For the first half or more of their sets, Mr. Darcy did not speak, his behavior what she might have attributed to his son before coming to know him. How he might behave in other settings among society with whom he was comfortable, she could not say. But his expression, so unlike what it had been when she had first made his acquaintance, was not at all censorious. So, Elizabeth contented herself with following his lead, knowing if he wished to say something, he undoubtedly would. That moment came with only a few minutes of the dance remaining.

"I hope you do not hold my behavior against me, Miss Bennet."

The comment had come so suddenly and without warning, it took Elizabeth off guard and rendered her silent for a few moments. Then she gathered herself and essayed to respond in an intelligent manner.

"Have we not had this conversation, Mr. Darcy?" said she, referring to his apology immediately before Mr. Wickham had been removed from Netherfield.

The sight of such a great man as Mr. Darcy appearing almost silly necessitated she stifle her laughter.

"Perhaps we have," replied Mr. Darcy, gathering himself. "But I should not wish you to misunderstand."

"The matter has been explained to me in great detail, sir. The history of your family, though perhaps I do not understand it completely, is prestigious, and I know I do not come from a level of society to match that of previous Darcy brides." Elizabeth paused, considering what she should say and then offered carefully: "I hope to learn, sir, so I may uphold the honor of a family of such impressive roots."

It seemed Elizabeth had said the right thing, for Mr. Darcy allowed himself a slow smile. "It would give me great pleasure, Miss Elizabeth, to assist you to learn the history of my family. There may be times when I appear overly proud of my forebears. I hope that will not provoke you to think me haughty."

"From what I understand, you have every reason to be proud of your history. It is very much my wish to become another in a long line of honorable Darcy wives."

The smile on the gentleman's face widened, and Elizabeth could see the close resemblance between father and son. "There are some ladies who would speak as you do, hoping to curry favor, to ingratiate herself when she has no intention of following through. In you, however, I sense an earnest desire which would be difficult to feign."

"I hope, Mr. Darcy, that I am always taken at my word, for I do not speak to mislead or with frivolous intent."

"Yes, I can see that," replied her partner.

The rest of the dance passed in silence. The shift, however, in Elizabeth's perceptions was immense, for the slightly uncomfortable silence of the past was replaced with something more endurable. It might be some time before she was comfortable with her husband's father, and perhaps even longer before he gained any ease with her. For the first time, however, she was hopeful it was possible.

While the stated purpose for hosting a ball had been to welcome their guests to the neighborhood, the true reason was not lost on anyone in attendance. The two engagements of the eldest Bennet sisters were much talked of, congratulations flowing in from every quarter. Some of them were even sincere! But there was another engagement of which Elizabeth was not aware though it shocked her when she learned of it.

It happened during supper that evening. The previous sets having been secured by Mr. Darcy, Elizabeth spent the meal in his company, along with close family and friends nearby. She took her turn at the pianoforte as was expected, with both Caroline and Mary, and accepted the applause with cheer. After she left the pianoforte, she was immediately approached by a close friend.

"Lizzy, I have something to tell you."

Nervousness roiled in her friend's eyes, and Elizabeth took her hands, squeezing them and saying: "Of course, Charlotte. What is the matter?"

"Nothing is the matter, Lizzy," replied her friend. "It is simply that I have some news which will shock you, though I must inform you that it is partially your fault."

"Then, by all means, do not leave me in suspense. What is this news of yours?"

Charlotte sucked in a deep breath and then said, in a rush: "I am engaged to be married."

"Truly?" gasped Elizabeth. "But I had no notion of you courting or even being called on by a gentleman!"

"As I said," replied Charlotte with a hint of a nervous laugh, "that is your fault, though it is also true we have not published our understanding far and wide."

"And who is the fortunate man?" asked Elizabeth. "Do I know him?"

"Oh, you know him very well, indeed, for it is Mr. Collins."

The man himself appeared at their side, as if summoned, and if he smiled at Elizabeth with a hint of the longing she had often seen in his gaze since his arrival at Longbourn, it was much muted now. When he glanced at Charlotte, Elizabeth could see the regard and respect for her, and Charlotte, who had never been a romantic, amazed Elizabeth by responding with a pretty blush. Delight filled Elizabeth's heart.

"That is wonderful!" cried Elizabeth, embracing her friend with a grip so tight, she heard the breath leave Charlotte's body. "You have both been sly, indeed, for I had no notion an attachment was forming between you."

Elizabeth pushed Charlotte out to arm's length, still gripping her shoulders. "Mr. Collins is an excellent man, Charlotte—I am certain you will be very happy with him.

"And let me commend you, William," continued she, turning a bright smile on Mr. Collins, "for seeing the worth in my dearest friend. You both deserve so much—I cannot be more delighted you will obtain happiness with each other."

"Thank you, Cousin," said Mr. Collins, his voice laced with feeling. "I know I shall be gaining a gem of the highest quality."

"I thank you as well, Lizzy," was Charlotte's quieter response.

"But should you not announce it?" asked Elizabeth. "Now is the perfect opportunity—I am certain Mr. and Mrs. Bingley would be pleased to oblige you."

"No, Lizzy," said Charlotte at once, Mr. Collins echoing her words. "Neither William nor I wish to take away from your celebration. We are quite content to court in private, allowing you and Jane to consume the attention of our neighbors."

A laugh was Elizabeth's response. "Now you are forcing me to become cross with you. I would gladly cede the attention, for I have no need of it."

"But you deserve it," replied Mr. Collins. "You are marrying into an illustrious family and will be ascending to the heights of society. I am naught but a simple parson."

"You have never been a simple parson," said Elizabeth, touching Mr. Collins's arm with affection. "You are an excellent man. Who knows? Perhaps someday your journey through life will take you to other places, greater positions and heroic deeds. The world is open to you, Cousin."

While Mr. Collins appeared embarrassed by Elizabeth's praise, Charlotte regarded her with a slightly shaken head. "I still maintain you read too many novels, Lizzy. William and I will be very content to live in Longbourn village and tend to the parish. But we are pleased with your felicitations. I hope you will attend our wedding."

"Nothing will keep me from it, Charlotte," replied Elizabeth.

After a few moments, Mr. Collins went away, but not without giving Elizabeth one last look. Elizabeth fancied she understood it — Mr. Collins, though he had never held any serious designs on her, was wishing her a final farewell in his heart, for he had succeeded in letting her go. The smile which Elizabeth bestowed upon him informed him she understood, that his happiness meant much to her.

"I wish to thank you again, Lizzy," said Charlotte when her fiancé had departed. "Some in your position might have responded differently to such news, particularly since you have known for so long how William feels for you."

"Charlotte," chided Elizabeth, "I could never be anything other than pleased. Mr. Collins has never hidden his admiration, but we have both always known our paths did not lie together." Elizabeth squeezed her friend's hands. "And you must know that Mr. Collins's previous infatuation for me has given way to much more powerful feelings for you."

Charlotte blushed, but she did not deny it. The sight of her friend so bashful when she was usually self-possessed induced Elizabeth to become playful.

"The one surprising thing of this affair is your father's silence on the matter — not to mention your mother's I might have thought they would be incandescently happy, proclaiming the match for all to hear!"

The ladies laughed together. "Perhaps you are correct. But you forget how much esteem my parents — especially my father — hold for *you*, Lizzy."

Sir William, who was speaking to one of the neighborhood men, found Elizabeth with his eyes at that moment. It was apparent he had a good notion of what they were discussing, for he bowed and grinned, to which Elizabeth responded. The man's jovial laugh reached her ears, and she shook her head. Her friend was correct as usual.

"Then will he announce it in the near future?" asked Elizabeth. "For surely he cannot remain quiet about it for long, and I suspect your mother will wish to have her share in the recent spate of matrimonial congratulations."

"I cannot say you are incorrect, Lizzy," replied Charlotte happily. "It will be announced soon, but there is no rush. We do not plan to marry until January or February at the earliest, so there is plenty of time for celebration."

The conversation devolved to Charlotte's expectations for the future and Elizabeth's questions concerning how it had all come about. Never having considered the possibility, Elizabeth still felt herself to be more than a little amazed, but with the excellent dispositions of her cousin and closest friend, Elizabeth was convinced they would do well together. In the end, they parted, each determined to retain their connection and maintain their friendship, though marriage, children, their duties as wives, and distance would separate them.

Still later, Elizabeth found herself back in the ballroom, a pleasant sense of sanguinity coming over her. It had been a wondrous night, one she would remember throughout the years of her life with nothing less than gratitude. The heat of the ballroom seemed to increase, and she felt like a little fresh air would be just the thing. Consequently, she moved to the door at the side of the ballroom and slipped through onto Netherfield's balcony beyond.

The crispness of late November invigorated her, the air refreshing after the closeness of a crowded ballroom, and Elizabeth walked to the bannister, looking out onto Netherfield's gardens beyond. But while the view was beautiful, the light of the moon casting a luminous glow on everything before her eyes, Elizabeth's attention was focused on the door behind her. As she had known it would, it opened after a few moments, allowing the light to spill out into the night, before it closed again. The sound of footsteps approached.

"I had not thought you would be so ungentlemanly to approach me in this manner, sir. Have you no care for the proprieties of the situation?"

"I have the highest respect for the proprieties," was his reply. "In the face of such loveliness, however, I find myself helpless before you."

With a smile, Elizabeth turned to gaze into the eyes of her beloved. "A pretty speech, sir. But I have proof of your rakish ways and little inclination of allowing you to steal another kiss."

"Oh, I am quite certain you are eager for me to steal another kiss."

Elizabeth arched an eyebrow. "Are you? I might wonder how you might have arrived at such a conclusion."

With exaggerated slowness, William leaned down and kissed her full on the lips. It was not a quick peck which caused her to start and flee as it had last time, but a warm, sensual brushing of his lips against hers, the kind which left her content, yet wanting more.

"Whatever am I to do with you?" asked Elizabeth as he pulled away from her. "You are incorrigible, sir. How many more maidens have you despoiled in such a manner?"

"Only you, dearest," said Mr. Darcy, leaning in again. "Only you."

*   *   *

"Are you convinced yet?"

Robert, who had been watching the dancers engaged in the last set—though trying not to appear as if focused on Fitzwilliam and Elizabeth—turned to her. Lady Anne took his actions as an encouragement to continue to speak. She grinned and grasped his arm, holding herself close to him.

"Of Elizabeth's suitability to be our daughter."

The huff with which Robert responded did not mislead her in the slightest. Much of his antipathy and displeasure had dissipated, and it was not all resignation left in its wake. It appeared there was much work yet to be done to bring him to full acceptance, but he was now on that path. That was the important point.

"She does seem to be a determined, genuine sort of girl." A pause ensued, during which Robert did not take his eyes from her. "Do you know she actually expressed her eagerness to learn about the family's history and to live up to the example of those who have gone before her?"

"That does not surprise me at all," replied Lady Anne. "But I am curious of your opinion. Do you suspect her of dissembling?"

"While it might be expected of a woman in her position, oddly enough, I do not. I have already said I consider her to be a sincere girl. Nothing she said impressed me of any other motive than to ensure her assumption of the title of the future Mrs. Darcy would not affect the family's standing."

"Again, I am unsurprised. Since we made her acquaintance, it has been easy to see she is not given to the artifice one so often sees in society."

"There was never a chance to dissuade him, was there?"

"It surprises me you feel the need to ask." When Robert looked at her, Lady Anne bestowed a gentle smile on him. "Fitzwilliam is quite as stubborn as you, Robert."

"Yes. I remember speaking those same words not long after our arrival in Hertfordshire."

"Perhaps more importantly," said Lady Anne, drawing his eyes to her again, "he possesses a different character from you, for all you are similar in essentials. Fitzwilliam would never have been happy with a society wife, a woman who would bring him prestige and wealth, but be more punishment than partner. He requires something more in a wife—he requires a woman who will love him, on whom he can shower his own love.

"Given what I am seeing before me now, it is clear she makes him very happy." The look of adoration Fitzwilliam was at that moment bestowing on Miss Elizabeth proved her point. "Does it not remind you of our courting days?"

A softness which was not often present in her husband's countenance entered his eyes. "Yes. It does very much."

"Then be happy your son has found what you found. Be happy he will share the same with his wife as we have shared all these years."

Robert looked on her with love, an ardency he rarely shared, but which warmed her whenever she witnessed it. "When you put it like that, it would be churlish of me to continue to disapprove of her, would it not?"

A grin stretched her lips and Lady Anne said: "I am glad you see it too."

The rumble of laughter built up in his breast, released in a chuckle. Robert caught up her hand, bestowing a lingering kiss on her wrist.

"I am blessed, indeed, Mrs. Darcy. To have married such a wise woman is a boast not every man can make."

"And I would have you remember it, Mr. Darcy, for I shall take great pleasure in reminding you of how correct I was in this matter."

Their shared laughter floated out over the dance floor, mingling with the final strains of the music. All would be well, it seemed. Her family would be whole, Wickham was banished, and her son would have all he ever wished. It was all she ever hoped for.

EPILOGUE

$\mathcal{C}$oming home to Pemberley was always something special. Though her first visit had impressed Elizabeth as to the beauty of the venerable estate, only living there had allowed her to come to a more complete understanding of what it symbolized, what it had meant to generations of the Darcy family and to those who depended on the estate for their livelihoods.

As she had promised her husband's father, Elizabeth had devoted herself to learning of the family's history. Coming to understand the legacy of which he had stewardship allowed Elizabeth to understand her father-in-law in some small way. Mr. Darcy, she thought, was pleased that she approached the matter with gravity. He never tired of relating the stories of his forebears. Elizabeth could understand why.

That was not to say they were at Pemberley always. The principal residence of Elizabeth and her husband had been Blackfish Bay on the coast of Lincolnshire. William had informed her it was the best of the Darcy satellite estates, and Elizabeth could well understand why. It was a picturesque locale, not far from the ocean, prone to breezes from the North Sea, the scent of which Elizabeth found particularly wonderful. She and her husband had spent several idyllic months there, coming to know each other as husband and wife, learning how to be a married couple. So happy was she there, Elizabeth thought she would never wish to leave, if it were possible.

But Pemberley was a world unto itself. The woods, the fields, the long valley in which it stood were scenes that had grown dear to Elizabeth. William was of the opinion that Pemberley was the best place in the world, and Elizabeth had quickly grown to agree. Yes, returning there was, indeed, special.

As the carriage in which they traveled crested the little prominence which provided such an impressive view of the house, Elizabeth leaned forward to look out the window, to accept the placid air of the place that always calmed her. As she did so, her husband of almost a year grinned.

"One might think you are impatient to reach our destination, Elizabeth."

"No more impatient than you, Husband," replied she. "Did you not inform me of your own feelings for this place, feelings even our comfortable home at Blackfish cannot satisfy."

"I did."

"Then I must suppose you are anticipating the coming reunion at your favorite place in the world as much as I am."

Though Elizabeth might have expected a response, her husband contented himself with a warm smile and a look out the window. The carriage proceeded apace along the road toward the stone building beyond, and soon Elizabeth could see three shapes emerge from the front door, waiting for them to arrive. While two of the figures stood at ease, waiting patiently, the third was bouncing on her heels, eager for the carriage to arrive.

When their conveyance swayed to a stop, William embarked before turning to assist Elizabeth from the carriage. Then she found herself engulfed in the embraces of her female in-laws, the soft welcome of the elder mingling—though much quieter than—with the squeals of the younger.

"How well you appear, Elizabeth!" exclaimed Lady Anne when the greetings had been made. "Is it not wonderful, Robert? Our first grandchild shall be born at Pemberley and not three months from now!"

"It is, indeed," said Mr. Darcy, his usual reserve coming to the fore. He executed a very proper bow over Elizabeth's hand, saying: "It is good to see you, Elizabeth, Fitzwilliam. But I must say you do not appear as . . . developed as I might have thought. I seem to remember Anne being much larger when she was as far along as you."

Elizabeth stifled a giggle, noting that Lady Anne had done so at the same time. Mr. Darcy was not prone to displays of humor, but when he did, it was always in an understated, droll way.

"It is not unusual for a woman to maintain her figure for some time into her first confinement," said Lady Anne. "Regardless, I should like to see Fitzwilliam and Elizabeth to their room so they can rest."

They all agreed, and Elizabeth soon found herself in her chambers with her husband. As it turned out, she was a little tired, agreeing readily to rest for a short time while William descended the stairs to see his father. Thus, it was some time later, when they all gathered together in the sitting-room, that an important communication was made.

"William, Elizabeth," said Mr. Darcy, his manner grave, "a matter has arisen of which I would speak to you both. It concerns Wickham."

The expression on William's face, which had become more open since their marriage, immediately shuttered at the mention of his onetime friend. His father must have seen his sudden anger, for he spoke to placate him.

"It is not what you think, Fitzwilliam. I have no more intention of supporting Wickham, for I now acknowledge the truth of what you told me of him over the years. As you know, I cut him off when he left Netherfield. He respected my wishes until about a month ago when I received a letter from him."

"I suppose he was asking for money," said William. He shook his head with disdain. "It is too much to hope he was able to make his way without incurring debt, for I know him too well for that."

The sigh which was Mr. Darcy's response confirmed William's suppositions. "Yes, that was the gist of his message. His circumstances, he assured me, were very bad, as his time in the position I had obtained for him did not go well. I hope you will not blame me if I kept in contact with that firm in order to be informed of his progress. He lasted barely four months."

"No, I cannot blame you for that," replied William. "I might have done the same."

Mr. Darcy gave a curt nod. "As his request was simple, I decided it was best to accede, on the condition he would not importune me again. The substance of his request was such that further contact is unlikely."

At William's interested look, his father assuaged his curiosity. "He requested my assistance in his taking a ship for the New World and expressed an interest in starting anew. It seems that not only were his circumstances bad, but the woman with whom he lived was on the verge of throwing him out, not to mention certain acquaintances were looking for him due to some substantial debts of honor."

"Wickham, Wickham," said William, shaking his head. "Will he never change? I have little hope of it." William peered at his father. "I suppose you agreed? If it had been me, I would have agreed for no other reason than to remove him from these shores forever."

"I did," confirmed Mr. Darcy. "The ship departed three weeks ago, with Wickham on it. Due to the remembrance of his father, I gave him one hundred pounds to assist him in making his way when he arrives. Whether it will still be in his possession when he disembarks in Baltimore, I cannot say. Regardless, our family association with him is at an end. For the sake of his father's memory, I hope he makes something of himself. But it is in his hands now."

"Thank you for informing us, Father," replied William quietly. "It was the correct choice."

Mr. Darcy nodded but did not reply. The conversation turned to other matters then, items of interest for Elizabeth, and for William, as well. The family was expected for Christmas on the morrow, both their Fitzwilliam and Bennet relations, including the Gardiners. It had been surprising, but Mr. Darcy had taken to Mr. Gardiner immediately, learning to rely on his judgment in all matters business. The Gardiner business had grown in the past year due to substantial investment by the gentlemen in the group. Knowing her uncle's acumen, Elizabeth suspected they would all make handsome profits in the coming years.

"You shall also make the acquaintance of the one member of my brother's family still unknown to you," said Lady Anne. "William's cousin Anthony has returned to England and will be joining us at Pemberley. My brother has informed me he is anticipating making your acquaintance."

"You will love Anthony, Elizabeth," said Georgiana. "He is as happy and amiable as Mr. Bingley!"

"Having heard much of him," said Elizabeth with a laugh, "I can hardly wait to make his acquaintance. Perhaps he might be able to share some stories of my husband." Elizabeth turned to regard William, noting his groan. "You *were* raised together, were you not?"

"They were," confirmed Mr. Darcy.

"But you should view whatever Anthony says with more than a hint of skepticism," said William. "He is renowned for his tall tales."

"That he is!" exclaimed Lady Anne. "But you shall judge for yourself. I also understand that your sister Mary will be bereft of her suitor since the Bingleys are to come to Pemberley."

Elizabeth looked to William and shook her head. That Mary had a suitor who had visited Netherfield in order to pay her attention had been a shock to Elizabeth. That it was Mr. Hardwick, the man who had seemed particularly interested in Elizabeth at that one ball they had attended in London was an even greater shock. But Jane had reported she was pleased with his ardency, though he was not too insistent for Mary's sensibilities.

"Mary is yet too young to wed," said Elizabeth. "Perhaps we can see more of them together during the season in London, for I am curious to know what he sees in Mary that would allow her to serve as a substitute for me."

"I think you do Hardwick a disservice," said William. "He is a good man." Then William paused and grinned. "And with Bingley, myself, and your brother all on hand to protect her, I doubt he will step out of line."

"It would also be best for you to take care in how you deal with Mary's feelings," said Lady Anne, laughter in her eyes and voice. "As much like you as she is, she will not be pleased with your interference."

Elizabeth huffed with annoyance. "Mary is the youngest of us — we have always been protective of her."

"And it is to your credit, my dear," said Mrs. Darcy. "But she is now nearly twenty and is capable of looking out for her own interests. A protective instinct is all well and good, but sooner or later, all young people must be allowed to spread their own wings."

As Lady Anne spoke, her eyes moved to her own daughter, confirming what they all already knew, that the time when Georgiana must be free was quickly approaching. Georgiana blushed under her mother's scrutiny, but she proved her increased maturity by refusing to look away.

"I look forward to seeing my family once again," said Elizabeth, turning the discussion slightly. "Though I will warn you that we are unlikely to see my father again once he is introduced to the library. You might never evict him from the house!"

They all laughed at the characterization of her father, for they all knew it to be the truth. This observation once again provoked a general conversation among them all, and for a time, news was exchanged, both of Pemberley and Blackfish, but nothing of much import was said. Through it all, Elizabeth felt the eyes of her husband's father on her, similar to what she had felt the previous year in Hertfordshire. But while that had been judging, there was some undefinable quality in his current scrutiny.

After a time, when William was engaged with his mother and sister, Mr. Darcy approached and sat beside her. They exchanged a few pleasant words about nothing of consequence, and Elizabeth became all that much more curious of his manner. This man was not one for small talk, though she had grown to respect his opinions when he did speak. This was something different.

"I know from your looks you are curious as to my purpose, Elizabeth," said he at length. "Perhaps you might even think me daft. But I wished to take this opportunity to thank you for making your husband so happy."

"It is nothing, Mr. Darcy, for I have derived as much happiness as has your son."

"Yes, I can see you have." He paused, considering his words, before speaking again. "I can see now that my son has chosen well, for you have brought so much more to him than any lady of society ever could have. That is something to value, something I had forgotten for a time. That he saw it is a measure of his own discernment. That he saw it in you, is very fortunate, indeed, though his choice of expressing himself was unfortunate."

The matter of their first meeting, William had informed his parents of before their wedding, insisting they should know of it, especially since the Bennets already knew. The embarrassment of the confession had become all that much greater when his father made his disappointment known. That Elizabeth could have demanded Mr. Darcy marry her to restore her reputation, and had avoided any suggestion of it, had raised her in his esteem.

"As I said, Mr. Darcy," said Elizabeth, "my feelings for your son render your thanks unnecessary, for I derive as much benefit as he. I could not be happier in my life."

"I am happy to hear it," was Mr. Darcy's quiet response. "In the future, I would like it if you and Fitzwilliam would spend more time at Pemberley, consider it your home, though I understand if you also wish for your own family home at Blackfish."

"I believe we will be happy to do so," replied Elizabeth warmly. "We both love Pemberley and all of you very much."

Mr. Darcy smiled and said no more, and after a few moments, the other three once again joined the conversation. That William knew his father had exchanged words with her was evident, but his countenance displayed no distress. His reconciliation with his father had been achieved, and as far as Elizabeth could tell, their relationship was as strong as ever.

The ability to once again be among those they loved in such a place as Pemberley was welcome to both Elizabeth and William, and they stayed together late that night, basking in the shared love of family. When they retired, it was with the anticipation of the other members of their family joining them.

When she told William of what his father had said, he looked at her, a question evident on his countenance. "Do you wish to spend more time here? Or do you prefer to stay at Blackfish?"

"It may be beneficial to spend some time there," said Elizabeth, "but I believe I have come to love Pemberley as much as you do. Perhaps it might be best to spend the majority of our time here."

William's countenance brightened, informing Elizabeth she had said the right thing. "I cannot agree more. Then it is settled."

They doused the candles and settled under the counterpane, Elizabeth with her head on her husband's shoulder. And as she drifted off to sleep, Elizabeth was struck by the rightness of the feeling of being at Pemberley. Yes, she had made the right decision in indulging her husband's love for his ancestral home. But more, she had decided correctly in forgiving him for his actions five years before. Perhaps his kiss had been an impulse, but it had led them to this point. Elizabeth could not have been happier.

The End

FOR READERS WHO LIKED
THE IMPULSE OF THE MOMENT

A Gift for Elizabeth
Sundered from her parents and sisters, a depressed Elizabeth Bennet lives with the Gardiners in London. When times seem most desperate, she makes a new acquaintance in Mr. Darcy, and the encounter changes her perspective entirely. With the spirit of Christmas burning within her, Elizabeth begins to recover from the hardships which have beset her life. Join Elizabeth in her journey to receive a special gift which will change everything.

A Tale of Two Courtships
Two sisters, both in danger of losing their hearts. One experiences a courtship which ends quickly in an engagement, the other must struggle against the machinations of others. And one who will do anything to ensure her beloved sister achieves her heart's desire.

Mr. Bennet Takes Charge
When Elizabeth Bennet's journey to the lakes is canceled, Mr. Bingley, along with his elusive friend Mr. Darcy, return to Netherfield, turning a quiet summer is topsy-turvy. Then Elizabeth learns her sister, Lydia, means to elope with a rake, and the very respectability of her family is at stake. Elizabeth takes heart, however, when her father rises to the occasion, in a way she would never have predicted. With Mr. Darcy's assistance, there may still be time to prevent calamity, and even find love, against all odds.

Murder at Netherfield
After the ball at Netherfield, a fault in their carriage results in the Bennet family being forced to stay at the Bingley estate, and when a blizzard blows in overnight, the Bennets find themselves stranded there. When a body is found, leading to a string of murders which threaten the lives of those present, Elizabeth and Darcy form an alliance to discover the identity of the murderer and save those they care about most. But the depraved actions of a killer, striking from the shadows, threatens their newly found admiration for each other.

Whispers of the Heart
A different Bingley party arrives in Hertfordshire leading to a new suitor emerging for the worthiest of the Bennet sisters. As her sister has obtained her happiness, Elizabeth Bennet finds herself thrown into society far above any she might have otherwise expected, which leads her to a new understanding of the enigmatic Mr. Darcy.

For more details, visit
http://www.onegoodsonnet.com/genres/pride-and-prejudice-variations

About the Author

Jann Rowland is a Canadian, born and bred. Other than a two-year span in which he lived in Japan, he has been a resident of the Great White North his entire life, though he professes to still hate the winters.

Though Jann did not start writing until his mid-twenties, writing has grown from a hobby to an all-consuming passion. His interests as a child were almost exclusively centered on the exotic fantasy worlds of Tolkien and Eddings, among a host of others. As an adult, his interests have grown to include historical fiction and romance, with a particular focus on the works of Jane Austen.

When Jann is not writing, he enjoys rooting for his favorite sports teams. He is also a master musician (in his own mind) who enjoys playing piano and singing as well as moonlighting as the choir director in his church's congregation.

Jann lives in Alberta with his wife of more than twenty years, two grown sons, and one young daughter. He is convinced that whatever hair he has left will be entirely gone by the time his little girl hits her teenage years. Sadly, though he has told his daughter repeatedly that she is not allowed to grow up, she continues to ignore him.

Website: http://onegoodsonnet.com/
Facebook: https://facebook.com/OneGoodSonnetPublishing/
Twitter: @OneGoodSonnet
Mailing List: http://eepurl.com/bol2p9

22852083R00203

Printed in Great Britain
by Amazon